"ONE KISS, ANGEL"

"I make it a practice never to mix business and . . ."

"Pleasure? Think of this as research."

His hands were beneath her robe, on her shoulders—rubbing. She tensed, but wouldn't allow herself to push him away.

"Open your mouth for me."

Angelica closed her eyes tightly. He took her lips, gently at first, then with the subtle force of experience.

When he finally raised his head, he gathered the neck of her robe into his curled fingers. "Mmm. I've decided to give you a chance to prove how thorough you can be."

Fear. He definitely frightened her. "Thank you."

"Don't thank me," he said. "I never *give* anything away."

Other Avon Books by
Stella Cameron

FASCINATION
HIS MAGIC TOUCH
ONLY BY YOUR TOUCH

STELLA CAMERON

BREATHLESS

AVON BOOKS ◆ NEW YORK

BREATHLESS is an original publication of Avon Books. This work has never before appeared in book form. This work is a novel. Any similarity to actual persons or events is purely coincidental.

AVON BOOKS
A division of
The Hearst Corporation
1350 Avenue of the Americas
New York, New York 10019

First Avon Books Printing: June 1994

AVON TRADEMARK REG. U.S. PAT. OFF. AND IN OTHER COUNTRIES, MARCA REGISTRADA, HECHO EN U.S.A.

Printed in the U.S.A.

RA 10 9 8 7 6 5 4 3 2 1

For Jerry Cameron,
my partner, best friend,
and hero.

One

"*You always were a bloody savage, Sinjun*."

Sinjun Breaker unbuttoned his shirt and shrugged it off. "Because I don't like unexpected visitors lurking in my bedroom? I'm wounded, Lorraine. And I thought I was being a perfect gentleman . . . under the circumstances." He was lying in wait for his own killer. Not an occupation for a *civilized* man. "What are you doing here?"

"Waiting for you." A single long fingernail slowly traveled the length of his spine. "This is the first time we've had a chance to be alone—really alone—since we arrived on the island. I'm crazy for you, Sin. A perfect gentleman knows what a lady wants and makes sure she gets it," Lorraine Hart whispered against his shoulder.

Beyond open French doors leading from his bedroom to an enclosed courtyard, the hazy gray-indigo of a young and deceptively tranquil Pacific evening slipped over sunset's last red wash. Palms bowed their shaggy heads, supple black silhouettes against a pewter sky. Less than two hours' flight to the east of Sinjun's private island fortress, Hawaii would be tuning up for just another night in tourist paradise. "Uh huh," Sinjun said, and concentrated, listening for the beat of the chopper's blades. What the devil was keeping

1

Chuck? He should have been back from Kauai hours ago.

"Uh huh *what?*" Lorraine slipped her arms around his waist. "Does that mean you're apologizing for neglecting me?" She pressed her breasts against his back and he felt her take a deep breath.

"Uh huh, you're right. A perfect gentleman probably knows what a lady wants and makes sure she gets it."

"So?" Her practiced hands splayed, flattened insistently over his belly, and she slipped her fingers under the waist of his jeans. "*So?*" she repeated.

"I'm thinking about it." He didn't have to look at the woman bent on getting him into bed—or anywhere else where her legendary sexual appetites could be momentarily satisfied—to see her. Lorraine Hart had an unforgettable face and a body that had mangled more than one sane, successful man's logic.

Sinjun Breaker was said to be many things—some of them anything but complimentary—but he'd never been accused of being other than a healthy male with healthy male instincts.

"Are you still thinking?" For an instant, Lorraine pulled her hands back—just long enough to unhook and tug away her bikini top. "Come on, Sin, before Chuck comes back and spoils everything." Her aroused nipples flirted with his tensed skin. She rubbed back and forth, sending her fingertips even lower into his jeans.

"And there you have your answer," he told her. Even as his brain remained on alert, the inevitable bodily reaction was rapidly making itself felt. Through gritted teeth he added, "A lady doesn't take advantage of her lover's absence to try and seduce his boss."

"This lady does. But only with you, Sin. You know you're the only man I want. *Eight* months. For eight months I've tolerated Chuck—and then having to be a prisoner on this godforsaken island—because I want you. And there's never been a time when we could really be alone. Until now." Her kisses were hot and openmouthed on his back.

"Chuck's already overdue," he told her shortly. "He'll probably be back any moment."

"Only because you took so long to come and find me. You don't have to worry about Chuck. You're the boss. Tell him I'm yours and he'll back off. He'll hate it, but he won't risk making you mad. Do it, Sin. Do what we both want you to do. *Take* me, lover."

She went for home, closed on the part of him he was helpless to disguise as other than ready for her, and laughed breathily. "Oh my, I'm so glad I happened along this evening. You poor, needy darling."

"That's *enough*." Sinjun grasped her wrists and yanked her out of his pants. He swung her around in front of him. "Go back to Chuck's cottage," he said, angry that his body betrayed just how successfully she'd turned him on. "And don't try this again."

Lorraine laughed aloud. A warm wind off the ocean billowed in sheer white drapes and sent her black hair tossing forward. The room was dark, but a rising moon made certain he saw the glitter in her violet eyes—and the full curves of her breasts, paler where her swimsuit had shielded them from the sun.

"Go, Lorraine." Releasing her, he swept up her discarded top and thrust it into her hands.

Swiftly, she trapped his fingers over her breasts. "You don't want me to go." For the first time since he'd arrived to discover her lounging on his bed, she sounded uncertain.

"Good night, Lorraine." He disentangled himself from her grip, not without experiencing another physical jolt.

"I'll tell Chuck," she said.

Now Sinjun laughed. "Yeah, sure. And risk having him kick your pretty fanny off this island? I don't think so, baby. I don't know exactly what you hope to get out of Chuck Gill, but I don't think you've got it yet." He wished, as he did a hundred times a day, that he could persuade his old friend and longtime employee to ditch this greedy nymphomaniac.

"Damn you!" she shrieked suddenly, and lashed out at him. Sinjun dodged successfully. "You know I don't want Chuck. I'm with him so I can stay close to you. You know I broke off a relationship that would have made me a wealthy woman because of you."

"Because when you met me you figured—correctly—that I had more money than Garth Lieber," Sinjun said without humor. "A lot more."

"That's a lie. It's not the money. We saw each other—you and I saw each other—and we both knew what we wanted. Don't deny that. I don't know why you keep putting off what's got to happen between us, but I do know you want me."

Impatience and disgust vied for first place in his crowded mind. Garth Lieber of Lieber Enterprises was one subject he'd rather forget tonight. Lorraine Hart was another. "Listen to me—" From the distance came a familiar throbbing. "That's the chopper."

"There's still time." She ran her hands up his arms. "*Please*, Sin. I can slip out the windows and he'll never know we were together."

Sinjun held her off and reached for the shirt he'd thrown aside. "Pull yourself together. And stay out of my way." Giving a gentle shove, he pushed her aside and started through the doors.

"Fuck you!" Her voice split air laden with the scent of plumeria and mango. "Fuck you, Sinjun Breaker."

He strode down steps toward the pool. "You should be so lucky, *lady*."

Halfway to the helicopter pad, Sinjun had changed his mind and returned to the house. Chuck liked a few moments alone after a flight to commune with his precious chopper and Sinjun usually tried to accommodate Chuck's passions. But forty-five minutes had passed and Sinjun was beginning to tire of lounging, feet propped on the desk in his study, supposedly engrossed in a report.

Finally the door flew open with the kind of force Chuck Gill put into everything he did. "Shit," he said by way of a salutation. "How many times do I have to tell you to quit tryin' to be your own goddamn army? I hope that female's as harmless as you think she is. If she isn't, you're running risks. Big risks."

Sinjun tossed the open folder on the desk. "Did we have a bad day?" He swung his feet to the floor, not quite missing his giant mostly-Irish wolfhound. "Move your hairy body, Swifty."

"Don't you waste that goddamn smart mouth of yours on me." Blond, blue-eyed and tanned, Chuck advanced, khaki shirt unbuttoned to display a muscular, hairy chest all the way to his navel. His fists—fists the size of camel hooves—bracketed slim hips. "We're both getting worn down by this."

Worn down in more ways than the one Chuck was talking about. "Before we hear about your day," Sin said, mentally preparing himself for a battle, "there's something I just want to mention."

"*Now*, for God's sake?" Chuck exuded frustration.

Sinjun had the feeling it was now or never. "Lorraine isn't any good for you," he said rapidly. "I think having her here on Hell is a bad idea."

Chuck's hands slid slowly to his sides. "Lorraine is none of your goddamn business."

"She is if she's here."

"Because you *own* everything that's here? D'you think you own me? D'you think you can treat me like a puppy dog and decide which treats I can have?"

"No, it's just that—"

"It's just *nothing*," Chuck ground out. "We're not kids anymore. This isn't Montana and you aren't finding ways to keep me on the straight and narrow with my father—or anyone else."

"I know—"

"I don't *need* you to make any more decisions for me." A big, blunt finger stabbed in Sinjun's direction. "I know you hate Lorraine's guts. You don't understand her. If you did, you'd know why I'm in love for the first time in my life. Back off, buddy. And if you value this friendship, don't ever try to interfere between Lorraine and me again."

Sinjun knew when to give up with Chuck. "Okay. Have it your way." Too bad Lorraine had to be the only woman Chuck had ever lost his head over. "Sorry. I was out of line. I care about you."

"Thanks." Chuck didn't sound grateful. "I only stay on Hell if Lorraine stays."

Sinjun should have expected that. "Does that mean you only stay with me if I decide I love Lorraine?"

Chuck said, "Let's just drop it. Okay?"

"Okay."

"We've got enough problems on our hands without the two of us sniping at each other."

Sinjun grinned wryly. "We sure do."

"You aren't handling this right," Chuck said. He didn't return Sinjun's smile. "Letting this journalist in could be the biggest mistake you've ever made. The next time you want to put your fool neck in the noose you're supposedly tryin' to avoid, go do it on your own. Don't send me to pick up the executioner."

Sinjun smothered a smile. "We've already decided Ms. Dean is probably exactly what she says she is—a bored journalist looking for a change of pace. Did you find her?"

"I found her." Chuck loped across koa-wood floors strewn with hala mats and hooked the stopper from a crystal decanter on a silver tray atop Sinjun's black lacquered credenza. He poured Chivas Regal to the brim of a highball glass, dropped in a single ice cube and swore when the liquor slopped over.

Sinjun waited.

"Goddamn engine trouble." Hunched over, flapping wet fingers, Chuck sucked scotch until ice displacement ceased to be a problem. "Took three hours to get clear."

"How is she?"

"I'm gonna want to spend a few hours checking her over again."

"Ms. Dean is that interesting?"

"Very funny. This has been a crappy day, Sin. Tread lightly, buddy." Chuck Gill was a tall man— not as tall as Sinjun—but close. He aimed a slit-eyed glare at his old friend and boss and dropped his long body into an antique cane-and-mahogany chair. He rested his glass on a delicately carved arm.

"Watch the chair," Sinjun said. "That sucker's seventeenth-century English and it cost as much as you make a year."

"I've been meaning to talk to you about that," Chuck said, but he shifted the glass to a knee. "I've already told you I think it's a mistake having the Dean woman on the island. Someone's trying to finish you, Sin. We're here to try and pull 'em into the open. So far, no takers, remember? Until this broad."

"Yeah." Sinjun nudged his dog with a toe. "Yeah. But if she is our man—woman—here on this island is exactly where we're going to want her."

Chuck dropped his head back and aimed his craggy, handsome face at the whirring wooden blades of a ceiling fan. "Three attempts in three months. Three times in Seattle someone tried to kill you and if they'd pulled it off, no sane cop would cry anything but *accident*. If this broad . . . and I only said *if* she's following you around looking for another chance to drop you, we're gonna need eyes on every side of our heads."

"Hell is my turf," Sinjun said quietly. He didn't scare easily, but even he was getting damned jumpy. "Hell is *my* island. No one comes unless I know about it and no one *leaves* unless I know about it. Whoever's trying to kill me will have to come here to do it and this is where I have complete control. If Miss Angelica Dean is bent on getting my blood in a bucket she'd going to have to figure out a way to get me *off* Hell and someplace else—presumably Hawaii— to do it."

"Why?"

"We went over this. Unless she—or whoever— intends to try knocking off not just me, but you, Lorraine and the rest of the staff—and then disappearing—it'll never work."

"Convince me."

Sinjun prayed for patience. "There's nowhere to land anything but a chopper here. Given the range, anyone wanting to get in and out fast would use a helicopter and a Kauai base rather than come by sea—which would take too long even without the reef.

"Bill Braden's monitoring all chopper flights from the islands. Our own radar's more than adequate. So there shouldn't be any getting through without us knowing someone's coming."

"What're you telling me?" Chuck asked. "You mean we've gone to a shitload of trouble—left everything you've got going at HQ and holed up here—and you don't even think those murdering bastards will come after you?"

"I *do* think they'll come. They'll find a way in. And we'll get 'em." He pushed his hands into his jeans pockets. "Surely this Dean woman isn't some hired assassin." Sinjun spoke more for his own benefit than Chuck's.

"Biography," Chuck muttered, tipping down more booze.

Sinjun pushed to his feet. "Hard to believe that anyone would want to write a biography of your childhood partner in crime, I know. But that's what the lady insists she wants to talk about."

"I guess that's what throws me. It seems crazy."

"I'm a fascinating man." Sinjun grinned cynically and headed in the direction of the liquor tray. "Everyone says so. Admit it. There isn't a gossip rag in the country—dammit—in the *world* that doesn't insist I'm the Alberto Tomba of finance. Sinjun Breaker, bad-boy manipulator of empires. Marauding vulture who finds the weak link in previously solid companies and splits them apart so he can buy up the remains cheap. Then there's that trail of lovely ladies I've reportedly used and left, weeping, behind me. Surely my notorious love life's worth a page or two."

"Yeah. There's that."

What love life? Sinjun poured himself a club soda over ice and speared in a wedge of lime. "I admit I'm skeptical, but her credentials look fine. A foreign correspondent with *Verity* for three years. Assignments all over the globe. And not a damn connection to anyone who might have a reason for wanting me out of the way."

"As far as you know."

"Right. As far as I know. And that's why I'm going to have her here. Not because I intend to spill my guts for some biography—but because I can't afford not to check her out. How did she take the delay?"

"Cool enough."

"What's she like?"

Chuck braced his hands on his thighs and drew up his shoulders. "Okay, I guess. If you like small, blonde women with big mouths."

Sinjun snorted. "Sounds appealing. I guess journalists have to be pushy."

"That means this one could just be a great journalist. She started firing questions about you while I was still knocking on the door."

"What time are you going back for her tomorrow?"

"Huh?"

"Tomorrow. What time are you going back to Kauai to pick her up? Or did she get so mad at you for canceling today that she'd decided not to show up at all?"

"What are you talking about, Sin?"

"I'll go slowly." Sinjun swirled his club soda. "Since it got too late for our meeting, we'll have to reschedule. I'm assuming you may have taken the liberty doing that."

"Shit. I've got better things to do than ferry some wise-ass journalist back and forth to Kauai. I brought her with me. She's in one of the beach cottages."

Sinjun choked on his soda.

"Jeez, I didn't think that'd make you sore. I had her bring a bag and I told her to take it easy tonight and expect a call from you in the morning. It saves me time and doesn't hurt you. Mrs. Midgely bitched but she said she'd scrounge up some eats and have Campbell take 'em down. No big deal."

Spreading his free hand, Sinjun set down his glass with a crack. "You've lost it. Holy . . . You've really lost it." He glanced at his bare feet and instantly discarded the idea of taking time to return to his bedroom for shoes. "I'm pretty sure she's harmless. But she might *not* be. There's an outside chance—a *way* outside chance that the lady may be toting a stiletto strapped to her thigh, or poison darts stashed in her panties. Don't you think it might have been a goddamn stupid idea to bring her here at night and *leave* her with the run of this island?"

Chuck leaned forward, then shot from the chair. "Oh, shit," he said, his jaw dropping. "What in Christ's name was I thinking? Stay here. I'll go down and make sure she's tucked up with a book."

"No, you won't." Planting a hand in the middle of his friend's chest, Sinjun dumped him back in the chair. He slid his Beretta from a desk drawer and checked the clip. "Which cottage is she in?"

"The one by the lagoon."

Sinjun shook his head. "Of course. Farthest away and the only one you can't approach without being seen."

"I wasn't thinking, Sin. I was so mad about the engine trouble. Let me—"

"No," Sinjun interrupted Chuck. "*I'll* check on our guest. Finish your drink. Then go to that . . . Go to Lorraine. She's probably waiting for you to keep her warm." If Chuck was lucky, the lovely Lorraine would still be more than warm—more than ready to give him a night to remember. At least Sinjun had learned one lesson tonight—he wouldn't be in a hurry to set his buddy straight about his girlfriend again.

The moon was his enemy.

Slipping from the cover of a dense clump of hibiscus, Sinjun hugged a fringe of shadow at the edge of the grassy slope that swept down to the lagoon cottage. A group of ancient hala trees, balanced crookedly on their teepees of air roots, offered a fresh blind. He threw himself across a swathe of light and landed against a ridged trunk.

Standing there, he felt stupid. He'd undoubtedly knock on the door and be confronted by a myopic female in a flannel nightie who wouldn't know one end of a gun from the other.

On the other hand . . .

Something cold and wet touched his wrist. "What the—" Fists curling, he swung around.

Instantly, a shaggy shape reared out of the gloom. Sinjun braced and whispered urgently, "Down, Swifty." *Too late.* Eighty pounds of unruly hound planted his front paws on Sinjun's chest and flattened him against the tree.

"*Down*, dammit." With both hands, he shoved the dog off. "And stay down. And *stay* put. Mangy, useless pest. Never around if you could be useful. *Down.* Go *home!*"

Swifty whined. Slowly, he lowered his belly and slunk away.

Sinjun turned back and peered out from the trees. The cottage had been built on a low, but sheer bluff above the small lagoon. From Sinjun's viewpoint, the building stood between him and the ocean. Glass backed by wooden jalousies formed most of the wall facing him.

The jalousies were open . . . all of them. And bright lights showed every detail of the living room that ran the length of the cottage.

Every detail included rattan furnishings, tapa wall hangings, a white shale fireplace, logs on the hearth, books on a glass-topped table, wood carvings of mythical gods—everything.

There was no sign of a woman, myopic or otherwise.

Sinjun waited, and watched . . . and fingered the Beretta tucked into the waistband of his jeans.

This was ridiculous.

But nothing moved.

Nothing.

Muscles in his belly clenched. He withdrew. She'd only been there half an hour—forty-five minutes at the most. Hardly enough time to cozy up in bed. And if she had, would she leave the living room lit up like a Christmas tree?

She could be expecting him to come after her.

She could be here somewhere, expecting to see him while he would be unable to see her.

Logic suggested he should ring the doorbell and introduce himself. Caution squelched the idea.

Ribbons of pewter cloud eased across the moon and the light over Hell went out.

Leaving the protection of the trees, Sinjun edged forward, keeping his head down.

The cloud passed. Silver stroked every surface once more.

Managing to stick to what shadow the shrubs threw, Sinjun made speedy progress to the corner of the cottage. There he rested and waited for his breathing to calm down.

Coming on his own might have been the dumbest move he'd ever made. Regardless of how confident he felt, he should have stationed Chuck as backup. Better yet, Sinjun's coolheaded, resourceful sidekick-cum-personal-servant, Enders Lloyd-Worthy, an Englishman who scorned Chuck's "vulgar tantrums," would have made the perfect shotgun for this occasion.

Then there was Willis—always Willis—the deceptively taciturn Samoan who tended the compound grounds with loving care. Willis's gratitude to Sinjun ran deep; it was Sinjun to whom he owed his life. Anyone who threatened Willis's benefactor would wish he'd thought longer, much longer, before drawing the attention of the strongest, most

physically impressive man Sinjun had ever person-
ally encountered.

Unfortunately, chances for careful contingency
planning had been passed up. And, according to
Chuck, there was only one small, smart-mouthed
woman to be dealt with. Sinjun pushed up
far enough to peer through the jalousies at
sill level.

This would all prove unnecessary anyway.

If Chuck hadn't said he'd dropped the woman
here, Sinjun would have thought some staff member left on the lights.

He frowned, and searched the room again . . .
and finally located what he'd been looking for:
something that didn't belong. Just inside the front
door stood a dark-gray suitcase.

Just inside the front door.

Still closed.

Placed where it could be grabbed by someone in
a hurry to leave.

Crouching beneath the windows, Sinjun ran rapidly past the front door and on until he could turn
a corner and reach a door that led to the kitchen.

Cautiously, he pressed his ear to a panel. No
sound came from inside. He eased the doorknob
to the left. The door swung silently open and he
stepped into the unlit room.

Moonlight sliced through skylights and back windows to print squares of white brilliance over pale
tile and stainless-steel appliances. Smiling grimly,
Sinjun softly closed the door behind him and pulled
the gun into his palm. On tiptoe, he crossed to the
short passage that led to the living room. Regardless of her reason, that small, mouthy blonde was
lurking somewhere, anticipating catching him flat-
footed.

Swiftly and silently, he moved into the cottage's
one bedroom and found it empty. The same proved
true of a small laundry room, a guest bathroom, a

sauna and a mudroom and shower at the back of the building.

Standing to one side, Sinjun peered through the mudroom window and into a small area between the cottage and the edge of the bluff. The cottage—built by the man who had willed the island to Sinjun—stood a short distance from a shallow drop into the odd, deep little lagoon.

He began to believe the woman wasn't there. Cautiously, he let himself outside and stood listening. A nearby chorus of bullfrogs, the rustling click of palm fronds overhead and a soft shush of surf into the lagoon were all he heard. The night wind brought a heavy scent of salt from the sea mixed with fragrant frangipani.

Letting out the breath he'd held, Sinjun walked toward the spot where the land fell away. Tension ebbed a little, but his muscles remained tensed. Damn Chuck. He'd left Angelica Dean here and she'd already sneaked out to go hunting. If he was lucky, all she hoped to find were some titillating snippets of information about his private life. If he wasn't so lucky, she hoped to find him—and really ruin his already lousy day by turning out to be an agent for whoever wanted him dead.

Who did want him dead?

He'd asked himself that question a thousand times in the six weeks since his first "accident," when he'd come close to being the victim in a drive-by shooting. And, as always, he began an inventory of business dealings, of people involved in those dealings who might have reason to think less than kindly of him. Unfortunately, there were more than a few. Investment magnates didn't always make a lot of friends, even if they were as scrupulously ethical as Sinjun Breaker.

He stepped back and froze. A movement at the edge of the cliff had caught his eye. He watched

long fingers appear and claw about until they dug
a hold in the bank.

The lord of the clouds had an evil sense of humor.
Grayness blanketed everything again.

With his eyes narrowed on the place where the
fingers had appeared, Sinjun waited.

A small grunt preceded the appearance of a
head. Next came hunched shoulders draped with
long, dripping hair and, finally, the rest of a body
that appeared to be clad in a transparently thin
white swimsuit. Evidently Angelica Dean, rather
than lying in wait for Sinjun, had chosen to
leap headlong into the sea and swim—alone—at
night.

She managed to haul herself up until she
crouched, knees jackknifed, like an oversized, pale
and dripping frog.

"Ms. Dean, I presume?"

The form at his feet didn't move.

"Are you having difficulty getting up?"

"No." Her voice was muffled.

"Good. Hasn't anyone ever mentioned to you
that it's dangerous to swim alone—particularly at
night?"

"Yes."

"Then you're a fool."

She muttered something unintelligible.

Sinjun began to lose patience. "I'm sure you want
to get off Hell as much as I want you off. I hadn't
anticipated your being brought here at this time of
day—or should I say night? But we might as well
discuss this project you've been hounding me with
now. Then you can be on your way first thing in
the morning."

Her next words were perfectly audible. "Arrogant bastard" wasn't something he enjoyed being
called, particularly by someone who'd been pushing him for a favor for weeks.

Still the woman hunched on the ground.

Sinjun stooped and touched her shoulder with his left hand.

She jumped.

"This is ridiculous. Give me your hand."

Without looking up, she did as he asked and he hauled her up. Standing straight, the top of her head didn't reach his chin.

Something broke in Sinjun. "Lady," he said, not caring how harsh he sounded, "I've had a hell of a day and I'm very, very jumpy. For your own good, I'd advise you to quit playing games."

"I'm not." The wobble in her voice suggested chattering teeth.

He couldn't afford to sympathize with his potential enemy, or an agent of a potential enemy.

"You're out of time," he informed her. "We'll do this my way . . . openly. I expect you to put your cards on the table . . . now. No holding back, Ms. Dean. Let me see what you're holding in your hand. We'll decide where to go from here."

He didn't imagine it, she cried out softly, as if anguished.

Slowly, very slowly, she raised her face and Sinjun swallowed once, hard, and with difficulty. Chuck hadn't quite painted an accurate picture. Small, yes. Blonde, yes. Mouthy? The lady had a beautiful, full, soft mouth—that much Sinjun could see in the moon-tinged darkness. And he could see that her face was oval, the chin pointed, the nose pert and slightly tip-tilted, the hairline heart-shaped above finely arched brows, and she had the biggest pair of eyes he'd ever seen. Blue? Gray? Green? That was one thing he'd have to look at in the light because the coy moon didn't tell him.

Muscles in his jaw flexed. "I told you what I want."

"Hands," she mumbled and, gradually, she lifted her arms until her hands were above her head. White teeth dug into her bottom lip before she whispered, "Are you going to shoot me?"

Sinjun frowned and glanced down . . . and his thighs locked. The muzzle of the gun he'd forgotten he still held was pressed into a full, white breast.

He started violently. Tension could make a man damned unobservant. His first impression had been *almost* accurate.

Ms. Angelica Dean was naked.

Two

🦋

*T*he muzzle of the mean, black gun was cold on her breast. The man's eyes, glittering in the moonlight, were aimed as unswervingly as his weapon . . . in the identical direction. And those blazing eyes were anything but cold.

Angelica deliberately straightened her back, then wished she hadn't. There was no missing the faint upward curve of male lips, or the flair of nostril. Showing him she wasn't afraid was one thing. Flaunting her bare breasts . . . and bare everything else . . . to a stranger with a gun was another.

It was madness.

Still, showing weakness was out of the question. "Do you intend to shoot me?" she repeated.

"Hardly."

She'd been right the first time, he *was* arrogant. "Are you—" Since her teeth were determined to chatter, she pressed them together before trying again. "Are you Sinjun Breaker?"

"I'm Breaker." His eyes returned to her face. "You don't spend much time in the sun, do you?"

Angelica pursed her lips, and shook her head slowly. None of her many rehearsals for this moment had covered the disaster it was.

"I didn't think so. You're so white you glow in the dark."

The immediate rush of blood to her face mortified her. If she hoped to pull off the role she'd designed for herself she'd have to control the blushes. Steel-skinned sophisticates probably never turned red—unless they got too much of his wretched sun.

"Put your hands down."

"What?"

"Your hands. Put them down."

"You told me to put them up."

"No, I . . . Forget it. Did you come down here like . . ." He waved the gun back and forth between her breasts. "Did you?" At least he didn't look down again.

"Of course not! What do you think I . . . Well, I did bring a robe actually. Just in case it got cold. It's over there. I'll just get it." Sidestepping, she moved—with forced nonchalance—toward the bush beneath which she'd left a robe she found in the bathroom. What would her friend Brenda tell her to do now? Dear Brenda was the most experienced woman Angelica had ever met, the coolest. *Cool*. "I'll just slip this on and then we . . . Well, then we can have that talk." Fumbling, trying not to show her haste and failing miserably, Angelica donned the dark-blue robe that brushed the tops of her feet.

He was Sinjun Breaker. *Sinjun Breaker!* A few feet from her stood the man who had become her obsession, the man who had changed everything in her life without even knowing she existed.

Angelica wrapped the robe tightly about her and tied the belt firmly. Just there, just behind her, the man she'd learned to hate lived and breathed—and had watched her walking, *naked*.

"Let's go." She swung around and squinted.

He'd gone.

Angelica searched the area—and saw the door to the house swing shut behind him.

"Arrogant bastard!" Arrogant and—from what she'd seen—every bit as physically arresting as billed. Holding up the too-long robe, she hurried after him. "I suppose you're used to women taking off their clothes for you. One look at six foot four inches of solid male muscle and they can probably hardly *wait* to rip off your clothes. I can hear those *bimbos*. 'Ooh, isn't he to die for? And all that lovely money.' *Wait* till I finish with you, *buster*."

She threw open the door . . . and walked into his chest.

"Were you saying something?"

Angelica stood her ground, even though it meant she had to tip her head back to see his face. "I said I could hardly wait to finish . . . unpacking."

"Ah. I see. I expect you'd like to dress before we talk."

"Yes." What had Brenda told her? *"Be comfortable in your body. Beautiful women who are used to having every male in sight snap to heel like drooling basset hounds move like they've got wheels instead of feet. Enough to make you sick as far as I'm concerned, but if you're after having this Breaker chap slavering over you, you'll have to roll with it, if you get my drift."* Brenda was English, from Yorkshire, and she had the most wonderfully unusual accent—once you learned to listen carefully so you understood.

"Do I have egg on my face, Ms. Dean?"

She started. "I beg your pardon?"

"You're staring."

"Be condescending. Sweep about a bit. Look up at him from under your eyelashes." Brenda, tall, handsome in a strong but feminine way, had shuddered at that. What, Angelica wondered, would Brenda say if she knew that rather than hoping to win the man's trust and write a predictably ho-hum biography, Angelica intended to sell a down-and-dirty exposé of Sinjun Breaker to the rag with the highest profile?

She tapped Breaker's arm with the back of a hand and swept by. In the doorway leading from the dark mudroom into a hallway, she paused and looked over her shoulder at the man she couldn't quite see in the darkness. "I'm perfectly comfortable as I am, Mr. Breaker."

"Good."

"Are *you* comfortable?" she asked.

"Oh, very."

"Good," Angelica said, experiencing a pain in her twisted neck. "Then let's talk." This was ridiculous. She couldn't keep up such crap.

In the brightly lit living room, Angelica clutched the lapels of the robe together and tried to think clearly. "A drink?" she said, spying several bottles on top of a glass-and-wicker trolley. "What will you have?"

"Nothing, thank you."

His voice was deep, yet very clear—and strangely still. The moment had come to face him, really face him in the light. She turned to find him disconcertingly near. The gun was nowhere in sight. That established, she studied his face.

Dear God, photos from news archives hadn't begun to show how knee-bucklingly stunning he was.

He tilted his head, raised his brows and stared back.

He felt her lips part.

Sinjun Breaker's lips parted, too, showing straight, square, very white teeth. His mouth was wide, the upper lip narrow, the lower full. The corners tipped naturally up—but only the tiniest bit.

Angelica looked at his nose. Straight, the bridge narrow. His brows slashed upward and were black, as black as the slightly curly hair that reached the collar of a loose white cotton shirt.

Then she studied the inevitable—his eyes—and felt the breath slip softly from her lungs.

Sinjun Breaker's gaze didn't falter. Green flecked with yellow-gold. Black curling lashes, spiky as if wet. And he seemed to look right into her mind.

Angelica passed her tongue over her lips—and Sinjun Breaker watched her mouth while she did so. And the tanned skin over the lean bones of his face tightened, shone across high, strong cheekbones and a square jaw.

Her heart began a heavy beat she heard in her ears.

The devil. What did they say about him? That he was the most beautiful angel of all? Before her stood the most elegantly, the most satanically handsome—the most beautifully masculine man she'd ever seen.

Angelica shivered.

"You're cold."

She didn't register what he said and when he moved, she started.

"Your hair," he said, matter-of-factly. "It's soaking that robe."

Before she could react, Breaker ran a hand around her neck, pulled out her sopping hair and let it fall. "Better?" His fingers rested lightly on her shoulder.

His touch was warm and firm . . . And he was loathsome. She must remember that.

"Rich men are used to getting their own way," Brenda had warned at SeaTac Airport when she'd dropped Angelica off for the flight to Hawaii. *"They use women like ruddy coats, and don't you forget I said as much. Pick out one they like—or one that's thrown their way. Put it on and try it out a bit. Use it—if you know what I mean. Then toss it aside when something a bit newer, or in a color that's a mite more appealing, comes along. Oh, yes, I know all about rich men—and good-looking ones. And if you put the two together, well, God help you then, my girl."*

Angelica heard Breaker laugh and glanced up at him, puzzled. "What's funny?"

"Nothing," he said, but continued to chuckle. "Perhaps we should put this discussion off until the morning when you may be less distracted—if I decide I'm going to have a discussion with you."

His words hit like a slap. "*If*, Mr. Breaker? You invited me to come. Why would you do that if you didn't intend to agree to my proposal?"

He considered for several moments. "Because I'm a curious man," he said. "I wanted to get a look at the woman who pestered me with letters and phone calls for weeks. Then followed me to Hawaii and, finally, to my island."

A curious man. What would he say if she told him right now that she intended to expose this curious man for the destructive, unscrupulous monster he was? "Curiosity can be useful," she told him, careful to keep her tone neutral. "I, too, am curious. Most journalists are."

"Are you a good journalist?"

She knew when she was being baited. "The best." Not the toughest. Not the one who didn't get ruffled by the world's rough elements, or its cruelty, but a journalist who'd been hailed as potentially the most sensitive and honest reporter of the coming age.

Breaker was watching her closely. "The best, Miss Dean? Also the most humble?"

That was one comment that didn't embarrass her. "Sometimes humility is spurious, Mr. Breaker. I assumed you asked a question to which you wanted an honest response. You got it."

He bowed. "Fair enough. Let's get down to business. Why does the *best* of journalists want to write my biography?"

She'd known this would come. Fashioning a detached smile, she sat at one end of a rattan couch strewn with soft cushions in shades of blue and green. "Even the best—at anything—can benefit from broadening their scope. My work is always slanted toward the human element. That's what makes me tick—people. People are what I portray best. But I want to try studying human nature from a slightly different perspective.

"You, Mr. Breaker, are going to make a perfect subject for what I've decided I want to do."

He paced to the windows and back, and dropped to sit in a deep chair with cushions that matched the couch. "I still don't understand what it is you want to do."

Angelica smiled ingenuously. "Why, I want to study you. Your life. A nobody kid from nowhere makes good—makes more than good—he makes a bigger fortune than the most optimistic of dreamers could conjure up.

"I want to start with the boy who grew up dirt-poor in Montana. The son of a drunk who never held a job. The kid who fathered his father and kept him going and mostly out of trouble until the old man got hauled away for killing a man. How did it feel—"

"Where did you get this?" he interrupted her. He remained in the same position in the chair, resting back against the cushions, one ankle on the other knee.

Until that moment, Angelica hadn't noticed his feet were bare—long, narrow feet with a sprinkling of dark hair on top, hair that became heavier on his ankles.

He remained in exactly the same position—except for his hands. His hands folded over the arms of the chair and the knuckles shone white.

"It couldn't have been easy to have the police come and tell you your father had smashed a whiskey bottle over a man's head and killed him."

"I asked how you know this."

She shrugged, but her stomach rolled. "Journalists are used to finding out the things they want to know." And sometimes they found out things they'd rather not know. "You are an incredible success story, Mr. Breaker. White trash to billionaire. I'd guess that makes you a minority of one."

He regarded her, his extraordinary eyes resembling green glass—broken green glass. "That was insupportable, Ms. Dean. And I don't have to take it from you."

"You don't have to take the truth?" What she was doing had been carefully calculated but she didn't have to like it. Her adult life had been dedicated to finding truth and trying to make it count for as much good as she could wring from it. Sometimes that wasn't possible and this was one of those times. This time it would be absolutely impossible. "Mr. Breaker, you may not like what I just said, but it is the truth and we both know it."

His hands relaxed . . . slightly.

Angelica gave him her most brilliant, most trustworthy smile before going in for the next thrust. "Have you ever tried to find your mother?"

He stared at her, unblinking.

"Is that yes or no?" When he didn't respond, she flipped wet hair away from her neck and continued, "She was a teenager when she became pregnant with you. Sixteen. Your father was thirty. I guess that means he was eligible to be hauled up on another rather unsavory criminal charge."

Still Breaker said nothing. The watchfulness that seemed part of him intensified. And Angelica's stomach turned and turned again while her heart thundered. "Anyway, as soon as Belle Ford—your mother—as soon as she dropped you, she dropped out of sight and no one seems to know what happened to her." With a puzzled frown and wide-open eyes, she flashed the message that this was one more mystery in the life and times of Sinjun Breaker, billionaire. "Given the way your father dealt with the man he thought cheated him at cards—hit him over the head with—"

"With a bottle," Breaker finished for her. "The guy had it coming. He called my father names I won't sully your pretty ears with, and drew a knife. Didn't you find that out in your snooping?"

"In my business we call it investigation. No, I didn't find that out."

"So it probably didn't happen that way? Think whatever you want to think, Ms. Dean. I know the truth. And my father didn't kill my sixteen-year-old mother after I was born, if that's what you're suggesting."

She shook her head. "I'm not suggesting anything. Just stating what crosses my mind. I'm like that. You'll always know what I'm thinking because I spit it right out." The charm she ladled into every word almost choked her. "But your mother—"

"My mother died four years ago. She'd been in a coma for almost a month following a traffic accident."

That caught her off guard. "Ah, I see."

"You didn't know that, did you? Your network must have slipped up. Give them forty lashes when you get back."

Angelica Dean wasn't considered the best because she was slow to recover from a blow. "What did she tell you about ducking out on you when you were a baby?"

He smiled, a lopsided smile she grudgingly acknowledged as endearing. "Nothing. I'd tracked her for years. I finally found her when she was already in the hospital after the accident. She'd made a life for herself, a decent life. There was no way I'd interfere in her family's grief or mess up the memories they had of her. I stuck around in the background until she died, then blew. Don't bother to try digging up anything about her. You'll be wasting your time."

His voice had become distant, and even more still. The smile hovered. Angelica leaned toward him. There was something vulnerable in that smile, something . . . Damn it! He was a pro at suckering people, but she wasn't about to become another of his victims.

Angelica got up and turned her back on him. "The man who flew me here is called Chuck Gill?"

"Yes."

"You've known each other a long time."

He exhaled loudly. "Just about all our lives. He's the best friend I've ever had. In fact, he's the best friend I ever hope to have. Does that answer a few questions for you?"

She tugged the belt on the robe tighter. "Together forever. Forever together. Something like that?"

"We've been through a lot, if that's what you mean."

"But you always came out better than Chuck, didn't you?"

He hesitated before saying, "Chuck hasn't always had good luck. And, like the rest of us, he's made his fair share of mistakes. But that's all changed now."

"Because you were around to pick up the pieces?"

"I think it's time to move on from here, Miss Dean."

"Chuck's father saved you."

After a short silence, Breaker said, "In a way, yes."

She walked to the windows, where she saw her own reflection against the moon-backed silhouettes of lush vegetation. "Chuck's father—Len—gave you jobs on his ranch in Montana. And he taught you to fly helicopters—the same way he taught his own son."

"That's right. What does—"

"It paints a picture of how you got where you are," Angelica interrupted him. "When you were twenty-two, a man by the name of Bruno Kertz employed you as his personal pilot and bodyguard."

"I don't think you needed to interview me, Miss Dean. You already know almost as much as I do. How about the size of my jockstrap? Did you find out that detail, too?"

Angelica frowned. Something had shifted through dense shadows on the lawn. She stared, searching for a form, but the shadows were still again. Tension must be making her jumpy.

"Miss Dean? Have I shocked you into silence?"

She returned her stare to her reflection and felt the rise of heat he seemed destined to be able to bring to her face almost at will. "All I have are the dry facts about you," she said flatly. And he was going to be shocked to the soles of his bare feet when he found out exactly what some of those facts were. "Bruno Kertz was a recluse, a very wealthy recluse. This island belonged to him."

"Bruno was a wonderful man. The best."

"I'd probably think he was the best too if he made me his protégé and then his sole heir."

"You're a cynic, Miss Dean."

"I'm a realist, Mr. Breaker. Tell me about the ruby peony."

He took a long time to exhale. "Go back to your source."

"I'd much rather have you describe it."

"A tree peony made of rubies. More carats than I intend to disclose. The stamens are of spun gold tipped with flawless diamonds. It's very beautiful and very old and I value it more than anything I own."

She visualized the piece. "Mr. Kertz had a name for it, didn't he?"

"He called it his ace in the hole. To him that meant it was his security blanket in case he ever ran on really bad times."

"I'd love to see it," she told him, completely honestly.

"You and a lot of other people."

He was as brittle as she'd expected. "Is it true you take the peony with you wherever you go?" she asked.

"Absolutely. My motto is, never fuck without one eye on your ruby tree peony. Next question?"

Angelica wouldn't let herself look away. She said, "You've obviously earned your reputation for being direct."

"Thank you," he said. "Why are you here?"

She felt suddenly sick. "My letters and telephone calls made that clear, I think."

"Do you? I don't."

This was it. This was the mine field she'd known was waiting on this island—with this man. "You are an international figure. You are also the embodiment of a fairy tale."

He gave a short laugh. "I beg your pardon?"

"Cinderella, Mr. Breaker. Surely you know the story. Poor little girl among the cinders gets swept—"

"I know the story." Sarcasm loaded his voice. "I fail to see any connection."

"Do you?" In the glass, she saw him rise to his feet and couldn't help bracing. "The only difference is that in your case the helpless victim of rotten parents was a boy and his savior wasn't a potential lover . . . or was he?"

"Son of a bitch!" Breaker hissed, not quite under his breath. "You want to bait me, don't you?"

"Perhaps." She willed her stomach to unclench. "Sometimes it works to make a witness angry.

Anger can cause a subject to be careless. Everyone knows how reporters like to lull—or infuriate—a source into indiscretion."

"Be ready to leave at dawn."

Angelica gathered the lapels of the robe to her throat. "I'd rather not."

"God, you're incredible."

"I know." If he knew how she felt, he'd laugh and walk out. "I'm incredible and so are you. We make quite a pair, don't you think?"

"Dawn."

"I won't be ready." She saw him move toward the door. "And if I did go you'd always wonder if you regretted not knowing more about me. Why is this island called Hell?"

"You wouldn't be interested."

"I'm interested. I'm interested in everything about you." *Everything*.

As she watched, he hesitated and changed direction. Slowly, he approached her. "My name is Sinjun. Don't ask me where my old man came up with a name like that. Mostly he was too drunk for me to ask. And if he was sober he was too mad for me to ask.

"My friends always called me Sin. Some said it suited me."

Some continued to say it suited him. Angelica drew a slow, deep breath. He was crossing the room, drawing closer.

"Then I grew up and there were people who still said Sin should have been my given name."

His presence, inches from her shoulder, was something she would have felt even if she couldn't see him.

"Then I got lucky—or what was considered lucky," Breaker continued. "Bruno Kertz realized I had more to offer than a mean pair of fists and a talent for flying just about anything with wings or blades. He decided I had a brain and he made

it his mission to push me into using it. Bruno gave
me a lot. But I gave back just as much. He was a
great man and I miss him."

"Hell," she prompted him.

"Simple." He lifted strands of her drying hair
and raised them to his face. "Nice. Spring roses—
and a little salt. Very nice."

Muscles in her thighs contracted; this man had
the power to arouse her. There'd been very little
time for Angelica Dean to play with sex. Very little
time and no one memorable enough to encourage
her to make more. But she knew a sexual pull when
she felt it. Breaker was feeling that pull, too, and he
intended to make use of it. "Hell," she repeated.

"Ah, yes, Hell." Very carefully, he gathered her
hair into his hand at the nape of her neck. "Honey-
blonde. It must look sexy as hell with the sun on
it."

She couldn't move. And she shouldn't, must *not*
respond to him, no matter how attractive he was.

"Mmm. What were we talking about?" he said.

"Hell."

The rough tip of one long finger traced the line
of her jaw from the touchy little dip beneath her
ear to the point of her chin. "Yes. Hell. My island.
Obvious, of course. The luck of the devil—that's
what I've got. And they call me Sin. Ergo, Hell.
Look at me."

The night must have grown warmer. She couldn't
fill her lungs anymore. A thumb had replaced his
finger and it rested at the corner of her mouth.

"Come on, Ms. Dean, look at me. Please?"

She turned her head sharply toward him.

"Yes, of course." His thumb brushed back and
forth along her lower lip. "They're brown. Soft,
soft brown. God, I bet they're something in the
sunlight, too."

"I—" He watched every move of her mouth.
"You're very good, Mr. Breaker."

"Good?" His eyes widened innocently. "What can you mean?"

"Have you ever met a woman who wasn't putty in your hands?"

He smiled and the light in his green eyes glittered. "I don't know. Have I?"

With those magical, smiling, incredibly hypnotic eyes he had the power to move anything and anyone. Almost anything and anyone. Unfortunately for him it wasn't his body she intended to undo, but his mind. "You might find it . . . stimulating to find out if there's a woman you can't seduce, don't you think?"

"Possibly." Gently, but firmly, he turned her to face him. "I thought you were here because you want to write my biography."

"I am." She dragged in another breath—and his gaze flickered lower. "Don't make too much of some of my questions, Mr. Breaker. I tend to wander a little sometimes."

"Do you?" He stroked the backs of his fingers down the side of her neck. "Somehow I doubt if you ever truly wander—not without knowing exactly where you want to wander to."

"You're amazing," she said. "You seem to read me too well."

"Do I?" His face bowed fractionally nearer. "You wouldn't try to flatter me into your corner, would you, Ms. Dean?"

He couldn't intend to . . . "I—no, Mr. Breaker."

"Good. My name is Sinjun. I think I'd like to hear you say that."

He *was* going to kiss her. "Sinjun." This was part of her plan to get what she wanted. She would lull him into trusting her, then take him apart, piece by piece. But she hadn't exactly considered how it would feel to be *touched* by him.

"Are you really serious about this biography thing?"

"I've never been more serious about anything."
Focus. She must focus.

"Do you suppose you could tell me—in very few words—why? Honestly?"

No, she couldn't quite do that. "You're a man of our times. Quite possibly one of the last of a kind we won't see again."

"Why?"

"Because the world's changing. People are forgetting about fairy tales. When they have—forgotten them completely, that is—then there won't be any more Cinderella stories."

"I don't think I like the Cinderella bit."

"I'll think of another fairy tale."

"Will you?"

She *wanted* to know what kissing him would be like. "Yes. Yes, I will." Angelica lowered her eyes.

His lips grazed across hers. "What do your friends call you?" he whispered.

"Angelica," she murmured. "Or Angel."

He chuckled softly. "Sin and the Angel. That has quite a ring to it. Open your mouth for me."

For some bizarre reason, he was playing with her. "I don't think so," Angelica said.

"I do. I definitely think it's imperative, in fact. We're getting to know each other well enough for you to write my biography the way it should be written—from experience." He bent to kiss her throat.

"I make it a practice never to mix business and . . ."

"Pleasure? Think of this as research."

When he drew her against his length her legs felt boneless. "Does that mean you're going to let me write your story?"

"It means I'm thinking about it."

His hands were beneath the robe, on her shoulders—rubbing. She tensed, but wouldn't allow herself to push him away. "Good," she said in a satisfyingly level voice. Why did he have to be so beautiful? And why did she have to react to him as every woman must have reacted to him since he was old enough to use his lips and his hands . . . and his body like a man. "Can we talk some more tomorrow?"

"Absolutely." He stared down into her eyes.

Angelica tried to look away but failed. "I think it would be a great idea if we said good night."

His smile was covert. "I think you might be right. And we will. Don't worry, Angel, I don't gobble up beautiful women on sight. Not even very little ones."

"Good night." Her voice cracked.

"Not even very little, very sexy ones with beautiful breasts."

The infuriating rush of hot blood sped over her face. "That's principled of you."

"I know. One kiss—*Angel*—then I'll go. I'll go and think about the next time we . . . talk." His white teeth pressed into his bottom lip.

"Right." Angelica rested her hands on his shoulders.

Predictably, he urged her even closer. "One kiss?"

Again she tried to look away.

"Open your mouth for me."

Angelica closed her eyes tightly. He took her lips, gently at first, then with the subtle force of experience. His tongue pressed past her lips, withdrew and thrust again. Heat burst from within Angelica. He was delivering a blatant little parody of how it would be if they were both naked and he was pushing into her body with all the force she felt shivering in the muscles beneath her fingers.

"Oh, yes," he said against her cheek. "I don't think it would be a good idea for you to leave at dawn after all."

"You don't?" A premonition sent goose bumps over her skin. She hadn't seemed to respond to him physically but he didn't care. He might even be the type of man who found resistance a turn-on. She said, "I'm glad you want me to stay. I'll be very thorough with the project, I promise you." Oh, very thorough. But what she felt was fear. She must be very, very careful with this man. He was one of those Brenda spoke of: the use-and-toss-away type.

He raised his head and gathered the neck of the robe into his curled fingers. "Mmm. I've decided to give you a chance to prove how thorough you can be."

Fear. He definitely frightened her. "Thank you." This bizarre little incident was all about control—his control. He'd shown her he could have what he wanted, when he wanted it . . . and *if* he wanted it.

"Don't thank me," he said. "I never *give* anything away."

Chuck was a fool. He really believed she loved him. Even while he'd been telling her about picking up some little tramp on Kauai and bringing her here, he'd been looking at Lorraine as if he never considered she wasn't crazy about him, too.

And now Sin was kissing the bitch like a man fresh out of longtime solitary confinement.

Lorraine stood on the lawn in front of the lagoon cottage, her arms folded beneath her breasts. They couldn't see her in the shade of a vast Australian fern, wouldn't even if they looked from their stage-lit set toward an audience of one. But Sin and the little whore had things in mind other than any thought of someone outside watching their disgusting mauling.

Sin would make love to that colorless nothing tonight. Already his hands were inside whatever she was wearing and he'd plastered himself on her like soft butter on warm bread.

he didn't think Garth should know about Lorraine and Chuck.

Chuck, for God's sake. He'd been supposed to help her get what she wanted, then get out of her way—quickly. By becoming his mistress, she'd made him her ticket to follow Sin—to follow him all the way to Hell. She couldn't stand waiting much longer.

She made fists and stared through the cottage windows at Sinjun's bowed head. He was kissing the mousy blonde like this was his last night on earth.

Fuck Sinjun.

She knew where to find what she needed.

Turning away, she headed through dense jungle toward the shore south of the lagoon.

"No," Sinjun repeated, "I never give anything away if I don't expect to be glad I did. Your intelligence on me is good, Angel. But you still have a great deal to learn."

He stepped away and she folded her arms tightly. "I'll look forward to . . . to the adventure. And I may just surprise you."

The smile slipped from Sinjun Breaker's unforgettable face. "Yes," he said. "Let's hope so. Oh, yes, I do hope you will."

With that, he left.

Angelica stared through windows at a night world she couldn't see, and imagined a tall, broad-shouldered, black-haired man striding away without looking back. And he went confident the woman he'd left behind would soon become one more of the conquests he considered his due—his right.

She had just kissed and been kissed by that man.

She had just been caressed by him and felt his desire to make love with her. Not love—sex.

Her own body had responded, even as she'd celebrated the first victory on the way to her goal.

There would be more intimate encounters between them, but next time she'd be prepared. Next time she would use him as he'd used God knew how many others.

Careless in his hunger to grab even more power, even more wealth, Sinjun Breaker had destroyed many men. And he had caused the death of one harmless, gentle woman.

For that he would pay.

Angelica would see that Sinjun Breaker was brought down for the death of Marlene Golden—her mother.

Three
❦

*T*he wind was still warm and it painted the
scarlet silk sarong against Lorraine's heated
skin.

She didn't have to be bored and alone. No. No,
tonight she'd follow up on an idea that had been
growing ever since she came to this stinking island.
Why not? Chuck had gotten back in a foul temper,
banged her with his usual "three strikes and I'm
outta here" style and drunk himself into a stupor.

All she wanted was to play a little game that
would bring two people some harmless pleasure.
She could regard the exercise as practice, a rehears-
al for the real performance. With Sinjun—and she
would be with Sinjun eventually—there would be a
command performance.

Raising her chin, anticipating, she pushed
through a tangle of vines and emerged onto a
grassy bank above a long strip of white beach.

She saw who she was looking for immediately—
exactly where she'd known he would be.

Almost skipping, Lorraine ran onto the cool,
coarse sand and advanced on the man who sat
facing the sea, a fishing pole propped beside
him. This wasn't the first time she'd followed
him through the night to this untouched stretch
of beach. On each occasion all she'd done was hide
and watch.

Not tonight. Tonight the watching was over and the fun was about to begin.

Chuck had warned her not to fool with Willis. So had Sin. But she knew why. They were afraid she'd have a good time, a real good time, and with a man whose silent stares had been inviting her to find out exactly what he had in mind for weeks.

When she arrived within feet of Willis's still form, Lorraine stopped. He was gorgeous, the kind of male masterpiece that turned a woman into willing jelly that wept just to feel him.

Lorraine wanted to feel him. All of him. Before this night was out, the cool, silent Willis wouldn't be cool anymore. When Lorraine had finished with him he'd be hot, and he'd stay hot—*be* hot whenever she wanted him to be, which could become real often until Sinjun wised up.

Willis's darkly bronzed shoulders were about a mile wide. In the moonlight, every muscle stood defined and alone, all the way to a narrow waist and slender hips. Tonight, dressed only in cotton shorts, he knelt on the sand, his massive thighs spread.

Lorraine pressed her hands against her belly. She wanted to feel those legs holding her down—and she wanted to make fire in his dark, watchful eyes.

Stooping, she scooped up a handful of sand and tossed it at him. "Hey, Willis," she said, low and seductive—coaxing, the way she knew a man liked to be coaxed.

He didn't turn around, didn't respond.

She took another step toward him. "It's lonely out here. Aren't you lonely here on your own?"

His right arm shifted and he pulled the fishing rod into his hands. In the silence, the reel swished and he tested his line before once more driving the handle deep into the sand.

Lorraine shivered and hugged herself. "I'm lonely, Willis. That's why I came out here, because I'm lonely and I know you are, too. I thought we could keep each other company."

"Keep each other company?" His voice was deep, rough, toneless. He turned and, still kneeling, stared at her. "Why do you want my company?"

"Because I like you." She swallowed. Even kneeling, his face was barely below the level of hers. With the moon behind him she saw the harsh shadows that slashed beneath his cheekbones and delineated muscles in his immense arms and chest. "You're like me, Willis. We're passionate people cut off from people to share that passion with."

"Are we?"

"Of course we are. And it doesn't have to be that way. We can have each other—be with one another."

"You're Chuck's woman."

Always the same old reminder. "I'm the woman Chuck comes home to. When he leaves the island, he has other women. Why shouldn't I have some fun, too?"

As far as she could tell, his face remained impassive. "Chuck leaves Hell to do things that have to be done. He's never gone longer than they take."

She hugged her ribs and laughed. "There are certain things that don't have to take very long at all, Willis. We both know that. Take it from me, Chuck is a *very* quick boy. Too damn quick. I need a man who knows how to take his time and make me feel all of him, a man with a whole lot of him for me to feel. I need you."

"Go," he said softly. "Go now."

Her need for him raged. "You don't want me to go. So I won't."

"What do you want from me?"

Her lungs expanded and she let her head fall back. "You know what I want, Willis. It's the same thing you want." The wind picked up her hair and tossed it across her face. "Let me show you."

She didn't hear him move, didn't even sense that he had until his huge hands slid around to cup her bottom.

Excitement bubbled out in her laughter and she braced her arms on his shoulders. "See," she said softly. "I told you we understand each other." Her gaze took in the fascinating angle of his black eyes. No hint of what he thought showed in those eyes and his full, clearly defined mouth didn't return her smile.

His grip tightened until the tips of his fingers dug deeply into her flesh. "I don't need a woman to tell me what I want. I don't want to take another man's woman."

"*I* want you to. I won't stay with Chuck, you know. Not for much longer."

He seemed to think about that and while he thought he tested her contours. "Maybe you're telling the truth."

"I am," she assured him breathlessly. "Chuck and I both know it's almost over."

He muttered something in his own tongue.

"What?" she said teasingly. "What did you say?"

"I said you can still leave."

"No." A trembly, wobbly sensation fluttered within her. "I'm staying. I'm inspired, Willis. Not many women know what I know. I know what a passionate man wants. I *know* what you want."

Through the thin silk sarong and satin panties, Willis's fingers pushed into the cleft of her bottom, shifted down, parted her. "Do you know?" He laughed, but there was no mirth in the sound. "You want to do what I want? Anything?"

She knew a moment's fear, but only a moment. "Anything."

"I've been watching you."

"I know."

He laughed again. "You make sure I watch. You flaunt your body. I never intended to touch you, but I'm a man and I've thought of how I'd take a woman like you."

"You have?" Hot, wet arousal darted deep. "Tell me."

"I don't like talking."

Raising one knee, he brought her down to sit astride his thigh. "Wet," he said, and his breath hissed. "Wet bitch."

She flinched. "Wet the way you like me."

"The way I'd expect a bitch to be wet."

"I'm not—" She bit back the rest of her retort. "I can teach you things, too, Willis."

"Teach me?" Without haste, he caught her wrists, took them behind her back and held them there with one hand. "No." The word was flat.

A frisson of panic welled. Lorraine stuffed it down. This was what she wanted. What she needed. "Then you teach me, Willis." She drew a deep breath, arched her back, knowing exactly what the moonlight would do to her body—right in front of his eyes.

Still holding her hands behind her, he stood and backed her to a volcanic rock that jutted from the beach. Without a word, Willis pressed her backward on the unyielding mass.

Fragments of shell dug into her wrists and shoulders. Lorraine wriggled. And then Willis laughed. "Good," he said. "Good. *Move* for me. I like that."

He ripped aside the sarong and grasped her breast. Squeezing with callused fingers, he bent to suck the nipple into his mouth, to suck and bite.

Lorraine struggled. She tried to draw up a knee but he trapped it with one powerful leg.

"You're hurting me!"

"You don't like that?" Wedging her arms between the rock and her own body, he stood astride her hips and ground into her pelvis. "Speak. Tell me you don't like my teaching. Tell me to let you go and I will."

She shook her head. He'd bruised her.

The next sound she heard was tearing silk. Willis ripped the sarong apart at the shoulder to bare her other breast. Rocking, smiling down at her with his mouth while no light touched his eyes, he let her feel the length and breadth and the unyielding hardness of him.

"You like that?" he asked. "You want to feel it—*all* of it?"

Lorraine nodded, but her throat closed against sick and mounting panic. He was cold. Exciting, but so cold.

Looking at her breasts, he surrounded and pushed them together. Staring, he bent to nip her flesh until she cried out and bucked.

"Yes, you learn very well."

Then his hand pushed up between her legs and past her panties. Still nipping her breasts, he drove his fingers inside her body. "Oh, God!" She clenched down and writhed wildly.

Caught off guard, he loosened his grip and in that instant, she dropped to the sand and scrambled away.

Her breath came in great sobs. And a thrill shot under her skin. When his hand closed on her ankle, Lorraine twisted and beat at him, shrieking, knowing she might incite him to the kind of sexual violence her dreams were made of and praying she could.

Slowly, face-down in the sand, she was dragged toward him.

"You came to make sure I wasn't lonely," he told her, his voice still without inflection. "You can't leave me now. I might keep on being lonely."

Lorraine pretended a fresh attempt at escape.

The grip left her legs. He shoved up her brief skirt and tore off the already destroyed panties. Whipping her to her back, he stared down at her an instant.

Deliberately enticing, she rested on her elbows and thrust her breasts at him.

"Lorraine," he said, speaking her name for the first time since they'd met. "I can still stop."

With a knee, she found his penis and pressed. "I can't," she said, and passed her tongue over her lips.

"Bitch," he ground out. "Horny bitch."

"And you love it." She rocked from side to side and giggled while he followed the sway of her flesh. "Say you love it, Willis."

Willis said nothing. Standing over her, he swept her up by the waist. When she stood before him, he grabbed the tattered sarong in both hands and twisted.

"Ooh, you're hurting," she said, pouting. The silk tightened about her elbows and she moaned. "I don't like that."

He twisted again. "Of course you do."

Willis used the silk bonds he fashioned to tie her arms together behind her back, then jerked until she fell to the sand.

Lorraine opened her mouth to scream, but his lips came down upon hers, swallowing the sound. She heard a zipper part, felt again his forceful fingers pushing inside her body. Then, while she lay helplessly squirming, he rammed in his big, beautiful sex and his hips moved like a well-oiled jackhammer.

At last she heard his control slip. His sobbing breath matched the pace of hers and Lorraine smiled through gritted teeth.

She felt him come, felt the warm slickness fill her. Then the world turned dark; dark and scorched at the edges. The climax broke over her so fast she felt herself falling through thick cloud that gave way, layer upon layer, until she landed, throbbing, sweating, pulsing—knowing she would come to him again and again.

* * *

It was a long time before he released her silken bonds. When she was free, he tossed the wreckage of her dress into her lap, looked at her long enough to show an echo of what she knew: Tonight was only her first time with him.

Willis zipped his shorts and turned his back on Lorraine. Returning to the spot beside his fishing rod, he sank to his knees once more.

"Willis," she called, getting up and walking to stand beside him. Her ruined clothes remained where they'd fallen. "You'll be here tomorrow, won't you?"

He nodded slowly. "Tomorrow, yes."

Lorraine felt his mind forming pictures of other nights, other hot dark releases with a kindred spirit. And her mind began to form a picture of its own. Chuck had said the pale whore meant something to Sin. He said she was here to spend time with him. Lorraine didn't like that and if it lasted very long, she might need help persuading Sin's little friend she'd rather be elsewhere.

"Good. I'll be here tomorrow, too, Willis." *Tomorrow and tomorrow and tomorrow*. Even while her bruises made themselves felt, she tensed against a fresh shaft of arousal.

Lorraine glanced down at Willis and smiled. Only a real woman would appreciate this man's special touch. Some might be repulsed. Some might even be scared . . . to death.

Four

"*G*ood morning, Mr. Breaker."

"Good morning, Enders."

Immaculate in khaki shirt, shorts and knee socks, Enders Lloyd-Worthy inclined his head smartly, giving a half-sideways view of gray, pot-scrubber hair that matched a square-cut thatch of a mustache. "Your melon is on the table, sir."

Sinjun sighed, let the kitchen door swing shut behind him and blinked against glaring rays of early sun that bounced over silverware and crystal set on a wicker-and-glass table.

He gave Mrs. Midgely, his very excellent cook, something he hoped resembled a smile and said, "Eggs, please. Fried." Then Enders Lloyd-Worthy, self-dubbed manservant and purveyor of *melon* and other items designed to make Sinjun live much longer than he cared to live, got the scowl he seemed to thrive on.

With Swifty loping beside him, Sinjun scuffed—barefoot—across cool terra-cotta tiles to the plant-filled solarium where he always ate breakfast when he was on the island.

"Cholesterol," Enders said without making eye contact, and scraped a chair back for Sinjun.

"Bacon with that, please, Mrs. Midgely."

Enders snapped a napkin across Sinjun's thighs. "Arteries," he murmured.

"What would we do without them?" Sinjun responded. "You're looking fetching this morning, Mrs. Midgely. Green becomes you."

She aimed a sly glance at Enders then smiled at Sinjun, her dark eyes warm through vaguely steamed glasses. "You want hash browns, Mr. Breaker?" Plump and fortyish, Mrs. Midgely's American heritage was barely visible through the larger Chinese influence—with pretty results. Inherited from Sinjun's benefactor, Bruno Kertz, the woman lived permanently on Hell. Despite the existence of her twenty-one-year-old son, Campbell, no Mr. Midgely had ever been seen or mentioned.

"Hash browns would be fine." A sheaf of fax printouts lay beside Sinjun's plate. "I see Fran's already at her post." Fran Simcox, Sinjun's secretary of eight years, went wherever he went. A powerhouse of efficiency, she'd spurned numerous efforts to woo her away. Sinjun made certain Fran's income and benefits were too impressive to be easily dismissed.

"We understand there's a person staying in the lagoon cottage," Enders said, pouring fresh-squeezed orange juice into a tall glass. "Evidently another of Chuck's diversions."

Sinjun smiled into his coffee cup.

"We don't *understand* she's there," Mrs. Midgely said. "We *know*. I had to send food down last night. Campbell took it. He said the lady was very nice."

Campbell, home for the summer from college on the mainland, chose that moment to enter the kitchen from a door to the gardens. Compact, with short dark hair and a pleasant, open face, he appeared at a glance to be any parent's dream son. Passing the table as if he saw neither Enders nor Sinjun, he went to stand behind his mother.

"Morning, Campbell," Sinjun said. In the past three years, since he'd left for school in California, the boy had become increasingly withdrawn. On closer examination, his dark eyes seemed either incredibly innocent—or vacant. "Enjoying your vacation?"

"I feel it more strongly than ever," Campbell announced, ignoring Sinjun. He touched Mrs. Midgely's shoulder. "There are a lot of negative influences. I'm going to be very busy here."

Damn strange, Sinjun thought. He'd suggest Campbell see a therapist, but Mrs. Midgely had already shown hostility at any interference with the way she dealt with her son.

"I was just telling Mr. Breaker that you took food down to the lagoon cottage, Campbell," the cook said. "I told him you liked the lady."

"She can't know about Chuck," Campbell said. "About Chuck and Lorraine. If she did, she wouldn't have come."

Swifty rested his great, shaggy head on the table and watched the cook set Sinjun's breakfast before him. "The lady's name is Angelica Dean," he said. "Chuck brought her here because I asked him to. She's a journalist. She came to see me."

Enders sniffed. "The one who kept calling in Seattle and on Kauai?" He waved for Swifty to get away from the table. The dog didn't move.

"The same. She was one of *Verity*'s lead columnists."

"*Was?* Has she been relieved of her post?"

"I don't believe she was involved in military engagements, Enders. She got bored and quit."

"How do you know?"

The grilling was expected from Enders, who saw Sinjun's safety and comfort as the reason for his own birth. "The lady told me she was bored," Sinjun said.

"Self-indulgence," Enders pronounced. "This new generation has no backbone. Sorry day when they abolished the draft. Mandatory stint in the army is what they all need. Give them a sense of honor. Determination."

"The lady isn't an adolescent." He was actually defending her. "If I understand correctly, she decided she needed to expand her talents." From Sinjun's point of view, she had talents that didn't need expanding at all.

"I take it her story has been checked?"

"It has," Sinjun agreed, growing irritable. "Call Fran, would you?"

"I don't believe I ever heard why this person wanted to talk to you," Enders persisted. "Hardly seems the time to give strangers the run—"

With a sharp shake of the head and a significant glance in the direction of Mrs. Midgely and Campbell, Sinjun silenced Enders. No need to worry the entire staff. "I think you can rely on me to do the right thing," he said, not at all sure he had done the right thing. If he had any sense, he'd send Angelica Dean back to wherever she'd really come from and hire professional round-the-clock surveillance.

The kitchen intercom buzzed. "Are you there, Sinjun?" Fran Simcox's high voice carried a perpetual hint of urgency.

"Here, Fran," Sinjun said before tucking in a mouthful of Mrs. Midgely's perfect fried eggs.

"What's going on here?" Fran said. "Did we open a resort? I thought we were in seclusion."

Miss Dean's presence was certainly not welcomed by all—if any. "Don't worry about a thing, Fran. I've got it all under control."

"You don't have a thing under control, buddy." As secretaries went, Fran was unconventional.

"Perhaps this should wait until I join you in the study?"

"Could I have an ETA on that? Just so I know how to direct traffic in the meantime?"

Sinjun frowned and picked up his coffee. "I'll be right there."

"G'day, mate," Fran said, and the intercom clicked off.

"What's with the Aussie lingo?" Sinjun raised his brows at Enders and instantly knew his mistake. As far as Enders was concerned, Fran could do no wrong.

"I'm certain Miss Simcox has a good reason for her mode of speech," Enders said. "I suggest you find out what it is at once."

"There are times," Sinjun said, slipping his untouched bacon to Swifty and getting up, "when I wonder if we've forgotten who's in charge here." Enders Lloyd-Worthy, expatriate Englishman, connoisseur of good taste and "the done thing," disdained Sinjun's staff to a man—and woman. With the exception of acid-tongued Fran Simcox.

Taking his coffee, Sinjun left the kitchen and trudged through the house to his study.

"G'day, Fran," he said. "Comfy, are we?"

She sat in his chair at his desk. "Why would someone called Brenda Butters be sending a fax to Angelica Dean at this number?"

He leaned, fingertips spread on the desk, and stared at her.

"Angelica Dean's that pushy bitch who says she wants to crawl inside your pants and check out . . ." Fran glanced at him and pushed a pen behind her ear. Light-brown hair curled wispily around her thin face. "The one who wants to know your innermost secrets?" She smiled innocently, showing a wide gap between her front teeth.

"Fran," Sinjun said, trying for patience. "You are the best secretary on earth, but you've got a disgusting turn of phrase. Clean it up, will you?"

"Yes, *sir*," she muttered, and read aloud from the fax, " 'G'day, Angel, thanks for the message. Sorry I missed your call. Not a thing going on here that can't wait. I'd be ruddy thrilled to come and bask on The Man's beach with you.' "

Fran removed the pen and pointed it at Sinjun. "She's talking about you, isn't she? It goes on: 'Remember what I told you. The Man has a reputation—quickest zip in the west. I'll look forward to hearing your up-close-and-personal impressions. On my way. See you soon, Brenda.' "

The pen hit the desk. Fran held the fax out to Sinjun. "Quickest zip in the west. *Brenda's* words, not mine. Sounds like you've got a couple of sex-starved groupies on your tail. Any idea how this woman would get this number? And why she'd send a fax here for Angelica Dean?"

"Angelica Dean's here." Damn the woman's nerve for inviting another unwanted interloper to the island.

Fran rose slowly to her feet. "On Hell?"

"In the lagoon cottage."

"How?"

"Chuck picked her up in Kauai last night and flew her here."

"Why?" Her pale-blue eyes had rounded.

Sinjun read the fax and shoved it into his pocket. "The lady asked for an interview and I was bored enough to agree."

"But—"

"End of discussion."

"Someone's trying to kill—"

"*End* of discussion, Fran."

She came around the desk. "Better watch your zipper, boss."

He let that pass. "When did this Brenda Butters's fax come in?"

"Just before I called you."

"Send one back saying she can't come. The Dean woman must have sent her a message before leaving Kauai. Evidently she wasn't prudent enough to point out that any communication sent here was likely to be seen by me. Our good luck. It could take Butters a day or so to arrange to get away from Australia and a good two days after that to arrive."

"She's not in Australia."

Frowning, Sinjun rubbed his jaw.

"Check the top of the fax," Fran said. "Seattle. She could be on a plane by now."

"*Shit.*"

"Look, boss. I know you don't like advice, but what the hell got into you? Why would you allow the Dean woman to come in the first place?"

"That was criticism, not advice. I don't owe you explanations. Let's just say I don't do thumb-twiddling well."

"So you invited some dirt-digging journalist to Hell." She ducked her head and raised both hands. "Okay, okay. I'm just gonna take the risk that you'll jump all over me. Someone's trying to kill you, Sinjun."

"Thank you, Frances. Revelation is always a thrill."

"Hear me out. We don't know who this maniac is. Do you have any guarantee Miss Angelica Dean isn't packing a gun?"

She hadn't been packing a damn thing last night. "No, I don't. And I don't like having my judgment questioned. I calculated every move here. She might just be our would-be assassin. Or intimately acquainted with whoever that is. Seems to me that since the police don't share our opinion that three life-threatening incidents should be taken serious-ly, we'd better jump into our own investigation. I thought I'd start by checking out Miss Dean. Any problems with that?"

Her tongue made a bump in her cheek.

"Good. I'll deal with Miss Dean later. What's on the agenda? Anything from Mary?" Mary Barrett was his chief financial officer, based in Seattle, who kept him up-to-date on the many business deals he had working at any one time.

"A report on Lieber."

Lieber. Just the name set Sinjun's teeth on edge. "Damn, I'll be glad to get either completely in or out of *that* one. Ten months of screwing around with him is ten months too long."

"Our Lorraine shared your opinion," Fran said without inflection.

Sinjun cleared his throat. He still found it hard to grasp that Lorraine had managed to fool Chuck enough for him to believe she was crazy enough about him to leave a fat ticket like Lieber.

Sin kept his thoughts to himself and asked, "Any sign of Chuck this morning?"

"Speaking of screwing around," Fran commented, and quickly added, "Not so far, boss. Should I buzz him?"

"Not yet."

"Mary says things are hopping with Lieber's SOS." Fran picked up the bulky file on Skins of Silk, Lieber Enterprises' proposed hot new product that would supposedly be within every woman's reach and knock Retin-A off the map. "There's been a flood of articles—and TV and radio attention."

Sinjun scanned the sheet Fran gave him. *"The world's waiting for this one?"* Would they be waiting if they knew Lieber was in financial trouble, that he needed to sell off controlling interest in SOS in order to keep the rest of his vast—and teetering—empire from sliding out of his grasp?

He'd have to find a way to meet with Garth Lieber and soon. "I want to review all this." He took the folder. "Then I'll get back to Mary. What else?"

"Preliminary figures on the Fanelli project look good. Mary says there's nothing to be done there at this point. Suggests you do take a look at Tucker's performance. She feels there could be something we're missing. She'll run the numbers again and get back to you."

Mary Barrett was more than good at her job. Too bad they'd once made the mistake of taking things a step beyond business. It hadn't worked. He'd gotten over the awkwardness but he was pretty sure she hadn't.

"Is there anything else that can't wait?"

"Nothing except this Brenda Butters. Are you going to allow our current visitor to throw her own private parties on your island?"

Sinjun grunted. "I'll deal with Miss Dean."

He looked through the windows at the pristine waters of the swimming pool in the center of his enclosed courtyard. Sleep hadn't come easily last night. Cameos of Angelica Dean, pale-skinned, wet and naked had intruded. She *couldn't* be the enemy. But neither could he allow himself to be convinced of that . . . just because he'd prefer to be.

"If Chuck shows, tell him I'll catch up with him later." With that, Sinjun pushed his feet into sandals and opened the door from the study to the courtyard. He skirted the pool and left the enclosure by a tall wrought-iron gate in a black lava-rock wall overhung with billowing magenta bougainvillea.

He'd been back on Hell for six days. This was his favorite place, bar none. But he was bored, damn it. *Itchy.* That's why he'd told Angel Dean she could come and pester him with her ridiculous biography notion.

Soft panting let him know Swifty was bringing up the rear. Sinjun clicked his fingers and the great mutt fell in beside him. In companionable silence, they made the walk through the jungle that ringed the compound, toward the lagoon cottage.

Birds trilled and fluttered among tangled vines that clutched the trunks of palms and looped between fronds that met overhead. Underfoot, the

hard-packed rusty-colored soil glimmered moistly
through shiny fallen leaves and pungent crushed
fruit. Wherever a ray of light punctured the green
canopy, captured droplets of mist swirled earth-
ward like veiled laser beams. Sinjun knew the trail
by heart, could negotiate it in the dark, or with his
eyes closed.

The vegetation thinned and he broke out onto
the slope that led downhill to the cottage. Surely
she wouldn't still be in bed at nine in the morning.

A fleeting vision of Angelica Dean in bed brought
a smile to Sinjun's lips and flared his nostrils—and
punched in his gut. He'd agreed to her coming
because he was at loose ends. That wasn't a lie.
He'd never as much as considered that she might
be an ethereal, intensely appealing woman with a
gorgeous body.

Sometimes a guy just lucked out.

He laughed aloud. Luck wasn't exactly his middle name these days and—although he knew of
absolutely no connection between Angelica and his
current shaky existence—the nubile nymph really
couldn't be blindly trusted.

He saw her before she saw him.

Facing the ocean, she hunched behind a hedge of
yellow hibiscus.

"Down, Swifty," Sinjun whispered. "And stay."
For once the dog followed orders instantly.

Sunlight glinted on the blonde hair she wore in
a single thick braid that swung back and forth
between her shoulder blades. Angelica dropped
to her haunches, waited, then shot to her feet
again, legs planted firmly apart. Slim, shapely
legs, smooth from narrow ankles all the way up
to short-shorts that hugged nicely rounded little
hips like blue denim brushstrokes.

Crossing his arms, Sinjun watched her repeat the
exercise several times.

Slowly, he let his hands fall to his sides. "Son of a bitch," he said under his breath.

Not under his breath enough.

She whipped around.

This time Angelica Dean was the one pointing the gun.

Five

*T*he sun blinded her. She squinted, but could see him only as a tall, wide-shouldered shadow.

Her eyes dropped to the gun, braced in both hands. It shook.

She suppressed an awful urge to giggle. "Good morning!" It wasn't necessary for her to see Sinjun Breaker to know he was the man facing her.

She could feel him.

"Are you planning to fire that thing?"

He was the enemy, not a friend dropping in for coffee. "Not immediately." She lowered her hands. He didn't have to know she'd bought the firearm—her first—only days ago. She'd decided that a woman alone among people she did not know or trust ought to take precautions. "It pays to keep in practice, doesn't it?"

"Does it?" He moved forward until she could see him clearly. A white, coarse linen shirt—open most of the length of a tanned chest—was tucked loosely into soft old jeans washed enough times to ensure a very intimate fit. A great, shaggy dog loped forward and flopped down behind him. "Do you always pack a gun?" Breaker persisted.

"Naturally."

He snorted. "Why?"

"We live in a violent world, Mr. Breaker."

"Sinjun will do. Sin if you feel particularly friendly. A little girl like you might get into more trouble carrying a gun than not."

Little *girl*? "You'll have to explain that to me."

He regarded her for a moment. "Simple," he said.

By the time Angelica had flinched, by the time his rapid move sent a current of air over her face, she no longer held the gun.

"Enough of an explanation?"

She only blinked. With the same hand that had taken the gun, he slid pressure up her arm and drew her smoothly, inevitably around him.

Her feet left the ground.

"Don't!" Angelica grabbed for any handhold and found none. "Oh!"

He directed her in a strange, slow-motion fall.

The instant she braced for impact with sandy dirt, his arms were beneath her and he swung her up against his chest. "Got you, Angel Dean," he said, laughing, showing those strong white teeth, driving in the laugh lines around his eyes and the vertical dimples beside his mouth. "Have I explained enough now?"

"I get your point."

One of his arms was beneath hers, pressing her breast to his chest. He looked down at her and the smile set. A muscle jerked in his jaw. "I wonder if you do get my point."

Her stomach dipped. "You're a big, strong man, Mr. Breaker. And I'm a small, weak woman. If that was the point you were making, I've got it."

His gaze flickered lower, to the spot where the soft swell of her breast made contact with hard, warm muscle through a thin layer of fabric—her shirt. Given the circumstances of their first meeting, it shouldn't matter, but in future she'd resist the temptation to go braless. The sun wasn't the only potential heat on this island.

"Something tells me the strongest part of you is the part I can't see." He removed the hand that was under her legs and, very slowly, let her slide down his body until her bare feet touched the ground. "Evidently you have a very good mind. Except when it comes to choosing firearms."

"Small and efficient," she said, parroting the gun dealer's words.

"Twenty-five-caliber Beretta," Sinjun commented, turning the weapon over before handing it back to Angelica. "Cute little ivory grip. I understand they do a nice job in pink, too. Amazing what they can turn out for the girls these days."

She pretended indifference. "All I ask for is peace of mind." If he expected her to get huffy about sexist crap he'd be waiting a long time. "As long as I know it kills, it's okay with me."

The downward curve of his lips jerked her spine straight.

"If you can get close enough to screw it in the guy's ear," he said. "It'll probably kill."

"You don't know what—"

"I'm talking about? Maybe. Of course, you could always customize it."

Angelica frowned. "Why would you . . . How?"

"File off the sight."

She frowned deeper.

"Smooth off the hammer."

"I don't think I want to hear the rest of this." Being too close to him wasn't helping her peace of mind.

Sinjun grinned. "You gotta let me get to the punch line. Coat the whole thing with Vaseline and watch the doc who tries to take it out get real mad."

"That's disgusting."

"I know. A clip might help. That peashooter's not loaded."

She'd forgotten! "I was only practicing."

"Yeah." He ducked his head to peer at her.

"Practicing. Word has it you're a very smart lady. I don't know nearly as much about you as you know about me, but the crack journalist who left *Verity* for no definite reason is very much missed. They'll welcome her back anytime she chooses to go. Did you know that?"

"It was implied and I'm flattered." Please, God, let her do what she'd set out to do without him deciding to dig any deeper into her past. "You've done all your homework."

He settled his hands at her waist. "There are times when intelligence doesn't quite cut it, Angel. There are big, dumb people in the world who take great pleasure in showing little, smart people how helpless they are."

She lifted her chin and tried to ignore the fact that his thumbs were making rhythmic sweeps over her ribs. "I should have remembered about you and guns, shouldn't I?"

His thumbs stilled—and dug into her. "I'm not aware that there's anything to remember."

"Perhaps not about guns, but violence, certainly."

He gripped her so tightly it hurt. "I doubt you'd find anyone who would call me a violent man."

Could the beautiful lines of his mouth become cruel? she wondered. Could he bare his strong teeth in rage? She placed her hands flat against his chest and pushed away. "I don't think it would be too difficult to find more than one person who might remember how you once earned your living with your fists."

She had her answer. The corners of his mouth turned down again and a white line formed around his lips. He could be cruel.

"You speak like a woman who thinks she's dug up some dirt."

"I've dug up a few things about you." Some of them very dirty, but she was only interested in them as weapons against him. "It's hot here. There's some shade at the back of the cottage."

Wordlessly, he gestured for her to precede him. Angelica walked away, feeling his eyes on her every step of the way. Any attraction to this man was something she hadn't factored into her plans. He was a user, a killer whose weapon was indifference—at least in his most recent crime.

But he did attract her.

Angelica reached a terrace shaded by profuse sprays of blue-violet flowers cascading from the branches of a petrea vine. "Would you like a cold drink?"

"No."

She set the gun on the edge of a stone planter. "Coffee?"

He pulled a deep bentwood chair to the edge of the terrace and sat down. "I've had coffee."

She cleared her throat. "It's nice of you to agree to allow me to interview you."

The hint of a smile touched his mouth, but not his eyes. "Last night's session showed promise. I could come to enjoy talking to you—"

"Last night I was caught off guard. Let's say you were, too, and forget . . . Why don't we just forget it. I appreciate being here."

"You are a very persistent woman."

"Reporting makes you persistent. The shy ones don't make it." He'd never know how she'd trembled every time she made contact with him.

"You have to be pushy, huh?"

"Something like that."

He tilted his head to one side. The breeze moved through his thick black hair. Sunlight curled into the plane beneath his upturned cheekbone and stroked the tough angle of his jaw.

"I don't suppose a knockout body hurts," he said suddenly.

Angelica was helpless to stop the blush. "I'm not usually in situations where people get to see me before they agree to let me talk to them."

His strange, intent, yellow-green eyes slipped slowly all the way to her curling toes and back. "When they do see you, though, Angel? Doesn't being built like a sexy little nymph increase your chances of holding your victim's attention? Sit down."

She bristled. "I'd rather stand. This isn't about me. May I ask you some questions?"

"Are you sure you have to?"

"Why else would I be here?"

He settled lower in the chair and rested an ankle on the other knee. "You tell me." A leather thong hung from his jiggling foot. "Just how many questions do you have, Angel? And how long do you think it'll take you to ask them all?"

As long as it took to expose him as a vicious opportunist who smashed anyone who got in his way. "To be honest, there are quite a lot of questions. For a biography to work well, there has to be the right mix of the professional and the private life."

"You mean you want this book to be a big success and it won't be if you don't get enough juicy, preferably unsavory detail?"

She made herself laugh. "That always helps. But I'll settle for good, solid human-angle stuff."

"Like anything you may have missed about my drunken father or the mother who deserted me? Is that going to be human enough?"

He was prickly on that subject. Good. She'd remember to use it if things got too tight. "I apologize for that. You caught me at . . . a disadvantage." She gave him her best innocently-charming smile. "I lashed out. Not very professional of me."

"Apology accepted." His glittering eyes rested in

the region of her breasts. "How long, Angel?"

She resisted the temptation to make certain her shirt was buttoned.

"How long will you need to be here?" he repeated.

Angelica started. "Oh, I'm not sure. I'll need a number of interviews, probably over some weeks. Sometimes things go quite quickly." They'd go as quickly as she could make them. Sinjun Breaker was a very sexy man and he knew it. There wasn't a doubt that he was eyeing her the way a very sexy man eyed a potential conquest. The safest place for her would be far away from this island.

He turned to slide a hand into one pocket. The long muscle in his thigh sprang solidly inside worn jeans. "Evidently you expect to be here enough time to entertain a guest." He thrust a folded sheet of paper at her. "Perhaps this is just the first of an entire gaggle of buddies you've invited along."

Angelica frowned at the fax she held, then felt a deep burning that flooded out to her fair skin. "*Damn.*"

Sinjun laughed. "I guess I wasn't supposed to see that?"

"This isn't what it seems to be."

"No? You mean you didn't invite an Australian friend to join you on beaches belonging to the fastest zip in the west?"

"Good grief. I could strangle Brenda."

"Answer my question first."

"No." She folded the fax again. "Brenda's English, not Australian. She's a very good friend. I simply let her know I was coming here from Kauai. This is just her idea of being funny."

"She seems to think she knows a great deal about me. A very great deal."

Angelica changed her mind about sitting down and plopped onto the legrest of a chaise. "Brenda doesn't hold . . . She isn't particularly fond of men."

"She's gay?"

"Not being fond of men doesn't necessarily make a woman gay," she snapped.

Sinjun pulled his shirt from his jeans, finished undoing the buttons and spread it open. "Cooler," he said, and smiled. "Is the suggestion that she's coming here just funny, too?"

Angelica squirmed inwardly. "Probably not."

"Don't you think the two of you should have asked permission?"

"I had no idea she intended to join me!"

"Don't shout."

"I am not shouting. Brenda Butters is a very strong-minded woman."

"And you're not?"

"She knows I don't have anyone else to—" *Fool.* Stupid, careless fool. "She knows I'm alone here and probably thinks there's no reason for her not to come and keep me company. Brenda's like that. Very thoughtful." He must not find out anything about her, least of all the fact that she didn't have anyone but Brenda to worry about where she was or what happened to her.

"This is a private island."

She poked at a fallen leaf with a toe. "I know."

"No one comes here unless I say so."

"I know."

"You seem to know a great deal."

"This isn't going very well."

Abruptly, he leaned forward, offered her a hand. "Relax, Angel. I'm not going to eat you."

He was quicksilver. One instant dark and foreboding, the next handsome, smiling charm.

"Give me your hand."

She did as he asked and flinched when his warm, strong fingers curled around hers.

"Your Brenda will have to contact us for permission to land. When she does, I'll have Chuck Gill go and pick her up."

Suspicion wound through her insides. "That's very good of you." Did he have some inkling about her reason for being here? Was this accommodating switch designed to help appease her and get rid of her quickly?

"You said you'd already *dug* up things about me." His grip tightened and he pulled her closer until she had to shift farther down the leg rest. "I can hardly wait to hear what you've been told."

Angelica swallowed. When would Brenda show? "I do intend to dwell on your achievements."

"Do you?"

She was near enough to see that his eyes were mostly clear green with bursts of yellow chips around the iris. They didn't waver.

She swallowed again. "My slant won't be anything clever or new. Poor kid makes good . . . Makes it really good in your case."

"Dull," he said, looking at her mouth now.

He was overtly masculine. His scent reached her, clean, touched with the subtle aroma of this island's red earth and the warm salt sea's tang.

So sexual.

Angelica averted her face. He knew his own power over women and he was deliberately using it on her, not because he had an inkling of why she was here, but out of habit. She must hold that thought: Sinjun Breaker expected to seduce every woman he met—every woman he might even toy with the idea of wanting to seduce.

At any other time and in any other place, she'd laugh. What did she know about sexy men? Almost nothing.

"What are you thinking about, Angel?" She felt him take her fingers to his lips and brush them gently back and forth. "All those terrible things you know about me?"

As a reporting journalist she'd held her own in a fair number of nasty situations. She was out of her depth here. "That's what I'm doing," she told him. Control was something she couldn't afford to lose for an instant until she could get out of here. "There's a lot of speculation about why you've chosen to run away and hide."

The brushing of his lips halted. "Hide? Who says I'm hiding?"

"People. The best, most beautiful people—especially those in Seattle who didn't get your apologies for failing to show up at their beautiful events."

"Too bad. I'm socially inept, I guess. Leave it at that."

"Even if I do, they won't."

"I don't give a rat's ass what they think."

Angelica pulled her fingers from his but remained sitting where she was. "Why are you hiding?"

The white line around his mouth reappeared. "Reporters. All the same. They teach you that in reporter school, don't they? Make 'em mad with rude questions and hope they get careless enough to tell you their secrets."

"Something like that."

"It stinks."

"You mean I'm making you mad and you may get careless enough to tell me your secrets?"

His smile didn't soften a single line in his handsome face. "I never did like women with smart mouths."

"Did Dee-Dee Cahler have a smart mouth?"

For a long time, Sinjun stared at her with narrowed eyes. Then he fell back in the chair and rested the back of a forearm over his face.

Bull's-eye!

"You do remember Dee-Dee? She was—"

"I know who she was."

Sometimes Angelica disliked what her job could

call upon her to do. She shouldn't mind hitting Sinjun Breaker with questions he'd probably tried to forget had answers, but she did. Still not tough enough, she guessed.

"She was very young when you—"

"Seventeen. You've sure as hell been doing your homework, too."

Whatever she heard in his voice mustn't be mistaken for pain—unless it was pain for the inconvenience this revelation might cause him.

"I went to Montana."

"Shit," he muttered.

"I told you I knew about Montana."

"You don't know a damn thing about Montana."

"There isn't even a dot on the map for that . . . For the place where you lived with your father. That made it hard to find. But when I asked in Dillon—"

"They told you where to find a bunch of condemned clapboard hovels with no running water and no plumbing—unless you count holes in boards over a stinking trench."

She didn't like the way his flat voice made her feel. "Yeah, they told me it was called—"

"Bliss." He'd removed his arm and dropped his head against the back of the chair to squint at a blindingly blue sky through the vine-laden frame that made the terrace a bower. "*Bliss.* Someone must have had quite a sense of humor, wouldn't you say, Angel? I bet you never saw anything quite like it before."

"It's not there anymore," she said softly. "Some people moved on and—"

"Died, you mean? Dying was a habit in Bliss."

"And some people were relocated. Mostly in a trailer park not far from where Bliss was." She seemed to have to swallow a lot. "Did you know that?"

"No."

"Guess what they called the trailer park?"

His squint found her face. "I think you're going to tell me."

"Bliss," she said. "Isn't that funny?"

"Because you think they should want to forget everything about their lives before they got moved into their sumptuous new trailers?" He sat forward. "Well, maybe you're right. Who knows? But I expect some of them thought they had things they actually wanted to remember."

She didn't want to feel any sympathy for him. "Look—"

"As far as I'm concerned, I never lived there. Forget it. I have."

"Dee-Dee Cahler probably wanted to forget it too."

He didn't answer.

"How do you feel when you think about her?"

"This is for the deeply personal touch, right?"

"Right."

"Shouldn't you be taking notes?"

"I've got fantastic recall." And she was hanging on his every word.

"I don't think anything about her. Never."

And she had a big fat bet that he did. It was in his voice. "I found her grandmother. She's the oldest woman I ever saw."

"*Shit!*"

"You say that a lot. Mrs. Cahler told me all about it."

"She doesn't know *all* about it," he said through his teeth.

"She knows you married Dee-Dee."

He rolled his face away. "That was a long time ago. A lifetime ago."

"Dee-Dee didn't have much lifetime afterwards."

His head shot back in her direction. "Make your point."

"You're one of the world's most eligible bachelors, Sinjun. And one of the world's most romantic success stories."

"Yeah, yeah. Cinder-fucking-rella . . . to use an immortalized line that should appeal to you. And I told you, I don't much like the parallel."

"I'll try to remember not to use it. Face it. If I don't write about you, someone else will. This will be an authorized biography. That makes you a very smart man because you've got some say in the end product. Cooperate with me and we may make it pointless for someone to write an unauthorized version because I'll have taken the sting out of the good stuff without stripping you naked in public."

He considered for a long, uncomfortable moment. "Maybe you will. Maybe you won't. I'll think about that some more. You've got something you're tip-toeing around, Angel. Give."

"We're going to have to work on trusting one another." Her throat was so tight it hurt. "We have to agree to be a team on this."

Sinjun stood up, stepped off the terrace and stared toward the area of the island that seemed completely choked with dense jungle vegetation. His profile was harsh and proud, not a profile one could imagine in what had once been Bliss, Montana—town without a name on the map.

"Will you trust me, Sinjun?" She was setting out to use a user. Use him and put as big a dent in him as she could. All she had to do was keep in her mind the picture of her mother as she'd last seen her—pretty, as blonde as Angelica and still young-looking. Marlene Dean Golden had looked quite lovely in her casket.

Angelica set her teeth. "Check me out. My references are impeccable." Impeccable, but damning if he probed far enough.

"Okay." Still he didn't look at her. "Okay, I'll go for it."

Triumph flooded Angelica. "Great. Thanks." Now for the first real thrust. "Are you up to whatever I may ask you? Anything?"

He nodded. "Yeah."

"Sometimes I'll make you mad."

"I know you will, Angel." His smile was cynical.

"Are you afraid something from your past may catch up with you?"

His fantastic eyes settled on her. "Catch up with me?"

"Something or someone?"

"Nothing and no one I can think of."

Angelica locked her legs. She said, "Not even the dead?" and knew from the fury that gradually turned his eyes to green ice that the dead face he was seeing hadn't belonged to her mother.

Six

*D*ee-Dee's face had been blue-white.
Transparent.

She'd stared at him while her life ran out and he
was never going to know if she stopped thinking
his name before or after the last faint breath trembled under blood-soaked cotton.

"*Sin,*" she'd whispered. And then her dark eyes
seemed to flatten, to lose focus. The end came within seconds. Sinjun looked at his hands. Dee-Dee
had been dead for hours before he remembered to
wash off her blood.

Angelica Dean moved. Sinjun heard the sound
of warm skin shifting on the rough fabric of the
cushion on her chair.

He'd forgotten, actually forgotten something that
had once felt like it would fill him up forever. At
twenty, looking at his dead wife, he'd expected to
see her—like that—for the rest of his waking and
sleeping life.

"Life got a whole lot better for you after that."

He looked at Angelica and pinched the bridge of
his nose.

Her soft brown eyes slid away. "Well, they did,
didn't they? Get better?"

"What are you saying?"

"After Dee-Dee Cahler . . . Excuse me, she was
Dee-Dee Breaker by then, wasn't she? But after

she died there wasn't much time for mourning. You had things to do. Things to accomplish. You were on your way to—"

"That's enough." Pain burst at his temples. What was the matter with him? All this was old. Dead. As dead as Dee-Dee and . . . And it was *over*. "Len Gill had a big spread out of Dillon. I was Chuck's friend—Len's son's friend—and Len took me in when I had no place else to go." He would get through this and be fine again.

"That was before Dee-Dee."

"Forget Dee-Dee," he told her.

"Have you?"

He returned to the chair and dropped down heavily. "You're good." He gave a short laugh. "Damn, but you're good. No wonder you can write your own ticket with one of America's most prestigious magazines. You don't feel a thing, do you? It's all business."

A yellow butterfly dipped past and Angelica watched until it flittered from sight. "My being here is business," she said finally. "This is a beautiful place. Idyllic."

"I like it."

"Bruno Kertz gave it to you."

What *didn't* she know? "He left everything he owned to me. I was his partner and he had no relatives." He'd been more than a partner. Sinjun had been the son Bruno never had.

Angelica watched him again. "No one to enjoy the fruits, as it were? How . . . fortuitous. Not even a kitty or a canary?"

"Not even a goldfish." Two could play at cute. "Are you absolutely sure you shouldn't be writing some of this down?"

"Absolutely. I'm getting a feel for you first."

Sinjun whistled soundlessly—and watched her. Downcast, her lashes were thick and dark with blonde tips that caught the light. Shit, he'd be writing poetry shortly.

"Is that okay—getting a feel for you . . ." She snapped her gaze up to his and cocked a brow. ". . . Sin?"

Oh, yes, she was *cute*. "You can get a feel for me anytime you like, baby."

Something flickered in her eyes. Awareness. They were supremely aware of each other. "Retreating into put-downs?" she said, all cool superiority. "Perhaps you're regretting that you've agreed to this biography after all?"

What in God's name did the woman want from him? And *why*? And why didn't he just call Chuck and tell him to get her the hell out of here?

He knew why.

He knew why she was here and he knew why he didn't send her away. And he wasn't sure which was scarier, knowing she was here to exploit him— or worse—or that he wasn't ready to send her away because looking at her gave him a big, beautifully painful hard-on.

A chill squirreled under his skin. Even in the rising heat of a Pacific morning, Sinjun felt flash-frozen. Cold shot up his spine and he shuddered.

Her tight little smile said she knew she was getting to him. And he was almost certain his first instinct had been right. Looking at him with big brown eyes was a woman who could have murder on her mind. His murder. "Whose idea was it for you to come here?" he asked her. The foolishness with the gun could easily have been for his benefit—to throw him off track.

"Mine."

Liar.

"Do you expect me to believe that out of all the fascinating people in the world, the most fascinating is Sinjun Breaker?"

Her eyes didn't waver now. "He is to me." She looked straight at him and honesty shone.

An angel with truth in her face and something poisonous with his name on it hidden elsewhere? "You're going to have to do better than that. Why not Trump?"

"Has-been."

How true. "Malcolm Forbes?"

"Dead men are too easy."

"How about Saul Steinberg? Should be plenty to get your teeth into."

"No surprises."

"His kid, then? Jonathan? He's a scrapper."

"Too young and clean."

He shook his head. "Annenberg?"

"Predictable," she said brusquely.

"You're very hard, Angelica."

"I don't hold a candle to you, Sinjun."

"You're a whole lot prettier than I am." He hadn't intended to say that. "But that's only important as a tool, huh? A deceptively charming exterior to cover all the pointy knives that make up your mind?"

She scooted her lovely little backside to the front of the chair and hiked an ankle up one thigh. "You have a persecution complex."

She could bet her sweet ass he did. He said, "I like to see if I can shake up the opposition, that's all."

Angelica tipped her face up to the vine-covered trellis overhead and held the toes of her propped foot in both hands. "I'm not the opposition. I'm a woman who asked if she could do a job. That job will be worth big bucks to you as well as to me."

Her position and his angle gave Sinjun a view of the tiniest rim of bright-pink lace-edged panty right where it didn't quite reach the crease at the top of her leg. The lace disappeared into shadow . . . Sinjun pushed back his shirt. How quickly a man's temperature could swing from cold to hot—burning hot.

"How do you know what the book's worth? Have you talked to a publisher?"

"Not yet. I want to generate plenty of excitement and then my agent will hold an auction."

"I don't need money."

She rocked her head from side to side, stretching her neck. "I do. Everybody does. No one ever has enough."

Sinjun shrugged. "I still think you've chosen the wrong guy. You need a household name."

Arching her back, she rolled her head. "Household name?" She sounded almost drowsy. Her throat was smooth and pale—all the way down to the tops of full breasts where her thin, white cotton shirt strained against its buttons.

Sinjun tightened his belly. It didn't help. The suspicion had definitely become close to a certainty that someone had sent her to Hell for very different reasons than the one she gave. But suspicion didn't govern his hormones.

"I bet you inhaled."

He breathed in sharply. "What?" If she looked at his crotch she'd know where his mind had been.

"You tried pot, didn't you?"

Sinjun crossed his legs. "What does pot have to do with anything?"

"You said household name and my mind wandered. I was looking for a reason why you haven't considered running for the presidency."

This was going all over the board. "You've lost me, lady."

"Never." She looked at him and smiled. "Nobody loses you unless you want them to."

Sinjun blinked. His mouth dried out and he knew exactly why. It hadn't happened lately, not for a long time, in fact. He was sexually aroused to a pitch that matched only one thing . . . the scent of victory after a long, hard battle. There had been times when his entire team had turned thumbs down on a project and he'd gone with it anyway—and sat back to watch his blessed instinct for winners pay off, and pay off some more. This was a time when he was both sides, the yea *and* the nay platoon, and Angelica was the project.

"I can't decide if I've had too much physical exercise for one day or too little," she said, her voice oddly husky. "I'm stiff." Smoothly, she slid down to sit cross-legged on the brick terrace.

He was tempted to offer help with relaxation.

Angelica folded forward until her brow touched the ground. She swiveled to grip one knee, then swung to repeat the process the other side.

"You're very limber."

Her response was to extend a leg out straight and walk her hands down until she could grip her ankle.

"Is it helping?"

"Mmm."

It wasn't helping him.

Sitting once more, she took one hand over her head and bent sideways.

God. Sinjun held his bottom lip in his teeth. His fingers curled on his thigh. One little move and he could fill his big hand with the right breast she so generously thrust in his direction.

"Better," she murmured. And the left arm came up—and the left breast.

His mouth, closing on her nipple, would soak cotton, paste it to budding flesh.

How would she look when she climaxed?

"Dee-Dee was pregnant, wasn't she?"

His elbow slipped off the arm of his chair.

Angelica sat with her back straight enough to thrill a marine drill sergeant. "When whatever happened, happened, she was five months pregnant?" If she'd been drowsy a moment before, the little limbering-up exercises had worked better than intravenous caffeine. Her eyes were wide open and boring into his.

"You're the kind of reporter who asks the color of the dead baby's eyes, right?"

"Not with a twenty-week fetus."

He shot to his feet. "*Fuck* you, lady."

"I hate it when people swear because they feel impotent."

"Son of a . . ." Not stopping to consider the wisdom of the move, he reached down, enclosed a slim arm in one hand and hauled her up. "Anytime you want to find out how potent I do or don't feel, just give the word."

She flinched, but didn't try to pull away. "I do believe this is going badly again."

"You aren't funny anymore."

"Neither are you. I warned you I was going to get tough."

"You haven't even *smelled* tough yet." He stepped closer.

She stepped back. "Hemorrhage. Her grandmother said that's what killed her."

Fury pounded in his brain. "You had no right—"

"Yes, I did. No one has the right to muzzle information. Not even you." Bright-pink rose in her cheeks. "More important men than you have tried to hide their pasts and failed."

He backed her up some more. "Dee-Dee hemorrhaged and died. We couldn't get help in time. Okay? Can we move on to the next subject now? Would you like to hear about my first wet dreams?" Dumb, dumb, *dumb*. He could already smell the way she excited him. More stimulation was the last thing he needed. He forced his shoulders down. "Let's talk about my career with Bruno."

"Eventually." She had to raise her chin to look a strong, angry man in the eye, but if she was afraid it didn't show. "Mrs. Cahler said Dee-Dee hemorrhaged because she'd been brutally beaten."

The sun switched off.

Sinjun closed his eyes and saw red-tinged black-

ness. From somewhere very distant came a small,
clear warning: There was more than one way to
kill a man. Where this woman was heading lay
professional as well as potential personal destruc-
tion.

He released her arm. "Congratulations," he said,
hearing his own, even voice as if it didn't belong to
him. "You've gotten deeper into my past than some
very seasoned reporters."

She spread her feet as if bracing for his attack.
"Are you still sure the going isn't getting too
tough?"

"I'll have a contract drawn up."

"I've already spoken to my agent. She'll be in
touch."

"My lawyers will want to go over any agreement."

"Naturally."

Nothing shook her. He said, "I'm out of time—"
The intercom chimed inside the cottage.

Angelica looked blank.

"Intercom," he told her, walking through open
French doors and into the bedroom.

"Where is it?" she said, and followed him past
the big bed where a demure white cotton nightie
had been discarded atop a dark-green-and-black
quilt.

Sinjun went to a mirror-fronted closet and slid
open a door. "Here," he told her. "And in every
room. Bruno was a very private man but when
he wanted to make contact it had to be *now*. As
in *at once*. You'll need that for your nonexistent
notes, too."

The intercom chimed again and he flipped it to
speak mode. "Yeah?"

"Sinjun?"

"Yes, Fran."

Silence, then, "Bedroom, huh?"

Fran had consulted the master board that indicated every receiver in every room—of every structure on Hell. She knew exactly where he was. "What is it, Fran?" In the mirrored door, he watched Angelica watch him. The expression in her eyes said she'd interpreted Fran's insinuation.

"I expected to reach Ms. Dean."

"She's right here."

"Is that a fact? That's okay. You're the man for the moment." There was a slight pause. "How are things going, by the way?"

Sinjun braced his weight against the wall and bowed his head. "Things are going just fine, Fran." When he looked up, he met Angelica's eyes. Apprehensive? The notion surprised him. "I'll be back at the house shortly."

"Shortly's not a good idea, boss. Now would be better."

More than apprehensive. Angelica's lips had parted and her teeth were clamped together . . . as if she expected bad news.

"Later, Fran," he said and moved to switch off the intercom.

"Nope. This is it. Decision-making time. For you and Ms. Dean."

Sinjun turned toward Angelica and, still speaking into the intercom, asked, "What exactly does that mean?"

Fran's reply was grim. "If I said this was the reservation desk, would that give you a hint?"

"This isn't the time for guessing games." Except for the game of guessing why Angelica was winding her hands together and staring at the intercom as if it had horns.

"You aren't trying. Do I say, 'Sorry, ma'am, we have no vacancies for the dates that interest you'? Or do I go ahead and tell Willis to clear a chopper from Fly Kauai for landing?"

"We aren't expecting . . . You're kidding. Now?"

"Yep. Those Australians must have real rapid air transport."

Sinjun shook his head and raised his brows at Angelica, who still appeared agitated.

No point in mentioning to Fran that their prospective new visitor wasn't Australian. "Give clearance."

"You sure? Chuck was saying this seclusion thing of yours is supposed to be taken—"

"I'm sure." As long as Angelica was around, he'd have to stop his nearest and dearest from talking openly—about anything. The rest of the staff didn't know about the close calls with death. Sinjun preferred to keep it that way. "You do want your Brenda to come and hold your hand, don't you, Angelica?"

Her arms slipped to her sides and her teeth parted. He saw her take a deep, deep breath.

"She's here already?" There was no mistaking the delight in that smile. "If you don't mind, I'd really appreciate having Brenda with me. She's such a help. And she's really a very interesting woman."

He nodded.

"We met in Australia, you know. Cairns. I was covering a story about the raising of a wreck."

"Really?" He glanced at the intercom.

"Yes. There was this Australian who kept hitting on me and things were getting . . . He was a nuisance."

"A nuisance?"

"Yes. There was the implied threat that if I didn't . . . Well, same old, same old."

"I can imagine. Why don't I just—"

"Anyway, I'd met Brenda. She's a systems analyst. Brilliant. She'd been out on a sheep station doing something with computerization. She fixed the guy for me."

Sinjun crossed one foot over the other and leaned against the wall again. The reason for the babble was obvious: relief. But why? Over what? "Was this Australian a scrawny little devil?" he said. "Or is she a black belt in something or other?"

"No! She told the guy to back off. Once he heard Brenda and I were an item and she was jealous, he lost interest real fast."

On the way to Sinjun's helicopter pad, Angelica fought a grin. At her announcement about Brenda, the expression on his face had slid through changes like an inept mime's. She hadn't intended him to take her literally, but, at least for now, she could use a break from the pressure that was building between them.

The dog—Swifty, she now knew—had abandoned Sinjun in favor of Angelica. He padded amiably at her side along the jungle path toward the compound.

The faint *phud-phud* of helicopter blades approached from the east. Sinjun strode ahead, broad shoulders swinging, never glancing back.

He thought he'd been coming on to a lesbian. Angelica couldn't muffle a giggle.

That turned him around. "What's funny?"

"Swifty," she said lamely, patting the dog's head. "He's so cute."

Sinjun narrowed his eyes and turned wordlessly back to stalk on through the jungle tunnel.

Moisture dripped from the broad, glistening leaves of vines that wound about the trunks of palms and hala trees. Geckos, their tails swishing, skittered from their posts atop fern fronds, and the occasional brightly colored bird shifted trailers hanging from mango and guava trees. Angelica trod on a fallen lemon and its sharp tang made her nose twitch.

The sound of the incoming chopper drew near and passed overhead where vegetation obscured the sky.

"How much time do you spend here?" Angelica called.

"The reporter reemerges." He plodded on. "It varies."

"Why are you here now?"

There was the slightest check in his stride. "I need a break. Nothing more interesting than that."

She didn't believe him. Something was going on that had caused him to duck out of Seattle fast—without telling some people who hadn't been pretending when they'd shown surprise at learning he'd gone.

"Planning to stay a long time."

"I don't know."

"That wasn't a question. You've more or less moved your center of operations here from Seattle. You don't normally do that."

He faltered and stopped. "How do you do it?" His elbows came up and he rested his fists on his hips. "What excuses do you give for asking the kind of questions that would get you the kind of answers you obviously get?"

"No particular kind." She caught up with him and smiled. Swiftly sat and leaned against her—which meant she had to lean back or lose her balance. "I find the direct, honest approach works beautifully."

"I'll bet. You just light up that big, beautiful smile of yours and the victim can hardly wait to tell you anything you want to know. Isn't that the way it goes?"

"Sort of. But there's always my gorgeous body to help me out, right?"

"Right. How long ago did you and Brenda—meet?"

"About two years ago."

"And you're still . . . getting along?"

Every little homophobic nerve in his body sent out shock signals. "Sinjun, I can't tell you how much I trust Brenda. She's helped me redefine human relationship. There's a special closeness that can exist between women, women who establish strong friendships and have the sense to nurture and cherish them."

"I'll take your word for it," he said, and started walking again.

The jungle path wound its way, a mile or so, uphill from the coast and emerged onto impeccably trimmed broadleaf grass. The grassy sweeps surrounded a high wall of black lava rock. Inside the wall, Angelica could see the low blue-tile rooflines of the house she'd barely been able to make out when Chuck Gill flew her in the previous night. After their arrival, Chuck hadn't suggested taking her to meet Sinjun. The morning would do for that. The last thing she'd expected was to see him standing over her above the lagoon.

The very last thing.

Angelica felt the rush of heat that had come with each recollection of that awful moment.

He'd kissed her and she hadn't stopped him.

Sinjun veered away to the right. The landing pad was a few hundred yards beyond the most easterly reaches of the compound wall. Sinjun's sleek white Eurocopter with its encircling, slender dark-blue stripe and discreet matching KB on the pilot door sat where Angelica had last seen it. A second, smaller helicopter was already setting down.

Angelica caught a glint of familiar carrot-red hair and waved wildly. "There she is." She started to run forward—and Sinjun promptly pulled her back. "Don't get in the way," he shouted.

"That's Brenda." Angelica pointed. "With the red hair."

"I can hardly wait."

She should remember to be glad that he made it easy to keep on hating him.

A door slid open on the arriving chopper and within seconds Brenda Butters emerged. Her short, thick hair glowed like a garish beacon. She tossed a bulky, soft-sided bag to the ground, leaned back to laugh and say something to the pilot and turned to survey her new surroundings.

"Brenda!" Angelica shrieked above the noise. "Over here."

Brenda sighted them and, even at a distance, Angelica saw her grin. Sweeping up the bag, she covered ground with her usual long-legged stride. "What ho, ducky," she boomed, drawing close. Dropping the bag again, she enfolded Angelica in a bear hug. "Couldn't stand not being in on all this. Thought I might as well trot over and take a gander."

Angelica didn't dare glance at Sinjun. "It's great to see you. How did you make it so quickly? You almost beat your fax."

"Don't take the mickey. If Seattle wasn't fogged in, I'd have been here yesterday, I can tell you that."

"Your fax didn't get here until this morning," Sinjun said, and frost coated each word.

Brenda turned her shiny, bright-blue eyes on him—eyes that, despite sensible flat shoes, looked directly into his. "You're having me on." Thick red lashes batted rapidly, signaling what Angelica knew to be intent assessment rather than nervousness.

Angelica looked from Brenda to Sinjun and encountered a blank expression on the latter's face. "Brenda thinks you're teasing," she translated. "To Brenda she added, "He's not. It did come this morning. Just as well you got held up. If you'd arrived yesterday I wouldn't have been here. I only got here last night."

"But I thought—"

"Yes, so did I. Mr. Gill—he's Mr. Breaker's pilot—he had engine trouble and we were late getting away from Kauai."

Brenda tutted. "Miracles of ruddy modern technology, eh?" At something more than thirty-five and less than forty—a subject never directly addressed—she was a flamboyantly handsome woman with the kind of lush figure that might already be blurring on someone less active. She hitched the brown leather belt at the waist of wrinkled, olive-drab linen slacks and tucked in an excess of matching shirt. "It's all miraculous as long as it works. And that goes for ruddy fax machines, too—or the people who supposedly use them for you. How come there's an armed guard, then?"

Following the incline of Brenda's head, Angelica saw a man she hadn't noticed before and at the sight of him her muscles felt suddenly weak.

"Willis," Sinjun said perfunctorily.

At that moment, the chopper that had brought Brenda lifted off again. Angelica glanced longingly at it, feeling a sense of being trapped and watching her only hope of escape disappear.

"So why's Willis waving a submachine gun, then? Does he think I'm a ruddy invasion?"

Reluctantly, Angelica turned from watching the departing helicopter.

"He isn't waving it," Sinjun said, and uttered an oath under his breath.

"Ooh," Brenda said, widening her eyes. "Hostility fair chokes you around here, doesn't it?"

From the corner of her eye, Angelica saw Sinjun's bemused face. He studied Brenda as he might a member of an endangered—or dangerous—species.

Angelica studied Willis. Dressed in loose white gauze pants—and nothing else—the man with the machine gun had taken up position a few yards distant. Huge, with the bulging muscles of a weight-lifter, and with long dark hair that brushed his shoulders and an exotically handsome face, he stood with his bare feet braced apart and the machine gun cradled like a baby in crossed arms.

Brenda ruffled her curly hair. "The scenery's spectacular, I must say." She made no effort to disguise the fact that she was referring to Willis. "Is that dog safe, then, Angel?"

Swifty continued to keep himself plastered to Angelica's shadow. "He's very safe." To Sinjun she remarked, "Brenda had a bad experience with a dog once."

Before Sinjun could respond, Brenda gave a sharp laugh. "Look what's coming now. Something from a ruddy time warp."

A stocky man approached from the direction of the compound. He wore khaki, all the way to his Bermuda shorts and tabbed knee socks. His lace-up buckskin shoes slapped the grass with military precision.

The latest arrival drew smartly to a halt at Sinjun's side. "What's all this, then, Mr. Breaker? According to Miss Simcox, there's somewhat of an upheaval. She seemed to think you might require reinforcements."

Brenda made an explosive sound.

Angelica bit her lip.

Sinjun narrowed his eyes and rocked from his heels to his toes. "Thank you for coming, Enders. This is Miss Butters. She's a friend of Miss Dean's."

The man with the machine gun came a step closer and flipped the gun around to rest against his other biceps.

"Eee," Brenda said, loudly enough for all to hear. "Puts you in mind of *In'ja* before the sun started to set on parts of the British empire, doesn't it? Expect a ruddy maharajah to come flapping along at any moment. D'you see the one with the arsenal, Angel? Makes you wonder what's so ruddy important it has t' be guarded like the ruddy crown jewels, doesn't it?"

Angelica cleared her throat. "Mr. Breaker—"

"Sinjun," he interrupted with a softness she didn't find reassuring.

"Yes, Sinjun. Sinjun likes his privacy, Brenda."

"Don't we all. I'm partial to it myself but I don't greet guests with—"

"I don't recall inviting you here, Miss Butters."

Brenda smiled, a truly remarkable event when she put her mind to it. Her brilliant eyes sparkled like deep aquamarines and her perfectly shaped teeth showed in a wide, white flash. She contrived to look charming and dangerous at the same time. "I'm so disappointed," she said, managing an amazing facsimile of coyness. "And I thought I heard someone on this island tell my helicopter pilot that we were to land. Who would have done that, d'you suppose, Sinjun? Shall I call you Sinjun, or would you prefer Sin? Somehow, Sin seems to fit—"

"Yorkshire," the bristly gray-haired man in khaki said suddenly.

"Aye." Brenda cocked a red brow. "What of it?"

He shuddered. "I was merely making an observation about your origins, Miss, er, Butters."

"Brenda will do. What's your handle, then?" When she got no response, she added, "Your moniker. *Name*."

Angelica groaned.

"Lloyd-Worthy. Enders Lloyd-Worthy."

Brenda stuck out a blunt-fingered hand. "Pleased to meet you, Enders."

Her hand was ignored. "I take it, Mr. Breaker, that Miss Butters will also be staying at the lagoon cottage?"

"Is that where you are?" Brenda asked Angelica, who nodded. "Right, then, I'd as soon be somewhere else if nobody minds."

Sinjun gave Angelica a long, questioning look.

"I've my own habits, if you know what I mean," Brenda said conversationally. "No sense straining a friendship, is there?"

"No sense at all," Sinjun agreed. "Where should we put Miss Butters, Enders?"

"There's the Koa cottage," Lloyd-Worthy said. "That's ready for occupation."

"Is it close to the sea, Enders?" Brenda asked.

He shuddered once more. "Very close to the sea."

"Are you catching cold?" Brenda said. "You're shivering."

"I am not catching cold. You are welcome to call me Mr. Lloyd-Worthy."

"Thank you. I'd as soon be somewhere away from the sea. Makes me nervous at night."

"If you'll excuse me," Sinjun said. "I'll leave you in Enders's capable hands."

"You live up to expectations," Brenda announced, deliberately dragging out her *a*'s while eyeing Enders Lloyd-Worthy's disdainfully raised nose with glee. "Oh, yes, Sin, you're every bit as handsome as Angel said you were going to be."

"*Brenda*," Angelica hissed.

"Am I?" Sinjun turned around. "Am I, Angel?"

She raised her chin. "You are an exceedingly good-looking man. But I don't have to tell you that."

"Is he as well-built as you expected?" Brenda asked, suddenly and deeply interested in the fingernails of one hand. "He doesn't have muscles like the private army over there, does he?"

A quick, quiet death might be nice, Angelica thought, closing her eyes—but not before she'd strangled Brenda.

"Oh, *really*," Enders said. "If you're ready, Miss Butters, I think we could find a place for you over the pool house."

Brenda hefted her bag once more. "What a funny place to find a pool house. Will it be noisy? Drunks make me nervous. They don't stay up all night and play, do they? Then fall about with the drink?"

There were times when Brenda pushed too far. "Pool *house,* not pool hall," Angelica said. "I think Mr. Lloyd-Worthy's referring to an apartment—or something—over a building by a swimming pool. Am I correct?"

"Absolutely." She was rewarded with a faint smile. The man turned a blank stare on Brenda. "The building is rarely used at all. I'm sure you'll find your accommodations to be more than adequate."

"Very well. You lead the way, Enders. I'll hunt you down later, Angel. Much later. I didn't get a wink last night so I may even sleep till tomorrow. After I explore a bit." Brenda set off after Enders, her bag banging against her leg. "I'm dying to find out what progress you've made on your project." She wiggled a finger at Sinjun as she spoke.

"See you later," Angelica said, grateful she'd decided to give Brenda the official excuse for being here. Maybe later, if she could persuade her friend to be circumspect, she'd share the whole story.

The man called Willis hiked his evil-looking weapon over his shoulder. He aimed a nod at Sinjun and easily caught up with Brenda. Without a word, he slipped the bulky bag from her fingers.

Brenda looked over her shoulder at Angelica, then up at Willis and thrust her lips out to say, "Ooh," in a breathy voice.

Left alone with Sinjun once more, Angelica sought to relieve the tension by scratching Swifty's shaggy head.

"That's the woman who helped you redefine human relationships?"

She'd lost her advantage. "Brenda is . . . not tactful. She's . . . zany."

"Loud, you mean. And she likes men—a lot."

"I never said . . . Well, I said she'd sort of lost faith in them. There's a difference."

"But she's not your lover, is she?"

Angelica glowed to the roots of her hair. "How dare you!"

"I dare. You deliberately tried to make a fool of me."

"You jumped to conclusions."

"I had help. How do you stand that woman?"

Angelica bridled. "Brenda's an individual. She doesn't try to fit into other people's expectations."

"She's rude."

Sometimes it was hard to defend Brenda to people who didn't know her. "She comes on strong because she trying to cover up for being . . . shy."

"Yeah." He shook his head. "I'm shy, too. I'm sure you noticed that."

She ignored the comment. "Brenda won't be any trouble. Forget she's here."

He faced her, came very close. "She won't be any trouble. Neither will you." The words were uncompromising. The voice was soft. "And I'm going to be the soul of agreeable charm."

The next breath Angelica took was too warm and it didn't fill her lungs. "Good. That's very good."

"This morning you made me lose my temper," he said. "I'm not happy about that. People seem to prefer not to play poker with me. They say it's because my face never gives anything away."

"That's . . . interesting."

"People also talk about the fact that I never give away what I'm feeling—in anything I do. I like it that way. Somehow you changed that. It won't happen again."

Her heart began to bump. "Are you afraid of losing your temper?"

His eyes became more yellow than green. "Obviously not. I've just told you I can control it." He dragged his bottom lip slowly through his teeth.

Angelica watched his mouth. "Is that something that took you a long time to learn?" Her heartbeat rose into her throat. There was danger here. *He* was dangerous.

"What do you mean, did it take me a long time to learn?"

"Controlling your temper." This man had a staff of gun-toting trained seals and she was baiting him, baiting the master. "How long did it take to be able to . . . When was the last time you really lost it, Sin?"

He tilted his head up and looked at her from beneath lowered lids. "A long time ago."

"Give me something to make a note of," she said, pressing her hands into her stomach. "You're into note-taking. Would around fifteen years be a good estimate?"

Lorraine crouched in a sandy hollow on the far side of the chopper pad from where Sinjun still faced that little mouse.

So much anger.

A splayed naupaka bush hugged the rim of the hollow. Through succulent leaves Lorraine saw the scene clearly. The red-haired Amazon type walked with Willis behind that tight-ass freak in Bermuda shorts who thought he was Sinjun's keeper—and that Lorraine was a whore. She couldn't hear a word from here but they were heading for the compound and the redhead was clinging to Willis's arm like an overripe tomato vine.

Willis looked and walked straight ahead and Lorraine smiled secretly. What Willis needed would be waiting for him tonight on the south shore and he knew it.

Chuck was being a son of a bitch. Because he chose to drink too much last night, she was supposed to put up with him not being in the mood this morning. He intended to stay in bed all day and she wasn't invited to make the stay more interesting.

She'd give anything to hear what Sinjun was saying to the blonde woman. The two of them faced off on the edge of the pad and Sin's body was so stiff Lorraine could imagine how it would feel to touch him: like touching sun-warmed steel cable. A thrill shivered along her nerves.

The good news was that body language said the lovebirds were arguing.

The bad news was that Sin didn't waste time around people he wasn't interested in.

Sooner or later Sin would realize he already had everything he wanted right here, that she—Lorraine—knew how to make him forget any other woman he'd ever met.

Lorraine didn't dare approach Sin again.

The blonde was another matter.

Why hadn't she thought of it before? Dropping back into the hollow, Lorraine sprang to her feet and ran, hunched over, toward the shore.

Within ten minutes she began skirting the jungle on the beach side. She stood straight now and sprinted. Another five minutes brought her to the front of the lagoon cottage. Breathing hard, she slipped around to the terrace at the back and entered through the French doors.

A journalist, Chuck had tried to insist. Someone from a big, fancy magazine who'd decided she wanted to write Sin's biography. Sure, and Lorraine was a marine biologist here to study the reef!

Sin had kissed the *journalist* like he'd never seen a woman before. He'd gotten inside her clothes like he'd never touched a woman before.

Unless there was enough to write about the way Sin fucked to fill a book, someone was lying to Lorraine.

Experience had taught her that there was always a means to dispose of any enemy. Often that means was something quite simple.

She opened one of the top drawers in the bedroom dresser and began searching.

Seven

*A*ngelica stumbled on a root hidden in the underbrush and barely stopped herself from falling. Somewhere in the seconds before Sinjun walked away, her stomach had gone into free-fall and it had yet to land.

She was out of her depth.

He gave off power in waves—and anger—the anger he said he always controlled.

But, and most dangerous of all, Sinjun Breaker attracted her as no man ever had.

God, she'd read about women who were drawn to evil men.

One step at a time, she told herself. One foot before the other. And she must ignore what he did to the sex drive she'd never thought she had.

Back to the cottage—as quickly as possible. Once there, she would retrieve the letter from its hiding place and remind herself of why Sinjun Breaker must be stopped.

Not that she'd really forgotten.

Her eyes stung and she blinked. There was no question of turning back now. She would find a way of proving exactly what he'd done and what kind of man he was. Then the world would know. Everyone would know that he'd never hesitated to sacrifice the weak on the altar of those he lived

97

to impress, those he'd vowed to best where they excelled most: making money.

She slipped on something hard and stopped, gasping to catch her breath. The dappled colors of the jungle swam before her.

Tears were a luxury she couldn't afford. Her mother had cried easily, retreated easily—been an easy victim.

The hard thing hidden in a bed of long, slippery needles and moist leaves was a casuarina cone from a fantastically gnarled tree. She blinked through the veil of tears and skirted a whole scattering of the ironwood's droppings. This place beckoned and repulsed at the same time. With fear pulsing in her brain, every crooked shape, every waft of warm, heavy, perfume-laden air became a seething threat. In the arms of a lover the shapes would become a sensuous cradle, the scents an aphrodisiac.

She had no lover.

Angelica reached the cottage.

He had been so coldly disdainful. *Why, why, why?* Deep in her consciousness, jabbing at places that tried to shut it out, hovered the question she didn't want to confront: Why had he allowed her to come here? Clearly her questions infuriated him. Clearly he didn't want the truth about his early years to be made public. So, *why?*

Wondering just how much she did know could be motive enough for his wanting to keep her where he might be able to put the brakes on whatever she wrote about him.

Obviously, if he had guessed her true reason for coming to Hell he'd have kicked her out already.

Her legs moved as if lead-weighted. Reluctantly, wishing Brenda had returned with her, she opened the front door and went inside.

She must find a really safe place for the letter—it was the last communication she had from her mother. The letter was the last communication her mother had made with anyone and what she'd written could help deal Sinjun Breaker a felling blow.

In the kitchen, Angelica poured a glass of iced tea and hovered before the refrigerator that Campbell Midgely, smiling all the while, had packed the night before . . . not long after Sinjun left.

She wasn't hungry.

Carrying the iced tea, she trailed toward the bedroom. First she would read the letter, then hide it until she was ready to leave the island.

The breeze turned long, sheer draperies into transparent sails. Angelica paused, frowning. Hadn't she closed the doors before leaving with Sinjun?

She shrugged. Evidently not.

Just the thought of looking at her mother's tear-streaked words sickened her. "Oh, Momma."

A pair of panties poked from the top drawer, jamming it open. Angelica tucked in the red satin and pulled the second drawer all the way out. Her fingertips located the envelope taped inside the back of the chest.

Early that morning she had discovered a small pond where the lawns behind the cottage dropped away on one side. Now, carrying the iced tea and the envelope, she trailed to a shady spot beneath the gently swaying fronds of a fan palm at the edge of the pond.

Sinjun had told her he would come to her, "when I'm ready. Whenever I'm ready." His hard eyes had swept from her face to her feet and back again, and then he'd left.

She'd all but accused him of beating his wife until she hemorrhaged and died. And his wonderfully controlled anger, delivered in his very silence, in the curling and uncurling of his fists, had been his response.

Angelica wedged her glass into sandy earth and slipped her mother's three-month-old Cabochard-scented letter from its envelope.

Whenever Sinjun had looked at her, she felt as if he touched her in every place his eyes covered.

For God's sake, she'd met dozens of good-looking men, been hit on by just as many, and never reacted to one of them like this. What was it that appealed to her—the fact that she couldn't have him?

Sick.

Did he leave her last night and think about the kiss afterwards . . . the touching?

It meant nothing to him. If he thought of it at all it was because he was amused at how easily she'd succumbed to his charm.

Heat crawled over her skin again.

She unfolded the creamy paper. At the top, engraved in deep-pink, was her mother's first name only. *Marlene.* Pink had been her favorite color.

MY ANGEL,

> *You're somewhere in Europe, Italy, I think, writing one of your wonderful stories about something I probably wouldn't understand. Expeditions to dig up old bones or something.*
>
> *You know I've always read your articles. And it's always made me feel wonderful—in a sad way— that you chose to use my dad's name. My dad liked to write—I've told you that so many times—but he never got to do anything with it. He used to laugh and say life got in the way of a man doing what he wanted to do. I know he'd have been proud of you.*
>
> *You'll read this here in San Diego, not in Italy. When you do, I'll be dead.*

Angelica hugged her shins and rested her forehead on her knees. If only Momma had picked up the phone and called Italy. Or *Verity.* The magazine would have tracked Angelica down.

She ground her burning eyes against her knees. How long did they say it took to get through grieving? Too long.

The sun was high and even the breeze didn't cool its heat. Buzzing came from tiny black flying insects that darted between lily pads and across the pond. The surface of the water lay still and glossy green, reflecting the wide-open mauve lilies.

Angelica continued reading, squinting against sunspots that danced on the page.

> *Don't feel sad, Angel. Save all your sadness and turn it into the courage you're going to need to do what must be done—for me and for the people I've loved most.*
>
> *No, that's not right. That's not what I mean. Do this for the one who never let us down. He never did, Angel. Not through it all. I was very young when Larry was killed, not much more than a girl, really. You were still very little. I don't know how I'd have managed without my dear, special friend (you know who I mean). Larry worked for him before the accident. He looked after us, Angel. He made sure we never wanted for anything—until someone turned him against us.*

Here the ink smeared so badly that Angelica could hardly read what Marlene Golden had written. Was that when she'd started taking the pills? Without looking, Angelica groped for the iced-tea glass and took a long swallow to ease her parched and straining throat. She read on.

> *I dare not write our friend's name (I don't need to, do I?) in case the one you must punish finds a way to get his hands on this letter. I know you wouldn't willingly share it, but he is a cruel, evil man and you're going to have to be very, very careful.*
>
> *The man who caused all this pain wants to cheat our friend in some business thing. To do this he needed to get rid of me because I was in the way.*

Oh, my darling Angel, I know you believe I left Seattle because I wanted to but it isn't true. Our friend sent me. At first he told me he was worried about something he couldn't discuss. He said I might be in some danger and he wanted me to be safe.

Angel, do not ever doubt that our best friend is innocent in all this.

I'm tired now. I have to write quickly and clearly so you'll understand what you have to do.

That other man, the man you must punish, used a disgusting woman to work her horrible little tricks on our friend so that she could get close enough to find out some secret information. The woman isn't important, only him. She was his lover, but she managed to make our friend believe it was he she loved and that she didn't want any other woman in his life. That meant me, so he sent me away.

Now she's engaged to our friend. He promised he'd keep on coming to see me once he moved me to San Diego but he never has. Money is all he's sent—as if he hasn't already made sure I had more than enough to be comfortable.

Angelica, I need him. I've always needed him. Do you understand what I'm telling you? Without my beloved friend I don't want to go on living.

When I found out about the other woman, I confronted her. She laughed at me. She told me about that awful other man and that they were lovers, and what they planned together, and that there was nothing I could do to stop them. And she told me my friend had only encouraged me out of pity and that now all he wanted was her.

I was an embarrassment and a nuisance. And I was too old for him now. She said he was sick of spending time with me when he could be with someone beautiful, sexy and young.

I am forty-six. Not young, but not so old.

Do you completely understand how important my beloved friend was to me now? Do not be shocked that he was my lover for all those years, Angel. Back at the beginning he had an invalid wife and you know how kind he is—he couldn't do anything to hurt her. When he was finally free to marry me, that grotesque man sent his whore to steal my place. She will marry the man who should have been mine.

I tried to warn our friend that she intends to destroy him, but all he did was get angry. Angel, that terrible, clever woman had already told our friend that I had approached her. She said that I'd made up an awful story and that I intended to tell it to him to get rid of her. The story I was supposed to have invented was the one she told me. I was trapped. He wouldn't listen to me. He said I was making it all up because I was jealous and he said I was never to go near . . . He said I had upset someone who meant a great deal to him and I must never speak to her again. Then he told me he wouldn't see me again.

So, you see, I cannot go on, can I?

He's kept on being kind. Sending money. He pays for this apartment, you know. Always has. And he paid for you to go to those expensive schools.

Angelica's back ached, and her head. The writing wandered now.

I'm lying, aren't I? Just a little? I do have choices about what I do. You'll have a right to be angry with me. I'm selfish and I'm a coward. I'm choosing to die rather than live while my lover is with another woman. Forgive me, please.

In my name, be the one to save the one who always loved us. Angel, I know he still does love us and that he always will. He's always been a

*man with—strong appetites, if you know what I
mean. This woman has managed to make him feel
like a very young man again and that's how she's
holding on to him.*

*Save him before they destroy him. Please do it
before it's too late.*

Three months had passed since this letter was
written. Angelica knew that the business deal her
mother referred to in the letter was still in progress,
but not how far it had gone.

*Please save our friend. All you need to know is
the name of the man who has taken my life: Sinjun
Breaker.*

There were two more pages, but she had to rest,
to think. Sinjun's trail had been pretty cold but
Angelica had carefully stirred the embers, pain-
stakingly turned up enough material to give her
a direct passage beneath his proud skin.

Unfortunately she'd found no clue to the identity
of the woman to whom Momma had referred.

A shadow slid slowly over her left shoulder.

Angelica's breath jammed in the middle of her
chest. As nonchalantly as she could, she folded
the letter and let it dangle from the fingers of her
right hand while she picked up her iced tea with
the left.

The shadow lengthened past her drawn-up knees
and onto the grass.

"Hello. Angelica Dean, isn't it?"

Angelica looked up and shaded her eyes.

Blue-black hair waved around a face no one, male
or female, was likely to forget. Thick, curling black
lashes outlined eyes of a color Angelica had only
seen in pictures—of Elizabeth Taylor.

"Angelica Dean?"

"Yes."

A slight smile rounded high cheekbones and showed off a neat little dimple to the right of the woman's mouth. "Chuck said you were pretty," she said. "And you are. I'm Lorraine Hart."

The name was said as if it should mean something. It didn't. Angelica said, "Hi," and waited.

"I suppose the best way to explain me is to say I belong to Chuck." She laughed, showing every perfect white tooth. Then she winked. "We know who really owns whom in these arrangements, don't we?"

"Yes," Angelica said, and agreed wholeheartedly in Lorraine Hart's case. Chuck was quite a hunk. Lorraine was larger-than-life gorgeous.

"I thought you might be as bored as I am so I came on over." Lorraine, in a soft, cream cotton shift that flattened to her body with each puff of breeze, struck a hip-thrusting pose and turned her face up to the sun. "I understand a friend of yours arrived today."

"Brenda. Yes."

Lorraine had large breasts. Her waist was small, her stomach flat and the prominent bone below shaded with predictably dark hair which Angelica could see through her almost transparent dress.

There was nothing between Lorraine and the naked eye but that creamy cotton.

When the breeze blew in the right direction— and it didn't have to blow particularly hard—there was very little about Lorraine that wasn't visible.

She walked—postured around this tiny island like that? In front of men? In front of men without a whole lot of sexual outlets?

"You're a journalist," Lorraine said. "What does your friend do?"

"Computers. She's an expert at setting up systems and troubleshooting."

Lorraine shook a hand from a limp wrist. "Sounds deathly. I'm a model."

I'll bet, "Yes."

"Are you with a paper or something?"

"At the moment I'm free-lance. I used to be with *Verity*."

"Oh, my." Lorraine was finally impressed. She dropped to her haunches, displaying a length of tanned leg all the way up to the curve of a buttock, revealed through a slit in the shift. "Why would you leave something like *Verity*? Trouble?"

Not the kind of trouble Lorraine was suggesting. "It was time for a change of pace. I may go back later."

"Chuck said you were writing something about Sinjun. About his life. What's that for?"

"A biography."

"The story of his life?" The woman tossed back her hair and laughed. "How interesting is that going to be?"

Angelica shrugged and tucked Marlene's letter back into its envelope.

Had Lorraine simply wandered over to be friendly, or had she been sent? Did someone hope that in a girl-to-girl chat Angelica would become comfortable enough to reveal exactly how much she knew about Sinjun? Each time their paths crossed she could tell he ached for the answer to that question.

"I'm thirsty," Lorraine said, eyeing Angelica's iced tea.

The last thing Angelica wanted was to spend time with this woman. "Would you like some tea?" she asked reluctantly.

"That would be nice." Lorraine bounced to her feet and waited for Angelica to join her. "Actually, there was something I wanted to say to you."

Angelica waited.

Lorraine hesitated, then turned away. "Let's go

back for that tea. We can sit and talk on your terrace."

The walk was accomplished in silence.

"Ah," Lorraine breathed when they moved beneath the petrea vine. "I love this island but the heat can even get to me sometimes. Is the tea in a jug?"

Angelica nodded. "Uh huh."

"I'll go for it, shall I?"

"I will." She didn't like the idea of Lorraine walking through the cottage, even if it was only a temporary home.

"Leave your glass, then. You'll need two hands."

Angelica gave up the glass and went inside. She hadn't crossed the bedroom before her stomach turned and she swung quickly around. Marlene's letter had been gripped against the glass. Both had passed into Lorraine's hand.

The terrace was empty.

Angelica's empty glass sat in the middle of the table.

"Lorraine!" Searching in every direction, she ran onto the grass.

"Here I am."

Angelica whirled about. Lorraine lounged against the wall at the corner of the cottage. "Oh, there you are," Angelica said, feeling foolish. The woman's hands were behind her back and there was no sign of an envelope.

"I'm so hot," Lorraine said. "I was just catching a breeze over here."

Angelica looked around. "There was an envelope," she blurted out. "I gave it to you with my glass."

Lorraine shook her head. "I'm sorry. I was going to put it inside the door but the breeze beckoned. Here it is." She produced the letter and held it aloft.

"Thanks." Angelica took the paper into her fingers and noted that it was warm—where it had been held against Lorraine's back. "I'll go and get that iced tea."

"Maybe I don't want it after all." Sauntering, Lorraine crossed the terrace and wound her arms around one of the wooden posts that supported the trellis. "I already knew you were here to write a biography."

Angelica dropped into a chaise. "So why did you ask those questions?"

"To see if your story checked out with the one Chuck gave me."

"Why wouldn't it?"

"This wouldn't be the first time Sinjun got Chuck to pimp for him."

No previous blush came close to the intensity of the one that hit Angelica now. "What a horrible suggestion to make."

"We're both big girls."

One of them was bigger than the other. "Well, in this case, you've made a wrong assumption."

"At least in part."

"What does that mean?"

Lorraine rested her chin on her shoulder and settled an expressionless violet stare on Angelica. "It means that writing a biography is the cover you've come up with for being here."

A sick little flip of the stomach sent Angelica's hand to her belly. There hadn't been time for the letter to be opened and read. "I don't have any idea what you're talking about."

"Maybe you don't. But maybe you do. Isn't it just a teensy bit possible that, in addition to deciding Sinjun will make a sizzling subject for your *biography*, you also wondered if this might be your opportunity to hook one of the world's most eligible bachelors?"

It took a moment, but then Angelica laughed. She bit her lip to try and stop.

"You aren't the only woman who laughs when she's nervous. Or when she's found out. You do find him fascinating, don't you? And not only as someone to write about?"

"Sinjun Breaker is a fascinating man, all right," Angelica said honestly.

Lorraine swung around the post. From the back, the crease between her buttocks was visible. From the sides, her breasts were revealed through the loose armholes of the shift.

"Okay." The swinging ceased abruptly. Lorraine stood, arms crossed, feet apart, like a beautiful creature stepped right out of a movie screen. "I don't owe you any help, but I'll give it to you anyway. Sinjun Breaker is one dangerous bastard."

Angelica's mind blanked.

"My advice to you is to pack up. Tell your red-haired buddy to do the same. Then get off this island. I'll persuade Chuck to say you asked to leave and—"

"No."

"If Sinjun pushes for more excuses, Chuck can tell him you had a sudden emergency and didn't have time to stick around for fond farewells."

"*No.*"

"You aren't listening to me." Lorraine came closer. "I think you're here for something other than a few juicy words for some little book. I think you've come to see just how much you can really get out of Sin. I'm sure I don't have to explain myself further."

"No, you don't. Please go away."

Lorraine leaned over Angelica, braced her hands on the arms of the chaise. "*You* are going to go away. I belong here. You don't know what you're fooling around with. Sinjun isn't your kind of man. He only relates to his own kind and you aren't it."

My God, the woman was jealous, nothing more. Lorraine Hart might be Chuck Gill's mistress, but it was Sinjun she wanted—Angelica would stake her life on that. "Thanks for the warning. I'll bear it in mind."

The beautiful face folded into a malevolent mask. "Listen to me and listen well. If you were any kind of a reporter you'd already know that Sinjun Breaker has never allowed anyone—particularly a woman—to get in the way of what he wants."

Angelica looked up into Lorraine's glittering eyes. "How can you be sure I won't tell Sinjun what you've just told me?"

"Because Sin and I are like this—" Lorraine raised a hand and crossed two fingers. "—and he'd never believe you."

"I thought you were Chuck's friend."

"I'm giving you a chance to save yourself. Take it. It's the last one you'll get from me."

Hairs rose along the length of Angelica's spine. "Maybe I should ask Chuck what he thinks about all this."

Lorraine threw back her head and laughed. She stood up and her breasts rose and fell with the force of the great breaths she took. "Chuck! Chuck?" Spinning away, she stalked to the edge of the terrace and back. "You won't tell Chuck because you won't dare. Everything Sin's been through, Chuck's been through. Chuck's been standing right beside him all the way. Sin's troubles are Chuck's troubles. What Sin has Chuck is welcome to, and vice versa. Do you understand now?"

"Like you?" Angelica asked, and was grateful her voice didn't wobble. "Do they share you? Is that what you're saying?"

"Yes!" Lorraine loomed over her again. "Yes, and I *like* it that way. Sin, Chuck and I, we understand one another and that's the way it'll always be."

"And you want me to butt out because you can't take the competition?"

Lorraine stood up straight and smoothed the shift.

"I'm going to say this once, then whatever happens is on your own head.

"There are people—men—who are too strong and too alive for the rest of the world to understand. They have needs that must be met and the rest of the world resents that. They are gods set loose among little people and they have to find ways to satisfy their hunger."

"*Jesus*," Angelica muttered.

"Don't laugh at me, you stupid bitch. Sinjun Breaker needs power. He *deserves* power because he's bigger than any other man. He knows that. His attention span is short in some areas—like women. When he wants one, he wants her. And he gets her. When he's done, he's done. And when someone gets in his way, there's only one thing to be done, and he does it."

"It?" Angelica slid sideways and got to her feet. She prayed Lorraine couldn't see how her legs trembled. "What does he do, throw you in the briar patch? Or just beat you to a . . . pulp . . . and . . ." Her heart felt as if it had shut down.

Lorraine backed slowly away. "And *nothing*. I think something finally clicked for you. I'm in the Pua-kali lodge. It's on the north side of the compound. Outside the walls. Get a message to me when you're ready to leave. In the meantime, remember—if Sin wants you, he'll have you. Then he won't want you around anymore."

"I take it you speak from experience."

"Oh, no." Lorraine shook her head. "I'm different. I'm enough like Sin to know how to handle him. You aren't like him. You're like all the rest."

"The rest?"

"The ones who aren't around anymore."

Eight

"***D*** you want to talk about it?"

Sinjun stopped in the act of feeding a sheet into the fax machine he kept on a leather-topped writing table in his bedroom. "Come in, Chuck," he said as the other man sauntered to pour himself a glass of seltzer from the bottle Sinjun had just opened.

Chuck raised his glass in salute. "I am in."

"I noticed."

"Ready to ship her out yet?"

Sinjun pretended ignorance. "What are we talking about?"

"The lovely blonde biographer. Ms. Angelica Dean. She who drives you to very uncharacteristic behavior."

"Ah." With thoughtful precision, Sinjun sent the Tucker figures Mary Barrett was pining for in Seattle. "What makes you think I'd want to ship her out?"

Chuck tipped up his glass and kept it there until ice cubes fell against his teeth. "The said uncharacteristic behavior was the clue." He wiped the back of a hand over his mouth. "Sinjun Breaker *shouting* in front of the whole world."

"Garbage."

"This morning? On the pad? Facing off with the lovely pen-pusher and looking as if you'd like to snap her smooth little neck with your bare hands."

The fax machine spat out an acknowledgment slip. "I thought you were *indisposed*. What did you do? Set up a telescope on the roof?"

"Campbell Midgely," Chuck said, grinning. He opened a jar of nuts and poured a small mountain into his palm.

"That kid could cause me to break a personal rule," Sinjun said.

"Such as?"

"Lose my temper."

Several peanuts fell to the hala mat at Chuck's feet and Swifty stirred himself to pad over and vacuum. "You mean you'd break a personal rule twice in one day?"

"Where the hell was Campbell?"

"Inside the Eurocopter."

"What the . . . What was he doing in there?"

"Kid's crazy about choppers. I took him up for a flip afterwards. Said he'd just been looking around and he heard you spouting off at the girl."

"Don't drop nuts," Sinjun snapped. "Bad for dogs. Tell Campbell to stay out of the chopper—or I will. I won't have to lose my temper, but he's not going to like it anyway."

"Leave it to me. Want some nuts?"

Sinjun shook his head. "Why did Campbell feel he had to tell you?"

"You don't know?"

"The kid never says two words to me. How would I know anything about him?"

"Seltzer?"

"No."

Chuck poured himself another glass. "I really thought you knew about Campbell."

Sinjun waited patiently.

"He's had a thing for Lorraine ever since he got here for the summer."

"Lorraine?" Sinjun sank into the chair beside the

desk. "Angelica Dean to Lorraine? Maybe I'm dense, but wasn't that a non sequitur?"

"Not really. He came to me weeks ago and said I should do something about the fact that you don't like Lorraine."

"This is coming from left field, Chuck."

Stuffing more nuts into his mouth, Chuck rolled his eyes.

"What does that mean?"

"Well, hell, I figured you knew the kid was odd. He seems to appoint himself as protector to any female who strays by. The point I think he was making today was that you're not to be trusted around what he calls *gentle* women. You're not kind—his words, not mine—to Lorraine and today you shouted at that poor, pretty little Miss Dean."

"*Shit.*"

"Yeah. I couldn't agree with you more. But that's not what interests me. I don't care if you give Lorraine the cold shoulder—particularly since we both know you don't and if you did she wouldn't give a damn."

Sinjun nodded. How could an otherwise intelligent man have such a blind spot when it came to a particular woman?

"The point is . . ." Chuck said, crunching. "The point is that poor, pretty Miss Dean managed what few people do: She made you pissing mad. According to Campbell, you walked away and left her in tears."

Sinjun wrinkled his nose. "Give me that." He held out his hand for the seltzer glass. "In tears? You're sure?"

Chuck gave up his drink. "According to Campbell."

There had been two bright spots of color on her face and her eyes had shone like polished amber. He'd been looking at triumph, not distress. "She wasn't crying. She was bloody thrilled with what she'd accomplished." The seltzer made him pucker. "I don't want her to go anywhere, Chuck. I want her right here until I find out exactly what she wants and how much she knows."

"What makes you think she knows anything at all?"

"Ah, yes, what indeed. How about Bliss, Chucky baby? Does that ring a bell? And I'm not talking about what you feel when you're playing pile-driver with Lorraine."

"Bliss?" Chuck said softly.

"Bliss. Did you know it's not there anymore?"

"You're kidding."

"There's a trailer park out of Dillon where all the folks from Bliss were moved. They're so nostalgic for the dear old township, they've named the park after it."

"Holy . . . Are you saying the Dean woman knew all this?"

"Uh huh. She went there."

"I can't believe it."

"She and old Mrs. Cahler are buddies."

Chuck's nut-hand stopped on the way to his mouth.

"For a successful biography, you need a good mix of the professional and the personal," Sinjun said. "That's what our journalist told me. Roughly translated, that means you can't sell a man's life story unless you can squeeze out enough dirt to keep 'em turning those pages."

"She found out about . . ."

"Yeah."

"How much exactly?"

"The hemorrhage. The . . . The baby." He stood up and turned away. "The story about the beating."

"*Christ*," Chuck said through his teeth. "I'm sorry she—"

"Don't be. She only knows what Mrs. Cahler

knows. Nothing. Nothing more than was written in the police report."

"You're sure?"

"Mmm. She tried to goad me. That's what Campbell saw at the pad. She's pushing, trying to get me to say something I'll regret."

"Get her out of here."

"And have her continue her fishing expedition until she catches the kind of fish she wants? No way. She let me know she could write a biography with or without my permission. You've seen enough unauthorized hatchet jobs to know how that goes."

"There's got to be a way to persuade her out of it."

"I'm sure there is. Just give me time." He looked over his shoulder at Chuck. "Leave it to me, okay?"

"If you're sure."

"I'm sure."

Chuck shook his head slowly. "Okay. End of topic. For now. Remember that charter chopper we talked about?"

Sinjun felt wrung out. "The one that's for sale?"

"That's the one. Turns out the owner's on hard times. Still catching up from the hurricane. It's a steal and it's a beaut. Probably exactly what we need for a backup. I looked at it."

"When?"

"I took Fran over to Kauai."

Frowning, Sinjun said, "When?"

"Right after you had your chat with Angelica. Got back a little while ago."

"Did Campbell ride shotgun?"

"You've got it. He didn't talk about you till we were on the way back, though."

Sinjun rubbed the space between his brows. "Why do I get the feeling I'm out of control here? Fran never told me she was going anywhere."

"I think it was generally felt that you'd rather

be left alone. Anyway, she's visiting those friends of hers. Spending the night. I said I'd pick her up tomorrow afternoon. She's going to be pissed if she has to wait around at the shop."

"The shop?"

"I think I'm hearing something in the Eurocopter's landing gear. The nose unit. I've made an appointment in Lihue to have someone go over it with me."

"That could take a while."

"Yeah. I guess you could come along and . . . Forget it."

"No. Great idea. I'll come with you and take up the other machine. I can check it out and bring Fran back at the same time. Kill two birds with one stone."

"I don't think that is a good idea, Sin."

"It's a fantastic idea. I'm starting to get cabin fever holed up here. And no one's going to know I've left Hell, so my neck is perfectly safe."

Chuck grimaced and chewed his bottom lip.

"Get out of here," Sinjun told him. "Go give Fran a call. Tell her she's lucking out. I'm running away with her. Make arrangements with the charter people, then tell her to meet me there. Fix a time with her."

"Sin—"

"Do it." The phone rang. "Go on. And stop worrying, will you?"

Chuck walked slowly to the door and Sinjun reached for the phone. "Chuck."

"Yeah?"

"Thanks, buddy. For everything."

"Anytime."

"Sinjun Breaker." Sinjun spoke absently into the receiver while Chuck gave a high-sign and left. "Who?"

"Are you okay?" the female voice on the phone asked.

"Who is this?"

There was a muffled word that sounded nasty. "M.A.B. Mary Abernathy Barrett. *Mary*, Sin. Your right-hand woman. She who holds the pieces of your empire together while you get a suntan."

He let out a breath. "Mary. Hello. How lovely to hear from you."

"You're with someone."

He cast his eyes heavenward. "No, I'm not." Using a remote, he turned on the TV and punched down the volume.

"You sound funny," Mary said. "We've got important things to talk about here. That fax you sent. You didn't include the numbers for the international group."

"I didn't?"

"Who's with you?"

"Not a soul. It's just you and me, Mary, I swear it," Sinjun said.

He flopped to the bed and stretched out on his back. His head, hanging off the other side of the mattress, gave him an upside-down view of the television screen. Kevin Costner was boyishly nibbling at a thumbnail.

"Did you look at Tucker's international numbers, Sin?"

He furrowed his brow. Blood was running to his head and he scooted into a more comfortable position. "Not in enough depth yet. Things have been a little busy around here."

Mary Barrett's silence was meant to remind him that he'd cut out of Seattle leaving her to deflect potential incoming missiles aimed at Kertz-Breaker. Mary thought what most people thought, that Sinjun had encountered an unusual series of accidents. Being a self-proclaimed tough, all-business cookie, she also thought he was scared and overreacting—and hiding out on Hell. She'd made not-very-subtle references to "the Howard

Hughes syndrome." He wondered briefly how cool she would have remained if a runaway cement truck had homed in on her car—while she was in it.

"You don't believe it's been crazy here," he said finally. "But I'm telling you this place has turned into Grand Central Station."

"How could it have? You said no one but your nearest and dearest knew you were there and that no one was going to find out unless you said so."

He considered what to say next. "I decided it was an appropriate opportunity to devote some time to a personal project I've had in mind." This had better be phrased just right. "I've settled on a biographer and we're doing some work together."

"A *biographer?*" The explosive amazement in Mary's voice wounded Sinjun. "Why in God's name would you want a *biographer?*"

This was the problem: When you couldn't come out and say you'd been hunted down for the project you sounded pigheaded. He said, "We could use less emphasis on entertainment types and more on business and industry personalities."

A mirthful little chortle got swallowed. "If you say so. A biographer, huh? And he's on Hell now."

"Er—yes."

"One biographer is hardly in invasion."

"Someone else came."

"Who?"

Holding out on Mary wasn't an option. If he didn't tell her, Fran—who lived to best Mary as Sinjun's confidante—would. "We've got a computer type in, too."

"What the hell for?"

He raised the phone receiver above his face and stared at it. "Communications glitch." Why not consider finding a use for Brenda Butters's expertise?

"What did you say?" Mary's voice was faint.

Sin clamped the phone back to his ear. "I'm streamlining our communications system here. We hit a glitch. Are we through with the niceties?"

"If you say we are."

What was the matter with him? Usually he could hardly wait to sink his teeth into a world-size problem. "We are. What do you have from Lieber?" Garth Lieber and his supposed miracle skin cream—the deal they were trying to finalize—were a major pain in the ass.

"When Lieber hit hard times, the sun was shining on our backyard. This is blowing out, boss. It's *huge*. Have you been keeping up on the news?"

Sometimes it was kind to lie. "No." Mary loved flaunting her meticulous attention to business.

"Jeez, it's a good job one of us is. By the way, that little fart Akers is cruising for a war with me. He seems to think he's gotten divine notice that he's in charge while you're not around."

Peter Akers, Kertz-Breaker's long-term planning specialist, was a bright, ambitious guy. Sin grinned. "Peter's okay. Cut him some slack. He's probably trying to be gallant and look out for you."

"*Shit*."

Sin held the phone away and flinched. "He knows *you're* my number two," he told her when his ear stopped ringing. "If you can't handle him, I will."

"I can handle him."

Predictability could be comforting. "I knew you could. Keep up on every move Lieber makes and feed whatever you get back to me."

"He says you need to meet with him."

He let out a long, soft breath. "Yeah." That's what he'd expected her to say. "Just as soon as I can, I will."

"We could arrange for me to bring him there, and—"

"*No*."

A short silence. "Every paper and magazine is running releases on the latest predictions for SOS face cream. According to the hype, a week or so using the stuff and you'd look like a ten-year-old."

"Instead of a twelve-year-old?"

"Don't fool around, Sinjun. There's a lot of hoopla about this stuff and we've got more than a fighting chance of getting our hands on controlling interest."

"You sound excited."

"And you're not?"

He was excited—but not in the way she meant. "I'm damned." He rolled onto his stomach, which only made him more aware of his physical state.

"What did you say, Sinjun?"

"I said I *am*. I am excited." For God's sake. Somewhere during the conversation, Angelica had walked, hips gently swaying, across his brain and he'd gotten an immediate physical reaction which was making him damned uncomfortable. "Mary, I'd like to put this Lieber thing off."

"Impossible."

He knew she was close to being right. "Not for long. Just until . . ." Until he could figure out how not to win a premature trip to a morgue.

"Lieber's pressing for a meeting."

"Soon."

Mary's sigh carried all the way from Seattle. "He suggested Tuesday. I think I can stall him a week longer. Will that give you time?"

Ten days. Ten days of waiting for Angelica Dean—or someone—to make a move. It would have to be enough time. "Tell Lieber a week from Tuesday." Any longer in this luxury coop and he'd lose his mind. Forced isolation was making him crazy—crazy enough to yearn to make love to a woman who'd proved she intended to make him miserable.

"Why don't you come in the day before," Mary said.

Sinjun grew still. "I told you it's going to be hard to get there at all." He picked at nubby threads in the white cotton spread.

"You'll need to be well-rested for the meeting. You know Lieber. He wants the money, but he doesn't really want to part with a piece of his action."

"Santa Claus is dead. It's a cruel world."

"We could have dinner, Sin." Her voice had grown soft. "Then go over everything we'll need for the meeting."

He dropped his forehead on a hand. "I don't think . . ." What would it hurt to give her a little of what she wanted? "Okay. Yeah, sounds great."

"It will be," she said with the purr that had stroked him in some of the right places for a while. "Let's make it dinner somewhere quiet, huh?"

"We'll eat at my place. That's real quiet."

Damn, he did not want that. "I don't want you going to any trouble."

"I like to cook—for you."

What the hell. At least he wouldn't have to look for a seat against a wall and check out the emergency exits. "Thank you, Mary."

"Thank *you*, Sin. We'll firm up the arrangements later."

He heard the receiver slip back into the cradle at the other end of the line.

A discreet knock at the door suggested that someone had been waiting for the telephone conversation to end.

"Come in!"

Enders came, chin jutting, his mouth pursed beneath the wiry mustache. "Sorry to disturb you, Mr. Breaker." He shut the door behind him and advanced across warmly glowing koa-wood floors. "I was . . . *told* to inform you that dinner will be at seven-thirty. Cocktails are to be served an hour previous."

Grunting, Sinjun stretched to replace the telephone. It was already almost six. He rolled to sit on the edge of the bed. "Is someone having a party?"

"It would appear so."

There were days when a man might wish he had no staff at all to tell him what to do. "Is there something you'd like to share with me, Enders? Something that's threatening to choke you, perhaps?"

Enders shrugged elaborately and raised one bushy brow. "Not unless you're interested in these annoying—or should I say *foolish* little household matters. Household matters that would not occur if we hadn't opened our shores—and our arms—to two total strangers at a time when we're all agreed that a certain *caution* is advisable."

"I'll bite. Tell me what this is about."

"Miss Butters called Mrs. Midgely."

The disdain in Enders's voice almost undid Sinjun. "Did she?" One did *not* laugh at Enders Lloyd-Worthy. Sinjun couldn't understand why, but his faithful servant hated the ground Miss Butters walked upon.

"She did indeed," Enders said. "Wished to give information about her particular preferences in the area of food. Her allergies. Those items that do not tempt her delicate palate, and so forth."

"Good God."

"As you say, Mr. Breaker." Enders picked invisible lint off one short sleeve. "However, Mrs. Midgely seems to have taken the bit between her teeth, as it were. Miss Butters—who, by the way, appears to have changed her mind about needing rest—said she's accustomed to regular meals of a certain variety and Mrs. Midgely behaved as if she regarded it as an honor to serve our latest *guest*."

"I hardly see what concern this is of mine."

"Mrs. Midgely has risen to the occasion. She informed me that she's certain you will wish your *guests* to be well looked after. Thus the dinner party. Mr. Gill and his friend that—Miss Hart, have agreed to be present."

"Chuck just left. He didn't say a word."

"Probably overwhelmed at the prospect, sir. Felt he lacked sufficient eloquence to express his delight, perhaps?"

"I don't understand a word of this."

"I informed Mrs. Midgely that you were unlikely to share her enthusiasm, but she seemed not to care. Campbell is to go to the lagoon cottage and extend an invitation in person. Then he will escort Miss Dean to the house. Apparently there's some notion that the lady may be in uncertain spirits."

Sinjun got slowly to his feet.

Enders's smile wasn't pretty. "As you probably know, Fran Simcox is away for the evening. Otherwise I'm certain she would be in attendance."

"Did anyone think to ask me if I wanted a bloody dinner party?" Sinjun asked.

"I'm asking you now, Mr. Breaker. A word from you and I'll make your apologies."

"Do that."

"Very good. I'll stop Campbell from going for Miss Dean. If the others arrive, I shall send them away. With luck we can reach Willis before he leaves his cottage."

"*Willis?*" Willis rarely spoke, let alone ate polite dinners with sizable groups. "Why would Mrs. Midgely ask Willis? And how in God's name did she get him to agree?"

"She didn't."

"But you just said—"

"Miss Butters invited him." Enders moved his neck like an irritable turtle. "And he accepted."

In that instant, Sinjun remembered how bored he was. "Oh, what the hell. Why spoil a little relaxation for everyone else just because I'm not in the mood? Let 'em all come."

This might turn out to be a very entertaining evening.

Nine

*C*ampbell Midgely's disconcertingly innocent smile and equally innocent dark eyes made Angelica want to look away. "Was there something you wanted?" she asked him. She'd answered his knock at the front door, but he had yet to say a word.

"Campbell?"

He breathed in through his nose and spread his hands over the front of his gray T-shirt. Partially obscured by his fingers was the inspirational message printed in purple: IN DEATH WE ARE ONE. His smile had become even more beatific.

Angelica knew a moment's uneasiness. "Would you like to come in?" She hoped he would refuse.

"Oh, yes." Campbell, a compact twenty-one-year-old with close-cropped dark hair, stepped into the cottage. "Are you better now? I would have come earlier, but I knew you would still be distressed. Sometimes one needs to be alone to heal pain."

"I'm very well, thank you." Apart from the residue of a headache that had struck within moments of Lorraine's departure.

"You're brave." He touched her cheek.

Angelica barely stopped herself from leaping away. "Thank you."

"And very, very beautiful." The touch became a fleeting stroke before he dropped his hand.

This day had been a lousy nightmare and it didn't show any sign of improving. "Thank you for being so nice," Angelica said. "Was there any particular reason why you came?"

"Yes."

She tipped her head to one side.

"I was sent to take you to *his* house. But first I must make certain you understand that you are not alone here. I will not allow anything bad to happen to you."

Creepy tightness crawled over Angelica's scalp. "That's nice of you, but I'm perfectly safe."

"I'm going to tell you something in absolute confidence because I know I can trust you."

She raised a hand to stop him, but he rushed on.

"My mother doesn't know because I haven't told her. She would be upset. I'll know when the right time comes to break the news. I am no longer in school at Berkeley."

Angelica wound her wrists together. She didn't want his confidences.

"Once I discovered what my true mission is, I could not stay there."

She expected to regret it, but she asked, "What is your mission, Campbell?"

"To find harmony with my fellow men—and women. I have been given the gift of deep empathy with those who suffer because they are too gentle. Especially women, because they are the most vulnerable. My task is to rescue and champion the weak ones. And to punish their aggressors."

"Oh." Angelica's stomach went into a descending spiral. "That sounds very heroic. If I ever need a champion, I'll let you know. But I do thank you for being concerned about me," she added quickly.

His smile became secretive. "I understand. You aren't ready to accept my help yet, but that's all right. Just remember that I'm here for you. And stay away from *him* as much as possible."

"You mean Mr. Breaker?" The question was reflexive.

"He is a cruel man. You are not the first woman he has victimized with his senseless anger. I will be watching him."

She looked into his intense young face. Such a pleasant, open face. "Yes, well—"

"I was fortunate enough to meet a group of people who have helped me to see what I am in this world to do. They were concerned about my taking this time away from them, but they need not have feared—I was meant to come. There is work for me to do here." His eyes lost their distant expression. "You are to come to dinner."

At first she thought she'd misheard. "I'm sorry?"

"I am to escort you to *his* house where you are to have dinner. Chuck will be there. And Lorraine." He closed his eyes briefly. "Also your friend, Miss Butters. Then there will be Mr. Lloyd-Worthy and Willis. Miss Simcox is on Kauai for the night. Naturally, Mr. Breaker will be present."

Face Lorraine again—and in the same room with Sinjun? "No!" Angelica straightened her spine. "No, I'm afraid that won't be possible. I have work to do. Please give my regrets."

"My mother asked me to tell you that she is cooking a special meal at Miss Butters's request. Miss Butters is helping with the preparations."

"Good grief." Brenda could be relied upon to make herself at home anywhere.

"That's what Mr. Lloyd-Worthy said." Campbell grinned and was instantly transformed into an engagingly normal young man. "You should see him watching her. Hah! Like she's from another planet. He keeps muttering about peasants and Philistines and *Yorkshire*. I don't think Mr. Lloyd-Worthy cares much for Yorkshire."

Angelica had to smile, too. "Dinner, huh?"

"Yep. And cocktails first. My mother's having a great time."

"What time am I supposed to get there?"

He looked at his watch. "Now for cocktails. Dinner in an hour."

She was going to have to get the rest of the clothes she'd stored in Kauai. "This is about as dressy as I can get." Spreading her arms, she looked down at the lacy white cotton tunic she wore over a tight red tube top and matching leggings. "I don't think it'll do for a dinner party, do you?"

When Campbell studied her outfit—with deep concentration—Angelica wished she hadn't asked the question.

"I think you look wonderful," he said distantly. "But perhaps you should put on a thicker sweater?"

He'd taken a *really* good look. She made up her mind. "I'll come. And what you see is what you get." And what Sinjun Breaker would get. If there was one thing she was certain of, it was that Mr. Breaker had a marked physical reaction every time he saw her. Perhaps she could use that to her advantage—even if it did scare her silly. She turned up the corners of her mouth at Campbell. "Just let me comb my hair and I'll be right with you."

To the casual observer, the scene on the veranda that hugged three edges of a lush enclosed garden might appear charmingly, appealingly civilized. To Sinjun it resembled a cross between a "Dallas" rerun and a bad situation comedy.

And she wasn't here yet.

He strolled to the farthest point from his "guests" and leaned on the wooden railing. A sudden, heavy rain had left the red earth popping and pungent. Drips fell from banana palms clumped in the corner of the garden. The gardenia-like fragrance of a coffee tree's white blossoms swelled on the damp air.

What the hell was taking her so long?

Sinjun peered outward at pools of flickering orange light cast from pole torches.

"When d'you suppose Mr. Willis will put in an appearance, then?" The Butters woman's full voice resounded.

"Willis," Enders said, far too tonelessly. Tonight he was apparently acting in the role of associate host.

"That's who I said."

"It's not *Mr*. Willis. Just Willis."

"What's his other name, then?"

"Something unpronounceable with a lot of vowels," Lorraine said. The vodka tonics she drank—mostly minus the tonic—already fuzzed the edges of her words. "Don't you worry your little . . . Well, anyway, don't you worry yourself about Willis. He won't come. This isn't his kind of scene."

As if a button had been pressed, a large form emerged through the gardens. Willis, who had tried, but failed to tame his appearance with a soft blue chambray shirt and gray chinos, prowled to the veranda.

Without a word, he disappeared into the house.

Brenda Butters threw back her head and laughed raucously. "Isn't he *marvelous*. So *sexy*. My God, he makes you feel like tearing off his clothes, doesn't he?"

In the well of silence that followed, Sinjun finally saw what he'd been waiting for. Angelica Dean, accompanied by Campbell Midgely, walked between plantings and mounted the steps to the veranda.

"Angel!" Brenda shouted. "There you are. What on earth took you so long? You're missing a wonderful party."

If her friend's ebullience embarrassed her, Angelica gave no sign. She bobbed to kiss Brenda's cheek and patted her arm before turning to the rest of the group. "Hi. Sorry I'm late, but I didn't get much warning."

Sinjun remained in the shadows. She was an understated knockout. Diminutive she might be, but every inch of her was pure woman. Her hair was drawn up into a soft heap at her crown but curls escaped to fall around her face. She wore a loose thing of some sort of wide-open cotton mesh. If it wasn't meant to draw attention to round, thrusting breasts inside a skinny, strapless little top, then it was superfluous. It sure as hell wasn't protecting her from drafts.

That snug red top would peel down so easily.

He shifted his weight to the other foot.

Campbell muttered something and hurried into the house. Lorraine, clinging to Chuck's arm, advanced on Angelica.

"How's the biography coming?"

"Fine, thanks."

Lorraine wore a knee-length dress of some flimsy silver stuff. A slit ran all the way up one smoothly tanned and elegant thigh. The boned bodice had a mind of its own and it wasn't particularly interested in covering Lorraine's overflowing breasts.

"What can I get you to drink, Miss Dean?" Enders asked. When she hesitated, he added, "My Chablis and lemon is very refreshing. I pour it over crushed ice."

"Thank you," Angelica said, so softly Sinjun barely heard. "That sounds lovely."

"Sounds like a friggin kid's party punch," Lorraine announced. "Join the grown-ups and have a vodka tonic."

"The Chablis and lemon will be fine."

Brenda had turned a chair to face the house. Dressed once more in green slacks and shirt—silk this time—she sat with her long legs stretched out.

"What do you suppose Willis is doing inside the house?" she said.

No one answered.

"What's for dinner?" Chuck asked Enders.

"Mrs. Midgely's being secretive, but—"

"It's a surprise," Brenda said. "You'll have to wait and see."

"God, I hope it's not some sort of health crap," Chuck muttered. "Sin'll have a fit."

"Will you have a fit, Sin?" Lorraine asked loudly. "Stop hiding over there. Come and join the party."

He separated himself from the railing and strolled toward them. "Good evening, Angelica. Glad you could come."

For a long time she looked steadily into his eyes. Then, abruptly, she turned away. "Spill it, Brenda," she said. "What have you talked that poor lady into cooking?"

Sinjun stared at her back, at her sweetly curved hips encased in red beneath the flimsy white top. He opened his mouth and felt a pulse begin to pound deep inside him. She really did turn him on—instantly.

"If they serve you alfalfa blintzes with cream of bean-curd sauce, I'll just have to take you home and feed you real-man food," Lorraine said, transferring her weight from Chuck's arm to Sinjun's. A provocative twist brought her breasts perilously close to escaping her bodice entirely. "I know I have what it takes to satisfy you." She leaned against him and while he looked into Chuck's expressionless eyes, Sinjun felt her tongue flick around his earlobe.

"Chuck's a lucky man," he said evenly, prying Lorraine's fingers from his arm. "No wonder he's always in a hurry to get home."

Chuck flashed an easy grin and relief loosened the tension in Sinjun's shoulders. What would it take to get rid of this bitch? When he had time, he'd figure out the answer.

"Do you like it?" Upon finding Willis already in the dining room, Brenda had steered him to the round table and taken a seat beside him. Now she watched him eat a mouthful of soup. "Don't the flavors fair jump out at you?"

Angelica studied Willis's impassive face and looked down at her own bowl of thin, greenish soup. She dipped in her spoon and unidentified objects drifted across the surface.

"Come on, then," Brenda said, her eyes glittering with mischief. "Give us a reaction, Willis."

Willis eyed her silently and continued eating.

Seated at her other side, Enders Lloyd-Worthy didn't quite hide his smile. "It is certainly, er, *full-bodied*," he said. "I'm not certain I quite recognize the primary vegetable."

"Fruit, not veg," Brenda said. "Chopped figs. Very good for you. They'll put hair on your chest, you'll see." She laughed and slapped him on the back.

Enders actually smiled and Brenda butted him with her shoulder. "I knew you had a sense of humor tucked away there somewhere."

"I don't see any men who *need* more hair on their chests," Lorraine said, leaning aside for Campbell— who was serving—to fill her wineglass. "Do you, Angelica?"

Angelica ignored the question.

Lorraine turned to Chuck on her right and slipped a hand inside his shirt. "Mmm. No." She stroked, gazing at his face. "Everything in order here."

Chuck removed her hand but he grinned before manfully continuing to eat the soup Angelica found too sweet.

"How about you, Sin?" Lorraine leaned to the left and tweaked at a button on his white shirt.

He pushed back the soup, folded his forearms on the table and watched her impassively.

"Dark-haired men are always so *animal*." She slipped the button from its hole and smoothed the backs of her fingers over the black hair she'd revealed.

Angelica felt sick. Why would someone as nice as Chuck Gill put up with a woman who got drunk and embarrassed him?

"That's enough, Lorraine," Sinjun said quietly.

For the first time, Angelica saw a flicker of uncertainty in the woman's violet eyes, but only a flicker. The next instant, she giggled and stroked her right breast, curling her fingers inside the skimpy top of the awful silver dress. "I definitely don't think I'll eat any fig soup," she said, openly cupping her own breast. "My chest is perfect just the way it is."

A wooden ceiling fan moved warm air about. No one spoke.

Sinjun sat opposite Angelica. She tried not to meet his eyes, but failed. He stared at her, his gaze unwavering. Lorraine had left his loose shirt gaping, showing hard collarbone and solidly defined muscle—and black hair.

He smiled, just a little.

Angelica smiled back. She couldn't help it.

From concealed speakers came the very soft strains of a soprano sax played to bebop rhythm. The effect was eerily discordant and hypnotic.

Sinjun moved ever so slightly with the beat.

"About time for the next course," Brenda said.

"It's coming," Campbell responded, removing soup plates.

Sinjun inclined his head, the smile still hovering about his clearly defined mouth. He raised one dark, winged brow.

Angelica opened her mouth to breathe.

Frowning in concentration, Campbell began placing fresh dishes before each diner. "A colorful feast," he commented, surprising Angelica.

"Well now," Mr. Lloyd-Worthy said. "This looks very promising."

Candlelight turned Sinjun's face to shades of shadow, all sharp bone and predatory hollows.

"All right, Willis," Brenda said. "Tell me what's in it."

Sinjun's lips parted a fraction.

Angelica's lips were dry. She wet them with her tongue.

Sinjun's gaze settled on her mouth.

"No," Angelica heard Chuck say.

She looked around.

"But I *want* some more wine," Lorraine was saying to Campbell. "Better yet, get me a vodka tonic."

"This is delicious," Mr. Lloyd-Worthy said. "Do tell your mother, Campbell. The chicken falls apart in your mouth."

"Hah!" Brenda pointed to his plate with her fork. "It's not chicken, it's tofu. Chanterelles, eggplant, peppers. The chanterelles were frozen, but they're not bad. Watch for the peppers. Mrs. Midgely's a marvel. She's got everything in that kitchen. The sauce is made from bitter melons and shoyu. This place is a ruddy utopia for vegetarians."

"It's good," Angelica said, picking out and eating pieces of eggplant. She didn't like tofu.

"Angelica, how did you choose Sin?"

Lorraine's sudden question startled Angelica. Recovering quickly, she replied, "As a subject for a biography?" This was a question she'd been waiting for. "I spent a lot of time reading financial publications. After a while, I narrowed my choices down to a handful and did more in-depth studies."

"Looking for the one with the juiciest private life?"

"Lorraine," Chuck said. "Maybe we should make this an early night."

"I'm having fun. Sin had the juiciest private life, didn't he? The juiciest *secrets?*"

"He certainly isn't a dull man," Angelica told her, trying for a light note.

"I'm Cinderella," Sinjun said, showing every sign of enjoying dinner.

Lorraine shrieked with laughter. "That's priceless. Cinder-fucking-rella."

"Really," Mr. Lloyd-Worthy said, and tutted.

Brenda tutted with him and grinned.

"Not too original," Angelica said, making no attempt to mask her own knowing smile at Sinjun.

"I've got to be up early." Chuck didn't appear to be having a good time.

Lorraine waved her glass unsteadily. "Is Cinderella cooperating with you?"

"We've made a good start."

"I'll just bet you have. How about giving us a performance rating? On his willingness to cooperate?"

"Lorraine—"

"Oh, shut *up*, Chuck. I'm having a conversation here."

"You going somewhere special tomorrow, Chuck?"

At the sound of Willis's deep, still voice, all conversation ceased.

"He speaks," Brenda said finally. She gave his massive biceps a friendly jab. "You should speak more often."

Willis turned his unreadable stare on her. "Why?"

"Because your voice makes me want to wiggle down in some dark, warm place." Brenda flattened the fingers of one hand over her mouth. "Ooh, I didn't mean that to sound the way it did."

Lorraine's mouth set in a hard line. "The hell you didn't. Bitch in heat."

"I've got to take the Eurocopter into the shop," Chuck said rapidly. "The forward landing gear sounds sticky."

Willis's attention had returned to his plate.

Mr. Lloyd-Worthy leaned over the table. "Will you be picking up Miss Simcox?"

"Yes."

"Oh, good. Will you be back by early evening, do you think? I received a communication from Seattle that I'd like her advice on. I need to send a response tomorrow night."

Lorraine snickered. "Need Fran's help with your love letters?"

"Actually, I'm in the process of purchasing a piece of art. Time is of the essence. I must have a message waiting for the dealer when she returns to Seattle from New York. But I respect Miss Simcox's opinion on these matters."

"I'll bring Fran back," Sin said. "I'm going over with Chuck and flying another chopper for the return leg. We need a backup for the Eurocopter and this one's a possibility. Don't worry. We'll be here in plenty of time."

"That's settled then," Chuck said. "I really do feel bushed. So, if you'll all excuse us?"

Without a word, Willis got up and left the room.

"I suppose he's bushed, too," Brenda said. "I'm staying for the lychees in brandy, myself. How about the rest of you?"

"Absolutely," Mr. Lloyd-Worthy agreed.

"I'll just have the brandy," Lorraine said.

Angelica pushed back from the table. "It sounds wonderful, but I'll pass. I've still got work to do tonight."

"I'll gladly walk with you." Campbell settled a hand on her back and Angelica felt again an inward shrinking.

"That's not necessary. Thank you anyway. After all, I don't have to worry about snakes and wild beasts, do I?" With the exception of the two-legged examples.

"There are boars," Campbell said seriously. "And in the dark the jungle can be fearsome to people who frighten easily."

Sinjun rose from his chair and came around the table. Beside Angelica, he gave a mock bow and offered her his hand.

She hesitated a moment before placing her own hand in his palm.

He helped her up. "Don't give it another thought, Campbell," he said. "I'll make sure the lady gets safely tucked up in her bed for the night."

Ten

❦

"**W**e're very attracted to one another, Angelica."

She missed a step and stumbled into Sinjun's back. He turned around, but she quickly put distance between them.

"You do admit I'm right?"

They'd walked through the jungle, Sinjun in the lead, not saying a word.

"Angelica?"

She made to pass him but he caught her arm. "I want to get back to the cottage," she told him.

"You will. Let me stay in front of you. I can find my way in the dark, you can't."

Almost no moonlight penetrated the foliage overhead. Sinjun started walking ahead and Angelica followed him. From the distance came the sound of surf breaking on the beach. Crickets kept up their zinging percussion. Somewhere nearby a bird's call ran a quickly descending scale.

"Avoiding the truth doesn't make it go away."

From the moment he'd ushered her from the house and into the soft night, she'd known she was in trouble.

She hadn't begun to realize just how much trouble until now.

"Okay," he said. "Let's try another angle. Which

138

particular Breaker rocks are you trying to turn over at the moment?"

"I'll be working on Breaker relationships for some time."

"In other words, my love life. How's it going?"

"I thought I'd wait and let you tell me the really personal stuff."

"Why do I find that hard to believe?"

Angelica felt utterly trapped. He was a big, powerful, supremely confident man. He was compelling sexually and he knew it. He knew right now that while she walked along behind him, trying not to trip over the myriad obstacles on the trail, her heart was jumping in her throat, her head was pounding and she'd lost the clear use of her brain.

What he didn't know was that the real Angelica Dean had reached the grand old age of twenty-eight without ever making love. Kissing had brought her pleasure on many occasions—so had physical closeness—but what came next had sent her into retreat every time. Heavy petting was something that happened to other women, but not Angelica. Until she'd had to stand up in front of him on the bluff that first night, no man had ever seen her naked. She'd always thought it a case of the right opportunity never presenting itself. When Sinjun had kissed her—fondled her—she'd responded, but the situation had been bizarre, her adrenaline had been pumping like fire. She'd wanted the kissing, and, for a little while, much more.

That moment had passed. Once again she was Angelica the ice princess.

"Did you discover that I don't go through women like sandwiches?" he said. "Did anyone tell you I'm reserved in that area?"

"As in shy?" she couldn't help asking.

He laughed. "Let's not push credibility."

"You sure cleaned up nice."

He stopped abruptly, but this time she didn't run into him.

"What does that mean?" he asked without turning around.

Her heart skipped, bumped madly and skipped again. "I was being a smart-ass. It goes with the Cinder . . . Well, there was another line in that movie about cleaning up nicely."

"I see. In other words, I've done a passable job of covering up my lowly beginnings. Thank you." He continued on.

Without warning, Angelica remembered the mantra Momma had intoned over and over again. "*Once you give yourself to a man you're used.*" Her mother's voice was so clear that Angelica suppressed a gasp. "*Men hunt and capture. Then the thrill's over for them. Remember that.*"

Evidently Momma hadn't lived by her own advice, but the warning must have stuck, Angelica thought. She was in fine shape to become one of the permanently hunted, and eventually, the ignored and the lonely.

Sinjun broke the silence. "Be careful here."

They emerged onto grass and he veered sharply to the left—away from the cottage.

Angelica hesitated, called, "Thank you for seeing me home. Good night."

"Come with me," he said, not missing a step.

She opened her mouth to argue, but couldn't seem to think exactly what to say.

"Come on, Angel. Live dangerously."

What made him think she wasn't already living dangerously?

The distance between them widened.

She was only here to spend time with this man.

Angelica hurried until she could fall in behind him once more.

"There's plenty of room beside me."

He waited until she caught up and strode onward

again, past the plantings at the eastern edge of the cottage lawns, downward through grassy hillocks where coarse sand mixed with earth until they arrived at a narrow band of flat rocks. The rocks, glistening in the moonlight, separated the land from the beach and the shimmering dark water beyond.

"You haven't seen the best of my island yet, ma'am." He offered her his hand as he had in his dining room and this time she didn't hesitate before taking it. "If you're going to write about me, you're going to have to see and understand what makes me tick. This is part of it."

"This?" Hanging onto him for support, she climbed gingerly over the slippery rocks.

"Back in the world of deals I have to be one man, one kind of man. He's okay with me. I like him well enough. Or maybe I should say I respect him for getting the job done. He's tough and calculating and he's a success. Here I'm different. This place, exactly as it is now, at night, is my flip side. At least, that's the way I think of it. It's serene. Peaceful. It's the part that's fed by the man I like to leave behind sometimes."

Angelica had forgotten to move. She stood, feet apart for balance, trying to see his face in the gloom.

"What is it? Is something wrong?"

"I . . . No." No man had only one dimension. But could she believe Sinjun had a kinder side than the one that had brought her here? And even if the answer was yes, did it matter?

"Relax. I won't let you fall."

She'd pulled it off. He believed she was nothing more complicated than an ambitious writer planning to exploit him. When they first . . . At first he'd been probing for more than her reason for choosing him as a subject. She had felt him weighing her authenticity; and he had judged her valid.

His hand was warm and strong, his fingers firm. He tugged a little and she followed him onto wet sand that sucked at her sandals. As soon as she found firm footing, he removed his hand from hers and pushed it into his pocket.

"Except for the little lagoon below your cottage, you can walk all the away around the island on the beach."

"How does it feel to own your own island?"

"I don't think about it."

She strolled along, the sea at her right, Sinjun at her left. He owned his own tiny paradise and he didn't think about it? "Imagine how it was when you were still living in Bliss."

"That's called memory, not imagination." There was a subtle change in his voice. The easiness had gone.

"Okay. Remember it. What would you have thought back then if someone had said you might own an island one day?"

"Those days were about survival. You dreamed about getting out alive. Nothing bigger than that."

"I didn't ask you about the reality of your dreams. The question was hypothetical. But surely there were moments of fantasy. Lying in bed half-asleep? Dozing on a hot day and looking at those purple Montana mountains?"

"Stay there." Several rapid strides inland took him to the top of an isolated rock.

Angelica walked slowly to stand below him. "King of your own mountain?"

"There's nothing very high on Hell. That's why the communications antennae are on the roof of the house. From up here I can see the light on a warning buoy over Lono's rocks." He nodded seaward. "Lono was an Hawaiian god. There are stories about him searching the islands for his lost love."

Against the silvered sky his profile was sharp,

his lithe body a dark shadow inside the loose white shirt.

"He never found his love, I suppose?"

"He did once. He thought she'd betrayed him, so he killed her. Hit her over the head with a rock. Then he spent the rest of his life looking for her spirit."

A chill raised goose bumps on Angelica's arms. "I don't think I like that story."

"Grim. But it makes you think." He planted his fists on his narrow hips. "Anyway, old Lono's rocks are out there waiting to grab unwary seamen."

"What is it about the story that *makes you think?*"

"Ah, yes, ever the gatherer of the whole story. It makes you think that we would all do well to be honest."

"You said he only thought she'd betrayed him. Perhaps she hadn't at all."

"*Perhaps.* Somehow she gave him reason to doubt. The moral of the story is: Always make your intentions absolutely clear or run the risk of getting your head bashed in."

For several seconds she gazed up at him. It was he who finally laughed. Angelica managed an accompanying chuckle. *Message received*, she thought. Apparently she hadn't entirely convinced him after all.

"You didn't answer my question." The best course was to hop right back onto the attack. "What would you have thought about this place—and it being yours—when you were a boy growing up in Bliss, Montana?"

"Your persistence is astounding. When I was a boy growing up in Bliss, Montana, subtropical islands were places inhabited by hostile natives— or the likes of Long John Silver. Neither appealed to me. I'm sorry, Angel, but I can't give you your answer because it's impossible."

"Fair enough. What about your love life?"

"In Bliss?"

She wished he'd come down where he was at least a little closer to her eye level. "Now."

"Oh, no, you don't. I'm not going to make your job that easy. Have you seen the little bucket I call my boat?"

"Not yet."

"You must. If you're here long enough, I'll take you out in it."

In other words, he was still counting the minutes until he could get rid of her . . . Wasn't he? Uncertainty made her turn her back on him. He'd said they were attracted to one another, but all that meant to him was a quick affair, so for now he might not want her to go.

"There's a reef all around the island. By the way, in case your intelligence missed something, Hell's approximately three square miles in size. But the reef makes a great barrier. Bit like a wall outside a moat with the island as a castle in the middle."

She chafed her arms. "There must be a way through the reef or you wouldn't have a boat. Or would you?"

"There's a way through. With the right tide and in a narrow window of time. You have to know what you're doing."

"Fascinating. Your love life?"

"You must have noticed how lush the gardens are—and everything else on this island."

Angelica smiled a little. "Yes."

"With no mountains, the rainfall is unpredictable. We have a desalinization plant on the north shore. It allows us to use seawater for all our needs."

"I'm impressed."

"Did I invite you to ask about my love life?"

"More or less."

He leaped down beside her and she flinched at the impact of his weight into the giving sand. "What do you want to know?"

Was it too much to hope that he'd instantly identify the woman who'd taken Momma's place? "The recent stuff."

"Let's walk. I get restless easily."

The wet sand made heavy going. Angelica paused to slip off her sandals before trudging on. "Is there someone now?" She almost held her breath.

"No."

"A little while ago?"

"Yeah. A little while ago for a little while."

"You got bored?"

The breeze had picked up. His shirt billowed behind him. "I don't think bored is kind in this context, do you?"

She snorted. "Are you *kind?*"

"Sometimes. About some things."

"Okay. So you were recently involved with a woman but you're not anymore. How about a name?"

"No."

She closed her eyes for an instant. "Biographies require statistics and they require names—lots of names."

"Forget it."

"You're too kind, right? But you did get bored with her."

"It wasn't good anymore . . . Not fun. Do you understand?"

Angel Dean might be a woman of very little personal experience but she was a walking reference library on the experiences of others. "I understand."

"How does it make you feel about me?"

"The fact that a woman has to keep on being all 'fun' to be a part of your life? You like honesty. Okay. I'm partly repulsed and partly fascinated."

He stood still and looked down at her. "You're a *lot* judgmental, lady. When you write your book—*if* you write your book—go heavy on the fascination. *Repulsive* isn't an adjective that appeals."

They walked against the warm breeze as far as a headland where trees screened the next stretch of shoreline from sight. "Are you getting tired?" Sinjun asked. "Or do you want to try for the whole tour?"

"Wouldn't that get us into bed pretty late?"

He chuckled and she saw his white teeth flash. Angelica blushed in the darkness.

"I'll forget you said that. Unless you don't want me to?"

"I'm not tired yet," she told him.

Surf curled over rocks heaped at the headland. Sinjun set an unerring course that threaded between craggy lava mounds and guided Angelica out on the other side.

"Can we begin by having you tell me about your women in general?" She'd been wrong about her objectivity. All her experience as an interviewer had not prepared her for this particular subject . . . with this particular man.

He turned and walked backward. Then stopped and waited until she stood in front of him. "*My* women? I don't actually own any."

"How many have wanted you to?"

His hand flashing out to grasp her wrist caused Angelica's breath to slam into her throat. "Where do you go to school to learn this muckraking craft of yours?" He pulled her close.

"It's called on-the-job experience. How many, Sin? And how about the most recent one? She must have been pretty special for you to be keeping her a secret. Not that you *can* keep her a secret. I'll find out. On the other hand, if you tell me, I may just choose to believe you and the end result will be *kinder*."

He yanked her near enough for her to have to raise her face to see him. "You're very sexy, Angel. And you like to make the best of it."

"We're not here to discuss me."

"Why not? I find you an engrossing subject. Every time you and I come within yards of each other, our hormones start homing in like guided missiles."

"I thought you didn't have an imagination."

"I don't. Except when it comes to erotic pictures of what you'd look like with a film of sweat turning your skin slick while you moved those round hips of yours under mine."

"Stop it." She felt weak, fluttery—and low in her belly—and lower still—the flutter became an ache that tightened every muscle. "We're strangers."

"I mustn't tell you the truth about what's happening very fast between you and me, right? But I'm supposed to allow you to twist every little word I say into an insult or a jibe you can use against me." He brought his face nearer to hers. "Every time you do that it makes me want to grab you. That's what I'm explaining to you here. It makes me want to grab you and find out what it would be like *with* you."

Her mouth was dry as a sandbox. "I'm going back. You don't need to—" She forgot what she'd been going to say.

"I don't need to what?"

Angelica looked past him, at two people who were too engrossed to have noticed that they were no longer alone.

"What the hell's the matter with you?"

"N-nothing." Her breathing speeded.

Sinjun kept his grip on her wrist but looked over his shoulder. "*Jee-sus,*" he said softly.

The sound of the surf—and passion—had closed the man and woman into their own world. The man was big—huge; the moon and the phosphorous glow from the surf showed his towering bulk. He leaned against the sloping trunk of a palm. The woman hung from him, her arms around his neck, her legs jackknifed and clamped to his sides.

Sinjun made no move to leave.

Angelica couldn't think beyond the crazed lust that drove the act she witnessed.

Not love. Not lovemaking.

Sex.

The woman's mindless sobs carried in jagged bursts as she rode the man's penis. Angelica saw the way his big hands gripped jerking buttocks.

Silver flashed. The woman was naked but for the ruined dress that bunched around her waist.

"Oh, my God." Angelica turned around and started walking.

Sinjun's touch, his hand settling on the back of her neck, made her panic. She shrugged violently away.

"Calm down," he demanded, striding along beside her. "That was no big deal. Just part of a couple of those love lives you're so interested in."

"Love? Let's not use that word for what they were doing."

"Why? It's not a word that means very much, is it?"

She broke into a run, but he kept up easily. The sand quickly tired her legs.

"You want to know about my love life. Maybe this is a great time to talk about it after all."

"Oh, please."

"You don't have to beg. Shall we start with my technique?"

"That's tasteless."

As her pace slowed, so did his. "Anything but tasteless," he told her. "Ask any expert witness."

She was aware that he knew that what she'd witnessed had shaken her and he was pushing the advantage. "Great. Point me to an expert witness and I'll—" The rest of the sentence froze. She couldn't help looking over her shoulder, although they'd passed out of sight of the "lovebirds." "Shall I go back there? Would I find an expert witness to talk to? *If* she's finished shrieking and grinding, that is?"

He said nothing.

Angelica saw the flat rocks ahead and lengthened her steps. "That was Lorraine."

"Thanks for enlightening me. And I do know when I'm being insulted."

The temptation was to tell him that Lorraine had already suggested something close to a *ménage à trois*. That wouldn't be smart. "Lorraine's a beautiful woman."

"She's a whore."

Angelica winced. "A man who spreads himself around is a *man*. A woman of the same ilk is a whore? Why not be *kind* and say she has a healthy sexual appetite, but it's different from yours?" Not that she'd necessarily believe him.

"Whatever makes you happy."

Ignoring his proffered hand, she negotiated the rocks and started through the grassy dunes. "She must have arranged to meet him. She had to have run all the way there and . . ."

"And jumped on him?"

She didn't thank him for finishing her sentence. "I thought she was Chuck's . . . I thought she was here with him."

"She is. Lorraine's a lusty girl. Chuck's a healthy, red-blooded guy, but apparently he's not enough."

"Does he know? About . . ." She couldn't say the rest.

Sinjun loped along at a leisurely pace. "Chuck had a rocky time as a kid. He never felt he lived up to Len's—his dad's expectations. Then I got lucky and made something of my life. Chuck never whined about evil fate, but he did have to listen to Len pointing out that his son's performance didn't match up to mine. And—as you already know—I was the boy from nothing with no advantages."

Angelica paused. "What does that have to do

with . . . Why does that mean Chuck would turn a blind eye to what Lorraine's doing?"

"Maybe nothing, except I can't tell Chuck what he should and shouldn't do with his private life. I've spent a lot of years telling Chuck he doesn't have to prove himself. Len's dead, but sometimes I think Chuck's still trying to show him he's a big boy who can make his own decisions."

"But—"

"Yeah, I know. So what? The fact is, Chuck loves Lorraine. Don't ask me why, but he does. He doesn't want my interference."

Angelica started walking again. "I still don't get it," she said. Her heart continued to pound. "She's making a complete fool of him."

"Chuck doesn't seem to notice. I wish to God he'd wake up and kick her ass where I wouldn't have to fall over it—not that I've got anything against spectacular female asses. In fact, given the right ass and the right—"

"Knock it off."

"Right."

He reached the bank before Angelica and stood aside while she scrambled up.

"I'm not opposed to rough sex now and again," he said conversationally. "Not the tear-and-leave-bruises kind, necessarily, although that does have its place sometimes."

"I can't believe you're saying these things."

"A little while ago you *asked* me these things. I thought you were the tough, unshockable journalist. You were the one who asked me if I could handle rough going."

She stomped on. "I . . . I did *not* ask you exactly." But she had given him the impression that she was sophisticated.

Sinjun darted around her. "Darkness is very, very sensual, Angel."

She attempted to dodge.

He was quicker. "This is good stuff. Too bad
you still don't have that notebook. Darkness and a
warm island breeze off the ocean. There's a seething
quality to nights like this. If I were making love to
you—we'll call it love for now. Kinder. If I were,
I'd go slowly, Angel. I have a thing for water. First
I'd lead you into the surf. I'd leave that damn white
thing you're wearing on the beach, but you could
keep on the little red top and tight pants."

"Let me go."

"Not until you know the whole story—about how
it would go if I was making love to you tonight. It'll
give you insight into what women can expect from
me—*generally*."

Her belly jerked inward. "Don't bother. I'll use
my imagination, thanks."

"I'll just bet you will," he murmured. "I'd lead
you out into the surf and beyond, until the water
lapped up to . . . your shoulders."

"Why are you doing this?"

"Stupid question. I'm enjoying it. You're tough
enough to take it, so why not? I'd take that tiny
waist of yours in my hands and swing you. Around
and around until you howled and grabbed for me—
and begged. I like the idea of begging a whole lot.

"Your hair would be down by then. Wet. I really
like wet. And then I'd kiss you. Not like that first
time. This time I'd kiss you till you forgot there
was a possibility you were making a mistake. And
while I kissed you, I'd peel your stretchy red *wet*
top down, and take the ass-hugging pants with it.

"I'd strip you in the water and float you on your
back and stare at you. I'd anticipate you with my
eyes before I tried you out for taste."

Angelica planted a hand in the middle of his
chest, gave a shove and marched past. This time
he contented himself with staying at her shoulder.

"When I turned you right-side-up again, I'd be
ready for some bobbing. Bobbing would be so good

with breasts like yours. You've got big breasts for a little woman. As a matter of fact, they're beautiful. And I'm one of those expert witnesses we talked about. Anyway, they'd be there, rising and falling, floating when I held you just right. And I'd suck your wet nipples into my mouth—"

"Stop it!" She'd reached the lawn and broke into a flat-out run.

"Hey, I just paid you a compliment."

"*Go away!*"

He got to the front of the cottage before her. "I will," he said, and threw open the door just as she made to head for the back of the building. "Please forgive my unruly mouth, it—"

"Get out of my way."

"Oops, I said *mouth* again. Sorry."

"You're despicable. And you are not sorry."

He propped an arm across the doorway and bowed his head. "Yes, I am. Damn, I don't know what . . . Yes, I do. *You* goad me into it. You push and pry and poke and dig for crud, Angel. And it brings out the bad in me."

"It brings out the disgusting in you."

"Hah." He looked up at her, then down. "I don't remember you fighting me off a few minutes after we first met. How come I didn't disgust you then?"

The memory hung between them. There was no defense.

"Tell me you aren't hot now. Tell me that just being told how I'd make love to you didn't make you hot and ready."

She shook her head. "Hot?"

Once again he held her arm. "Don't play games with me. I didn't get quite as far as how I'd push inside you, but you were anticipating it. And you were ready. I know a passionate woman when I see one. You've been giving me nothing but come-and-get-me signals, lady."

He meant he thought she . . . "Go and . . ."

"All by myself? What a waste."

Effortlessly, he pulled her against him. Her face was pressed to his chest where the shirt gaped. Beneath her cheek, the hair on his chest was smooth. He smelled of sea salt.

"Feel me, Angel," he said, resting his chin on top of her head. "Then tell me whether or not you're burning."

His hand cupping her bottom, lifting, pressing her hips to his, left no doubt as to his meaning. He was hard and huge and pulsing.

Angelica's body did what he'd told her it would. She trembled, ached and the pulsing between her legs matched his. And she burned.

All strange. She would not let herself give in to a man she must keep on hating. She struggled, but he was too strong.

"Are you burning?" he whispered against her temple. He kissed her there. "Aching?" He kissed her ear, licked the sensitive folds until she shuddered. He kissed her jaw and her neck. He kissed her collarbone and slowly, so slowly let her slip down to stand on tiptoe.

"Are you, Angel?"

She closed her eyes. "Let me go."

"Of course." Sinjun slackened his grip, ran his palms down her arms, moved away a little and clasped both of her hands. Raising her fingers to his lips, he kissed each one, slowly. Between breaths he murmured, "I do want you." At the second index finger, he drew it all the way into his mouth and sucked, drawing it out with the slightest pop. He continued to hold her hands.

"Please, let me go."

"I wonder how much—or how little more persuasion it would take for you to ask me to stay with you." He dropped her hands. "At least you've got a good start. Don't they say something like 'Write what you know'? Nice going, kid. You'll be able to bring true realism to that biography."

He walked away and she heard him say, "I've got a whole lot more willpower than I ever knew. Don't count on it holding out the next time. See you tomorrow."

Angelica slid to sit in front of the open door. "Not if I see you first." She couldn't stand up anymore.

She'd lost her sandals.

Eleven

❧

God, her head felt like an overinflated ball. Lorraine propped herself on her elbows, adjusted her sunglasses and tipped her floppy straw hat lower over her eyes. If she had the energy, she'd slip into the pool and cool off. She didn't have the energy.

If Sin thought she didn't see him there in his bedroom—watching her—he was a fool. But Sin was no fool. He knew she saw him and he wanted her to.

She smiled to herself, winced at the pain that shot through her brain from ear to ear and managed to keep right on smiling. "Campbell!" That beautiful boy would be nearby. Campbell was always nearby, particularly when she stretched out by the pool to work on her tan. "Campbell!"

"Yes, Lorraine."

She didn't bother to twist around and look up at him. "You are such a sweetheart. Would you do me a great big favor and go ask your mom for a tall glass of—" She'd been going to say lemonade. A hair of the dog was what she needed. "Ask her for one of those Chablis-and-lemonade things Enders makes. Would you do that for me, sweetie?"

"Do you feel all right?" He sounded anxious.

Irritation burst inside Lorraine's poor, aching head. "I feel just fine, thank you. Chablis and

155

lemonade." All she needed was another fucking caretaker. Chuck was driving her nuts with his shrewish nagging about what she did and didn't do to his liking. Sin's every glance in her direction was a superior judgment. Enders treated her like a nasty child . . . The list went on.

"Campbell?"

"Chablis and lemonade. I'll get it for you."

"You are a *dear*. Oh, and Campbell, my lotion is all gone. Could you see if you can round up some more for me?"

"I'll do it. You need to take very good care of yourself, Lorraine. I feel your woundedness."

Drivel. She closed her eyes behind the blessedly concealing glasses. "Thank you for caring about me." He was a little wacky, but the body was great. Maybe if she did some work on the body, his undoubtedly ready hormones would take care of the other.

Sin was still there, a tall sentry staring straight at her. She squashed the temptation to wave at him, pulled an inflatable pillow under her crossed arms and rested her chin.

She still wanted him.

The journalist and her big, brassy friend were in the way. They must be persuaded to leave Hell. Maybe, if she could pull something off quickly, they'd decide to leave with Chuck and Sin today and not come back.

Not enough time.

There was always her idea for enlisting Willis's help with Angelica Dean. A swimming expedition. Just for *fun*. No way did that little bitch have what it took to be enough woman for Willis. He'd eat her alive.

What if things went wrong and she didn't just crawl away and disappear afterwards? What if she whined to Sin?

Lorraine breathed in through her nose, long and

slow. She'd given up too much not to get what she wanted.

Sometimes people went swimming and didn't come back . . .

Then she had to figure out a way to bring Sin to heel.

Lorraine stared at his bedroom. He wasn't standing in the window now. She'd gone into his room and waited for him before. He'd been angry, but that was because he didn't want to upset Chuck.

No doors were locked on Hell.

Of course! Grinning, she flapped her feet up and down. Sin needed a little help to see things the right way. *Her* way. Why hadn't the thought presented itself before? A little blackmail—just a little—would help if anything went wrong. All she needed to do was decide on the appropriate night.

But those women had to be gone.

"Chablis and lemonade." Campbell had arrived without her hearing him come. "I put mint in it."

"How clever of you."

"I thought you'd like it."

He crouched at her elbow and set the glass where she could reach it easily.

Lorraine followed the lines of supple, flexed muscle up his calf, along his thigh to the frayed edge of cutoff jean shorts. Languidly, she shifted a little and curled one hand around his calf. She rubbed up and down, then ran the backs of her fingers beneath his thigh.

He became utterly still.

Lorraine sighed. "Thank you *so* much, Campbell."

When he spoke, there was no missing the squeak in his voice. "I would do *anything* for you, Lorraine. You know that. You are one of the ones who must be protected in this place."

Behind the screen of her glasses, she rolled her eyes. "And I'm very grateful to know I have you."

"There is so much evil here," Campbell said. He

had not moved away. Lorraine's fingers still played with the underside of his thigh. "Everywhere you look," he added.

Lorraine heard a woman's fulsome voice and did look. She propped an elbow and rested her head on her hand to see past Campbell to the adjoining side of the pool.

Oh, my God. She wanted to leap up and dash to where Willis, in a teensy slip of a royal-blue bikini, skimmed a net across the surface of the pool to catch fallen leaves and needles.

She felt the weight of her breasts. Her nipples hardened and a fiery stab arced upward from between her legs.

Last night had been almost too much. Almost. Tonight she could hope that it *would* be too much. Yes, too much would be quite marvelous.

"Willis shouldn't walk around in front of ladies dressed like that."

Lorraine wanted to howl and shout, *What ladies?* Instead she made a meaningless noise.

"I hope Angelica doesn't come. He would embarrass her."

Angelica. What a hatefully appropriate name for a little tart with an innocent expression on her boringly predictable face. She minced around in front of Sin and the poor fool was getting sucked in by the aura of mystery her so-called project gave her.

She was hiding something, and the letter Lorraine had intended to take a look at—before Angelica rushed back with panic written all over her—might very well explain what that something was.

Willis straightened and looked toward the pool house, a two-storied structure built of the same black lava rock as the house and with a matching dark-blue tile roof. Brenda Butters, her red hair blazing, emerged from one of three sets of double doors on the ground floor.

She waved at Willis.

He waved back.

Damn. Willis never communicated with anyone— not in the expected way.

Wearing backless sandals with high wedge heels that must make her almost six and a half feet tall, Brenda strode confidently toward Willis. The brilliant-yellow swimsuit she wore was the kind worn by racers and it hid not one millimeter of her astonishingly voluptuous, well-toned body.

"*Good God,*" Lorraine muttered, not caring if Campbell heard. "That's obscene. She'd be better covered in nothing at all."

"A brash woman," Campbell said, mollifying Lorraine slightly. "I think she's interested in Willis. He may like her, too."

She brought her back teeth together. "Nonsense." As she said it, her gaze came to rest on the bulge in Willis's bikini and she swallowed. "Like"— for anything or anyone—wasn't programmed into whatever made the big man tick, but Brenda Butters certainly reached parts of his mechanisms very nicely. The big man was getting bigger by the second.

Brenda's laugh reached Lorraine clearly. The high-heeled sandals were kicked aside. Two steps to the edge of the pool and Brenda executed a clean, shallow dive. She glided a distance beneath the surface of the water, bobbed up—laughing again—and slicked back her ugly orange hair. Keeping her hands at the back of her head, her elbows pointed to the sky, she waded toward Willis. Lorraine was yards away but she could see how the thin yellow suit became transparent when wet.

Willis dropped into a crouch and extended a hand to Brenda.

He never responded to Lorraine—except when they were naked and having sex. Afterwards he walked away and didn't look back.

Brenda caught Willis's hand in both of hers and yanked.

He shouted and lunged into the water.

Lunged, not fell. Lorraine shed her hat and took her sunglasses all the way off. Willis dived beneath the surface and in a moment Brenda went down, shrieking, arms flailing. When Willis surfaced, Brenda's arms were around his neck. And he was grinning . . .

"I've never seen Willis smile," Campbell said.

Neither had Lorraine.

"That woman is one of the evil ones."

"Isn't she just. Did you bring the lotion, Campbell?"

He produced a bottle and began uncapping the top. "My mother said—"

Lorraine put her hand over his. "Did you mean it when you said you wanted to be my friend?"

He frowned and sincerity shone in his dark eyes. "You know I did."

"Well—" She threaded her fingers into his. "—I've been trying to pretend I didn't know what you meant. About people not being kind to me here. And about my woundedness." God, this stuck in her throat.

"Yes," Campbell said. "Has something happened to you? Tell me."

It was so goddamn easy. "I can't talk about it all yet, but I think I am going to need your help."

"Ask," he said urgently, his fingers tightening. "Anything. I'll do anything."

"It's all so complicated. There's . . . Well, I used to be a close friend of Sin's, but now he hates me."

Campbell's nostrils flared. "You don't have to explain any more. I understand. I told Chuck to do something about the way Sinjun treats you but he laughed at me."

Lorraine was alarmed. "You mustn't say anything more to Chuck about any of this. Do you understand?"

He hesitated before saying, "Yes," but sounded very uncertain.

"Trust me. Chuck's a good man but he's too close to . . . Well, you know *who* he's too close to."

"D'you want me to go to Sinjun and—"

"No!" she hissed through her teeth. "Sinjun isn't the real problem. There are others who've influenced him against me."

Campbell inclined his head to look at her face. "Do you want Sinjun to like you?"

Every word must be carefully chosen. "He was my friend. Even before I knew Chuck, I knew Sinjun. We were like—brother and sister." Sure, and she thought of him like a brother. Lorraine almost laughed.

"What happened?" Campbell's earnest concentration threatened to break Lorraine's shaky composure wide open. "Was it Chuck? Did he do something to turn Sinjun against you?"

She weighed her response. "No." The Chuck issue would take care of itself when the time came. Dangling her glasses from a finger and thumb, she indicated the cavorting couple in the pool. "It was her."

"Brenda Butters?" Campbell looked over his shoulder. "I thought . . . Didn't Sinjun just meet her for the first time yesterday?"

Lorraine rested her brow on the back of one hand and let her hair swing forward.

After a moment a hand passed gently, shakily, from her crown to the center of her back.

Lorraine grinned, and sniffed loudly.

"Oh, no," Campbell said. "Please don't cry. I'm sure—"

"You've got to promise me you'll never tell another soul what I'm going to tell you," she whispered urgently.

"I *promise* you."

"Oh, thank you." Folding her arms under her face, she sighed deeply. "Thank you, Campbell. Will you be a love and rub lotion on my back?"

Another pause, and she heard him squeeze lotion into his hand. Very tentatively, very carefully, he smoothed the cool, slick cream over her hot skin. Lorraine shuddered.

"What is it?" Campbell stopped rubbing. "Lorraine?"

"I've been in so much pain. Your touch gives me hope, my friend."

He resumed stroking and said in a low voice, "I don't understand how Ms. Butters—"

"They *already* know each other," she said harshly. "I don't know for sure why they're both pretending they don't, but they do. And they also know that *I* know the truth. I saw them together in Seattle. I think she may be a private investigator. That would fit. There's definitely something weird going on with Sin. Why else would he decide to hole up here with no warning?"

"I wondered about that."

"You're smart," she told him. "No one's going to put one over on you. This is what I think. I think someone—probably a woman—someone's been threatening Sin. He hired Brenda to find out who. Angelica Dean's probably just a front, an excuse for Brenda to be here."

His hand stilled. "Oh, no. No, Angelica is truly good. I feel that."

She screwed up her eyes and cursed under her breath. "I don't mean she isn't a journalist. In fact, I believe Angelica's absolutely for real. To serve her own purposes, Brenda put her up to approaching Sinjun about writing his biography and Angelica thought it was a great idea. She's as much a victim of that woman as I am."

"My God," Campbell muttered.

"Angelica doesn't know she's being used." Whatever happened, Campbell would have to be kept firmly under control. "It's no good trying to tell her the score because she'd confront Brenda and we can't risk that."

"Why is that woman turning Sinjun against you?"

"This is still only a theory and it's got to remain between us, Campbell. You can see what she's like—how she *uses* herself with men. She'd make Sin believe her over me. You must only do what I ask you to do."

He murmured assent.

Lorraine took a deep breath. "Brenda's turning Sin against me because she's the one who's really behind whatever's threatening him. She cooked the whole thing up to take advantage of him. That's the only answer that makes sense. But she's worked out a way to put the blame on me."

"Jesus," he said softly.

Lorraine smiled again and said, "Undo my top."

"Your . . . top?"

"Mmm. Please."

Slowly, he untied the bow.

"Thank you. I think I'm burning. Where I'm paler. Be a dear and spread some lotion."

Using both hands, Campbell shakily swept her length from elbow to underarm to waist. And on the way his fingers passed over the sides of her breasts.

"Mmm," she murmured. "Do that again. I like the way you touch me. You're strong and you make me feel safe."

Campbell stroked, and stroked some more.

Whatever needed to be done would be done. Willis wouldn't risk having his precious boss—and Chuck—told that he'd raped Lorraine. No, he'd be happy to make sure she didn't tell that little lie. Willis could pay the asking price for her silence by taking Angelica swimming. And Campbell—poor, unbalanced boy who'd probably been suppressing violent impulses for years—Campbell would be available to visit Brenda and avenge his idol in her darkest hour.

Or Angelica and Brenda would wise up and fly off into the sunset—and toward safety. Either way, Lorraine would finally have Sin all to herself.

"I'll do *anything* for you, Lorraine," Campbell said, his voice thick.

"I know you will," she said. "Thank you."

She had him.

"Holy . . ." Sinjun moved back into the window.

Chuck shifted behind him. "We'd better get going. You know how Fran gets if she's kept hanging around."

"Fran's a trooper," he responded absently. "Chuck, you and I need to have a chat."

"Sounds like woodshed stuff. What did I do this time?"

"*You* didn't do anything."

"Good. We'll talk on the way to Kauai."

Sinjun said, "Come here," and kept on staring through the window.

"Sin—"

"It *won't* wait. This has already gone too far."

Chuck arrived at Sinjun's side. "We *have* to leave," he said without glancing outside. "What the hell's gotten into you?"

"Lorraine," Sinjun said simply.

Chuck made an exasperated noise. "Lorraine isn't your problem, Sin. She *isn't* a problem, period. She drank a little too much last night. That's why she got out of hand. It was nothing. I can control Lorraine."

"Chuck—"

"*End* of topic. I've been known to suck a few too many myself on occasion. You're squeaky-clean these days, but you've had your moments."

"Chuck—"

"*Leave* Lorraine to me."

Sinjun's patience ran out. "That would be a fine solution. Only you aren't doing too good a job right now. Take a look at the woman you *can control*." He inclined his head. "By the pool."

Chuck looked, and his brows drew together.

"Yeah," Sinjun said. "Some control. She's coming on to that kid with all guns blazing. He's a kid, Chuck, a babe in the woods."

Chuck's expression grew blank. "He's putting lotion on for her."

"She's all but naked," Sin pointed out. "If good old Campbell isn't about to pop his shorts I'll eat my hat."

"He's asexual," Chuck said flatly.

Sinjun rounded on him. "The hell he is. D'you think all this preoccupation with who is or isn't kind to poor little Lorraine is harmless? He's got the hots for her and she's using that to try and get attention."

"Whose attention?" Chuck asked tonelessly.

Sinjun turned back to the window. "Jesus, I hate this."

"*Whose* attention?"

He couldn't bring himself to tell his friend that the woman who warmed his bed was angling to move into this very room. "Yours," he said finally. "For some reason the Lorraines of this world like to live on the edge. She wants to make sure you see her cozying up to Campbell and get jealous."

"I'm not jealous of an empty-headed kid."

"It's not his head she's working on. *Shit!*"

"*Shit,*" Chuck echoed, but softly, as Lorraine pushed up onto her elbows, leaving her bikini top on her towel. "She doesn't think sometimes."

"She's thinking now," Sinjun said, narrowing his eyes. "Bet on it. You're a lucky man. She must be quite a handful—or two—in bed."

"Lorraine knows what a man likes."

Sin watched out the window as Campbell Midgely leaned back to sit on his heels and glance nervously about. Lorraine tossed her hair aside and transferred all her weight to one elbow. She twisted to look up at Campbell . . . and to give him an up-close and intimate view of her big, beautiful breasts.

The kid looked away.

Lorraine ran her hand along his thigh and Sinjun saw the boy jump.

"Damn," Chuck said. "She's got a lot of energy, is all."

Sinjun gave a short laugh. "She's permanently in heat, friend. Which is okay if you want to be a twenty-four-hour stud service. Evidently she's not getting enough with you."

"Goddamn—"

"Cool down," Sinjun ordered. "I don't mean to rile you, but what's going on out there isn't going to wash in confined quarters like this."

"She wouldn't . . . She wouldn't *do* anything with Campbell. Not really."

"Are you sure?"

"I . . . Sure, I'm sure. I—" He swallowed. Lorraine was slipping her hand over Campbell's crotch.

"What would you call what she's doing now?" Sinjun asked.

Chuck scrubbed at his eyes and mumbled, "Forget it. I'll have a word with her when we get back tonight. She's teasing the kid, is all. Trying to have a little fun. Any minute now and he's going to bolt."

"Mmm. But probably not before he finishes putting a shine on those tits. The boy's only human."

"She wouldn't let him . . ." Chuck held his mouth

open and clicked his jaw. "I ought to *kill* the little bastard."

Blocked from the view of Willis and Brenda Butters in the pool, Campbell put lotion into a palm, hesitated again, then went to work oiling Lorraine's breasts.

Chuck made a move toward the French doors but Sinjun put a restraining hand on his arm. "Do that and she'll be getting exactly what she wants," he said quietly. "She knows we're watching."

"No, she—" Chuck retrained his eyes on the engrossed couple. Without warning, he pivoted away and prowled to the center of the room. "I'll deal with it later. *Okay?*"

"See that you do. We've got enough on our plates without worrying about Lorraine drawing my housekeeper's virginal son into some sort of sex game."

"Virginal?"

"You heard me. I know when I'm looking at a repressed kid who's experimenting. I won't have Mrs. Midgely upset. She's special to me—the same as she was to Bruno before me."

"For God's sake. Do we have to be bleeding hearts over the *housekeeper?*"

Sinjun stared directly into Chuck's eyes and said, "Yes." He considered and discarded the notion to tell Chuck about Lorraine and Willis. He'd only use that if all else failed. "Fix it."

Chuck executed a sloppy mock salute. "Aye, aye, sir. Are we ready to leave?"

"Yeah. Just let me ask Enders and Mrs. Midgely if they need anything."

"Sin—"

"It won't take a minute." Swinging open what appeared to be a closet door, he revealed the master intercom panel and pressed the button for the kitchen. He said, "Mrs. Midgely?" as soon as he heard the connection open.

"Yes, Mr. Breaker?"

Sinjun grinned and tucked in his chin. Mrs. Midgely invariably shouted into the speaker. "I'm going over to Kauai with Chuck. Anything you need?"

"Nothing, thank you, Mr. Breaker. Shall I ask Mr. Lloyd-Worthy?"

"Do that."

The sound of retreating footsteps followed.

Chuck paced, checking his watch every few seconds. "We've *got* to go."

Sinjun nodded. "Calm down."

"Hello, Mr. Breaker." Enders's well-modulated voice was precise. "You will remember that I'm hoping to enlist Miss Simcox's help this evening?"

"I haven't forgotten."

"Could you acquire some starch, sir? A spray would be best. Collars are simply not at their best without starch."

Sinjun saw Chuck raise his eyebrows and stare pointedly at his watch.

"Spray starch coming up. See you later—"

"Would you also be kind enough to procure a quantity of lilikoi? Miss Butters has expressed interest in a passion-fruit chiffon pie."

"Not a problem."

Chuck spread his arms. "Passion-fruit pie? That broad moves in, takes over and demands *passion-fruit pie*? And Enders clicks his heels and . . . Jesus H. Christ."

"I do hope you'll control comments like that in front of the lady concerned," Enders intoned.

Chuck made a face at the lit panel. For Sinjun's ears only he said, "One day I'm going to teach that tight-ass a lesson."

"Spray starch and passion fruit," Sinjun said, grinning. "Will do."

"Much appreciated." Enders cut off the intercom.

Chuck gathered a file he'd set on the writing table. "Let's get out of here. I'm ready for some fresh air and very little conversation."

"Sounds great to me." Fresh air, very little conversation—and a few hours away from captivity.

The fax bell rang.

"Leave it," Chuck said, on his way out the door.

Sinjun leaned to see the sheet coming out of the machine. "Hold it!" he called to Chuck. "This might be important."

"*Everything's* important around here," Chuck muttered, visibly exasperated.

"Something on Lieber." Sinjun removed the transmission. "Will you look at that? Our Mary's a genius."

"Are we going, or should I put my slippers on?"

"We'll go, we'll go. Look at this. Remember Lieber's industrial park in Kentucky?"

Chuck remained in the doorway. "What about it?"

"Nothing as far as the world's concerned. But the world doesn't know Lieber just used it as collateral against an eighteen-million loan to keep the San Diego and Seattle software outfits operational."

Chuck whistled.

"Every day another dollar, as they say," Sinjun commented. "Every day he's deeper in."

"And every day he needs you more?"

Sinjun looked sharply at Chuck. "You've got it. But if he doesn't expect to give me something I want for my money, the deal's going to fall apart."

One corner of Chuck's mouth jerked upward. "How did that little kid I used to know get to be *so* tough?"

Sinjun had heard enough references to his past lately. "Let me put a call through to Mary. Then we'll be on our way."

"Fran's going to be royally—"

"Pissed. Yeah, I know. You already told me. This won't take any longer than it has to."

An hour later, he hung up and turned around to find Chuck had left. Before Sinjun could go looking for him, he came back into the room. He carried a glass of seltzer and an open jar of nuts.

Sinjun snorted and accepted the seltzer. "I thought you said we had to hurry."

"Not anymore. I called the charter people and tried to locate Fran. I was going to tell her we'd be late. She'd just left. The guy who owns the chopper we're interested in agreed to bring her over."

Sinjun consulted his own watch. "Damn."

"No sweat," Chuck said, pouring nuts into his hand. "This'll work out fine. I'll take the Eurocopter over to Kauai on my own. You wait for them. You can fly the return leg with the owner to see what you think about his machine. We'll come back from Kauai together. But I don't want to keep the mechanic twiddling his thumbs so I think I'll cut out now."

"Sounds good to me." Making no remark about the route past the pool being shorter, Sinjun followed Chuck through the bungalow's cool interior to the front door. Outside in the atrium, swaying clumps of bamboo lined trails of river rock.

"Why don't we plan on catching a cool one while we're over there?" Chuck said, pushing open an ironwork gate in the outer wall. He still carried his jar of nuts.

Sinjun said, "I'm easy." He and Chuck could use a little one-on-one in neutral surroundings. "When will the other chopper get here?"

"It'll be a while. The guy I spoke to said he thought it had just left. When you get to Kauai, catch a ride to Lihue. I'll meet you in the arrivals lounge at the airport. Have me paged."

Chuck walked along the path that led to their own helicopter pad. Sinjun didn't miss the determined way his buddy avoided glancing in the direction of the courtyard surrounding the pool. Only an unconscious man could fail to hear the shrieks and splashing sounds that rose in bursts.

Sinjun set his jaw. Chuck hadn't had a whole lot of luck. Len Gill had been a good father, but he hadn't taken time to show Chuck the ropes he'd need to handle when he took over the family ranch. After Len's death, the once-thriving Gill place had taken a nosedive under its new owner's influence. From then on, everything Chuck touched turned rotten—including his relationships—until he'd shown up on Sinjun's doorstep, flat broke and asking for a job. That had been a good day—for both of them—but Chuck still hadn't learned to pick the right woman.

"Shoot," Chuck said. He tossed a handful of nuts into his mouth and handed the jar to Sinjun. "Sorry. Take this back, would you?"

Sinjun grinned. "Anytime."

Pausing abruptly, Chuck shoved his hands in his pockets and stared at the ground. "You always said that. *Anytime*. Whenever you've had to bail poor old failure Chuck out of another hole that's what you've said: *Anytime*."

Discomfort made Sinjun look away. "Friends stand by each other," he said. "Let's get you on your way."

"Sure." Chuck walked on, faster this time.

When they reached the pad he made his customary circle around the Eurocopter before approaching the door. In the act of climbing up, he changed his mind and faced Sin once more.

"I'll see you in Lihue," Sinjun said. He stacked the jar inside his empty glass.

Chuck studied the ground again. "Yeah. See you."

The faint intrusion into the silence by the *phud-phud* of another chopper's blades broke the awkward moment. Sinjun gave Chuck a long, assessing gaze and shaded his eyes to peer toward the horizon.

"Get going," he said, concentrating on the speck coming out of the distance. "Don't dwell on what happened back there. You're probably right. Lorraine's just bored."

"Yeah."

"We all have lapses in the judgment area. She's no different." He didn't want to back off on the topic, but he hated to see Chuck miserable.

"Thanks, Sin." Chuck gave Sin's biceps a thump. "For everything."

"Looks like Fran left a lot earlier than you thought."

"What?" Chuck seemed to notice the other aircraft for the first time. He followed Sin's lead and shaded his eyes. "That can't be it. The guy said it just took off."

They both watched the helicopter close in on the island.

Sinjun chuckled. "It's her, all right. Trust Fran. She hates to be dependent upon anyone. She must have decided to try and get here before I left."

Chuck was frowning. "I must have forgotten to tell her what time we were arriving in Kauai. If we'd gotten out on time we'd have missed them."

Sinjun set down the glass and began waving. "She handles nicely," he said, watching the little craft swoop toward the island. "Compact. I think it's going to work for us."

"Yeah."

"Wait till he lands the thing. We could take a look at it here."

"Okay."

The other helicopter, light-tan with a gold chevron on its nose, approached the reef.

Sinjun's arms stilled over his head. "What . . . Chuck—" He started to take a breath, but flinched instead. "My God! Oh, my God!" He began to run and heard Chuck pounding along behind him.

Even in the brilliant blue of an early-afternoon sky, the exploding aircraft sent up a black-streaked ball of fire that painted the heavens red . . . blood-red.

Angelica turned her face from the fading circles of fire and the rain of debris that peppered the ocean.

The helicopter had been making its approach to the island. It had almost made it.

She pressed her hands over her ears as if the splitting noise that still echoed in her brain could be shut out.

Even as she skirted the cottage and headed toward the jungle path she knew there was nothing to be done. Her feet thudded on the bed of fallen foliage and the sound of her own breathing became a roar.

As soon as the chopper had come into view she'd known it was Sinjun returning in the charter craft.

He'd died in that shattered blaze.

They'd both died, Sinjun and his secretary—Fran. That was right; her name was Fran.

By the time Angelica broke onto the lawns that sloped up to the compound, sweat ran between her shoulder blades and stung her eyes.

Then she saw Brenda. And Willis. Willis quickly pulled away from Brenda and raced from the grass to the beach and toward the sea. A few forceful thrusts of his powerful legs through the water and he launched into a driving crawl, heading for the reef.

"Brenda!" Angelica's shout came out as an hysterical whisper. "Brenda!"

She pounded over the grass, her long gauze skirt wrapping around her legs like a rope. How could he be dead?

Why did her throat burn? She couldn't care that the man who had ruined her mother's life no longer existed.

She *could not* care.

Brenda saw her and stopped.

"It . . . It's gone," Angelica gasped. "It just disappeared in all those . . ." She reached Brenda and stood panting, staring after Willis.

Brenda bent over and gripped her knees. "My God." She took in great breaths. "I never saw anything like it. Poor devils."

Angelica pressed a fist into her middle. "It *was* the helicopter they intended to test-fly?"

"Aye. Willis said it was."

"What's he trying to do?" Angelica asked, pointing to Willis now. He had become a diminishing blob that occasionally cleared a wave.

"I don't suppose he knows," Brenda said, straightening slowly. "He's doing all he can do. Swimming and praying for a miracle."

"It's pointless. He shouldn't risk going out there."

"He's a strong swimmer." Brenda gave a short laugh. "He's a ruddy machine."

Angelica closed her eyes and saw Sinjun's face. She *did* care.

"Hey." Brenda patted her back. "You feel sick. Bound to. So do I. Take it easy, Angel. Breathe through your mouth."

"Willis won't find anything," Angelica said. She dropped to sit cross-legged on the grass. "No one will."

Brenda crouched beside her. "I wonder what happened. I didn't actually see the thing explode—just heard it. Then saw the smoke and flames."

"One minute it was flying in." Angelica looked toward the spot where the helicopter had been. "Then it turned to fire and disappeared."

"Aye. Well, that's that, then."

Angelica gathered her loose hair into a bunch at her nape. "You're right. That's that." An accident had done her job for her and she ought to be glad.

But she hadn't wanted Sinjun to die.

She heard running feet and looked over her shoulder, into the sun. Two silhouettes, with a big dark shape slung between them, approached from the compound.

Brenda shaded her eyes. "Oh, dear. They're going out there, too. I wish they'd wait for the proper authorities to come."

One of the figures blocked out the sun and Angelica squinted. "Who is it?" She pushed to her feet.

"Sinjun and Chuck," Brenda told her.

"But . . ." She turned toward the sea, then back again—and looked into Sinjun's drawn face. "But you're . . . You were . . ."

He checked his stride only for an instant. An inflated black Zodiac, its large outboard already in place, made an unwieldy burden that he shared with Chuck Gill.

Sinjun's narrowed eyes remained on Angelica's face. "I'm what?" he asked. "Dead?"

Twelve

❦

Sinjun covered the mouthpiece on the remote phone he carried. "You're sure she's up there with Brenda?"

Chuck sat in Sinjun's chair behind the study desk. He said, "Yes," and sounded as weary as Sinjun felt. "Willis said she went to the pool house early this morning and hasn't left."

Sinjun held up a silencing hand and spoke into the phone. "The day before yesterday. It would have been early in the morning. Or it could have been the night before. Late. Yes." He nodded and paced. "Okay, but make it fast, please."

"The FAA guys don't think there's been any foul play, Sin," Chuck said.

"They don't *know*. The divers have been at it for two days and they haven't found anything suspicious. They haven't *found* anything, period. The bottom line is that a woman died but she doesn't have any relatives kicking and screaming for answers. The world won't stop for the guy who was with her, either. 'Engine fire leading to an explosion' works just fine at the bottom of a report."

"It works just fine for me, too," Chuck said. "Yes, someone could have found out you were supposed to be flying that chopper and arranged for it to blow up. I guess. But what about the timing?"

"What about it?"

"I don't know, but I can't figure out how you could time a thing like that. Damn it all, Sin, *how* would Angelica Dean pull off what you're suggesting she pulled off?"

Sinjun dropped into a chair. "If I knew the answer to that, we wouldn't be holed up here hoping I've got at least five more lives."

"Every one of those accidents could have been just that—accidents."

Sinjun knew a moment of cold helplessness. "You sound like the police. I was almost the victim of a drive-by shooting, but that was a case of being in the wrong place at the wrong time."

"Perfectly possible. it happens all the time."

"Then someone tried to force me off the road. In the Cascades. With a drop that looked about a hundred thousand feet deep from where I was."

Chuck picked up a pencil and fiddled. "But you weren't forced off the road."

"Only because another car fell in behind and the guy had to give up." He massaged the back of his neck. "The *woman* had to give up. I still say it was a woman wearing a scarf and dark glasses."

"You thought it was a woman who took a potshot at you, too."

"It was. Same thing. Something tied around her head, and glasses."

"If you start giving positive identifications of Angelica I'm going to have you committed."

Sinjun picked up a glass of seltzer and drank thirstily. "I'm not a fool. I'm not about to accuse anyone without being certain. Chuck, I didn't imagine that car in the mountains. It drew alongside and started edging me over."

"It was dusk. Maybe he—or she—was trying to overtake you and—"

"Don't." Sinjun jabbed a finger in Chuck's direction. "I've heard all the excuses. You'd have had to be there, buddy. You wouldn't be making excuses if you had. But go on, tell me the brakes on that cement truck just didn't hold."

"They didn't."

Frustration almost choked Sinjun. "No, they didn't. Someone made sure of that." The phone rang and he pressed the speak button. "Sinjun Breaker here . . . Yes. Yes. Why not? I see. Thank you," he finished quietly, and swung the phone by its antenna.

Chuck sat upright. "So?"

"A phone call was placed from the lagoon cottage to Kauai early in the morning of the day before yesterday." He let the words hang. "The day of the crash. You want to know the receiving number?"

Chuck shrugged.

"The air-charter field out of Princeville. The field—"

"I know, I know. The field Fran flew out of."

"Not positive proof," Sinjun admitted. "But too close to ignore."

The pencil slid out of Chuck's fingers and clattered on the desk. "Who did she talk to?"

"The telephone company said it's just a general office number. Anyone could have picked it up."

"I was afraid of that. You'd have to question everyone who works there—or happens by, for that matter."

"Damn, I wish I could turn the clock back." Sinjun felt an unaccustomed stinging in his eyes—not for the first time in the past couple of days. "Fran was . . . Fran was good people. She was great people. I'm going to miss her. So's Enders. He's hardly said a word since it happened."

Chuck said, "It's about time shit stopped following us around."

"Sometimes I think it has." There was no need to ask Chuck if he was talking about the lousy years they'd put on their shoes—individually and collectively. "We've shared a lot, Chuck. Good and bad. It's been more good than bad for quite a while, or it was until this mess started."

"Yeah." Chuck laughed without mirth. "And I intend for us to share a whole lot more good. From here on I'm gonna be your skin, buddy. Where you go, I go, and I don't want any arguments."

"I can handle myself."

"That's great, but I'm gonna be right there watching your fingers. I've got to make sure you don't forget to hang on tight."

A shred of warmth curled around Sinjun's rigid gut. "I'm impressed by your maternal instincts. I'll have to go to Seattle and deal with Fran's affairs."

"Great. We'll go together."

Sinjun stood up and said, "I'm going to talk to the police first."

"I wish you wouldn't."

"I want them to confront her. Then I want to confront her myself."

"I know," Chuck muttered. "But the police are going to say you're nuts and if you're right—if the girl is involved—you'll make sure whoever she's working for gets alerted. Hell, I don't know. Maybe you *should* try to persuade the police."

Two sleepless nights were taking their toll on Sinjun's concentration. "Uh uh," he said slowly. The only realistic approach to the problem was equally slow in coming. Finally he said, "No, I think your instincts are good. I also think it's time Angel Dean got really serious about my biography."

"Tell me what she was like." Brenda lay on the bed in the apartment above the pool house.

"I never met her."

"You didn't?" Brenda raised her head off the pillows to stare at Angelica. "I thought you said she was efficient."

"I said she sounded efficient. On the intercom."
Seated on a cane stool beside one of two windows,
Angelica kept her sights trained on the activity
below. "I heard her on the intercom at the cottage.
Efficient and cheerful—and smart."

Brenda dropped back onto the pillows. "And now
she's dead. She's been dead for two days."

"It's all crazy," Angelica said, watching yet
another group of official-looking men leave the
compound and head toward the pad where a large
police helicopter waited. "I keep getting the feeling
Sinjun thinks it was *my* fault."

"Don't be daft. How could he?"

"I don't know. But he looks as if he'd like to hit
me." Her stomach turned, as it had so many times
in the two days since Fran Simcox and a man called
Jim Allen were blown out of the sky in front of her
eyes. "When I tried to talk to him this morning he
walked away."

"We should get out of here." Brenda turned onto
her side. "He's probably not going to want to carry
on with your biography thing. Not now, anyway."

"Sinjun's given orders that I'm not to think about
leaving." Telling Brenda the true reason for coming
here would be such a relief, but explaining the circumstances of her mother's death would take more
energy than Angelica had. "Chuck Gill told me."

"Breaker can't order you about."

"He's upset."

Brenda propped her head. "Enders is more upset.
I think he had a thing for Fran."

"I was sure Sinjun was dead," Angelica murmured.

"So you've said." Rolling to her feet, Brenda stood
up. "I think you might want to consider not saying
it anymore."

Angelica pleated a leg of her shorts.

"Listen, I wasn't going to tell you this, but I think
you need to know." Keeping her eyes on Angelica,

Brenda tucked in her shirt. "I heard Chuck tell Sinjun to watch what he says to you. Why, I don't know, but I reckon . . . You're right. He *does* seem to have it in for you. Chuck said something like, 'If you're right, you'd better make sure she doesn't guess.' "

Angelica buried her face in her hands. "I don't know what it all means."

"Maybe it's nothing to do with this awful tragedy. Maybe he's pulling a fast one. Stringing you along while he finds out what the market's likely to be for his biography."

Angelica's head shot up. "What do you mean?" Her heart made double time. "You think he's talking to people in New York about it?"

"He could be. Some publishers, maybe. He's got plenty of contacts, so that shouldn't be hard. He could also be trying to find out if he could get a better split on the money with someone else."

"We haven't talked money," Angelica said.

Brenda's feathery red brows rose. "Why ever not? This is a ruddy money-making scheme, isn't it? You said you picked Breaker out because he's had a weird life and people will find him fascinating." She grinned, and the result was wonderfully wicked. "He certainly is fascinating, Angel. And— until this fiasco—I could have sworn he found you fascinating, too. The night of the dinner party—you remember—when he took you back afterwards?"

"I remember." How would she ever manage to forget?

"I'll just bet you do. What happened? Is he a good kisser—among other things?"

Angelica felt herself turn red. She didn't answer.

"Quite so, my pet," Brenda said, almost purring. "I won't push it for now, but later you'll have to give me all the lovely details. I rather fancy Willis, myself."

"Brenda!"

"Don't *Brenda* me like I was a kid. You should have felt what I felt when we got playful in the pool." She made owl eyes. "My-oh-my. If I was an easy girl, I'd already have his blue bikini hanging on my rearview mirror."

"You're impossible," Angelica moaned. "I'm tired and I need to decide what to do next. I think I'll go back and try to sleep."

"I don't think you will," Brenda said, leaning to look past Angelica. "Unless Sinjun's just out for a stroll around the pool, we're about to have company."

Angelica jumped up. "He's coming here?"

"Um . . . Yes, he certainly is. As I speak he's coming into the pool house."

"He could be getting ready for a swim."

Brenda sighed theatrically. "I should be so lucky. If I believed that, I'd sneak down the stairs and peek."

"Brenda!"

"Brenda, *Brenda*. If he wants to swim, all he's got to do is walk out of his bedroom." She inclined her head. "I hear fairy footsteps on the stairs."

The solid thud of climbing feet made Angelica retreat to the farthest corner of the room.

"Come on," Brenda said. "Wipe that scared-kid look off your face. Put *him* on the defensive. He's probably coming to apologize for his nasty temper, anyway."

Brenda didn't wait for Sinjun to knock more than once before flinging open the door and greeting him with a cheerful "Morning, Sinjun. Come in. Angelica and I have been keeping each other company. Not a time when anyone wants to be alone, is it? Normally I like my own company, but—"

"Good morning," Sinjun said formally. He barely glanced at Brenda before walking to stand a few feet from Angelica. "How are you?"

She had a ridiculous urge to cry. "Tense," she said honestly.

"Aren't we all?"

"I'm very sorry—" Angelica wiped her palms on her shorts. "That's pretty lame, but it's the best I can do. Campbell told me that . . . He said that Fran was something special."

"She was." When his lips came together, muscles flicked in his cheeks. "I'll be leaving for Seattle early tomorrow morning. Fran didn't have anyone close. I'll be attending to her affairs."

"Of course." Looking into his face—at this moment—Angelica could see only a man who was suffering. "If I can do anything to help . . ." Even as she let the offer trail away, Angelica couldn't believe she'd made it.

"There's nothing you can do." In the bright light of morning, his eyes were as much yellow as green and no vestige of kindness lingered there. "This is the time for Fran's friends to do what must be done."

"Yes, of course. I expect Enders—"

"Enders wants a memorial here on Hell. Somewhere he can go and remember—even if we don't have anything left of her to put there."

Her stomach made another sickening revolution. She said, "I'm sorry" again and wished she could escape his intense stare.

"I'd like you to be ready to leave at seven in the morning."

Angelica felt her lips part.

He turned toward Brenda. "Do you have anywhere you have to be in the next few days?"

"I . . . No. Nowhere at all. I'll be glad to come along."

"Thank you, but I'm going to ask you to remain here."

Panic welled in Angelica. "What are you saying? Why—"

"For some reason, Enders seems to think Brenda's the kind of woman to have around in a crisis."

"Yes." Swallowing with difficulty, Angelica continued, "People always feel that way about Brenda. But—"

"Good. That's settled then. Brenda stays to help stop Enders from falling apart." He returned his attention to Angelica. "You come with me."

What he said didn't compute.

"Willis will also remain. He can be trusted to give me accurate intelligence reports—on how things are going here. Chuck will be with us."

"I don't understand why—"

He talked over her. "I already had business to see to in Seattle. It wasn't scheduled for a few days yet. It'll be shifted forward."

"What does all this have to do with me?" She took a step toward him.

He matched her step with one of his own and stood close enough to look down into her face. "It's simple. I'm going to Seattle. You're coming with me. You and I have an agreement. Sinjun Breaker's biography will be written by Angelica Dean. It's time we got going on this project, don't you think?"

"I thought you'd want to wait."

So unexpectedly that she jumped, Sinjun settled a heavy hand on her shoulder. "I *don't* want to wait. And I want you to do the best job that's ever been done on any life. You're going to get a real scoop, *Angel*. You're going to get to crawl into my eyes and under my skin. Personal's going to take on a whole new meaning."

"Well . . . Thank you." He was frightening her.

His smile stretched his mouth. It did nothing for his green-ice eyes. "Don't mention it. Consider it my contribution to the chronicles of an age. Where I go, you go. It may get tedious—for both of us. Somehow I think I'll hold up better than you will."

He was threatening her. Why? Was he reacting to grief over Fran's death? Lashing out at the only one he felt free to hurt?

"I don't really think it's a good idea for me to intrude while you're dealing with personal things," she said, hoping he couldn't hear her anxiety.

"Well, I think it's the best possible idea. I've decided to give this biography my all. You must be wondering why I'm suddenly so keen, right?"

"Yes," she murmured.

"It's because I can't quite believe that explosion was an accident. Can you?"

Angelica covered her mouth.

"You can't, can you? You thought I was aboard that helicopter and you weren't the only one. I'd bet a lot of money that *I* was supposed to die the day before yesterday. And I'd bet just as much that there'll be another attempt to kill me."

She smothered a cry.

Sinjun smiled anew—a disturbing sight. "I knew you were a sensitive woman. I'm concerned for your safety, too, Angelica. It could be that someone's anxious to make sure I don't ever tell all my secrets, couldn't it? All this could be an attempt to make sure you don't get to write my biography.

"I'm going to make sure you do, but I'll have to look after you in the process. I can't risk anyone getting at you . . . hurting you."

"Don't!"

"Sorry. I'm frightening you and I don't mean to. Trust me, Angel. I'm going to look after you because I feel responsible for your welfare."

Brenda started toward them. "Excuse me, but—"

"*Be quiet.*" Sinjun silenced her. "You'll be well taken care of here until we return. Meanwhile, I'm going to keep Angelica with me at all times—just to make sure she's safe."

"Please don't worry about me," she managed to blurt out at last.

"Oh, but I do. Pack, Angelica. I think you'll enjoy my home in Seattle. You can have the room next to mine and there's a perfect little study where you can work on your notes. You will need to take notes. There'll be a lot going on."

This was the answer to a prayer, yet she was terrified. "Thank you," she said, aware of a fine tremor in every muscle.

"Don't thank me. We'll think of this as a kind of marriage of convenience. Together as a means to ensure we both get what we want. Together . . ." His laughed chilled her. "Until—or should I say *unless* death do us part?"

Thirteen

❦

*U*nless death do us part.

Angelica felt the confidence and vitality of the man who walked beside her through Seattle-Tacoma Airport. He set a course straight ahead and people automatically stepped out of his path. Women stared—and more than a few men. Angelica didn't blame them.

Unless death do us part.

The jacket of his dark suit was slung over his shoulder. A white shirt emphasized his tan. Rather than making him appear travel-weary, the loosened knot of his red tie added to the air of casual command.

Sinjun Breaker expected to control all he touched —or wanted to touch—and the expectation showed. Angelica hovered on a knife blade between fearing him and longing to be someone important in his life. Focusing on destroying him had become a torment. Somewhere on the journey between Hell and Seattle, probably around the time she'd watched him when she thought he was asleep in his plane seat—then been startled to realize he wasn't—she had begun to hope her mother had made a mistake.

He'd let her look at him for a long time before opening his eyes and staring at her, totally alert. She'd thought what she saw in him was a struggle, and, maybe, regret . . . and desire.

They'd hardly spoken in the many hours since leaving Hell, yet she'd never been more aware of a man's presence, had never thought it possible to feel such awareness.

She asked, "Where's Chuck?" and her voice sounded out of practice.

"He went ahead to collect the baggage."

"I'm going to have to buy a few things," she told him. "I wasn't prepared to be away so long."

"That's easily fixed."

At an escalator, he stepped aside for her to get on, then held her elbow all the way down.

Unless death do us part.

A panicky sensation attacked Angelica's insides. At the bottom of the escalator, the doors of an underground shuttle stood open and Sinjun propelled her rapidly into a car.

"Sit down," he said, indicating an orange plastic seat.

"I've been sitting for hours," she said, grasping a pole. "I'd rather stand."

He stood facing Angelica, his broad, long-fingered hand resting above hers. His knuckles showed white.

She concentrated on his smooth shirtfront. He was a man of many faces: relaxed lord of the tropical manor; wanderer of beaches and king of the rocks with a bag of myths to share; angry man of many secrets; and now, forceful commander of a powerful financial empire.

And would the real Sinjun Breaker please stand up?

The thumb of his right hand, coming to rest lightly on her cheek, startled Angelica.

Very softly, with his fingers spread over her ear and jaw, he stroked. "You look tired."

She was powerless to suppress a tremor. "I'm fine."

"Is there anything you'd like to tell me, Angelica?"

Her throat dried out. "Tell you?"

"Anything that would make you feel better?" His fingers slipped into her hair and he tilted her face up. "I keep getting the feeling there's a barrier between us. It's as if you say one thing and mean something entirely different. Or perhaps you *think* something entirely different?"

She was the only one hiding the truth? "That's funny," she said. "I get the feeling you don't always reveal very much of yourself. Do you think that's what you're feeling? Your own self-protection, only you're projecting it onto me?"

His response was to tuck a loose piece of her hair behind her ear. Dropping his hand, he studied the lit panel above the door and listened with apparent absorption to the high female voice that repeated departure instructions in Japanese.

Angelica bowed her head and let out the breath she'd been holding. With every moment she became more entangled with him. And she wouldn't escape even if she could. Because, of course, the closer she got to the man, the closer she got to her goal.

She bit her bottom lip. Her goal wasn't clear-cut anymore.

At the main terminal, he again clasped her elbow to steer her through the crowd. "I just remembered a question I haven't asked you," he said. "Where do you call home?"

A moment's confusion dissipated. "Nowhere." In this case, honesty was easy. "My job takes me . . . Used to take me all over the world. When I was in New York I bunked in a friend's apartment. That's where I store my possessions. Not many. I'm not a collector of things."

"Male friend?"

She glanced sharply up at him. "Does it matter?"

"No."

But he had asked. Angelica hid a smile and understood what had pleased her. For some perverse reason it was becoming ever more important that Sinjun be aware of her as a woman.

He moved with even greater purpose and she had to run to keep up. They left the building by automatic doors and went directly to the edge of the sidewalk outside. Taxis and shuttles and limousines came and went in a jostling jumble, spewing forth and sucking up travelers.

Angelica barely had time to feel the light summer air on her face before a dark-gray Lexus sidled to a stop and Chuck, loaded down with baggage, appeared from behind them. The trunk of the Lexus popped open and he deposited his burdens inside.

"Get in," Sinjun said, and Angelica jumped. He held open the car's back door.

She hesitated for a moment, then did as he asked.

Sinjun slid into the front passenger seat and Chuck joined Angelica in the back.

A woman with dark hair bobbed to fall sleekly from center part to jaw sat behind the wheel. She spared Angelica one long, gray-eyed gaze through round tortoiseshell-framed glasses before concentrating on Sinjun.

Boy, did she concentrate.

Angelica sank back into soft tan leather and observed how the woman leaned, subtly but definitely, toward Sinjun. "Everybody's talking," she said in a low, clear voice. "I've done my best to shut off the gossip, but—"

"This is Angelica Dean," Sinjun said perfunctorily. He hooked an elbow over the back of his seat to see her. "Angelica, meet Mary Barrett, my chief financial officer."

Angelica got another cool stare—and a raised brow.

"You two may cross paths a bit," Sinjun said. "Angelica is my biographer."

The dark-brown brow rose another notch. "Really? How surprising."

Angelica decided a polite noise was the safest response.

"I told you I had someone working on a biography," Sinjun said.

"Yes. You did." Mary Barrett's tone made it clear that she hadn't expected a female writer. "I thought we should get together at my place as planned."

"We're about to get moved along," Chuck said, breaking his silence for the first time as a traffic cop approached the Lexus.

Mary eased from the curb and skillfully slid through the slalom course of vehicles until she could gun the powerful car toward the freeway. She didn't speak again until they passed the first sign for Seattle.

"The meeting's set for tomorrow. I—"

"We'll talk about it later," Sinjun said.

In other words, they would talk about "it" after they got rid of Angelica. So much for the carte blanche she was supposedly going to get on the life and times of Sinjun Breaker.

"Have you been to Seattle before, Angelica?" Chuck asked.

How strange that she'd actually pulled it off. They really knew so little about her. "Oh, yes. I like it." She'd grown up on the Eastside and lived there until she left for Sarah Lawrence at eighteen.

Chuck looked through the window at silver birches, their bright leaves trembling in the breeze. "Too cool for me," he said. "Give me Pacific heat any day."

Or Montana heat? Angelica wondered how much information she could get from Chuck Gill, if he could ever be persuaded to let his hair down and talk about the man he idolized.

"Where do your people live?" Mary Barrett asked. She checked over her left shoulder, maneuvered across several lanes of traffic and merged smoothly onto the interstate.

Women like Mary Barrett spoke of "people," not families. Angelica was mildly surprised to catch an amused glance from Chuck. Once again, the truth would serve very well. "I don't have any living family. I never knew my father—not really. My mother's dead, too. My mailing address is in New York." All absolutely true—or almost. "Didn't you know Fran Simcox?"

The element of surprise worked. Absolute silence, the kind that was loud enough to deafen, filled the car before Mary Barrett said, "Of course I knew her. I know everyone Sinjun knows."

Except me. And what a very unusual comment. Angelica was tempted to echo, *Everyone?* but thought better of it.

"It must have been awful," Mary said, and Angelica saw how the other woman's hands tightened on the steering wheel. "Blown up. Just like that."

"It's never 'just like that,' " Chuck said, his face turned to the window again. "They say there's always at least a second and it's the longest second of your life."

"Garbage," Mary said. "Pure speculation. No one ever lived to talk about it."

"Ever heard of black boxes?"

"Drop it," Sinjun said, but mildly. "It's too bad that chopper didn't have a recorder. Not that we were likely to recover it. Let's leave it at that."

Chuck remarked, "Might have been nice if Mary hadn't had to be prompted to mention Fran."

Sinjun half-turned in his seat, shook his head and turned back.

"We all deal differently with grief," Mary said.

Chuck snorted. "Fran and Sin were friends as well as employer-employee. They had the kind of relationship that's rare between a man and a woman because it was just that, a friendship. That made you green with envy and you hated Fran's guts for it."

"That's *enough!*" This time Sinjun shot around and fixed Chuck with a narrow glare. "We're all suffering. End of topic."

"It's okay," Mary said in the kind of humble tone that set Angelica's teeth on edge. "The problem here isn't poor Fran, it's me, isn't it, Chuck?"

"Sinjun said the topic was closed."

"Fine. But let's not pretend about who's really jealous of Sin's friendships."

"Good God." Sinjun pressed his head into the rest. "I hope that imaginary pencil of yours is racing, Angel."

Mary's face came sharply around and she darted a shrewd look from Sinjun to Angelica. She hadn't missed the familiarity in Sinjun's comment—or the name he'd used.

"There she blows," Chuck announced as the sky-scrapers of Seattle came into view. "It's gonna look like the Big Apple soon, right, Angelica?"

She studied the blue and bronze, the marble-white and glassy black of the elegant city and smiled with pure pleasure. "I don't think so. Not quite." To their left, the sun turned the waters of Elliott Bay into glittering blue chips. On the horizon, the Olympic mountains rose, rugged and dark to their snow-capped tips. "Nope. Something's always going to make this different."

And it was home.

"I'm taking Sin to my place," Mary said. "Where can I drop you?"

"I've got an errand or two to do." Chuck leaned forward. "Downtown. Let me out by the Columbia Center. I'll pick up my car from the office. Stay at Mary's until I get there, Sin. Okay?"

Sinjun took a long time to say, "Okay," and he didn't sound thrilled.

"How about you, Angelica?" Mary asked.

"She'll come with us," Sinjun announced promptly.

"But—"

"That'll work out for the best." Sinjun stretched his arm along the seat behind Mary's shoulders. "Best for me."

And there would be no more argument, Angelica thought, while she wondered if she should be considering giving up on what had become an even more complicated venture than she could possibly have anticipated.

"Where do you buy things?" Sinjun asked.

Mary glanced at him. "Things?"

"Clothes. That sort of thing."

A frown creased Mary's smooth brow. "Nordstrom. Ann Taylor. Helen's Of Course. Bally. Depends what kind of things."

"Good." He sat straighter. "Remember those stores, Chuck. Angel wasn't expecting this trip. You can run her around town first thing in the morning."

Angelica felt suffocated. "I don't think—"

"You don't have to," Sinjun said. "Your job is to concentrate on me. I'll take care of you."

Even if she'd missed the possible double meaning, Mary Barrett wouldn't have. At any moment, the Lexus would be minus a steering wheel.

Chuck got out of the car at the soaring black Columbia Center and Mary zigzagged across town to an elegant condominium complex overlooking Lake Union.

Once out of the car, Mary slipped a hand into Sinjun's and smiled up at him. "It's so good to have you back. It's been frightening here the last few days."

He returned the smile and didn't attempt to remove his hand. "It's been frightening where we were, too." They walked close together, Mary press-

ing her compact, shapely body against him and
holding his arm. "There can't be anything much
more horrifying than watching an aircraft explode,
right, Angel?" he added.

She walked behind, feeling like the bridesmaid
who stuck around too long. "It was horrible."

"I'm sure it was." Dragging, Mary turned the
walk into a stroll and kept right on gazing up
at Sinjun. "Thank God you weren't . . . Well, you
know what I'm saying."

They all knew what she was saying.

Mary Barrett's sumptuous home was on the third
floor of the complex. Sinjun went into the green-
and-gold living room like a man who knew his way
well. Hovering on the perimeter of lustrous, dark
wood floors that surrounded a beautiful antique
rug, Angelica observed the scene. Sinjun let Mary
take his jacket, then he sank into a dark-green leather
couch.

"Seltzer?" Mary suggested. "Or club soda?"

He nodded and closed his eyes. "Seltzer, please.
Angel's tired, too, aren't you?"

She regarded him silently until he opened his
eyes.

Helpful Mary bustled to hand Sinjun his glass
and promptly carried on to a passage leading
off the living room. "Forgive me," she said, too
pleasantly. "We get so caught up in our own little
worlds, don't we? Let me make you comfortable in
my room. Sin and I have things—business things to
catch up on."

Angelica glanced at Sinjun but he made no comment. She said, "Thank you."

With instructions to "make herself at home" and
to "take a nap if she wanted to," Mary shut Angelica quietly but firmly into a bedroom so white it
chilled the eyes.

Half an hour later—thirty-two minutes, to be
precise—she tired of studying first the view, then

her watch and wandered into the bathroom.

Kertz-Breaker definitely paid more than minimum wage. In a pinch, the white marble tub would make a lap pool; bathing alone would be a desolate experience.

Angelica let a breath whistle out through her teeth.

She wasn't really losing her touch. The events of the past crazy week had slowed her down a little was all.

If not shared, this bathroom would be wasted.

She shut the door and locked it without being sure why.

On the back of the door, twin white hooks held twin white terry robes—twin except for one being considerably longer than the other.

Mary Barrett could be *Mrs.* Barrett.

Mr. Barrett's razor and cologne sat beside the right of two white marble sinks set in a long white marble counter. Mrs. Barrett's perfume bottles, her lotion and a pair of pearl earrings decorated the side of the left sink.

Angelica tiptoed closer and opened a square cloisonné box beside the razor.

It was filled with little foil packages.

She swallowed and closed the lid quickly.

This was silly, and it was wrong.

Mary's towels, ranged along a rail to the left of the tub, were emblazoned in green script with the initials M.A.B. Tasteful. But then, Mary was tasteful.

Angelica's eyes shifted to matching towels on a rail to the right of the tub. No initials this time.

The green script announced simply, SIN'S.

Fourteen

❦

*T*he Lexus belonged to Sinjun. So, evidently, did Mary Barrett.

By the time he had driven Angelica to the Seattle mansion he called home—with Chuck tailing them in a nondescript tan Ford compact—the long summer day had waned into darkness.

Sinjun's home sat behind a high stuccoed wall in the best of the best sections of plush Queen Anne Hill. Once the electrically operated gates had closed behind the Lexus, Chuck sped away.

Sinjun unlocked the front door and ushered Angelica inside. "I'll show you directly to your rooms," he said shortly, indicating for her to precede him upstairs.

As she climbed she glimpsed rooms opening off the foyer, rooms furnished with antiques, many of them Oriental.

"This is breathtaking," Angelica told Sinjun, turning a slow circle at the top of a staircase that rose from the entrance hall in a single wide span, then bifurcated to form a gallery around the second story. Overhead, mythic frescoes in shades of palest-blush to blood-red took the eye all the way up to a circular dome of rich stained glass.

Sinjun placed a hand in the small of her back and steered her to the left. "Most of what you see—the best, in many ways—is exactly as it was when I bought the place. Any credit for design goes to the former owners."

"I suppose it does. But you get the credit for recognizing exquisite taste." Which led very naturally to a more important topic. "Mary Barrett's home is certainly lovely."

"Yes."

"She must be very good at her job."

"She is."

Surprise, surprise. Sinjun didn't want to talk about Mary Barrett. Was Mary the woman in Momma's letter? The woman who was Sin's lover and then set out to ensnare Momma's friend? "How long have you . . . How long has she been with you?"

"This will be your room." Leaning past her, he threw open a door and gestured her inside. "I think you'll be comfortable here."

Angelica laughed and he looked at her sharply.

"Sorry," she told him, only a little sheepishly. "What an absolutely fabulous room. I've never slept in a four-poster before." Neither had she found herself assigned to quarters composed of acres of silk carpet worn to a marvelous dark-red-and-blue patina upon which stood a complement of French antiques. Angelica was no expert and tended to get her Louises muddled, but she recognized the rococo exuberance from one reign and the neoclassical grandeur of another. The dauphin's dolphin motif decorated the corners of a gorgeous flat writing table placed where, by day, the light from three tall, narrow windows would brighten its surface.

"I take it that means you like it," Sinjun said.

She'd felt him watching her reaction. "Were all the furnishings left in the house, too?"

"No." He lifted her lone suitcase onto the magenta-and-violet-draped bed. "Mrs. Falon lives in. She's my housekeeper and guardian angel. The rest of the staff don't sleep here. Mrs. Falon's rooms are on the ground floor at the back of the house. Pull the cord beside the fireplace if you need anything. She'll get back to you by telephone."

Angelica grinned. "You're joking."

He had the grace to grin in return. "Put it down to remnants of the child I never got a chance to be. Everyone said the bell cords had to go. So I kept 'em."

They laughed.

As quickly as the moment of closeness was shared, it dissipated.

Angelica continued to feel close to Sinjun, but the connection was purely physical. He made her intensely aware of her small stature—just as she was intensely aware of how large he was, and how little defense she would have against any attempt he made to . . . He was a civilized man, not an animal.

He'd admitted the importance of controlling his temper.

Angelica had seen him lose it.

Dee-Dee Cahler Breaker had been beaten until . . . *until* death did she part from her young husband.

"What's the matter?"

She jumped. "Nothing. Absolutely nothing. I'm overwhelmed and a little tired, I guess. This has been a long day."

"Of course. I'll leave you to settle in." He walked to a bathroom that opened from one side of the bedroom. "Everything looks ready for you. Would you like me to show you the study now?"

Angelica ordered her thoughts. "I think I'd prefer to work here." She indicated the writing table. "Unfortunately things haven't gone exactly as I'd planned. If I'd known we'd be jumping into the project like this I'd have brought my computer from New York. I'll have to make do with that invisible pencil of mine for a while."

He didn't return her smile. "I'll arrange a laptop for you. Someone from my offices will call for specifications."

"Thank you, but—"

"Tomorrow morning you'll want to sleep in. Mrs. Falon will bring you breakfast. She'll call up for your preferences."

"How nice." The gentleman was really into authority.

"Tomorrow afternoon I'm going to take you to Kertz-Breaker. To sit in on a meeting. I think it would give you an interesting insight into the way I operate—professionally."

Apparently he'd decided he could choose every word she wrote. "That would be very helpful." She doubted that whatever innocuous event he'd invited her to attend would be helpful at all, but she'd go along. With any luck Mary Barrett would be there and Mary had become very important to Angelica. She believed this was the woman he'd supposedly ceased to consider "fun."

Without preamble, Sinjun asked, "What size are you?" While Angelica gaped, he openly assessed her body. "What do they call clothes for little people?"

Little people? "Is petite what you had in mind?"

"Exactly. Petite. What size? About eight?"

"Six," Angelica said, letting the chill factor build.

"Great. Six, petite. Chuck's good at picking things out. He does it for Lorraine all the time. Get some rest in the morning. He'll go around those shops Mary mentioned and have people help him fix you up."

Lorraine of the topless, bottomless silver dresses and thong bikinis? "No, he won't," Angelica said, taking pride in the even tone of her voice and the guileless smile on her lips. "Even if I could afford a new wardrobe—and on a temporarily-between-jobs journalist's salary, I can't—I assure you I'd prefer to pick it out myself."

His expression didn't alter. "If it makes you more comfortable, we'll call whatever I spend on you a retainer. After all, you are here on my account. We can make adjustments later, when the huge advance on my fascinating biography rolls in."

Angelica knew an instant of fear. He did suspect her of being something other than what she'd inferred. She could *feel* his antagonism.

"Let's not talk about this now," she temporized. "You're probably tired and I know I am." And no doubt he was expected back in the white room. Mary had made a poor attempt to cover her disgust when Chuck had showed up and Sinjun insisted upon leaving with Angelica.

He worked his red tie completely loose and let it hang. "I should mention that there's a very complicated—and efficient—alarm system in the house and grounds."

"I would expect that."

"Yes. Of course. So you do understand that you can't simply come and go from the house at will? Mostly you'll be with me, but if you want to go outside during the daytime and I'm not around, contact Mrs. Falon. You won't be wanting to leave at night, but if you should have some sort of emergency, you'll have to come to me."

Apprehension crawled over Angelica's skin. "I see. I suppose I reach you by phone, too?"

He went to a door on the opposite side of the room and turned the key in its lock. "Quickest thing would be to come through here." He waited for her to join him and met her eyes as they entered a bathroom dominated by an oversized Victorian-style tub on claw feet. "This is an arrangement left over from the days of separate beds. Your room, with its own bathroom, would have belonged to the wife. I rather imagine she signaled her interest in . . . Well, when she used her key to this bathroom, her husband probably figured she didn't have a headache."

On the last occasion when he'd decided to discuss sex with her, he'd been a whole lot more basic. "Perhaps it was the husband who did the signaling."

He drew his bottom lip between his teeth and raised one eyebrow. "If you'd been the woman on the other side of that door, Angel, he'd have been on call at all times."

"Why is it you manage to make even a compliment sound . . ." She bit back the rest.

"Sound?" The tilt of his head dared her to continue. "Sound what? Like an invitation? Probably because that's exactly what it was. But don't let me make you uncomfortable. I'll spend all the nights you're here hovering somewhere between semierect and erect, but don't give it another thought."

"Do you speak to all women like that?"

He shook his head. "Now that's odd. Now I come to think of it, I've never even considered speaking to another woman the way I speak to you."

"That's insulting."

His smile was angelic. "I imagine that depends on the way you look at it. After you." Another door stood open into a bedroom even larger than Angelica's. Sinjun guided her over the threshold. "Sometimes I don't rouse too easily. Don't be afraid to come in and shake me."

She stood—as far from him as was possible without dashing back through the adjoining bathroom— and looked at a room remarkable for its starkness. Ivory silk covered the walls and ivory satin sheets were turned down on a big bed with no head or footboard. Ivory carpets lay on mahogany floors so dark they appeared black, even beside the black lacquer furnishings reflected in its sheen.

"So?" Sinjun said, his smile becoming a smile as old as time between men and women. It said that they were alone here and they both knew it—and that he definitely liked the idea.

The best Angelica could manage was "Very nice," before scuttling back to the magenta-and-violet opulence of the room she'd been allotted.

"By the way," Sinjun said behind her.

She willed her heart to slow down and faced him. "Yes?"

"I don't lock the door on my side. You might want to follow suit. Safer that way." He walked back toward his bedroom.

Safer? Good grief.

Angelica shut the door behind him, being careful not to bang it. As soon as she dared, she'd try to put a call through to Brenda. Even if Sinjun found out, the excuse would be simple; she'd be checking up on her friend.

Shortly after she closed her door into his bathroom, she heard him leave and go downstairs. Her windows looked over the front driveway. Within minutes, the Lexus swept toward the gates—which opened smoothly—and slipped away into the night. And Angelica had no doubts about where he was headed.

He spoke of death threats and fear, then left her a virtual prisoner. She'd told him she had no family. He had no reason to believe that, apart from Brenda, she had a soul in the world who would search for her until long after . . . long after something awful had happened to her.

Nothing awful would happen to her.

And Brenda did know where she was.

But Brenda was also a captive—on an island with no escape except by a boat Angelica had never seen, or a helicopter that was parked in Honolulu.

Cautiously, Angelica lifted the telephone and listened to the dial tone. Jitters attacked viciously. She let the receiver slip down again and concentrated afresh on the quiet in the house.

Instead of panicking, she should be congratulating herself. With patience, she'd get her story on Sinjun. She'd expose him and save the man her mother had loved from whatever schemes Sinjun might have to ruin him.

Sinjun should be arriving at the Lake Union condo by now. It shouldn't bother her to think of his long, lithe limbs tangled around Mary Barrett's athletic body in her white bed, but it did. Angelica's cheeks turned hot and she ached in all the places he'd made her ache that night on the beach . . . and before he'd left her at the cottage.

What would he do if he knew she was a virgin? Sneer?

Laugh?

Or simply not believe it?

She'd given him plenty of reason to assume she was no stranger to sex.

What was it really like? What would it be like with *him?*

She wasn't too innocent to visualize him lying awake on his satin sheets. Nor was she too naive to get a vivid picture of that part of his body that was going to be "hovering somewhere between semierect and erect" when he thought about her joining him on his slick sheets.

Everything tingled—and burned.

Saving herself for Mr. Right was becoming really old.

Damn. How could she be fantasizing about the man she intended to ruin?

Angelica snatched up the phone again, consulted her address book and dialed the number for the apartment over the pool house on Hell.

Almost at once the receiver at the other end was picked up. "Hello?" Brenda's voice was unusually subdued.

"Brenda," Angelica whispered hoarsely. "I can't believe I got through so easily. It's me. Angel."

"Oh, Angel. Boy, am I glad to hear your voice. Are you okay?"

"I don't know."

"Why are you whispering?"

Angelica bit her lip. "Because I'm afraid of being overheard."

"By whom?"

"I'm at Sinjun's house—more like a little palace, actually. The only person here is the housekeeper. I haven't seen her yet but she lives in rooms on the ground floor. Sinjun's not here, but the housekeeper's probably around somewhere."

"Why don't you go out and find a call box?"

Carrying the phone, Angelica clamped the receiver between shoulder and ear, pulled a fragile-looking gilt chair close to the window and sat down where she could watch for Sinjun's return.

"Angel?"

"If I try to get out of here without telling anyone, an alarm will go off."

"Jee-sus. Aren't we a pair?"

So Brenda also understood they could be at risk. "Yes. Both in cushy jails. Is everything okay there?"

"On the surface. Enders is a good sort, I think. Completely broken up by Fran Simcox's death—"

"That's it!" Angelica jumped up. "The authorities are bound to go back and investigate further. You can ask them to fly you out."

"According to Enders, they aren't coming back."

Angelica stared at her dark reflection in the window. "You could call a charter service to come and get you."

"I thought of that. Any incoming aircraft would be picked up on the radar. That might be fine, but before I try it, I've got to be sure that wouldn't cause someone to do something hasty."

"What would . . . Like what?"

Brenda let out a loud sigh. "Like bump me off and tell whoever arrived that I'd already left."

Angelica sat back in the chair with a thud. "Why would anyone do that?"

"Because Mr. Breaker's got something big to hide and he intends to keep it hidden, maybe? Angel, I don't know what you've started to dig up, but I think it's nasty. Look, there are a lot of interesting people in the world—why not have a go at bowing out from this one and choose someone else?"

Telling Brenda everything might put her into even more danger—if she was in danger at all.

"Angel," Brenda said. "Apart from Mrs. Midgely and Enders, I'm being given the silent treatment. Willis seems to have all but disappeared. Lorraine slinks around, glaring. And that little weirdo, Campbell, is just plain threatening."

Angelica glanced at the bedroom door, then at the door to Sinjun's bathroom. Still everything was silent. "Campbell's an earnest kid. He's into saving the world from the forces of evil. Why would he want to threaten you?"

"Simple. He's decided I *am* one of the forces of evil. Look, don't waste time on that now. Tell Sinjun you've changed your mind. Honestly, I think that's what all this is about. He's got a grubby past—or present—and he wants to make sure he puts a stop to any ideas you've got about finding him out and going public. He's afraid for his *reputation*, Angel. I swear he is."

Bull's-eye. "You're right. But I can't stop now."

Brenda's scrambling thoughts were almost audible. "Of course you can. Tell him you've changed your mind. Say you've decided to go back to *Verity*. Say *anything*, but get out of there."

Angelica made up her mind. "Listen to me and don't interrupt. This is personal. I know I told you otherwise, but I lied. I'm going after this man because someone close to me asked me to.

It's personal and it's a matter of honor. I *have* to do it. Do you understand?"

Too long elapsed before Brenda said, "Not really."

"Then *accept* it and don't question me now. In time I'll be able to explain everything. If I go along with the restrictions here and keep my nose clean, and you play the charming houseguest there, we'll come through okay."

"Sinjun told you he thought someone was trying to kill him."

As if she could ever forget. "I know. And I intend to find out why. The problem is, he's definitely behaving as if he doesn't trust me and I'm not sure how to get around that."

Brenda clicked her tongue. "I've seen the way he looks at you. There's nothing like the promise of a good fuck to take the edges off a man's reasoning."

Angelica covered her eyes and felt her legs go rubbery. Was she the only twenty-eight-year-old virgin in the world?

"Did you hear what I said?" Brenda asked.

"Yes."

"And you get my drift?"

"You think I ought to use sex to get what I want from Sinjun Breaker?"

A pause. "In a word, yes. Now, if he were less than any red-blooded girl's dream I might try to think of something else. Angel, just looking at the man's a turn-on."

She couldn't deny the truth. "Before I left to look for Sinjun in Hawaii you told me I should try to persuade him to agree to the biography by letting him think I was interested in him . . . sexually. You said it would stroke his ego and make him more likely to consider my proposition. I sort of . . . Well, I didn't intend it to go quite the way it did, but I definitely gave him the impression that I . . . He doesn't think I find him repulsive."

A familiar, uninhibited laugh rolled along the line. "No kidding? That's encouraging."

"I don't intend to . . . I don't approve of, well, going all the way to get what you want."

Brenda laughed again. "Going all the way? I haven't heard anyone say that since I was a kid. It's up to you to decide how important this thing is to you. Then you'll do what you have to do to get it. That's the end of my lecture."

"Thank you."

"How important is it?"

"Very," Angelica said. "When it's all over I'll explain and then you'll understand. Do you think you're safe there?"

"*Yes*. Don't worry about me. Enders is sane and I think Willis is, too, in his way. There may be some nutty connection between Lorraine and Campbell and she hates any woman under a hundred and ten. You can work out the rest."

Angelica didn't want to work it out. She glanced at the door to Sinjun's bathroom again. "Okay, Brenda. Sit tight. This call was easy to place. But tomorrow I get sprung to go to Kertz-Breaker for some meeting Sinjun's having. I'll find a way to get through to you then."

She was still looking at the bathroom door when the good-byes were said and the phone was back on the desk.

She would see headlights and hear the electric gates open as easily from Sinjun's bedroom as from this one.

Kicking off her shoes, she dumped her oversized purse upside down on the bed and fished a pocket flashlight from the heap that emerged.

Quickly, she let herself into Sinjun's dark bathroom and crossed toward his bedroom.

The door stood open.

The room beyond was dark except for the moon's pale illumination.

No previous assignment had caused her to creep around in the dark—in a very possibly dangerous man's bedroom—searching for something the dangerous man definitely wouldn't want her to find. The fact that she didn't have any idea what the something might be did nothing for her confidence.

But she desperately needed some leads.

The moon showed her the way to a tall chest against the wall opposite the foot of the bed. Starting at the bottom because it was easiest, Angelica shone the pencil-thin beam of her flashlight into the drawers, working her way up, carefully lifting and dropping the contents. Thoroughness wasn't an option, but she found nothing unusual.

She switched off the light, flattened herself against the chest and looked around the deeply shadowed room. There was a sound, but it was only the pounding of her pulse in her ears.

Bedside drawers contained papers, none of which meant a thing to Angelica. Without removing books from floor-to-ceiling bookcases, there was no way to find out if something secret was hidden behind them.

A chest with a mirror on the wall above it stood between two of the windows. Angelica approached it slowly and turned on the flashlight again.

The drawers were shallow. The second one contained a worn flat box secured in each direction by a dirty rubber band.

With fingers that shook, Angelica took off the bands, set them carefully on top of the chest and opened the box.

Just a photograph. She realized her shoulders were hunched and let them drop. A black-and-white photograph in a cheap ornate frame. The flashlight beam picked out a couple standing on the single step before the entrance to a peeling white clapboard building. Angelica looked closer

and stopped breathing. The man was a very young
Sinjun Breaker and beside him, clinging to his arm,
stood a too-thin, dark-haired girl wearing a dress
that did not hide her pregnancy.

Angelica forced herself to breathe. By the door
of the pictured building was a notice board. She
couldn't read what it said, but she knew she was
looking at a dilapidated church and that the woman beside Sinjun was Dee-Dee Cahler Breaker. This
pathetic thing was a wedding picture.

The world would pore over this image—the proof
of Sinjun Breaker's beginnings—and they'd be hungry to know what had become of Mrs. Breaker.

Working so fast she almost dropped it, Angelica
turned the frame over and eased off the back. From
the look of the box that had contained the photo,
Sinjun hadn't opened it for years. If she was careful—and clever—he wasn't likely to notice it had
been touched.

She slid out the photograph, replaced the back of
the frame and returned it to the box. Blessedly, the
fraying rubber bands didn't break when they were
stretched again. She might not be so lucky when
she returned her prize.

With the box back where it came from and the
drawer closed, Angelica noticed writing on the back
of the picture. The penciled words were faded and
she had to peer closely. The initial M and a date.
The date of the marriage. The thought that the girl
had probably done the writing and that she must
have held hope for a brighter future with her new
husband and baby constricted Angelica's throat.

She stared at the writing again and remembered other writing. Her own . . . And the same
date. She'd made a note of that day and year
herself.

"Oh!" She couldn't stop herself from crying out.
That was the day Dee-Dee died . . .

Angelica's gaze flew up—to the mirror.

Moonlight struck a blue-white blade over the face of the man who stood in front of the closed bathroom door.

"Keep your hands where I can see them," Sinjun Breaker said.

Fifteen

"**W**alk toward me," Sinjun told her. "Slowly. And keep those hands exactly where they are."

She didn't move.

He edged sideways, toward the nearest bedside table. Holding the Beretta in his left hand, he reached to press the switch on the lamp. Its immediate glow was subdued by a black glass shade but he could see what he needed to see.

No gun in sight.

"Come on." He motioned her toward him with his free hand. "Come to me, Angel. Show me what you've found."

The mask of panic slipped slowly from her face, but fear still shaded her eyes. "You're into picking on defenseless women, aren't you?"

His thighs tensed and he sucked in his belly as if she'd hit him. "Defenseless?" If he gave her the smallest advantage she'd use it well. Smart, this—this whoever or *whatever* she was. "Don't tell me that cute peashooter of yours isn't tucked away where it should be fun to find."

"You always go for the cheap shot. Even in the little things."

God, but she was something. Haughty even when he found her searching his room—even when she was alone in his house and he was pointing a gun at her.

Sinjun advanced. "If you won't come to me, I guess I'll just have to come to you. Don't move those hands."

"I went through the drawers in your room," she announced loudly. "There, I've admitted it."

"Thanks for telling me. For a minute back there I thought I was imagining things."

"You're trying to stop me from doing my job."

"We're going to get to that," he said, all silk. He passed the foot of the bed and arrived in front of her. "In fact, why don't you start talking about your *job?* You might begin with the name or names of whoever's paying you to do whatever you intend to do to me."

"No one's paying me." Her brown eyes were huge, her parted lips moist where her tongue had made its nervous pass. Worn loose, her blonde hair looked mussed and so did the short camel-colored linen tank dress that had been crisp when they left Hell. The dress clung to her breasts, her hips and thighs.

Sinjun moved his eyes slowly from the dip of wear-softened fabric between her thighs, to her breasts. If she wore a bra it was one of those great little numbers that offered up their contents without covering the hot spots. Her nipples made enticing bumps in the dress.

He'd seen her naked once, but he hadn't touched her—not really. He wanted to touch her now.

For the first time he realized what she held, like a platen, before her.

"You told me I was a prisoner!" Her voice skated upward. "You said I couldn't leave without setting off alarms, then you left me all alone in this house."

"No, I didn't."

The photograph shook in her fingers and he

smiled grimly. She talked a great line but she was one terrified woman.

"That . . . Your housekeeper's somewhere in the house. Big deal. Are you going to tell me she'd help me if you'd told her not to?"

"No. I'm not going to tell you that. Give me the photograph."

"I didn't hear you come back."

He eased the picture from her. "I didn't leave. Mrs. Falon did. In my car."

Her mouth opened but no sound came out.

"It's just you and me. That should make you very happy. You've got me all to yourself for . . . For as long as I decide that's the way it's going to be."

"You're threatening me."

"You bet I am."

She tried to jerk away but had nowhere to go. "You're . . . You're *horrible*."

Sinjun laughed. "And for a lady of the world, you do say some cute things. Your nipples are cute, too. Real cute."

"*Stop* it."

If shocking her would loosen her tongue, he had no intention of stopping.

Bundling her wrists together in the same hand with his gun, he made himself look at the photograph. And he made himself show nothing of the old rage he felt. "Not much of a wedding, huh?"

"So you don't deny that's what it is?"

He feigned amazement. "Why would I deny it? Dee-Dee got married. To me. This is the picture of the happy couple." Edging Angelica aside, he cracked the top drawer of the chest and pushed the photograph inside. "I can't tell you how disappointed I am that you're not interested in writing my biography after all."

She raised her chin defiantly. "I *am* interested."

"You're a liar. Is someone . . . Jeez, how could that be? There's no one who'd bother."

"Is someone what?" she asked through clenched teeth.

"Okay. Is someone trying to get even with me through you?"

For an instant the fearless jut of her jaw wobbled. Her eyes slid away.

"I see," he said softly. "For some reason you know and I don't, there's a contract out on me. Right?"

She shook her head.

"Oh, I think so. And killing me isn't enough. My reputation's supposed to be assassinated right with me."

"I don't know what you're talking about."

He backed her against the chest and anchored her there with his hips. Her flinch and the shift of her body made certain they both knew the condition he was in.

Finally, panting, she said, "I thought you'd gone out."

"Obviously." He ground into her a little. "And obviously, you were wrong."

She moistened her lips again and he came close to losing control.

"I . . . I want to know things about you."

He wanted to know things about her, too. "What things?"

"Personal things."

"Ask."

"I have. You've refused. You toss me canned speeches about business and Bruno Kertz. You want to make it all pretty, and it *isn't, is it?*"

"Oh, I like fire in a woman." He liked the faint sheen on her skin and the way her breasts rose and fell.

"Let me go."

"I don't think so, lady. Not until you tell me the name of the bastards who hired you."

"*Damn.*" She wrenched her wrists within his

hand. A futile effort. "There is no one, I tell you. But I want to know why you think there is. This is the stuff I need from you, Sinjun. I *need* to know the things about your life that make you think someone would hire a killer, for God's sake! Trust me, damn it."

He laughed and wrapped his free arm around her. "Trust you? Don't you know that men like me learned how *not* to trust in the cradle? There are a very few people I trust and it never comes easily. The men I do trust earned it, just like I earned theirs." He began slipping down the zipper at the back of her dress.

"What are you doing?" Either he was seeing panic in those big brown eyes again, or she was as aroused as he was. He'd bet on the latter.

Sinjun quickly gripped and lifted her to sit on the chest. "I'm undressing you," he told her.

She became absolutely still. "Why?"

He laughed again. "Dumb question."

"Stop this."

"Tell me who you're working for and I will."

A giggle bubbled from her throat. She was breathing heavily now. "I'm it. I'm the big bad army you think is out to ruin your reputation—and *kill* you. My God."

The Beretta had to be hurting her. He switched her wrists to his right hand and tossed the gun to the bed behind him. "Why do you want to kill me?"

"I *don't!* I do not have the vaguest idea what you mean. You say the helicopter explosion may have been deliberate. Are you suggesting I could arrange that? It's preposterous!"

He put her wrists back in his left hand. "I'm not convinced." It was a gamble, but he said, "When I look through your things, I'm going to find a black scarf and dark glasses."

She struggled afresh. "You're mad!"

Sinjun used one leg to nudge her knees apart, pushed her skirt up to her hips and pressed himself into the notch of her thighs. "We'll see. When I've done what's got to be done here, I'll let you help me search."

"I don't have a black scarf. I do have sunglasses. Who doesn't?"

True enough, but he wasn't convinced because he couldn't afford to be. He resumed attending to the zipper, sliding it down, watching in the mirror behind her as first the back of her black bra was revealed, then the slender line of her spine all the way to lacy black bikini panties.

She wriggled, but only succeeded in making the dress start to slip off her shoulders. "What are you going to do?"

"Simple," he said, while his blood pounded harder—and he grew harder—if that were possible. "I'm going to see exactly where you've hidden that little gun of yours."

"I don't have it."

"Forgive me for finding that difficult to believe."

Her shoulders were smooth and white, more so against the thin black bra straps.

The dress traveled farther down her arms.

"I was wrong to come in here and poke around."

"You're right." He couldn't resist bending to press his lips to the curve where the side of her neck met her shoulder. She trembled wildly. Sinjun's eyes closed for an instant and he breathed her in. "I like the way you smell—and the way you taste."

"We can forget this evening ever happened. I'll write my story and I'll clear everything I do with you."

"I don't believe you." Her bra strap needed little encouragement to go the way of her dress. His mouth gave that encouragement. "Do you expect me to accept that you picked Bliss, Montana, out of thin air and then just *stumbled* over old Mrs. Cahler?"

Her breathing rasped. "I'm a reporter. A journalist. I look for facts, then a hook, a slant. It's no secret that you came from Montana. People know you were poor. When you aren't around they enjoy talking about . . ."

"Yes?" He smiled cynically into the hollow above her collarbone. "When I'm not around they take the only pleasure they can when it comes to me. They sneer about what you so aptly referred to as *white trash*. White trash who beat them all out. They hate it and that suits me. I don't need them."

"I followed your trail backwards to Bliss, Montana. That's the truth."

"And you don't know anything about trying to shoot me from a car on Broadway here in Seattle?"

"My God!"

"Is that shock that it happened, or shock that I'm connecting it with you? How good a driver are you?"

The rasps became sobs. "A damn good driver."

"I'll bet you are." In two swift moves, her arms were free of the dress and the "damn good driver" sat before him, bared all the way to bunched linen and black panties that scarcely covered her mound. Bared except for an inviting bra that was exactly what he'd pictured. Black satin, and fastened in front where a tiny red satin rose nestled between her breasts, the cups stopped just below stiff pink nipples.

All expression slipped from Angelica's features. "Do you see any guns?"

He inclined his head. "Not yet. But . . ." Letting the words trail off, he rested his index finger on the red satin rose.

"Well, make sure."

Her defiance sent a fresh thrill into places that had already been tested too far. "I will." He kissed her then, full on her lips. Just like the first time, there was the slightest resistance before she let him part her lips and curl his tongue inside.

The kiss was long, and slow and hard. He released her wrists and she rested her hands flat on his chest. He still wore the white shirt but he felt her heat.

"Put your arms around my neck," he murmured.

She did, and he went to work on the red rose. It parted and he filled his hands with her breasts.

Angelica whimpered into his mouth, but she didn't try to stop him. Her nipples were hard buds against his circling palms.

He didn't know who she was. Not really. Minutes ago he'd been prepared to try her for attempted murder and find her guilty.

Feeling her breasts on his chest—minus the shirt—became imperative. Sinjun ripped his buttons undone and layered himself against her.

They kissed like starving people, their mouths rocking and biting, their tongues reaching.

He slid his hands down inside her panties and cupped her bottom. Somewhere in his numbed brain a small voice said the lady was hiding no gun.

Her fists, clenched into balls on his shoulders, made him raise his face. "What?" he asked her.

Frowning, she looked into his eyes. "This is . . . I . . ." Her gaze shifted down and she stroked his chest, his ribs, his belly. "I didn't even remember to bring the gun with me."

He almost smiled. Almost. "If you did, you aren't carrying it on you." Still rubbing her breasts, he slowly bent to take a nipple into his mouth. She gasped, started to pull away, then moaned and pressed closer. Sinjun applied the very tip of his tongue to erect, wet flesh and, reluctantly, lifted his head again. "What are you, Angel? What are you really?"

"I've told you. I'm a—"

"A journalist."

"*Yes.*" Her fingers bit into his arms. "I know nothing about any attempts on your life," she said. "And finding out about Dee-Dee was just dumb luck."

"Luck?" His eyes flew to her face.

She sighed. "*Yes, luck.* When a journalist hits on something that looks like a fresh angle, that's luck. Surely you can understand that."

"I understand that you've cooked up some grubby theory about me and the girl who was my wife for . . ." He pressed his lips together. "She was my wife."

"For less than a day?"

His heart seemed to stop beating.

"The date of your wedding's on the back of that picture. That is what that date is?"

Now he could hardly remember what had made him keep the damn picture. "Yes." Or maybe he could.

"Dee-Dee died that day."

His hands circled her neck loosely. "That night." The woman before him was so lovely, so desirable— and she was hurting him more than she could imagine.

"Murdered?"

He had an absurd urge to yell. He said, "*Yes.* Yes, she was murdered. Not the way you think of murder, but murder just the same."

"Someone beat her and she died because of that?"

"Do we have to keep doing this?"

"Let me into all of your life. Let me ask questions and give me honest answers." Her grip on him softened and she smoothed his shoulders soothingly. "Stop suspecting me of being something I'm not. I'm nothing more than a recorder."

He'd like to believe her. If he did, it was back to square one. There was a killer out there somewhere and his was the last name the bastard thought of before he went to sleep each night.

When he focused on Angelica's face, he saw how her eyes shone with intensity, how her full, very-kissed lips trembled.

"Come on, Sinjun," she said. "*Trust* me. Let me do the best job possible on telling your story."

She leaned toward him, her mouth parted in invitation, her beautiful breasts begging for much more of what he'd already given them.

"It'll be good," she told him. "With you and me working together, it's got to be more than good. It'll be great."

"Hell." He shook his head and stepped back.

"Sinjun?"

"Look at you." Sinjun looked at her and he saw how she shook with excitement. "You want this so badly, you'll do anything to get it. *Anything*." Her thighs remained spread, showing the black satin triangle that covered very little. "Oh, lady, I do believe you will do one fantastic piece of work on your story. I believe you'll do a fantastic job on whatever you decide to do in this life."

"I—"

"No." He held up a silencing hand. "Holy *shit*. Regardless of what you think about what just happened between us, I've never made a woman have sex with me."

She crossed her arms under her breasts.

"Get out." He couldn't trust his control much longer. "Get back in that room before I do what you're weeping for me to do."

"You won't regret—"

"Shut *up*, damn you. You decided to do what I'm sure you'd do very well: *Fuck* this stupid bastard's brains out until he lets you have anything you want."

"No." Holding her dress, she slid to the floor.

"Save it. You can have your story."

"Yes." With jerky steps, she edged around him. "But I didn't try to do what you said—"

"The hell you didn't, *Angel*."

She reached the bathroom door. "Thank you. I—I wouldn't know how to do what you're saying."

"I never forced a woman. And sure as hell, no woman's going to *force* me. To do anything."

"I just want to write your story."

"*Good*," he roared, following her through the bathroom and pushing her into her bedroom. "We start tomorrow."

Clutching her dress with one hand, trying to shield her breasts with the other, she backed away.

Sinjun looked at her, all the way from her staring eyes to her toes, and back. "If and when you and I get around to fucking each other's brains out, it'll be *my* decision. I already know what you want. See you tomorrow."

He slammed the door, stripped off his clothes and stepped into his shower. For a few moments before turning on the water, he listened. No sound came from the room with the four-poster bed.

Icy water blasted his skin.

Other parts of his body hardly seemed to notice.

Sixteen

❦

$\mathcal{A}$t 8:00 A.M. a man who identified himself as one of Mr. Breaker's assistants called and asked what kind of laptop Angelica preferred.

"Just about anything," Angelica said, reluctantly sitting up in bed. "I use WordPerfect. Thank you." She hung up.

The night still draped her mind, a collage of images and sensations from what had happened with Sinjun, and what had happened after she'd left him, when she'd hovered between sleep and consciousness and the world became a tilted, terrifying place.

At 8:10 A.M. a woman who cheerfully identified herself as Mrs. Falon called to ask what Angelica would like for breakfast.

"Toast, please," Angelica said, falling back onto the pillows. "And coffee with lots of cream. Thank you."

She would have to pull herself together, shower, dress and set about facing a day when she couldn't avoid looking at Sinjun, listening to Sinjun—*feeling* Sinjun whether or not he touched her.

Angelica struggled to sit up again and allowed her legs to dangle over the side of the high bed. If she'd actually slept for three hours she'd be amazed.

Water had run in Sinjun's bathroom for far too

long after he left her standing, almost naked, staring at the door he'd slammed.

She shuddered. How could she look him in the face again? They'd both be remembering last night. And he'd be thinking she responded to him only to get what she wanted.

"Don't think," she muttered. "Don't think. Don't think."

All the way to her own bathroom, gathering clean underclothes, trying not to look at the ruined heap of clothes she'd discarded in the early hours of the morning and finally climbing into the shower, she repeated the mantra.

She said, "Don't think," as shampoo ran down her face, but saw the whole lamplighted scene like a video replay.

The instant Angelica turned off the water, sounds came from the bedroom.

With agonizing care she slid open the shower door and grabbed for a bath sheet.

"Good morning!" a woman's voice caroled. "Shall I bring your coffee in?"

Angelica almost said no. Rapidly, she wound the bath sheet around her body and said, "Yes, please." Friends were in short supply around here.

The comfortable, gray-haired woman who entered, wearing an unremarkable navy-blue dress and sensible matching flat lace-ups, was any orphaned child's fantasy mother. "Good morning!" she announced again, setting a substantial, black-glazed mug of creamy coffee beside a ruby-toned sink. She put a plate of toast beside the mug and regarded Angelica with kind brown eyes. "Don't mind me. Nibble what you want and let me know when you're ready for some fresh."

Angelica blotted her hair. "I won't need anything else, thank you." She wanted to ask questions. Lots of questions. What did Sinjun have for breakfast? What time did he eat? Had Mrs. Falon taken him his coffee yet?

"Mr. Breaker said you had a very hard day yesterday." Mrs. Falon appeared concerned. "He said you were to take it easy and he'll be back for you at twelve-thirty sharp. He said to tell you the meeting's at one. Oh, and Mr. Gill will be along with some things for you, but he won't be stopping, and someone's bringing a computer for you."

Sinjun had already left. "Thank you very much." There seemed nothing else to say, except that she didn't want any *things* Chuck Gill might be likely to bring. Mrs. Falon could do nothing about that. "Thank you," Angelica repeated.

"Don't mention it." Mrs. Falon bustled away. "You will call when you want something?"

"Yes," Angelica said, surveying her reflection in the bathroom's mirrored walls until she heard the bedroom door close behind the housekeeper.

Within seconds, she hurried to look down from the windows onto the driveway. Inside the tall stucco walls lay perfect lawns and beds of massed roses in full bloom.

She could dress and walk out . . . and give it all up.

Last night, when Sinjun had asked if someone was trying to get at him through her, there'd been a split second when she'd thought he knew the whole story.

A tanned girl in a cotton shirt, jeans and rubber boots came into sight below the windows. She carried a bucket and pruning shears. While Angelica looked on, the girl inspected rosebushes, cutting off wilted blooms as she went.

Sun and flowers. A warm, peaceful morning. All so normal.

But not a single thing was normal for Angelica.

The phone rang.

Angelica let it ring again, and again, and again before she picked it up.

"Finally," Sinjun said. "What took so long?"

She waggled the cord. "Maybe I was asleep."

"You shower in your sleep?"

Angelica felt slightly sick. "Does Mrs. Falon have instructions to inform you of every move I make?"

"Mrs. Falon is very dedicated. Toast, and coffee with lots of cream. You're pretty. The pink towel suits you but you need fattening up. A few good meals would improve you, to be precise."

Angelica couldn't help smiling. "I see. I don't think I like feeling watched."

After a pause, he said, "Yet that's how you make your living, isn't it? Watching people? But I guess that's different."

"I think we both know it is. Who does Mrs. Falon think I am?"

"A biographer," he said promptly. "Who should she think you are?"

Every question seemed designed to trip her. "It was a simple inquiry. I didn't want her to think I was . . ."

"If I'd brought you home in that capacity, you'd be sleeping in my room."

In that capacity. He made sexual liaisons sound casual—or maybe even clinical. "Do you really think someone's trying to kill you?"

"I know they are."

The little hairs on her spine prickled. "And you think I'm that person."

"As I told you when . . . I told you I *don't* think so anymore."

"But you do think I'm unscrupulous." Her heart drummed. "You think I'm the kind of woman who will go to any lengths to get what she wants, including . . . Well, any lengths."

"Including offering sex to someone she doesn't want to have sex with?" He waited an instant before finishing. "Yes, that's what I think. And now you know I'm not interested under those circumstances."

"Yes." But that's not what she'd been doing, not in the end. In the end, she'd wanted him as she'd never wanted a man before. She *had* never wanted a man before, but she couldn't tell him that. He'd laugh and call her a liar.

"We seem to have run out of conversation," Sinjun said. His voice was so cool and distant.

"Someone called about a computer."

"It's on its way."

"I don't want Chuck to bring me clothes."

He cleared his throat. "He's going to anyway. A woman who does that sort of thing is picking them out. You're bound to find something that works."

"I don't like feeling as if I'm a prisoner."

"You aren't," he said shortly. "When I first invited—or told you to come with me, I intended to keep you where you'd have difficulty hurting me without hurting yourself. I'm not worried about that anymore. But I can't stop you from walking out if you want to anyway."

"The alarms—"

"Just tell Mrs. Falon you want to leave."

"I don't," she said, without ever planning to.

"Because of your precious story."

He wasn't asking her a question. "Yes." And she was no longer telling the whole truth.

"I think you're even more ambitious than I am and I didn't think that was possible."

"You tested me last night."

His laugh brought goose bumps to her skin. "I tested you and you passed. You'll give your all for the cause."

The cause. Now she was convinced he still had no idea what that cause was. "Last night was unfortunate," she told him. "But if it convinced you I'm not an assassin it served a purpose."

Her purpose had become fuzzy as her desire for Sinjun grew. But she couldn't forget her mother's dying wish and the rest of what Marlene Golden had disclosed in her letter.

"Angelica," Sinjun said softly. "I don't think you plan to stick a knife in my back, but I'm not convinced of another single thing about you."

Including the possibility that she was falling in love with him? "I understand you expect to pick me up at twelve-thirty." Prisoners fell in love with jailers. Kidnap victims became infatuated with their captors.

Sinjun had already told her she was free to go when she pleased.

"If you still want to come," he said.

"Yes," Angelica told him.

Kertz-Breaker occupied the first and the top five floors of a twenty-seven-story black glass building on Third Avenue in the middle of downtown Seattle. Kertz-Breaker owned the entire building.

The drive from Queen Anne Hill had been short, yet Angelica felt as if endless extra miles had been put on her nerves.

"The meeting you're going to sit in on is important," Sinjun said as they swept into an underground garage. "And touchy. To fill you in as much as you need to be, the people we're dealing with want a great deal for very little."

How informative. "Isn't that what everyone wants?"

He looked sideways at her, bringing the car to a full stop at the same time. "Some of us still think in terms of equity—in all things."

It was the first time he'd actually met her eyes since he'd arrived at the mansion and Mrs. Falon had come to take Angelica downstairs.

Now—still staring at her—he turned off the ignition. "What do you think about honesty and fair play, Angelica?"

She thought that concentrating on anything

around Sinjun Breaker was becoming too difficult for comfort. "I've always believed in fair play." And she was going to have to switch off the havoc his yellow-green eyes and slightly smiling mouth could create for her.

"As you've already suggested, we're going to have to get past last night and attend to business," he said.

She nodded, but felt heat rising in her cheeks.

Sinjun turned sideways in his seat. "The reason I went to the island when I did was because it was obvious my skin was a hot-ticket item in Seattle."

"You could be mistaken about that," she said quietly.

He let out an exasperated breath. "Did you attend the police academy?"

Angelica smiled a little. "No. But I know what you probably mean. They do tend to want to see the corpse before they put down their coffee cups."

"You said it."

She was the first to look away. "Maybe you shouldn't have come back here."

"Why, Angel, you almost sound as if you care."

According to Momma, there was a debt to be paid and Sinjun was the debtor.

She averted her face. If she made him pay off that debt, the rest wouldn't matter anymore. Sinjun could never be any part of her life then.

"I was rough on you last night."

Angelica closed her eyes.

His fingers, slipping to cup her jaw, seemed to pluck the air out of the car. "Look at me," he said.

She let him ease her face around, but kept her eyes downcast.

"It didn't come easily, did it?" he persisted.

The next breath hurt her throat. "It?"

"Coming on to me for the good of the cause?"

"I . . . didn't . . ."

"Not at first, but you did when that was what you thought it would take."

She shook her head.

"Look at me."

Slowly, she raised her eyes to his.

"What do you see?"

"I . . ." Her swallow clicked. "A man."

His eyes narrowed. "I don't know how to read you. I thought I did."

"I'm not very complex."

He gave a short laugh. "You don't joke well. You're the most complicated woman I've ever met."

The garage was dimly lit. A yellow beam cast a panther gleam into his eyes. His dark hair was still too long for convention; it curled where it touched his very white collar. The bones of his face—cheek, jaw, nose—were blades against lean shadows, his eyebrows bold arches.

Not a gentle face.

Not the face of a man who would easily forgive.

Angelica's gaze shifted to his mouth. A mouth only barely short of being beautiful, the outline clear, the texture firm. And it could feel . . . Somehow she would get through this and forget him.

Sure she would.

"So tell me," he said. "Now you've studied me so carefully, what do you really see?"

"I see someone I'd rather know was alive . . . somewhere." Her voice broke and, horrified, she closed her mouth.

Sinjun frowned and said, very softly, "Why do I get the feeling *I* may be the one who's not seeing clearly?" He cursed, just as softly. "I don't need this now, but y'know—and I'm almost sure I'm going to regret saying this—but I hope there may be a chance for something between you and me. Something that might bring us both pleasure."

Angelica's heart hit bottom—and then it ached. Damn fate. Why now? Why with this man? "I'm a really terrible game player," she told him, meaning every word. "Why don't we go to your meeting."

Moments slipped by before he reached beside her and unhooked her seat belt. While she held very still, he tilted his face, observing hers, detail by detail—so close she felt his clean, warm breath on her lips. "Let's do that," he said. "But afterwards, tonight, why don't you and I try to start over?"

She couldn't answer him.

"Angel? I'm not suggesting we go to bed." He smiled and the effect was devastating. "Not that I think that would be such a terrible idea. But maybe we should start with something expensively romantic like fish and chips on the waterfront— and maybe a walk by the bay in the dark."

Her own smile was reflexive.

"Starting to sound interesting? Honest, I'll be a perfect gentleman. And think of the opportunity to learn more about Sinjun the man."

"The meeting," she said, wanting desperately to say *Yes, oh, yes.*

"Fish and chips and a dark walk?" he persisted, still smiling.

Angelica pushed her hair back. "The meeting first."

He sounded boyish when he said, "It's a deal."

Soon he was ushering her into the hushed, gray-carpeted corridors and reception areas on the ground floor of his home offices. Conversation ceased whenever he was spotted and it didn't resume while he was still within earshot. Angelica noted that his employees showed respect that didn't seem to have an undercurrent of dislike— or fear.

All the way, he held her arm and each time he glanced at her she saw the battle he was fighting: to trust or not to trust? She didn't even have that luxury. For Angelica the battle was to stop *wanting* to trust—stop wanting him.

"This elevator only goes to my suite," he told her when they'd walked from the back to the front of the building. A man in a dark suit sprang forward to press the button and Sinjun nodded at him. "I see Chuck did a nice job finding you some clothes."

"This is mine," she told him of the russet silk jacket, shell and walking shorts she wore with matching flat suede pumps. "Mrs. Falon is a whiz with an iron."

The doors closed and they started up.

"Chuck didn't come by?"

Angelica grimaced. "He certainly did. My . . . The room is half-filled with boxes."

"But you don't like anything?"

She lifted her chin. "I haven't looked at it."

"You are one stubborn little female." But he said it with a grin. "We'll continue this later—maybe over those fish and chips. You do like—"

"Fish and chips? As a matter of fact, I do." The net was growing so tight, the cutting free could only leave her bloody.

"Good. Chuck will be at this meeting. He sits in on most things. It's an arrangement most people don't understand, but they don't have to. Apart from him, you'll only know Mary."

Ah, yes. Mary. For a few, foolish minutes she'd forgotten sweet M.A.B. of the monogrammed towels, the twin robes . . . and the pretty box of foil packets.

But he hadn't gone to her last night.

"Here we are," Sinjun said.

She couldn't let herself care for him. He'd said there had been a woman in his recent past who wasn't "fun" anymore. It now looked as though that woman was Mary and that meant—if Momma had been right about him—that it was Mary who Sin used in his plot to get whatever business information he needed from Momma's . . . *friend*.

Her first impression of Sinjun's suite was of filtered light through a tinted glass wall. Light turned a softly silvered gray and spread airy strokes that both contrasted with and complemented bold Oriental screened walls and more of the black lacquer she already knew Sinjun favored.

"Exquisite," she murmured.

His pleasure was in his deep voice when he said, "Thank you. The meeting will be in the boardroom."

A short walk across steel-gray carpet took them to double rosewood doors that stretched from floor to very high ceiling. Sinjun threw open the doors and a rumble of conversation rolled out.

The company gathered at the opposite end of an astonishing Chinese-red conference table—one woman and several men—turned to face the newcomers.

"Good afternoon, Mary," Sinjun said, "gentlemen."

Standing a pace behind him, Angelica had an instant, desperate longing to lean against a wall . . . to stop herself from fainting.

Sinjun was speaking. He glanced back at her and she saw his smile as if through a veil.

" . . . Angelica Dean," she heard him say, and she stared across the room.

"Angelica, this is Garth Lieber. We're hoping to become partners on a project that's very dear to both of our hearts."

She saw the tall, silver-haired, powerfully built man Sinjun indicated.

Finally, she met Garth Lieber's brown eyes, the eyes of the man who, for more than twenty years, had been her mother's secret lover.

Seventeen

"I told Garth you'd insist he take the seat with
the best view," Mary Barrett said—gushed.
"Tell him yourself, Sinjun."

"By all means," Sinjun said.

This was it. The end. Angelica clutched the notebook she carried so tightly, its edges bit into her
palm. Garth would open his mouth and say, *"My
little Angel!"*

She stood as if her feet were one with the soft
gray carpet.

Garth smiled at her . . . *politely.*

He smiled as if he'd never seen her before in his life.

And he shook his head, so imperceptibly Angelica couldn't be certain she'd seen it at all. "Pleased
to meet you, Miss Dean," he said, walking toward
her, large hand outstretched. "A biographer, eh?
Can't say I've ever actually met one before."

She loosened her grip on the notebook and put
her hand into his. "Yes," she said woodenly as he
pumped her fingers.

"So our Sinjun's got hidden depths, has he? Something even more interesting than what we already
know? Come on, Sin, let us in on some of the dark
secrets."

"You'll have to read the book," Sinjun said, all
jovial nonchalance.

Angelica looked quickly from Sinjun to Garth

to Mary. If her mother's letter had any truth to it, Garth was the only one here who didn't know about Sin's plot with Mary.

Mary Barrett fluttered around the distinguished-looking man. "How about that drink now?" she said. "I'm sure Sinjun will join you and I know I will."

"Well . . ."

"*Scotch.*" In her mind, Angelica heard Garth speaking to her mother in the kitchen of the lovely Seattle home she'd been forced to leave. "*And just kiss it with soda.*" Momma used to come alive whenever Garth visited . . .

"By all means, we'll have a drink," Sinjun agreed. "Perhaps Peter would do the honors. Meet Peter Akers, Angelica. He's our long-range planning expert."

Angelica managed to say, "Hello."

"Hello," Akers echoed. A stocky man, thirtyish, with a thin blond crewcut and guileless blue eyes behind wire-framed glasses, he went to slide open a panel that concealed the bar.

"What will it be, Garth?" he asked.

Garth met Angelica's eyes again. "Since Miss Dean is the most interesting member of our company—so to speak—let's serve her first. What would you like to drink, Miss Dean?"

"Angelica," she said automatically. "Nothing for me, thanks."

He wasn't going to give her away.

"Fair enough—Angelica." Garth turned to Peter Akers. "Scotch," he said. "And just kiss it with soda."

A fresh wave of weakness rushed over Angelica. She sought the nearest chair and sat down. After all, she was a simple scribe and not part of the proceedings here—except as an observer.

Garth didn't want Sinjun to find out who she was. Angelica opened her notebook. Her silk blouse stuck to her back and she prayed the fact wouldn't become evident. She risked another glance at Garth, found his eyes upon her again and grew still.

He was willing her to join him in a lie. But why?

Garth had to be reeling from the shock of seeing her. And he also had to be questioning such a coincidence.

Drinks were served.

"Are you sure you aren't thirsty, Angelica?" It was Chuck Gill, wearing a dark suit, white shirt and tie with an ease that belied his usual attire, who smiled at her across the red table.

She shook her head. "No, thanks." She was confused and she wanted, more desperately than she'd ever wanted anything, to get out of here.

Garth, Sinjun and the four other men present took places at the table. Mary pulled a chair close to Garth and sat with her arm almost touching his.

Skins of Silk was mentioned frequently. A revolutionary beauty product that would replace cosmetic surgery for many. Heavily shrouded in secrecy, enough had been leaked about the preparation to ensure that "age-conscious women of the world awaited with desperation." These women were "panicked at the thought of the product coming onto the market too late." They would "pay anything for the hope of fresh youth without use of a scalpel."

In an odd monotone, Peter Akers reminded Garth that Kertz-Breaker had already signed an interim agreement with Lieber Enterprises and that it was time for more than vague projections for the release date of Skins of Silk.

Chuck simply listened.

Two other men, both accompanying Garth, took copious notes but had little to say.

Mary Barrett seemed intent only upon assuring Garth of Kertz-Breaker's absolute confidence in

Lieber Enterprises and in Skins of Silk in particular.

Angelica looked at Mary's left hand. No ring. But, after all, Marlene wouldn't have had to see a ring to believe there was an engagement—not when Garth had apparently backed up Mary's story.

And Garth would be likely to keep a relationship with Mary secret. After all, he'd have every reason to be afraid that Sinjun wouldn't approve of his chief financial officer's intimate involvement with a potential partner.

The possible reality of the situation stunned Angelica: Garth thought that he and Mary were the only ones who knew what he believed to be the truth about their relationship.

She looked away from them, through windows that spied upon the roofs of buildings that were giants in their own right. Angelica felt tears threaten and blinked. Truth was clean, like the innocent blue sky outside. Deception seeped from every side in this roomful of privileged people and she detested that she'd been drawn into the ugliness.

Garth was speaking again. "We don't expect our integrity to be questioned, Sin."

Integrity. A frightful urge to laugh passed blessedly quickly.

"Kertz-Breaker certainly doesn't question your integrity," Mary said earnestly to Garth.

The lady's your enemy, Angelica wanted to tell Garth. *You should have listened to Momma. She was right. Your sweet young thing repeats every word you speak in the dark.* But she couldn't tell him because—until she found a way to convince him otherwise—he wouldn't believe her, any more than he'd believed Momma.

For a long time Sinjun listened silently to the negotiations that flowed about him but at last he said, "You're asking Kertz-Breaker to make a considerable commitment."

The room grew still.

"You already knew that," Garth said.

Angelica watched, and scribbled—not knowing exactly what she wrote and not caring.

Sinjun consulted papers that Peter Akers had set before him. "We've already started making advances in accordance with the original agreement. These figures are double what was initially understood."

"*Initially?*" Garth gripped the edge of the table.

"Exactly. And that was more than eight months ago. Things change."

"Not unless I say they do. Not when *my* money is involved."

"Sin," Mary said. "Let's hear Garth out."

Garth drummed his fingers impatiently on the shiny red tabletop. "There's nothing to be heard out. You want fifty-one percent of Skins of Silk. I've agreed to sell it to you."

"You *asked* me to buy," Sinjun retorted. "I agreed on a price and now you think you can double it and still hold forty-nine percent?"

"I'm asking you to show stronger support. The project has *cost* double what we expected. *I'm* paying double, too."

Sinjun turned sideways in his chair. "What's going to make me want to show what you call *stronger* support?" He hung a sheet of paper between finger and thumb. "Your cost analysis isn't my problem and it doesn't make me want to give you a blank check."

"I'm not asking for a blank check." Garth leaned over the table for emphasis. "I'm asking a fair price for the biggest action to hit the beauty industry—*ever*."

"So you say," Sinjun remarked evenly.

One of Garth's men dropped his pen on the red table. "So we say?" he blustered. "So six years of research and incredible test results say." The pen rolled along the table, click-clicking, its gold surface winking.

When the pen arrived in front of Sinjun, he slapped his left hand over it. "Show me the results."

The pen's owner surged to his feet and fussed with an overhead projector.

"I'll see to the screen," Chuck said, rising at a more leisurely rate and pressing a button that operated another disappearing wall panel.

"No," Sinjun said abruptly as the image of a woman's lined face stared morosely from the first frame. A second frame, this one of the same woman, but smiling and virtually wrinkle-free, followed before he pushed back his chair and stood up. "You don't understand me, Garth. Before and after shots are the stuff of any cheap ad campaign."

Garth got to his feet. His face had turned a shade of mottled red. "What the fuck is this?"

"Save it," Sinjun said. "Give me facts and figures and projections. From the labs."

"Are you suggesting we've lied about this product?"

"No! Unless it's by omission. I think you've told us only as much as you think you have to, to get my money in your pockets. I didn't come here to be snowed with a bunch of snapshots.

"I want to know dates and figures. The dates are more important than the figures right now. You've already got a chunk of Kertz-Breaker money. When or *if* you get any more—"

"You signed an agreement," Garth roared.

"Agreements can be rescinded," Sinjun said smoothly. "As I was saying, whether or not you get any more money from us depends upon the date this product is scheduled to hit the market."

"Wait, wait, wait." One of Garth's people, a plump, sandy-haired man with a face reminiscent of a concerned spaniel, spread all ten fingers in the air. "Let's not get hasty here."

"Let's not," Mary agreed, turning on a scorching smile. "In fact, let's get these drinks freshened. I'll have coffee and sandwiches sent in for anyone who wants them."

In the crossfire of responses that followed, Angelica excused herself and slipped from the room.

"Ladies' room?" she said to the disinterested woman on sentry duty behind a reception desk.

Angelica followed directions, made the appropriate turn that took her out of sight of the receptionist and dropped gratefully into a convenient leather bucket chair. The chair was flanked by a table with a telephone on its shimmering top. She leaned sideways to rest her head against the cool, wood-paneled wall.

It was possible Sinjun didn't know a thing about Momma. Mary could have told her story out of spite. Afterwards, she'd be unlikely to admit to Sin that she'd bragged and repeated their plans to another party.

Brenda would be waiting for a call. Angelica picked up the phone.

She could tell Sin her whole story and ask him to be equally truthful.

And he could deny everything and kick her out.

Would he make up a tale about attempts on his life? She pulled the slip of paper with Brenda's island number on it from her pocket and pressed buttons.

The phone rang on Hell.

Angelica stretched out her legs, crossed her ankles and visualized the warm, peaceful serenity of the island.

Nothing was what it appeared to be anymore.

A muffled footfall brought her face up.

Garth stood a few feet away with his hands sunk deep into his pockets.

The sound of ringing continued. Angelica held the headset away, glanced at the earpiece and slowly hung up.

Garth said softly, "My little Angel."

Eighteen

❦

"*W*hat are you doing here?"

Of course he hadn't bought the coincidence theory. "You heard what Sinjun said, Garth." He looked somehow different, as if the interval since she'd last seen him had blurred all the lines she remembered. "It's been a long time."

His brown eyes pinned her. "Sinjun approached you to write his biography?"

The chair and telephone table were just inside a short hallway where men's and women's rest-room doors faced one another. Behind Angelica, a blank paneled wall formed the far end of the hall. Leaning against the corner, Garth effectively filled the space that was the only way out. She felt hemmed in—trapped.

"Whose idea was the biography, Angel?"

She pushed Brenda's telephone number back into her shorts pocket. "It was my idea." He asked what was she doing here. Not how was she recovering from her mother's death, or if she'd forgiven him for not making it to the funerral.

"Did you know I was in negotiation with Sinjun?" he asked.

Lying didn't come easily. Angelica said, "Why did you pretend not to know me?" Attack might be her only defense.

242

He jingled coins in his pockets. "I didn't want to embarrass you," he said finally.

"Embarrass me? Why would you embarrass me?"

Garth shrugged. "I don't know, really. You didn't attempt to say anything."

"You shook your head," she said. "And you called me *Miss Dean.*"

He wet his lips. "Let's say we both misunderstood and leave it at that. But I did think you might prefer to keep your personal life out of it. Out of what's supposedly a business arrangement . . . between you and Breaker."

"It is a business arrangement," she said shortly. "The flowers you sent for the funeral were beautiful."

The corners of his mouth jerked down. "Good. Sorry I couldn't be there."

So sorry he hadn't contacted her since and hadn't even mentioned the event until she prompted him. "I'm sure Momma would have understood."

" 'Course she would." He visibly grasped the escape she'd offered. "Reasonable woman, your mother."

Reasonable? For the second time in far too short a period, Angelica's eyes stung.

"You can be up-front with me, y'know, Angel."

Startled, she looked at his face. "What do you mean?"

"Did . . . Are we still friends?"

Her insides clenched. "Yes." He was asking if she knew about his affair with her mother.

"Yes?" He tipped his head and smiled. "Is that all—'yes'? I thought you and I were more than friends. I thought we were buddies."

Angelica trained her eyes on his. "So did I." She would not let him know how much his indifference had hurt her. "I've been traveling, but you could have reached me—if you'd wanted to."

The smile fixed. "I don't like being hemmed in, Angel."

Especially not by a gentle woman whose love for him made her so fragile. "Consider yourself unhemmed," Angelica said, making certain her own smile was jaunty. "Now what?"

He raised a quizzical eyebrow. "What do you mean?"

"Do we go back in there and say, 'Guess what? We've remembered we know each other. In fact, we've known each other all of Angelica's life.' Will that cover it, d'you think?"

"You know we can't do that."

She knew she could not tell him what had sent her in search of Sinjun—not yet, if ever.

"You understand, don't you, Angel?"

"Make it clearer."

A white line formed around his compressed lips. "Don't get smart. You won't say anything."

Angelica stood up and wished she hadn't. "I'm not a child anymore, Garth." At least when she was sitting his height advantage wasn't so obvious.

"No." He massaged his jaw. "I would have come to San Diego if I could. You know that."

"You've always been a man who did what he wanted to do."

"*Damn*, you sound like your mother."

She breathed deeply through her nose. "Thank you. My mother was a sweet woman."

"Yes. Yes, she was. Look, I'm sorry. I can't say more than that. I couldn't get away. I had commitments. You know how it goes."

She could imagine how things had probably been going between Garth and Mary. No doubt attending the funeral of his lover of more than twenty years hadn't met with his new woman's approval.

"How've you been, Angel?"

Now he would try platitudes. "Wonderful, thank you."

"Good." He smoothed his shirtfront in a gesture so familiar Angelica looked away. "Why Breaker?"

"He's an interesting man."

Garth considered before saying, "Yes, but how did you choose him?"

He was getting too close. "By chance really. I was reading the clip files, just poking around for something different, and I came up with him."

Garth looked anything but convinced. "Surely you've heard of Skins of Silk—*had* heard of it before today?"

"Of course." She forced a laugh. "Who hasn't?"

"Didn't you know Lieber was the developer?"

"Everyone knows."

"Not quite everyone." He dropped his head and looked up at her.

"It's very public, Garth. And I have a reason to notice, remember." She let him think about that. "After all, we do have a long shared history."

"We do indeed. You didn't expect to see me this afternoon?"

"I certainly did not." This was where the lines between lying and avoiding the truth blurred. "The connection between Lieber and Kertz-Breaker isn't general knowledge."

"No," he said thoughtfully. "No, I suppose it isn't. I thought you were happy with *Verity*."

"I was. And I may be again, but I needed a change of pace. That's why I decided to look into writing a biography." She was almost beginning to believe the story herself.

"And no one actually suggested Breaker to you?"

The woman who loved you sent me. She sent me because she loved you. "No one spoke to me about him."

"Are you sure?"

Angelica had always liked him, always looked forward to his visits. At this moment it was hard to remember exactly why. "Who would suggest

Sinjun Breaker to me?" she asked him quietly.

He managed to appear admirably blank. "No one in particular."

"Oh, I think there is. What other reason could you have for grilling me like this?"

"I—" He drew up his shoulders. "I—You do see what it looks like from my point of view."

"Tell me."

"It looks damned fishy," he blustered. "But if you insist it's the coincidence of the century, so be it."

Angelica frowned. "I can't imagine what else it *would* be." She decided to gamble on a bluff. "But we should tell Sinjun we're old friends. If he finds out later he's going to think it's weird."

"He won't find out," Garth said rapidly. "Why would he? *How* would he?"

"Why wouldn't he?"

Garth's shoulders rose again. "Did people know . . . Do you tell people you know me?"

Angelica shook her head slowly. "No. Momma always made it clear that you didn't want us to. She said it was because the two of you had known each other since before she was widowed." She paused and watched him, and saw him hold his breath. He was expecting her to say she knew he and Momma had been lovers. "Momma was puritanical in her way. She said she wouldn't risk having your name soiled by any talk about . . . Well, you can imagine."

"Yes."

She'd let him off the hook. Not because she wanted to, but because this wasn't a game she could play. "Momma was such an innocent, wasn't she?"

"Yes."

"How she could imagine that anyone would think her capable of some sort of clandestine relationship with you, I can't imagine."

Angelica kept her eyes on his until he chuckled unconvincingly and said, "That was Marlene. She had the simple soul of a child in some ways."

And you treated her like a child. And if Sinjun Breaker was responsible for her death, weren't you equally responsible?

"Well," Garth said, looking more relaxed. "This is really something. When all this is over with Kertz-Breaker, we'll have to get together."

She found herself smiling. "We will." Some part of her still wanted, very much, to be friends with Garth—for the sake of the many old times they'd shared.

He sighed. "Who'd have expected you to be in that boardroom?"

"Several people agreed with me that Sinjun would make a good subject. He's a complex man."

"You don't need to tell me. Do something for me, would you, Angel?"

Feeling too warm, she took off her jacket. "If I can."

"You're getting pretty close to him, aren't you?"

Closer than Garth could possibly imagine, or maybe not. "I guess I am."

His voice became conspiratorial. "If you hear anything you think I ought to know, will you tell me?"

"He always looked after us, Angel. Never doubt he was our special friend and that he loved us." In the end, whatever he'd felt for them hadn't been enough to stop him from betraying Momma.

"Angel," he pressed. "Will you?"

"Do this for me. Stop that man from hurting our special friend." Still she hesitated before saying, "I'll try." Perhaps the day would come when she'd be able to forgive Garth and . . . and trust him again.

"Thank you." His smile was the old, charming, reassuring smile. "Are you . . . Is he anything more to you than a business proposition, Angel?"

"No!"

He held up a palm. "Whoa. It was just a question. No need to get angry—unless you're not telling me the truth."

"Why would you think of such a thing?"

"Men know certain things about other men."

He had her full attention. "What things?"

"Ooh." He pushed out his lips. "Like when they're interested in a woman—if you know what I mean. Watch out for Breaker, Angel."

The temptation was to tell Garth she knew better than anyone how careful she had to be with Sinjun. "I know what I'm doing," she said.

"You may think you do. Breaker's unscrupulous. If you've done any work at all on him, you already know he had to be one hell of a scrambler to get where he is."

"He didn't do it entirely by scrambling."

Garth split a wide grin. "You have been doing some work. Good for you. The guy had a shitload . . . A whole pile of luck, didn't he? But he had it because Bruno Kertz decided to give it to him. Bruno was one tough son of a bitch. He knew he'd found a mind that matched his own and he grabbed it. Sinjun Breaker is like a reincarnation of Bruno and the old man crowned him his prince. And eventually, when Bruno died, he made Breaker king."

"Thanks for the insight," Angelica said, without sarcasm. "I appreciate any help I can get. But don't worry about me with Sinjun. I can handle him."

"I wonder if you can. He's interested in you."

Angelica stopped breathing entirely.

"Like I said, men know these things about one another. He's cool—cold. But the cold ones have to be watched the closest. Was he all for the biography?"

It could not hurt to be as truthful as was safe. "Not at first."

Garth's laugh was a nasty bark. "But he changed his mind? I'll bet he did. What changed his mind was you—and I don't mean it was *your* mind that changed his. He looked at you like . . . Mmm. Breaker would like to be more than a business arrangement with you."

Her heart drummed. "Sinjun's one of those men who aren't easy to read. On this occasion, I think you've misread the male-to-male thing."

"I don't. And I don't want him taking advantage of you."

She heard genuine protectiveness in his voice. "Thanks for caring."

He looked her full in the eyes and gave the old kind grimace that had once made her feel important to him. She smiled back.

Angelica heard a woman say, "Garth?" and recognized Mary Barrett's voice.

Garth straightened and looked over his shoulder.

"You'd better get back in there," Mary said urgently and in low tones. "It'll be okay now. I've promised to produce the necessary data in a day or so."

"Mary . . ." Garth glanced in Angelica's direction.

"I know, I know," Mary rushed on. "This isn't safe. There's no other way. With any luck I've bought us enough time."

Angelica gathered her jacket into a bundle.

Garth turned his back on her and Mary came into view. "Tell them we passed on the way to the rest room," she told him. "Be casual—" Then she saw Angelica.

"Go back, Mary," Garth said calmly.

Instead she held her ground and gave Angelica a hard look that didn't quite hide her surprise.

"Angelica and I were discussing this biography business," Garth said, and laughed. "I'm thinking of hiring her to write mine. If old Sinjun's worth a few pages, I'm worth a few more, wouldn't you say?"

Mary didn't smile. "I wouldn't be surprised." She passed them both and went into the rest room.

Garth shook his head. "Temperamental, our Mary."

"Is she?" More than ever, Angelica felt alone and vulnerable. "What if she goes straight back to Sinjun and suggests we might not be newly acquainted?"

Garth's eyes narrowed and a muscle flicked rhythmically in his jaw. "Don't worry about Mary," he said. "She's on our side."

Our side? And which side would that be? Garth's, or Sinjun's? One thing was certain, Angelica's own side was very select—she was the only member.

"That'll do it for now, then," Sinjun said an hour later.

Everyone rose from the boardroom table and, after handshakes, Garth and his contingent filed out.

Mary gathered papers together into a folder. "I'll get right to this, Sin." She'd returned to the room a few minutes after Angelica. Garth had taken a while longer and come back making innocuous comments about having had to make some calls.

"Do that," Sinjun said to Mary. "Thanks for your input, Peter. Efficient and concise as always."

Peter Akers's pleasure showed. He followed Mary's lead, shuffling papers into a heap. "We'll speak in the morning then, Sinjun?"

"In the morning," Sinjun agreed. He went to the windows and looked out until the door closed behind Mary and Peter. "What did you think of all that, Angelica?"

She thought she'd just witnessed a room filled with almost as many agendas as people. "Impressive," she said.

"That's a safe catchall." Sinjun turned around. A tightened quality about his features suggested the afternoon's tension hadn't left him unscathed. "I'll be glad to answer any questions later. I've got an appointment to deal with . . . Ah, hell."

"Hey, Sin," Chuck said. "You okay?"

"Yeah—*no*. I'm going to attend to Fran's affairs and I hate it." He arched his neck. "Who could have dreamed up what happened? I still find myself thinking I'm going to ask her this or that."

Angelica started to go to him, but stopped herself.

"She was the most irreverent, the most irritating and the one of the funniest people I ever met." Sinjun smiled bitterly at Chuck. "I'm not ashamed to say I miss her. I do. And I feel responsible for . . . I feel responsible."

"You weren't," Angelica blurted out. "No one was. It was an accident."

Sinjun met her eyes. "Chuck will take you back to the house. I'll pick you up later. Okay?"

It wasn't really a question. "Okay," she said, and wished she could offer him some comfort.

By the time Chuck opened the door for her, Sinjun had returned to his study of the world outside.

On the way down to the first floor, Angelica tried to think of something to say, but failed. When her eyes caught Chuck's, he smiled thinly.

The car stopped with a soft thud and the doors slid open. Angelica stepped out and murmured a response to the dark-suited attendant's greeting.

"I'm in the garage," Chuck said, touching her arm.

She glanced toward heavy glass windows fronting Third Avenue and said, "Why don't you do whatever you have to do? Don't worry about me. I think I'll walk for a while. I can easily get a cab back to Sinjun's." And, in the meantime, she could think—try to sort out the jumbled mess this afternoon had been.

"Sin wanted me to take you home."

Angelica looked up at him. "I'm not ready to go there," she told him quietly. "I need to walk. I'm not used to being cooped up."

His extravagantly masculine mouth drew open a fraction and he worried the inside of his bottom lip with his teeth.

"See you later," Angelica said.

She'd barely taken two steps toward the street before Chuck joined her. He walked ahead, pushed open a heavy door and followed her outside into an afternoon that tossed gusts of warm, dry breeze.

When they had descended steps to the sidewalk, Angelica gave Chuck a cheery wave and turned determinedly away from him.

At the corner, she felt his presence near her shoulder and grimaced.

"Where are we going?" he asked as they crossed the street.

"I'm not going anywhere in particular," Angelica told him, and knew at once that she most definitely *was* going somewhere.

"I'll tag along if it's okay with you."

Madison Street rose sharply uphill between Third and Fourth Avenues. Angelica blinked at the scintillating dazzle of sunshine on roofs of cars lining the curb. Two golden dogs and a fat gray cat lay in a contented heap beside their man-of-no-means owner.

"Poor critters," Chuck muttered.

Angelica dug some coins out of her pocket and dropped them into the man's proffered paper cup. "Street animals don't do so badly," she said, warming to Sinjun's sidekick. "There's a volunteer vet service for them in the city. Where did Swifty come from, by the way?"

"Honolulu."

Leaning into the hill and starting to climb, Angelica scrambled for a way to get rid of Chuck. "Sinjun just picked him up in Honolulu?"

"You've got it. The dog almost got hit by a truck. Sin picked him up—he was only a pup then—and took him to Hell."

"Sinjun has a way of appropriating whatever he wants, doesn't he?"

"You could say that."

"You don't have to baby-sit me, Chuck."

"I can't think of a baby I'd rather sit with," he said.

Angelica was too anxious to smile. "Thanks. I think. I'm going to get some coffee."

"Great."

She swallowed a groan and set a course for the nearest green-and-white Starbucks sign.

Her hand was on the brass door handle when inspiration hit. "Is there a library in the city?" She knew there was and that it was barely a block away.

Chuck ran a hand through his thick, sun-streaked blond hair. "Seattle Public. Fourth and Madison. Why?"

She wrinkled her nose. "Just some boring scut work I need to get done."

"Why?"

"Because it needs to be done," Angelica said, allowing her pleasant expression to slip.

"For Sin's biography?"

"Yes," she said, entirely straight-faced now. "I want to take a look at whatever I can find on Kertz-Breaker."

"We can give you that."

"From your point of view," she said shortly.

"Let's get that coffee."

"You get some," she told him. "I think I'll pass after all."

"Okay. The library it is."

"No, Chuck," she said, leaving the doorway of Starbucks and putting distance between them. "I'm not under house arrest, or any other kind of arrest.

If you talk to Sinjun before I do, tell him I'll be fine."

"Why are you trying to lose me?"

Angelica started uphill once more.

Chuck's long strides made short work of eliminating her lead. "Sin's worried about you."

"I'm not."

"Has he told you about the attempts on his life?"

"Yes."

"And you realize there's a possibility—a slight one—that the chopper explosion was designed to get rid of him?"

"Sinjun said something to that effect."

Ahead, a changing crossing light loosed a tide of walkers, humid-faced men in business suits and clomping, sneakered women—in business suits. They rippled downhill, separating Chuck and Angelica.

At the next corner, Chuck made his way back to Angelica. "Sin's afraid you may be in danger because of your association with him."

"He's already told me all this."

"Yeah. So you understand why I can't leave you alone."

"No." She faced him. "No, I don't understand. And I don't think you understand that we're not on Hell anymore. This is the mainland in the good ol' U.S. of A. and I get to decide what I do or don't intend to do—and with whom."

Chuck pretended to ward off blows. "Ouch." He grinned and, yet again, Angelica couldn't fail to notice how good-looking he was.

She had to grin. "I do appreciate the concern, but I doubt if anyone even knows I'm working with Sinjun."

"We can't take any chances. The price of a mistake would be too high."

Angelica settled a hand on his flexed biceps and guided him out of another gathering crowd at the crosswalk. She drew him close to a concrete planter filled with blindingly raspberry-colored impatiens.

"This is probably a good place to talk," she told him. "Safe."

He circled the planter and faced her. "How do you figure that?"

"No one thinks anything of a man and woman talking in the sunshine on a busy downtown street. You and Sinjun have known each other since you were kids."

"Just about all our lives. I told you that the day I picked you up on Kauai."

"I know. I'm thinking aloud. Feeling my way." She hesitated for a moment, then asked, "Did you know his father?"

He shifted his weight to one leg. "Yeah. If anyone did, I guess so. Look, let's—"

"He was a bastard, wasn't he?"

Chuck whistled through his teeth and fixed her with searing blue eyes. "One hundred percent son of a bitch," he said. "I hope I don't offend you."

"My ears are asbestos-coated. D'you think Sinjun's the way he is because of his father?"

Chuck swore under his breath.

"Is that yes or no?"

"*No*, dammit. What the—What are you talking about? Buck Breaker was a shiftless drunk. He never stuck to anything and he never did a damn thing for Sin."

"Sinjun doesn't drink."

Chuck looked blank. "Not anymore."

Angelica watched him closely. "He used to."

"Some."

"He's an alcoholic like his father?"

"Goddamn—" He shut his mouth on the rest of the word, but not before he'd reached across the planter and closed a huge hand on her upper arm. "Sinjun is not an alcoholic. He just doesn't drink anymore."

She would not give him the satisfaction of seeing her wince. "Because he's afraid he could be an alcoholic? Makes sense. Recent studies—"

"Stuff your recent studies. Sinjun like to know his head's clear. Anything that might cloud his judgment isn't in the cards."

"He's a control freak." Angelica looked pointedly at his hand on her arm. "And evidently he isn't the only one."

He released her immediately. "Have it your own way. I'll let him know you decided to take a taxi home."

She'd rattled him. "Did you know Dee-Dee Cahler?"

Chuck's hand went to the knot on his tie. His gaze lost focus.

"You did, didn't you?"

"I just told you—Sin and I have been together since we were little kids. Sure, I knew Dee-Dee."

"What was she like?"

He set his lips firmly together.

A dust eddy flipped up from the sidewalk to sand Angelica's ankles. "What did you think when she and Sinjun decided to get married?"

Chuck looked at the sky. So did Angelica. A jet, like a miniature silver-white arrow, unrolled its showy contrail across the blue heavens.

"What did you think?" Angelica pressed.

"They got married. The end. There wasn't any great decision."

"Maybe the decision was made when they had unprotected sex."

"Listen." Bringing his chin down, he moved to stand beside her, so close she had a ringside seat on his red-and-black tie. "Don't waste your time trying to see if Sin and I will contradict each other on the subjects that fascinate you most. It won't work. When you question Sin, he tells me what

you ask him. And I'm going to tell him anything
you ask me. Got that?"

"Yessir."

"Great."

"Were you there when Dee-Dee died?"

"For God's sake!"

She tilted her head and studied random black
patterns on the tie. "Were you?"

"No."

"Was she beaten?"

"*No!*"

"You're very defensive, Chuck."

"You're very pushy."

A row of small children, each one holding a knot
on a length of hefty rope, marched by under the
watchful eye of two women. When the procession
had passed, Angelica said, "Sinjun has authorized
this work. I can't write about nothing but how
wonderful he is and always has been."

"I can't understand why he did agree," Chuck
said through his teeth.

"Mrs. Cahler said her granddaughter had been
beaten and that's why she aborted."

Chuck considered for several moments before
resting the tip of a large forefinger on Angelica's
collarbone. "Go to the library." He tapped, tapped.
"And while you're there, make a list of any questions you want to ask me."

"Why? So you can share it with Sinjun and make
certain your stories agree?"

The next tap ground into bone and stayed put.
"Sin and I have been looking out for one another
for a very long time, Angelica." His nostrils flared.
"If you know what's good for you, you'll tread
carefully. I think he's going for your so-called project because you're getting to him in places that
tend to have a mind of their own. Don't push that
advantage too far because it won't last too long."

Heat washed up under her skin.

"Pretty blush," he said. "I'll just bet you're pretty all over."

"I'm going to the library now."

"Sinjun's good, y'know. Or so I've been told."

Standing at the curb once more, she looked up at Chuck. "Good at what?"

He smiled broadly. "I think you can work it out. And I think you know he wants you. Why not forget all this biography crap? Let down and have some fun." His gaze turned lazy and made a slow sweep all the way to her toes and back. "You want him, too. I've seen the way you look at him."

"Good-bye." She willed the lights to change.

"Sin doesn't tend to stay interested, but while he is he'll give it his all. That's what he intends to do, y'know. He intends to start sleeping with you every opportunity he gets until he's bored with you. Then he'll pass on to something fresh and so will you. But don't worry, he'll make sure the pay's good."

"Shut up," she hissed.

"Drop the phony cover-up and tell it like it is. You read about him in some magazine article. Then you got interested and decided to go take a look. And you liked what you saw. Every woman does."

Finally the walk light turned from red to white and Angelica shot across the street.

Chuck was right beside her. "He isn't the marrying kind," he said conversationally. "A lot of women have tried to change his mind on that. Never works. But you can do nicely—"

"*Look.*" She pivoted into his path and pounded a fist into his chest. "I have never been insulted the way you've just insulted me. I'm a journalist, not a prostitute."

"There's a difference?"

Angelica took several calming breaths. "Okay. You've done your best to scare me off. You've failed. I am not interested in Sinjun Breaker for personal reasons, other than those that relate to the project we both already know about. If you ever speak to me like this again, I'll go directly to Sinjun and complain."

"Good luck."

This was impossible. She started up the library steps.

"You passed the test," Chuck called from the sidewalk.

Slowly, she turned and looked down at him. "What did you say?"

"I said you passed the test. I pushed and you didn't crack. You may just be what you say you are."

Angelica planted her hands on her hips.

Chuck patted his pockets. "I almost forgot to give you this." He produced a folded piece of newsprint, climbed to press it into her hand and walked away again, but not before adding, "Could be that this will help you decide to rearrange your angle. It surprised us as much as it's going to surprise you."

By the time Angelica looked up from reading, Chuck Gill was striding out of sight.

The clipping was from a recent issue of a Dillon paper and it announced: *Cahler, Sarah-Mae, approx. 90 years old. Died suddenly. No surviving relatives.* To the right of the death announcement was a short paragraph about the tragedy of older people living alone. *According to Joshua Simms, who thinks he may have been the last to see the deceased alive, Sarah-Mae Cahler was a remarkably spry woman who looked "good for a heap of years yet."* The article concluded with a dry suggestion that looks could be deceiving.

Mrs. Cahler had certainly looked in fine health four weeks ago. In the summer warmth of a late Seattle afternoon, Angelica shivered.

Nineteen

❦

Seattle loved Sinjun Breaker. It also loved to hate him.

Seated before a microfilm viewer on the busy main floor of the library, Angelica hooked her arms over the back of the chair and stared at blurred, four-year-old entries from the *Seattle Times*. She'd gone through them all before and they hadn't changed since then.

For a man who purportedly picked women like daisies and didn't stick around long enough for their petals to droop, remarkably little had been written on the subject of Sinjun's love life. What little there was classified him as *the* man to catch—and the man least likely to be caught at all. Angelica still gained the impression that in some quarters there were probably wagers in place against the odds of Sinjun ever marrying, on who might be the lucky woman in the unlikely event that he ever did marry and on how long such a marriage could possibly last. There was no doubt that among the available elite—and undoubtedly a great many others—he was considered a hot-ticket item.

Surprisingly, he was referred to in all instances as a bachelor. Evidently his marriage had been short and historically obscure enough to allow him to lose it. If Angelica hadn't had the astonishing luck to encounter old Mrs. Cahler, she wouldn't have found it either.

And now Mrs. Cahler was dead—suddenly.

Ninety. That, and the attendant probability of simple lack of breath, was a perfectly good cause of death.

Chuck's message had been implicit: *Back off*.

Angelica had no intention of backing off.

On microfilm there was a mountainous accumulation of copy about Sinjun's business dealings. The fact that he was apparently closely related to Midas garnered sleekly coated, mostly inaccessible commentaries by formally well-fed brains that seemed permanently poised to point I-told-you-so fingers when the upstart crashed.

Angelica rewound the reel and flipped off the viewer. What she wanted to find wouldn't be on microfilm—not yet.

She glanced toward the front of the building. The sidewalks were crowded with homeward-bound workers. Soon she'd have to head out herself.

Garth thought Mary Barrett was working on his side, against Sinjun, in the Skins of Silk venture. Sinjun thought the reverse . . . didn't he?

Slowly, Angelica returned the reel of film to its box.

Momma had believed absolutely the story she'd written on the night she died.

But it didn't have to be true. Sinjun didn't have to be the villain. In fact, Sinjun had given her no reason to be certain he intended to engineer some ruinous plot against Garth. On the other hand, Garth's exchange with Mary in the hallway at Kertz-Breaker made it plain that he thought she was helping him with something he didn't want Sinjun to know.

Angelica couldn't ask either Garth or Sinjun to take her into their confidence, any more than she could warn them of potential intrigue.

All Angelica knew about Garth was what she remembered and what Momma had told her. Regardless of any growing doubts about him, a promise was a promise even when made to someone already dead—*especially* then.

She rubbed her tired eyes.

Then she did what she'd known she would eventually do.

The place to start was Seattle; the date, something more than twenty years earlier.

It was time for Angelica to make another, more thorough examination of the man who had been Momma's "dear friend."

"Are you sure?" Angelica asked the man she'd called at the state records office.

The voice in Olympia, the state capital, said, "If you've given me accurate information, I'm absolutely sure."

She let her head fall forward. "Thanks."

"You're welcome."

They hung up.

The sun had faded. People passing the telephone booth wore end-of-the-day faces.

"There's no record of this Garth Lieber being married," the man in Olympia had said.

Momma had believed a lie. Angelica pushed open the door and stepped onto the sidewalk in front of the library. She wanted to see Sinjun. The longing broke like a powerful wave and left her weak and scared. He was the man she was supposed to hate and fear. Hate and love were said to be barely separable. She couldn't possibly love him, but what she felt when she thought of Sinjun definitely wasn't hate. And the only fear he made her feel was for her supposedly untouchable heart.

Without planning to, she began retracing the route she'd taken with Chuck and by the time she reached Third Avenue she was running.

The lobby of the Kertz-Breaker building was deserted. A clock over the elevator bank amazed her. It was seven-thirty. Sinjun had probably left.

She punched the button on his private elevator and waited.

Five minutes later, she was still waiting and the lit panel showed that the car remained on the twenty-seventh floor.

Chuck must have reported her trip to the library. Sinjun wouldn't necessarily expect her to be at his home on time.

Impatient, Angelica took another elevator to its termination on the twenty-second floor, got out and climbed the ten switchbacking flights of stairs to the penthouse office suite.

The stairway door thudded softly shut, closing her into muted silence. Wall lights cast white wedges upward to the high ceilings.

Faintly over the sound system came the strains of a soprano sax. Angelica took several steps and stopped. She didn't know where Sinjun's office was.

The sax reminded her of him, of his yellow-green eyes watching her across his dinner table on the island and later, on the beach . . . In her mind, the surf and the wind had sung into the night with a high, searing insistence that moved with the man.

If she discovered that there was no need to help Garth, then why should she stay?

To do what Momma had asked her to do?

Or because the thought of leaving—of never seeing Sinjun again—knocked the bottom out of her insides?

"Angelica?"

She spun around. Sinjun stood in a doorway to her left.

"Chuck said you'd gone to the library. Mrs. Falon was going to call me when you showed up."

He was annoyed by her intrusion. "I'm sorry. I intended to go back there, but I thought . . . That is, I wanted . . ." What exactly did she want?

"What did you want?" Sinjun slouched against the doorjamb. The suit and tie had been discarded in favor of casual khaki slacks and a cream linen shirt open at the throat. Moisture clung to his hair as if he'd just gotten out of a shower.

"Angelica?" he prompted, shrugging upright. "Shit! What's the matter with me? Something happened, didn't it?"

Before she could respond, he covered the space between them and clasped her shoulders. "Tell me. Now."

She shook her head. "Nothing happened—not really."

"Come in here." Slipping an arm around her, he took her through the doorway and into a room only identifiable as an office by a huge, paper-strewn desk consisting of a dark-gray marble top supported by rosewood pillars.

Angelica allowed herself to be led to a seating area flanked by acres of books in rosewood shelves.

"Sit here," Sinjun ordered, all but pushing her onto a creamy leather couch. He sat beside her. "Take your time, but I want to know every detail."

She studied him. He thought someone had tried to hurt her and that she'd rushed here because she was frightened. "It isn't what you think," she told him, but her heart tripped. There was no mistaking that Sinjun Breaker was concerned for her welfare.

"You're trembling," he said, taking one of her hands in both of his. "Don't try to cover anything up, Angel."

Telling someone what she now knew would be such a relief. Unfortunately, this was a man she absolutely could not confide in—not completely. "I've had a shock," she said simply. "I'll get over it."

His grip on her hands tightened. "Was it on the street? A car? These people like cars. Easier to get away afterwards."

"No, Sinjun." She should remove her hand but didn't want to. "It was at the library and there was no threat to my personal safety. I found out something and it shocked me. That's all."

"But you came straight here."

She looked into his eyes. "Yes."

"Should I be flattered?"

Angelica considered before saying, "I don't have anywhere else to go—except to where you are," and then felt foolish for revealing her vulnerability.

Never shifting his gaze, Sinjun straightened his spine. The corners of his mouth turned up a fraction more. In his elegantly casual linen and cotton, with his tanned skin gleaming faintly and moisture glistening in the thick, black hair that touched his collar, he resembled a time-traveling pirate in almost-civilized clothing.

"So I win by default?" he said. "I'm still glad you felt you could come to me—that you wanted to. I won't push, but if you want to tell me what's on your mind, I'll listen."

"Someone I loved a great deal was betrayed—by a friend," she said obliquely, never having intended to do so. "I thought I knew this *friend*, too. I was wrong." Although she'd had her doubts since earlier this afternoon.

"Go on."

"No," she said, withdrawing her hand. "It isn't interesting to anyone else. And it isn't even important anymore."

"It's important, Angel," Sinjun said. He touched her cheek with the backs of his fingers. "The way you looked when I saw you out there told me there's something very wrong. You don't know where to turn, do you? What to do next?"

He was so right. "It's hard to accept disappointment—the kind that comes when people let you down."

"Who let you down? You said you're all alone."

Another mistake. "I'm alone here," she temporized. "Actually, it was someone who used to be
very dear to me who was betrayed. By someone
she loved more than . . . more than anything."

"Brenda?"

"No." Angelica smiled. "Brenda guards her heart
carefully. No, not Brenda."

"Sorry for pushing," he said. "Would you like a
drink?"

"No, thanks." She was still reeling from disbelief.
How could Momma have been so foolish and so
trusting? "What happened isn't so complicated. A
gentle woman put her faith in a man she thought
was strong and true. She thought he was honorable
and that he would never willingly do anything to
hurt her."

Sinjun's chest expanded with a deep breath.
"Honor tends to be a scarce commodity."

"Yes. Unfortunately I believed what she believed,
so we were either both stupid or he'd have done well
on the stage."

"What did he do? Or don't you want to tell
me?"

"He ruined my . . . my friend's life. He was her
lover. She thought he couldn't marry her because
he was already married—to an invalid he'd never
loved but was too kindhearted to abandon."

"Ah." Sinjun raised his flaring eyebrows. "I think
I can guess the rest."

How odd, Angelica thought, that the story felt
unique and utterly personal, yet it was a cliché.
"I'm sure you can guess. Today I found out he
was never married at all. While she was making
excuses for him and accepting what he told her,
he was laughing at her. He manipulated her whole
life and she never stopped thinking he was Mr.
Wonderful." She squeezed the bridge of her nose.
"Come to that, I thought so, too. He never intended
to marry—at least not my friend."

"Sounds like a real winner. Can't your friend put it behind her?"

"Oh, yes. She's done that now."

"Good." His gaze became distant. "We all have to forget things sometimes. You should follow her example."

"She killed herself."

Angelica covered her mouth. She'd never meant to say it aloud.

Sinjun's eyes narrowed. "Jesus."

"It's over now," Angelica said. She stood up. "I think I should get my things and find somewhere else to stay."

"No." He was on his feet. "No, I'd rather you didn't do that."

"Why?"

He only hesitated a moment before saying, "We have an agreement. Nothing's changed about that, has it?"

She didn't know anymore, didn't know what she thought or what she wanted. "I guess not. But there's no need for me to take up space at your place."

"I think there is. When you said you'd had a shock, I absolutely believed someone had tried to hurt you. Do you believe me?"

"I . . . Yes."

"I have no reason to think there won't be another attempt on my life. And I'm still afraid someone might try to get at you, too."

"I don't—"

"Please, stay where I can keep an eye on you."

She shouldn't want to. "I suppose I could for a little while."

"Great." His smile made him look boyishly young. "Things have been so messed up. Maybe when they settle down I can really give you the help you need—if you're still as set as you were on writing about me."

"Thank you." This was what she'd set out to do: make him trust her.

He went to the desk and picked up some keys. "Are you still game for those fish and chips?"

She wasn't hungry but she said, "You bet."

"Great. Are you up for a walk?" When she agreed, he added, "We'll come back for the car," and put the keys into his pocket.

"I should have followed your example and gone back to change."

Sinjun nodded toward a closed door on the far side of the room. "I didn't go home. I've got everything I need here. Sometimes—if I work late—I don't bother to go home at all." He waved her past him and into the reception area. "And you don't need to change. You look great."

A simple, polite compliment shouldn't please her so much. "Thanks. So do you."

Laughing, he went to press the elevator button. "You're never going to be boring, Angelica Dean." As the door slid open, he offered her his hand and stepped back.

And Angelica screamed.

Where the elevator car should have been, empty blackness yawned.

Twenty

❦

"**S**injun!"

He heard Angelica scream his name, felt her grab his wrist, saw her fall and slide toward the elevator shaft.

And for a suspended instant, his weight hovered on the brink of the drop that would shatter his flesh and bones.

Angelica shouted, "No! No! No!"

His right shoe slipped on the metal threshold. Pain shot through his straining left leg.

Her feet must have jammed into the wall. Her knees began to buckle, but she held on.

In the second when he would have tilted away into space, her weight jerked his elbow behind him—against something solid.

Clawing toward safety with his free hand, Sinjun rammed his elbow against the wonderful wall and threw himself forward, away from the shaft.

He landed face-down on top of Angelica.

Instantly, he rolled to his back, pulling her with him.

"Oh, my God," she said, sobbing against his throat. Her hands burrowed under his shoulders and she seemed to try to cover him. "It wasn't there. There's nothing there."

Sinjun kept his eyes shut. His pulse pounded in his temples.

Gradually, his heart slowed down. Nerves and muscles twitched.

Angelica Dean—sinister nemesis—had used every ounce of her less-than-substantial weight to try to pull him to safety.

Sinjun opened his eyes and looked first up at the distant ceiling, then down at mussed blonde hair.

She hadn't just tried to save him; she'd pulled it off. If her fall hadn't turned his body, he'd probably be lying on top of the elevator car, somewhere below this floor—God knew how far below this floor.

"Holy . . ." Finally he made his limbs answer commands and he wrapped her in a crushing hug. "You're incredible. Christ, I was on my way. Down and out. You saved me." The idea was incredible.

"You saved yourself," she said and her voice cracked. "I thought you would fall."

Sinjun loosened his hold on her, but only slightly. "What just happened isn't possible," he said, massaging her back and shoulders with hands that shook. "The elevator door can't open if the car isn't there. That's what tells it to open."

"But it did. And it *isn't*."

"Damn, I must be hurting you." As carefully as he could, Sinjun maneuvered to his knees and stood up, helping Angelica to her feet at the same time. "I fell on you."

Pushing back her hair, she smiled up at him. "I'm tough." Her gentle golden eyes smiled, but her lashes were spiky and damp. "Would you please hold on to me? If you don't, I'm going to fall down again."

He threaded her arm through his and laced their fingers together. "I'd carry you, but I'm not sure I wouldn't drop you."

When they had all but collapsed onto a sofa in his office suite, he punched a button on the intercom system that connected with the lobby of the building. "Colin? Are you there?"

There was no response.

"Wasn't there a man in the lobby?" he asked Angelica.

She shook her head. "No. I tried to get your elevator, but it showed it was on this floor and it wouldn't come down. I thought maybe you had a way of keeping it up here if you were alone. I don't know. I took another one up as far as it would go, then used the stairs the rest of the way."

A garbled blast of shouting voices blared from the intercom.

"That's coming from the lobby," Sinjun said, and hit the buzzer again. "Colin?"

"It's Mr. Breaker," a man's panicky voice announced. "Mr. Gill, it's okay. Mr. Breaker's okay."

"No damn thanks to you," Chuck said in the background. "Goddamn *fool*."

"Chuck," Sinjun said loudly. "Get up here and bring Colin with you." He shut the connection without waiting for a reply.

Angelica caught his chin between a finger and thumb and turned his face toward her. She wrinkled her nose. "You've cut your cheek on something. It's not bleeding much but it ought to be cleaned."

"It will be. Later. I've probably bruised your entire body and it ought to be put to bed." He wasn't inclined to acknowledge his double entendre. "As soon as I get to the bottom of what happened here tonight, I'll take you home. Stay and rest while I talk to Chuck and Colin."

She didn't argue.

Sinjun paced the foyer, unable to bring himself to go near the gaping elevator.

The door to the stairs opened and Colin, the tall, thin night attendant, rushed in. "You all right, Mr. Breaker? I never thought someone might be trying to get at you, honest I didn't."

"What makes you think someone was?" Sinjun asked, deliberately calm.

"Mr. Gill was coming in from the garage and he saw me. He just about tore my head off." Colin's light eyes protruded and blue veins showed through the pale skin at his temples. "He wanted to know what the fu—What I was doing away from the lobby. I told him there'd been a call telling me someone was going to rip off cars parked down there. I went to take a look."

Sinjun felt something change and looked up in time to see the elevator doors slip shut. His eyes went to the lit panel above where the indicator flashed for the twenty-sixth, then the twenty-fifth floor and stopped.

"Chuck said I should never leave the lobby for any reason if you were up here alone. He said I wasn't to ask why but he's worried someone might try to do something to you. Is that right?"

"Could be."

If he didn't have Angelica as a witness, someone might suggest he'd imagined almost falling into an empty elevator shaft.

"Where's Chuck now?"

"He went back to take a good look around the garage before coming up. Told me not to leave you till he gets here. He seemed as mad at himself as he was at me."

Chuck spent too much time trying to be the father, mother and brother Sinjun had never had.

"Sin?" Chuck shot through the door. "Jesus *Christ*, I just lost ten years of life. Someone called Colin down to the garage for some nonexistent emergency. I thought you were going to be lying up here in little pieces."

"I almost was lying in little pieces. But it wouldn't have been right here. The elevator malfunctioned and I came close to finding out how I'd take to skydiving."

Chuck's face whitened. He wore a navy-blue cotton jacket and from a pocket he pulled a handful of something dark. "I should have listened to you after the explosion," he said, holding out a black scarf. "This was caught on the steps to the garage. She must have dropped it."

Sinjun took the square of silk. "The only way to make that door open without the car being there would be to override the system. Am I right?"

"Yeah." Chuck scrunched up his face. He looked at the closed elevator doors, then at the panel. "Yeah. You'd have to make it think the car was where it wasn't. Not something your average little journalist could do. But there isn't much about Ms. Dean that's average, is there?"

"Follow me," Sinjun said, and led the way back to his suite. Once inside, he stood back to let Chuck see Angelica. With any luck, she hadn't heard the suggestion that had just been made. "Tonight my life was saved by a ninety-pound weakling."

The smell of fried fish, and chips liberally doused with vinegar, mingled with a strong aroma of tar and salt. Angelica breathed in the scents and listened to the waters of Elliott Bay lapping at pilings beneath the waterfront piers. Once Chuck had left, she'd persuaded Sinjun that she needed to eat and walk more than she needed sleep. He'd been easy to persuade.

"I weigh a great deal more than ninety pounds, y'know," she told him and took another bite of crispy-coated fish.

"Sorry. Ninety-one?"

"I weigh enough to help stop a large man from twisting his ankles."

In the red and pink neon light from the Ivar's Fish Bar sign, his aggrieved expression was almost funny. "I'd have done a lot more than twist my ankles."

"Twisting your ankles and bruising your knees, then."

"I came damn close to dying of a heart attack."

She touched his arm. "That makes two of us." Experts from the elevator company had arrived at Kertz-Breaker within thirty minutes of being summoned. They quickly determined that when Sinjun "supposedly" opened the doors, the car had been two floors below. They said they found no evidence of tampering, but agreed that didn't mean there couldn't have been any. Evidently *if* was a big word among everyone—including the police— who'd been called to investigate. *If* the doors had really opened onto an empty shaft, they had closed again and the system now appeared absolutely normal.

"The police seem to think I'm some sort of crank," Sinjun said. "I could almost swear one of them said 'What next?' when they were leaving."

"He probably said '*What's* next,' " Angelica said. But she'd heard the same thing and was still angry. "As in what did they have to do next."

Sinjun stepped away from the fish bar. He went to lean on concrete railings and looked down into the water.

Angelica joined him. "I wasn't going to ask, but what did Chuck mean about me? Before you brought him into your office?"

"Do you hear that?" Sinjun leaned farther over. "Sea lions under the pier."

She listened, but didn't hear any honking. "He said there was nothing average about me. What did he mean? I didn't hear what went before."

"Forget it."

"No."

"Yes." His face, when he turned toward her in the gloom, was tense and sharply drawn. "Don't look for more trouble than we've already got."

They'd become *we*? "Chuck thought I had something to do with what happened to the elevator, didn't he?"

Sinjun studied the bay.

"He thought I was involved in the helicopter explosion, too. I can't even begin to imagine why."

"The night before it happened, or the same morning, you made a call to the strip at Princeville on Kauai." Sinjun looked at her again. "I should say, a call was made from the cottage and it seemed likely that you made it."

She frowned, then remembered. "Yes, I did. I called to ask about getting the rest of my things sent over to Hell."

"What things?"

"My clothes. All the clothes I took with me to Kauai and left in storage at Princeville when Chuck flew me over to see you. They quoted me a shipping rate that would buy an entire new wardrobe. I told them to forget it."

"I see."

He saw now, Angelica thought. "You believed I caused that horrible accident, too. You almost said as much."

"I still don't think it was an accident. But I was wrong about you."

Her heart seemed to turn over. "But you did think it—at least for a while."

He ate several chips—slowly—before saying, "Someone is trying to kill me."

"And you thought it could be me."

"Yes."

"Oh, great." Angelica tossed her food into the nearest garbage container, leaned back against the railing and crossed her arms. "I'm a journalist. A good journalist. I do an above-average job writing stories. I use a computer because it makes sense, but I still jump if something buzzes, and if I get anything as threatening as a 'disk full' warning, I go *cosmic*. I shriek and wring my hands and get out the blood-pressure cuff because I'm afraid I'm going to have a stroke."

"Point?"

She pursed her lips and glowered straight ahead.

"Make your point."

"*Okay*. My point is that the word *technophobic* was probably invented for *me*. *How* would a person begin to know how to blow up a helicopter?" She flapped a hand in front of his face. "Go on. Tell me how to do it in case I've forgotten. After all, I'll undoubtedly want to do it again someday."

"I've already told you I made a stupid mistake."

"You made an asinine mistake. And *bypass an elevator computer system*? Oh, right. Absolutely. No need to remind me how to do that. It's real fresh in my mind."

"I'm sorry, Angelica. Okay?"

"You jam a whole bunch of wads of chewing gum into the control box—or is it the control center? Or the control *tower*? And then—"

Sinjun, grabbing her, pulling her to him and holding her face against his shoulder, shut off the rest of her tirade. "Okay, okay," he said softly. "I was an ass. Actually, I never even considered you might have done anything to the elevator. You were with me, remember? And you stopped me from falling down the damn shaft."

She'd begun to shake again.

"It's all right," he said, stroking her hair. "We've both had a hell of a shock, but it's all right now."

Angelica realized she was perilously close to tears. "It's all right for *now*," she told him, filling her hands with his linen shirt. "Something is going on. There's no doubt about it—regardless of what the police think. Sinjun, there'll be another attempt."

He slipped his hand under her hair and rubbed the back of her neck. "That isn't something you have to worry about."

"Yes, it is. I'm scared."

"Don't be. I intend to make sure you're very safe."

Angelica closed her eyes tightly. "I'm scared for you, not me." It was true, but she should never have told him.

Sinjun grew quite still. "Why are you scared for me?"

This way lay a very slippery path. "Because I don't want you to be hurt."

"Why?"

Oh, no. She would not allow him to pry the absolute truth from her. "Because . . . Because I want you around so I can write your stupid story. There. Now you know the truth."

"Do I?" He held her away. "I'm tired, how about you?"

Keeping her eyes lowered, she nodded.

"Why don't we walk back up to the building and get the car? I think I should take you home."

They were close, and growing closer—whatever that meant.

People, ones and twos, couples with children, still strolled the waterfront. A crossing bell rang and the trolley rattled by on the opposite side of the street, close to the viaduct.

Sinjun had grown silent and Angelica couldn't think of a thing to say. At the foot of the hill-climb to Pike Place Market, a man sold plastic glasses with bulbous white eyes on springs where the lenses should have been.

"How about it?" Sinjun said. "Might come in useful if I need a quick disguise."

"Don't joke," she said, but he bought a pair anyway.

As they climbed the steep flights of steps, Sinjun

put on the glasses and the eyeballs bobbled in the region of his upper lip.

"Take them off," she hissed. "You look ridiculous."

"But would anyone recognize me? That's the point."

"You have to take this seriously," she told him. "You have to go somewhere safe until you find out who's doing this, or they lose interest."

"I tried that," he said, and tossed coins into the open violin case of a musician who sounded to Angelica as if he belonged in a symphony. "That's what I was doing on Hell."

"You should probably go back there. Immediately."

Sinjun took off the glasses. "Someone almost blew me up in the islands, remember? At least, they may have, and poor Fran's dead as a result."

"It could have been an accident." She wouldn't look at him. "Go back there and don't let anyone else come."

"I can't stay there like that forever."

"You can't let yourself be murdered."

"You really do sound as if you care."

She'd already revealed too much of herself. "Why would someone want to kill you?"

"I don't know. I'd tell you if I did, but I don't."

They arrived on Western Avenue and started down the dimly lit street. At Madison, they crossed the road again and began climbing the hill past the Alexis Hotel where a liveried doorman was closing the doors on a sleek black limousine.

"It's a wonderful night," Angelica said, feeling as if she was noticing for the first time. "How can there be anything sinister on a night like this?"

He laughed deep in his throat. "This city has a way of making the world feel clean and honest and infinitely kind. It isn't Seattle's fault that bad things happen here."

The streets between First and Third Avenues were almost deserted, yet Angelica felt watched and said as much.

Sinjun reached for her hand and pulled it through his elbow. "Relax. They say criminals stick to their patterns. Whoever wants me dead is going to keep trying to kill me when I'm all alone."

Angelica shivered. "Or when they think you're all alone."

In the silence that followed, she knew they were both thinking that if she had not gone to him at Kertz-Breaker, and if he had been unlucky enough to be looking the other way when the elevator doors opened, he would probably have fallen.

"Two floors isn't so far," Sinjun said.

Their minds were running parallel. "Far enough to break your neck if you fell just right—or wrong."

They reached the building and Colin, still looking shaken, greeted them in the lobby. "You all right, Mr. Breaker?" he asked.

"Great, thanks, Colin. We'll be on our way back to Queen Anne now."

"Right then," Colin said.

Once in the stairwell, Sinjun started not down, but up.

"Where are we going?" Angelica asked anxiously.

"Where they'll think I'm not going to be tonight. Save your breath. you'll need it to climb twenty-seven floors."

"*Climb?*"

"We can't use the elevator. Colin might notice."

"You think Colin—"

"No, I definitely don't. But I'd rather he didn't know we're up there, just the same. I'll let Mrs. Falon know where we are and give instructions for her not to tell anyone else."

By the time they reached the twenty-seventh floor

Angelica *wished* she might die—or at least collapse into blessed oblivion.

Sinjun appeared to be breathing only moderately hard. He pulled her into the foyer and let her fall into the nearest chair. "Leave me here," she said, and when she could, turned sideways to drape her legs over one arm and allow her head to loll on the other. "I'll be just fine. You go to sleep . . . wherever you sleep when you stay here. You'll be perfectly safe. If anyone else comes through that door, I'll claw their hearts out."

He smiled and dropped to his haunches, then turned and sat with his back against the seat of Angelica's chair and his head resting on her middle. "We'll both stay here. Then we can both claw their hearts out."

"We could lock the door," she said thoughtfully after a pause.

"Sterling idea. But I can't until I can stand up again."

Angelica hitched herself up and looked down into his face. "We never cleaned that cut."

"Who cares?"

"Get up. It could get infected. What was I thinking of?"

"Narrow brushes with death, maybe?"

"Get up."

Grumbling, he did as she asked, locked the stairwell door and led the way into his office. "Leave the lights off," he told her. "Just in case someone's watching from below."

Moonlight made it easy to locate the door he'd indicated earlier.

"The bathroom's interior," he said when they'd entered a bedroom painted by the moon from a palette of shades of gray. "No windows in there—except for the skylight. Light through that wouldn't be visible from below. Come on. I'll show you where everything is, then you can sleep here."

Angelica said nothing. She stepped behind him into what was obviously a bathroom and stood in the darkness while he shut the door.

"Stand still," he said shortly, and she heard him scuffling.

"What are you doing?"

"If you need to whisper, I'm wasting my time." The light came on. "There. I put a towel along the bottom of the door, just in case."

"I see."

He grimaced. "Pretty dumb now I think of it. I must be jumpier than I thought."

The bathroom was exactly what she expected: stark masculine lines and all white except for lush green plants hanging from stainless-steel cross-beams below a skylight with a gorgeous view of a star-sequined, black-chiffon sky.

She felt Sinjun watching her and turned busily toward the sinks. "Where do you keep first-aid stuff?"

"I don't need first-aid stuff."

"Of course you do." Briefly, she met his eyes in the mirror. "Don't worry. I'll blow on it so it doesn't hurt."

Sinjun didn't smile.

Angelica hesitated before opening the louvered door over a wall cabinet. It was empty.

She glanced at white towels and had a fleeting recollection of initials embroidered in forest-green . . . and of a pretty, cloisonné box.

"I'd rather not go through all your cupboards," she said in a voice that sounded too high. "Sit down somewhere and tell me where I can find what I need."

"There's alcohol under the sink."

"It'll burn."

"It's the best I can do."

He hadn't attempted to move from behind her.

Angelica bent over and opened the cupboard

beneath the sink. A bottle of alcohol stood alone on the bottom shelf.

Sinjun's hands settled on her hips.

She opened her mouth to catch a breath. "Got it. Sit down."

His hands moved upward and came to rest— loosely—at her waist.

Muscles in her thighs felt suddenly useless. And in deep places she began to burn as she had that night on the island—and in his bedroom on Queen Anne.

Holding the bottle of alcohol, Angelica straightened and took a white washcloth from a stainless-steel bar beside one of two sinks.

"Sit," she said, twisting away.

He didn't try to stop her.

"Over here." She pointed to the edge of a bath that was the double of the Victorian she'd seen in his bathroom at home.

He smiled a little and did as she asked.

Angelica ran hot water on the washcloth and went close enough, just close enough, to dab dried blood away from the small wound on his cheekbone.

"Don't be afraid of me," Sinjun said. "I won't bite."

"I'm not afraid." The wound wasn't as deep as she'd feared. "Stay put for the alcohol."

He stayed put and Angelica poured a small amount of alcohol onto the cloth.

When she approached Sinjun again, he tipped up his face and closed his eyes. "Don't forget to blow on it."

Her stomach turned. "It's not too bad. I was afraid we ought to have had it stitched, but I don't think it'll scar."

From as great a distance as possible, she reached to blot the cut.

Not enough distance.

This time he went straight for her waist, but his touch was casual enough, relaxed—not threatening. Or it might not be threatening to someone less uptight than Angelica was.

"Done," she said.

"No."

She dragged her bottom lip through her teeth.

"It stings. Blow on it."

Her stomach flipped over again, and the burning drew the little muscles between her legs tight. "It can't sting."

"Believe me. It stings."

"It'll pass."

"Everything passes." He opened his eyes and looked directly into Angelica's. "Everything passes when it's taken its natural course. Some things need a little soft breath from a woman's mouth if they're ever going to feel better."

His eyes were purely green tonight. Green and glittering—and conveying his message with absolute clarity.

Pursing her lips, Angelica leaned and blew—very softly—on his cheek.

"Oh, God," he murmured, and his big hands spread.

His fingers splayed over her stomach and the heel of one hand drove down against her mound.

He wasn't stopping her from running away.

He didn't have to.

"Is . . . Is that better?"

Once again he was looking into her eyes. "No, Angelica. It isn't better. It's worse."

"Oh."

"Oh. Yes, *oh*."

"It'll pass soon."

"The pain I've got isn't going to pass at all without some help."

She might be inexperienced, but she knew what he meant.

Beneath his hands, an ache fanned—fanned wider and deeper until Angelica felt as if his ten fingertips were points of fire and she didn't want the fire to go out—ever.

Sinjun was watching his hands on her belly. With his thumbs, he smoothed the silk over her hipbones and traced the dips in front of them all the way down her groin.

Angelica jumped.

He'd brought his thumbs to rest at the very center of the notch between her thighs and pressed. She felt him part her, felt his deliberate probing.

The next sensation shocked her. "Oh." Her breath rushed out.

"Feel good?" he asked, absorbed, still studying his hands, still following the little stroking motions of his thumbs.

"Don't."

He stopped, but didn't remove his hands. "Walk away, Angel." His voice was low and rough. "Walk away. That's all it'll take."

Angelica stared at him.

"You don't want me to stop?"

What she wanted had become centered in her body, all feeling, all needing—all separated from thought.

She grasped Sinjun's shoulders.

"I'm glad you want what I want," he whispered, and smiled. "You don't really like bras, do you?" His right thumb pressed into the spot that made her jump again. "Do you?"

"What?"

His attention shifted higher. "You're not wearing a bra tonight."

"How do you know?"

"I can see your nipples. They're hard."

Oh, God, she'd forgotten. It was warm and she'd left her jacket behind before they went to the waterfront. She blushed wildly.

He glanced up at her face and said, "I love it when you go all pink." Then, slowly lowering his gaze, he leaned to moisten the silk over one of her nipples with his tongue.

Angelica heard her own moan. His thumb moved more insistently and her legs began to give out.

"It's okay," he said against her breast. "Go with it, sweetheart." Very gently, he drew the nipple into his mouth and settled his teeth lightly.

Angelica made fists. Where his mouth rested, sharp, intensely pleasurable tension mounted.

She *ought* to run.

He sucked, opened his mouth wide and nuzzled, moving his head slowly.

"Sinjun?" She'd never felt anything like this. *"Sinjun!"*

"Mmm?" He pulled her blouse loose and smoothed the skin around her midriff.

Angelica tingled where he touched her now, and swelled with need where he no longer touched her.

Gradually, his hands rose until they rested beneath her breasts.

Sinjun looked up at her then, raised his face, watching her eyes intently. "Kiss me," he said.

Angelica felt her lips part.

"Kiss me, Angel."

She was drawn closer.

"Yes," he murmured. "Come on, sweetheart. *Kiss me.*"

Closing her eyes, she settled her mouth on his, felt him draw in her breath and softly return his own. And while he caressed her mouth with his tongue, he took the weight of her bare breasts into his hands, pushing up, pushing in, covering, kneading—playing fingertips over their desperately aching points.

They kissed . . . and kissed. And Angelica could not think of anything but his mouth and his hands, and her own seared body.

Again his hands left her, but only to allow him to unbutton her blouse and slip it from her shoulders.

Their mouths stilled, but remained together.

Sinjun framed her jaw, pushed his fingers into her hair, pulled—just a little—and then began to caress her.

Their lips parted and he held her away, enough away to allow him to look at the skin he stroked.

Angelica felt a flush begin, felt a rushing of heat into her face, into her breasts.

Sinjun glanced at her face. "You blush a great deal, Angelica." He didn't smile.

"I always have." But she hadn't always stood naked before a man. She had *never* done that, except on the extraordinary night when he'd found her at the edge of the cliff on Hell.

That night had been nothing like this one.

His gaze passed slowly over her face. He lifted her hair and pushed it behind her shoulders.

She wanted to touch *him*.

With fumbling fingers, she began to undo the buttons on his shirt.

Sinjun looked down, watching while she finished. Then he offered his wrists and she loosened the cuffs. He took the shirt all the way off himself.

Her breath fled once more. Sinjun Breaker was beautiful. Broad and muscular, but in a lean, elegant way. The sleek, dark hair on his defined chest narrowed, to run in a slender line to his navel.

"Will I do?" he asked when she finally let herself look at the bulge at his crotch.

She swallowed and felt the heat in her face glow.

"You *really* do blush, don't you? I like it. Funny."

She swallowed again. This was a moment she'd known could exist, but, somehow, had stopped expecting. He thrilled her, yet made her so very unsure and afraid . . . and so desperate to know that he wanted her as much as she wanted him; at least for this moment.

"What is it?" He ducked his head. "Angel?"

"You are . . . I like looking at you."

"Oh, lady. Not nearly as much as I like looking at you."

She met his eyes. "Yes, I do."

His smile made a muscle in his cheek quiver. "Shall we hold some sort of contest to find out who wins? In the liking-to-look category?"

Angelica shook her head and managed to return his smile.

"I want to make love to you."

Her heart fell away, and her stomach.

"Do you want that, too?"

She opened her mouth, but couldn't tell him yes.

"Yes," he said, as if speaking for her. Sliding a hand around her waist, he began again the rhythmic forays between her legs.

And again Angelica sank her fingertips into his hard shoulders. A fiery surge made her gasp.

In one motion, he took away the sweet burning and pushed his hands inside the legs of her shorts, inside her panties, gripped her bottom and pulled her to sit astride one of his thighs.

Sinjun rocked her back and forth against flexed muscle. Sensation mounted and the light began to dim for Angelica. Her head fell forward against his neck. She kissed his jaw, nipped at his earlobe.

"My God," he breathed. "You are something. How did I get so lucky?"

Angelica heard his voice as if from a great distance and smiled. She found his flat nipples, and copied the motions he'd made, rubbing the small nubs and smiling wider when a shudder passed through him.

"Little magician," he murmured. "You know exactly what you're doing, don't you?"

She knew only what instinct taught her . . . as she went along. Openmouthed, Angelica explored the slightly salty skin along his collarbone.

"I want you so much," Sinjun said.

Pushing his hands under her arms, he splayed his big hands until he could flip his thumbs over her nipples.

Angelica's face came up.

Sinjun laughed, and lifted her to stand in front of him. Swiftly, he stripped off her shorts, taking her panties with them. When they'd fallen around her ankles, he pulled them away and backed her to the tiled wall so fast, she almost tripped.

"Trust, sweetheart," Sinjun said when she gasped. "I won't let you fall." His face had darkened and his eyes glittered as if with fever. "You are so sweet."

Her back met cold tile and she spread her arms.

"Yes," he said raggedly. "Oh, *yes*. I like you like that."

Covering her breasts, pressing them urgently, his face went . . . He pried her legs apart with his face.

Angelica's eyes rose to the black, star-pricked sky beyond the glass dome.

His mouth was between her thighs, his tongue darting deep into swollen folds. He shifted, slipped his hands around her hips and parted her until he could open his mouth over the part of her no man had ever seen, much less touched.

She tried to move, but the next flick of his tongue sent her arms hard against the tile. There was pain where her wrists hit. But there was another pain—a surging, exotically suffocating pain that burst from the flesh he probed.

Angelica heard her own thin wail—and Sinjun's laugh.

He laughed.

And the burst shot upward in a hot sheet.

She shuddered, and shuddered—and grasped his head, holding him to her.

When Sinjun rose, swinging her into his arms, she was helpless to do anything but wrap her arms around his neck and hang on.

In the bedroom's sultry gloom, he stripped back covers from the bed and sat her on the edge of the mattress. Holding her legs apart with his own, he unzipped his pants and pushed them down.

Angelica watched him and her lungs refused to fill. He was a big man. Or were all men as big? How did a woman stretch to take so much? Women did, that was all. It happened every day—but not to her—never to her.

When he was completely naked, he bent to kiss her, all the while caressing her shoulders, her arms, her breasts. He pressed his fingers into the still pulsing place between her thighs and she jumped.

"I'm going to make love to you now, Angelica," he said, kissing her after each word. "I want to feel you around me. Hold me."

He took her hand to his penis and folded her fingers around him.

Automatically, she gripped. The smooth, rigid flesh pumped.

"Yes," Sinjun whispered urgently. She heard him fumble for a drawer in the bedside table. He turned aside briefly before pushing her to her back and looming over her.

Then he was nudging the end of his shaft against the opening into her body. And she felt her own wetness.

"You're ready for me, Angel," he said, seeking with a finger while he pressed more insistently.

She wanted him. It was time.

He began to enter.

Angelica's body inched away.

"Oh, Angel," Sinjun murmured, licking her ear. "You are so perfect. So perfect for me."

He *was* big. And he pushed, and pushed.

"God, Angel. Oh, God." His voice broke and all

the power in his long, lean, hard body gathered into the thrust of his hips. "Oh, God!"

"Aah!" Angelica's own cry caught in her throat. The drive of his sex stretched and scalded.

Sinjun withdrew and pushed into her again.

Angelica panicked. She couldn't take him into her. Her body clenched. "No!" With her fists, she beat at his shoulders. "No!"

He didn't seem to hear her. "You're small," he gasped, and thrust again.

Something gave inside her.

"My . . ." Sinjun's hips jerked again—and once more—then he was still, so still. "What the hell . . . Are you? . . . Oh, *Christ!*"

Violently, he pulled out of her and stood up.

"Sinjun, I—"

"How old are you?" he said, his breath rasping.

"I—" She fought to breathe. "Twenty-eight."

"How the hell does a woman who looks like you, and responds like you, get to be twenty-eight without . . . *without?*"

She couldn't answer, couldn't speak.

"You're a *virgin.*" It sounded like an accusation.

"Yes," she told him clearly. Her heart pounded. She closed her eyes and turned her face away.

"Correction." She felt him leave the side of the bed. "You *were* a virgin, goddamn it!"

She heard the door slam as he left the bedroom.

When her eyes flew open, she saw multiple fiery beams sparking from an object on the bedside table. Pushing onto an elbow, she reached out and traced the intricate facets of what she instantly knew was his precious, priceless ace in the hole.

What a naive fool he must think her.

Falling back onto the pillows, she covered her face. "*My motto,*" he'd told her, "*is never fuck without one eye on your ruby tree peony.*"

She could never be in his league.

Twenty-one

❦

No sound came from the bedroom.

Sinjun stood a few feet away, listening. He'd snatched up his pants as he left, but hadn't bothered to put them on.

Twenty-eight.

A journalist who'd traveled the world with a major publication.

And last, and most, an achingly lovely, desirable woman.

So . . . So, for some impossible-to-imagine reason, she'd chosen to remain pure.

Pure. Even the word stuck in his throat.

And why him? Why tonight?

He scrubbed at his face.

Dammit, he was still erect. Turning away from the door, he grimaced. His dick still wanted her.

He still wanted her.

Angelica Dean had saved his life tonight. And she hadn't been the one to make the move afterwards. Sinjun thought about that. She'd never made any move at all on him—which figured. From what he'd felt a few minutes earlier, Ms. Angelica Dean was virtually untouched by human hands.

Something scuffled in the bedroom.

Or sniffled.

He closed his eyes and raised his face to the ceiling. He didn't want to feel like an animal. He didn't want to be like a fighter who'd narrowly missed death in battle: proving he still lived by fucking the first thing in sight.

Sweat broke out on his brow.

He wasn't like that, could never be like that. He'd never been with a woman who didn't want him—at least as much as he wanted her.

Angelica was different, and . . .

She didn't deserve to be treated as he'd just treated her.

Sinjun went slowly to the bedroom door and knocked.

Something rustled, but she didn't tell him to come in.

He went in anyway.

The moon touched a sheet-covered ball in the bed.

He cleared his throat and moved closer, tossing his pants aside before he reached the side of the bed. "You shocked me," he said, and swore inwardly. *Clumsy, obtuse fool.* "I'm sorry if I frightened you, Angelica."

She didn't move or respond.

"Hey." He lowered himself to sit beside her. "Hey, bump-in-the-bed. Come out."

He heard what definitely sounded like a sniff. "Are you crying?"

"No."

"I didn't think so." And he didn't feel like making jokes. "Can we talk?"

Silence.

"Angel, please talk to me."

The bump rotated. She pulled the sheet down from her face, but remained curled on her side.

He couldn't see her features, but he said, "Hi."

"You can sleep in your bed," she said. "Give me a few minutes, and I'll get out of here."

"You're not going anywhere," he told her. His temper began to rise, and other things rose right with it. "At least, you won't go anywhere without me."

"You can't make me stay."

"Try me."

She started to pull the sheet back over her head. Sinjun stopped her. "*Don't* do that."

"Leave me alone, please."

"Why?"

Her sigh shuddered on for too long. "I'm embarrassed." She shifted partially to her back and light glittered in her eyes. "And maybe I'm . . . Well, it doesn't matter to you."

"Yes, it does. Maybe you're what?"

"Just embarrassed."

Sinjun found her hand. When she tried to pull away he held on and laced his fingers through hers.

"I'll go down the stairs," she said, her voice muffled. "I won't give you away."

"I don't give a flying . . . You aren't leaving."

She averted her face.

"Talk to me," he said, and raised her hand to his mouth. He kissed each finger, and the spaces between—slowly—and pressed his lips lingeringly into her palm. Then he folded her fingers over and held her fist against his chest. "Talk to me, Angel. Make me understand what just happened here."

"I can't."

"Sure you—"

"I *can't*, because I don't know, damn it."

Hesitantly, Sinjun stroked her hair. "You got frightened."

"I . . ." He felt her hold her breath. "Yes. Yes, I guess I did. Then I felt stupid."

"Why stupid?"

"You know why."

He knew Angelica was different from any other woman he'd known. And he thought she was wonderful. "Whatever you are, sweetheart, it isn't stupid." And she scared the hell out of him. "If

I'd . . . If I'd guessed, I wouldn't have . . . I wouldn't have."

She spoke softly. "I wanted you to."

Sinjun leaned over her and said, "Why?"

"Why did you stop?"

He caught his bottom lip between his teeth. Deep water with women was something he'd always avoided—except for once—and that once had clinched the depth of his relationships from then on. Until now.

She was waiting for his answer.

He stroked her hair again, moved it aside and kissed the side of her neck. "Maybe I realized you were too much for me." Or too good. He moved the sheet from her shoulder and kissed her there.

"I wanted you." She sounded shaken—and stubborn.

He smiled ruefully in the darkness. What a night. Someone tried to kill him—again—and the astonishing woman who foiled the attempt decided to sacrifice her virginity to him.

"You're trembling," he said.

"No, I'm not. I'm shaking. I'm cold."

With only the slightest hesitation, he lifted the sheet and climbed into bed behind her. She hunched into a ball again.

Sinjun pulled her back against him and wound his arms around her. "Warmer?" He was warmer.

"No."

He grinned. "As in, not yet?" Carefully, he began to chafe the tops of her thighs, then her belly, then her middle. "Are we getting there?"

"No!" She captured his hands and adjusted until she could hold them over her breasts. "I'm not a kid. I like this, Sinjun. I *really* like it."

He gritted his teeth. His damned erection had more than a mind of its own. She had to feel it on her cute little butt.

She held still before saying, "You like it, too."

Nuzzling forward, he took her earlobe between his teeth.

"Don't you?" she persisted. "I can feel you do."

"Oh, yes," he breathed, and played his fingernails over her nipples. When she squirmed, he held her fast. "I like it, Angel. Do you want me to make love to you?"

"I want *us* to make love."

"You aren't scared anymore?"

"I'm scared . . . I'm scared out of my wits. But I still want it."

Could she possibly know how much she excited him? "Okay, sweetheart. You've got it. *Yes*, sweetheart, you've got it." He turned her to her back and pinned her with a thigh. "This is your last chance. Speak now, or hold your peace."

He saw her lips part and she said, "Kiss me."

Groaning, he covered her mouth and drowned. Her arms snaked around his neck and she arched her lithe body into his. He kissed her and filled his hands with her breasts.

He felt her withdraw an arm and go in search of his penis.

"I won't be able to kiss you for long if you do that," he said, and sucked in a sharp breath. "Don't say I didn't warn you." Her fingers slid around him, and beneath.

Sinjun grinned through gritted teeth. The inquisitive minx was exploring. "Find anything interesting?"

She paused.

"Don't stop, baby," he breathed. "I was only inquiring."

"You're interesting," she told him. "I am scared."

"I know. God, you can't do that, love. Not unless you're ready for what comes next."

Before she'd finished saying, "I'm ready," Sinjun positioned himself between her legs and began to press inside.

This time she didn't clench up on him until he was all the way in, and then he couldn't have turned back even if he'd wanted to.

"Go with it," he panted against her temple. "Go-with-*it*."

Angelica's breathing rasped. She hissed a tremulous "Yes."

"Wrap your legs around me." He was pumping now.

Her heels rammed into the backs of his thighs and rose higher. Then her calves were clamped around his waist and her agile hips jolted off the mattress to meet each thrust he made.

His climax broke too fast, rolled over him, poured out of him—heated him from the inside out.

"Angel!" He heard his voice calling her name, felt her legs hold him even tighter.

Shuddering, he started to fall, caught himself on his elbows and rolled to his side, keeping her layered against him.

He screwed up his face and cradled her head beneath his chin. "All right? Are you all right?"

She whispered, "Yes."

"I hurt you, didn't I?"

"No."

His lungs burned. "Too fast. I came too fast."

"No."

"Yes, I did. Next time it'll be better, sweetheart." He held her too hard, but he needed to feel her joined to him. "There'll be a next time, Angel. And a next time."

"Yes."

He grew still and forced his clamoring nerves to calm down. "You hated it." He held his breath.

She shook her head.

"Yes, you did."

"I loved it. I absolutely loved it." She raised her face and in the moon's subtle touch, her eyes shone and he could see her smile. "Thank you."

He felt . . . He felt he might die from not knowing what he felt. "Don't say that." He felt something dangerous. This woman was not going to
fade easily into his past.

"I'm sleepy," Angelica said. "But I don't want
you to come out of me."

"Hell," he exclaimed, and kissed her, deeply and
quickly. "You're what's known as a fast learner."

"A quick study?"

"You're incorrigible."

"And you're incredible."

She was like no woman he'd ever been with. "Go
to sleep."

"I will. Promise me something."

"Anything." The damnable thing was that he
meant it.

"When I wake up, I want to do this again."

Angelica had been watching him for a long time
in the darkness. She'd awakened before him and
taken deep, almost painful pleasure in studying the
silvered lines of his naked body.

When he stirred, she closed her eyes and pretended to sleep. Carefully, he pulled himself up
on the pillows and stacked his hands behind his
head.

As soon as she was sure he'd settled, she dared a
slitted-eyed look at him. His profile showed clearly, and the sheen of his eyes. A long, slow breath
raised his chest, then slowly escaped.

Sinjun Breaker was thinking and she'd give anything to be inside his head.

"You're awake."

He spoke suddenly and she started. "Uh huh."

"I'm a confused man."

"Are you?" Her insides were jumpy.

"I want to make love to you again."

She breathed out as hard as he had and crawled
to rest her face on his chest. "So do I."

"Questions first." He took a hand from behind his head and fiddled with her hair. "Why, Angel?"

"You'll have to be specific," she said, playing for thinking time.

"Why were you a virgin until tonight?"

Hoisting herself higher, Angelica nestled her head into the hollow of his shoulder. "It doesn't matter, does it?" She made small circles over his chest.

"It matters very much—to me. And it sure as hell has to matter to you."

"It's personal."

Sinjun's fingers stopped winding through her hair. "I realize that, but given the circumstances, could you try sharing it with me?"

"I didn't mean that." He wouldn't understand, but she'd explain anyway. "The act of . . . It's personal. The most personal thing there is. That's what I've always thought. And I still think it."

"Making love, you mean?"

Angelica sought his stubble-rough jaw. "Making love. It should *be* . . . It should be love," she finished quickly. "Your body is all you ever really own. I could never just . . . I couldn't just use it casually. I don't mean I judge other people for feeling differently. I'm only trying to explain how I feel."

"I see."

She doubted it. "How can it *not* be personal to accept someone else inside you? Or to enter someone else?"

His fingers trailed lightly over her shoulder, but he didn't reply.

"You asked," she said. "And I told you. I expect you to think I'm weird."

"I don't. Tell me, why did you decide you wanted to make love with me?"

Angelica turned her face into his shoulder. She had gone too far, said too much.

He shifted down in the bed, curled over her. "Please tell me."

She shook her head.

Sinjun stretched on his side and rolled onto his back, lifting her with gentle hands until she lay on top of him. "Do you feel like doing the most personal thing with me again?" he said.

Did he understand what she'd told him?

"Angel, I think I . . . I think I feel what you do."

She stopped breathing entirely.

"Were you saying you might be in love with me?" He felt for and found her thighs. "Sit up. I want to see you."

With his help, Angelica straddled his hips and braced her weight on his shoulders.

"God," he murmured, running the backs of his fingers over her breasts. He pulled her down until he could take a nipple into his mouth and suckle. Pushing her away a little, he said, "I'm ready again," and she felt him nudging her vagina.

Angelica rose just far enough to allow a smooth, downward swoop that swallowed his shaft to the hilt.

The next time she awoke, it was to an empty bed, but she heard water running in the bathroom, and the low, rumbling sound of an off-key bass singing what might have been "It Had to be You."

By the time she slipped from the bed and went quietly into the bathroom, Sinjun was reclining in the tub, his head resting back, his eyes shut. He was definitely singing "It Had to be You."

He didn't notice her until her first foot entered the water. "Is it warm in here?" she asked innocently, positioning herself over him as he'd positioned her only an hour earlier.

His eyes were serious and he didn't smile. "It's going to get warmer very soon." He studied her face. "I want to tell you something first."

Angelica eased back to sit on his thighs.

"Let me say this fast. The day we were married, Dee-Dee had an abortion."

Angelica's hands flew to her mouth.

"She'd already arranged it. She told me as much that night—when I found her at her grandmother's house."

"No," Angelica whispered. "Why would she do that?"

"Because she didn't want a baby. I've stopped judging her for that. She wasn't much more than a baby herself and neither was I. But I wanted that child."

She saw remembered pain flare in his eyes and said, "Sinjun, don't."

"I have to. It's important for you to know. Dee-Dee wanted to marry me. She was a lost little kid and she needed someone to care for her. She appointed me. I think I loved her—in a way. We made love a few times and she got pregnant. She went away without telling me and came back . . . She came back the way you saw her in that picture."

Angelica felt tears rim her eyelids. "I'm sorry. For both of you."

"Yeah. I said we'd get married and later I found out she went right out and arranged for the abortion. The idea was to have some sort of rosy arrangement for just the two of us. No babies allowed. She slipped away that night and the next thing I knew someone came to tell me Dee-Dee was ill at old Mrs. Cahler's place. When I got there, Mrs. Cahler said Dee-Dee had been beaten up and that's what caused the miscarriage."

"Are you sure that wasn't what—"

"I'm sure. Dee-Dee couldn't face telling Mrs. Cahler the truth. The beating story was supposed to get her off the hook, but she died. End of story."

"I'm sorry." And she hated herself for having accused him of things he couldn't be capable of doing. "I never meant . . . I wish I hadn't pried."

"I would have told you in the end, anyway."

She studied him.

Sinjun stared back, unblinking.

"Why?" she asked at last. "Why would you have told me? For the biography?" For the biography she'd forgotten about for hours—together with a lot of other things?

"No. Because I don't think you can love someone and not tell them everything about you."

Her heart seemed to stop beating. "Sinjun?"

"No one ever gave me what you have," he told her. "And I don't mean the obvious. You've given me yourself, haven't you?"

"Yes."

"You wouldn't do that if you didn't love me?"

"No." She could suffocate on this emotion.

"I find it hard to believe I'm saying this, but I may be feeling the same way about you." He drew her head down and kissed her. "Are you all alone, Angel? Except for Flaming Brenda?"

She knew very well what he'd just suggested. "*Flaming* Brenda?" There no longer seemed any need to be cautious with him.

"Seems to fit. Flaming ruddy Brenda."

Angelica chuckled. "Brenda is a gem and I love her."

He traced the small bones in one of her hands. "Who else do you love?"

She stopped chuckling.

"Isn't there anyone else? Anyone at all?"

"No."

"Did you . . . Have you ever been in love? . . . Have you?"

"Before?" she said gently. "Mildly infatuated, yes. In love, no. And I think you probably believe me."

"I do," he said, and sought her lips.

The shrill ringing of a phone made Angelica raise her head.

"Damn." Sinjun looked at an instrument on the wall above the tub. "Mrs. Falon's the only one who knows I'm here."

"Maybe there's an emergency."

The grating tone drilled the humid air, twice, three times—four.

"It could be that someone's on a fishing expedition just to see if I'm here."

"But there could be something wrong." Angelica held the edges of the tub. "I'm going to answer. If it's anyone but Mrs. Falon, I'll say I'm the janitor."

"No."

"*Yes*. It's the only thing that makes sense." She lifted off the receiver and brought it to her ear. "Hello?"

There was a faint sound of music on the line before a woman's voice said, "Is Sinjun there?"

Angelica gripped the handset tighter. "Who is this?"

"Who are you?"

She considered and discarded her janitor idea. "Who are you trying to reach, please?"

"Angelica." There was a flat, venomous whip to the way the woman said the name.

"Yes." Why deny it now? "Yes, this is Angelica."

Sinjun moved and water lapped.

"This is Lorraine. Let me speak to Sinjun. *Now*."

Angelica gave him the phone and said, "It's Lorraine."

He shook his head, but said, "Yes," into the receiver. Seconds passed before he snapped, "That's none of your damn business."

Angelica began to feel cold. He'd told her he loved her, hadn't he? Looking at his angry face, she felt a deep fear and a premonition of loss.

"Chuck shouldn't have told you where I was," Sinjun said. "And Mrs. Falon shouldn't have told him."

Falling in love with this man was something she couldn't have guarded against because she would never have dreamed of such an eventuality.

"Forget it!" Sinjun started to take the receiver away from his ear. Then his eyes narrowed and he pressed his lips together while he listened. "Explain."

Angelica moved to climb out of the bath but his hand shot out to restrain her. He shook his head.

"Why can't you tell me on the phone?" His forehead puckered. Gradually, his lips parted and he looked at Angelica. "That won't be possible. No. Absolutely not possible. If Chuck confirms that he believes what you're saying, I'll come. Angelica will come with me." He hung up.

"What is it?" she asked.

"If I can believe the woman, she's found out who's trying to get rid of me."

Twenty-two

❧

*B*renda Butters was ugly. Ugly, too big and too sure of herself.

Standing a few feet from Sin's breakfast table in the sun room, Lorraine poured wine into a water glass and pretended to be disinterested in Brenda's conversation with Enders.

Enders took off his reading glasses and pushed aside the book in which he'd been making notes. "I don't think Sinjun should come back here."

Lorraine paused with the wine bottle in midair.

Brenda leaned across the table and said, "Why ever not? I'd have thought you'd be glad to see him."

"I don't care what the police think," Enders said. "That helicopter blew up. I saw it."

"So did I," Brenda agreed. "But that doesn't have to mean it was deliberate. And if someone was trying to hurt Sinjun, I still think he'd be safer here than in Seattle."

Yeah, yeah, yeah. Lorraine set the bottle down with a crack on a kitchen counter, lifted her glass and looked down into the white wine as she drank. All she'd listened to for days—ever since Sin left—was constant rehashing of the stupid helicopter crash. That and the revelation that someone had supposedly been trying to kill Sin for some time.

Even the damn dog wouldn't quit whining.

Lorraine had something more important than fairy tales to deal with.

Thanks to the letter she'd found at the lagoon cottage, she could win everything—or lose everything—when Sin got back to the island. There wouldn't be any neutral outcome.

"You'll be glad to have Chuck back today, Lorraine," Brenda said. Sun through the windows turned her hair orange. "You seem a bit at loose ends on your own."

Lorraine tipped up her glass and took a long, long swallow before responding. "I'm never at loose ends."

"That's nice." Brenda returned her attention to Enders. She patted his hand. "Fran must have been something special."

"She was," Enders said, and sighed hugely.

Lorraine tuned them out. The only topic of conversation around here was *Fran*. Fran this and Fran that.

Where was Willis this morning? Swimming with Brenda at this time each day had become one of his rituals. Jealousy made Lorraine ache. Being horny made her ache more. She looked sideways at Brenda and wondered, yet again, what Willis saw in her. He had to be fucking her. As far as women were concerned, nothing else about them interested him. And he'd made it plain he didn't want Lorraine near him anymore.

Damn him. *Damn them all.*

Brenda yawned and stretched, locking her laced fingers behind her neck and arching her back. She wore a white swimsuit today. Thin, and banded with transparent mesh in deliberately provocative places, it showcased her breasts. Her nipples were dark, the centers puckered. Lorraine glanced at the vee between the other woman's legs. Dark hair there. And it showed, for God's sake.

Looking up, Lorraine met Brenda's eyes. Brenda smiled. She felt superior, damn her. She felt sexy, sexier than Lorraine—because she, not Lorraine, was screwing Willis.

Had Willis talked about her?

Had he said he didn't want her anymore?

Rage rose like bile in Lorraine's throat.

It was time to make her move. But she had to be careful, more careful than she'd ever been with anything.

Mrs. Midgely, pushing backwards through the kitchen door with a pile of clean laundry in her arms, diverted Lorraine.

"Morning, Mrs. Midgely," Brenda said, all syrupy good humor. "Ruddy lovely morning, too."

"Ruddy lovely, yes," Mrs. Midgely responded, smiling cheerfully. Her glasses were sliding down her shiny nose.

"Why don't you get into a suit and come for a swim?" Brenda said to the housekeeper.

Mrs. Midgely laughed. "You like your fun, Miss Brenda. I work here. I don't swim."

"You could if you wanted to," Enders said shortly. "We both know Mr. Breaker prefers us all to be comfortable."

Mrs. Midgely chuckled on.

Brenda had them all fooled. They all thought she was a charmingly eccentric pet, one they should indulge and fuss over.

Even Willis thought so.

"Oopsy," Brenda said suddenly, bouncing up from the table. "Look at the time. Places to go and people to see. See you all later, darlings." She pointed a long finger at Lorraine. "Go easy on the joy juice, lovey. Ruins the skin if you drink too much of it."

Lorraine waited until Brenda had left before draining her glass and pouring another.

"You might want to consider Brenda's advice,"

Enders said, returning to his notebook.

Sweeping up the bottle, Lorraine passed him without a word and went outside onto a shady terrace at the back of the house. She caught sight of Brenda's white suit and the flash of her red hair. Then she saw Willis jog into view and fall in beside Brenda. They started downhill at the far side of the compound lawns and disappeared.

There wasn't much time to decide how to work things. Sin would arrive in the middle of the afternoon—with Angelica. When Lorraine called him yesterday, she'd begged him to leave the journalist behind, but he'd refused. She'd been hoping he would agree and then Brenda would have had no excuse to hang around any longer. Sin had made what had to be done more difficult, but it would be managed.

With help, Lorraine would manage. Angelica must go—permanently—and so must Brenda. Unless she could figure out a last-minute way to change Willis's mind, he was no use. But Campbell was still panting to be a lapdog and today he was going to get his chance. Today Lorraine would make sure Campbell would do whatever she told him to do. And by tomorrow she wouldn't need anyone's help because she'd have what she wanted. She would have Sin—wonderful, forever grateful Sin.

Swinging the wine bottle by its neck, she set off in the direction of the Midgelys' cottage. During the late morning and early afternoon—Mrs. Midgely's busiest time at the house—Campbell meditated.

Lorraine grinned. She would go and help him meditate.

She reached the place where the lawns began their dip toward the coast and, in the distance, beyond the compound walls, saw Willis and Brenda, hand in hand, walking toward a dense thicket of orange-blossomed hau trees that screened part of the beach on this side of the island.

Lorraine hesitated. It wouldn't take long to convince Campbell that he must do exactly what Lorraine wanted him to do when Sin and Chuck arrived.

Slipping swiftly downhill, she thought about how she would control Campbell, and how she would use Campbell to control Chuck and, ultimately, Sin.

It was too bad she couldn't just take precious Angelica's secret letter and show it to him.

When she'd first found the folded pink envelope beneath the bottom drawer in the bedroom of the lagoon cottage, her luck had felt perfect. But it wasn't perfect. That sniveling hag she'd made Garth get rid of hadn't actually stated Lorraine's name, but Sinjun wouldn't have any trouble figuring out that she was the woman Marlene Golden referred to. He knew it was Lorraine who had been engaged to Garth Lieber and he'd soon figure out that she'd lied to Marlene. Sin would learn the one fact that would destroy every plan Lorraine had worked for: he'd know that she'd told Marlene Golden she was having an affair with him and that they were working together against Garth.

At the time it had been fun to torture Marlene. The story had just grown all by itself. Lorraine had known she would leave Garth and that she intended to get Sin. All she did was invent the truth a little early . . . with some complete fabrications that made everything sound more interesting. Now she wished she'd ignored Marlene. If she had, Angelica Dean and Brenda Butters would never have come to the island.

Lorraine reached the hau thicket and walked in its landward shadow looking for a break that would give her a view of the beach.

Who would have believed all the things Marlene Golden had written about Garth in her tear-jerking little letter? And most of them were going to be so useful.

The first thin patch in the trees looked over nothing but rocky beach and ocean. Lorraine took a sip of wine and stole on.

She smiled secretly. Angelica thought she was so smart—tracking Sin down and doing whatever she planned to do to him. But evidently she hadn't figured out that Lorraine was the woman who had taken Marlene's place with Garth—or if she had, she'd decided to buy good old Momma's theory completely and concern herself only with punishing Sin.

The breeze carried the sound of voices.

Ahead, Lorraine saw another area of sparser leaves. She reached it and peered cautiously through. That bitch Brenda would die when she found out Lorraine had watched her with Willis.

At first she couldn't locate them.

Her breathing speeded up and she started to feel wet. Watching had its benefits. It wouldn't be the first time she'd been turned on by a good show. Then she'd go and play with wonderfully innocent, wonderfully ready Campbell who'd been groomed quite long enough.

She started to duck under the gap, but then she saw them. Sitting on a rock with her knees drawn up, Brenda looked toward the water's edge where Willis bent to wash something Lorraine couldn't see.

Willis stood up and waved.

Lorraine pulled back, then realized he was waving not at her but at Brenda.

When Lorraine looked again, Willis was walking back to Brenda. He held out a hand and now Lorraine could see that he held a piece of coral.

"Beautiful, this one," Willis said, giving his find to Brenda. "Mushroom coral."

"It's so purple," Brenda said.

So purple, Lorraine mouthed. What the fuck was this crap?

"Out by the reef you see every color," Willis said. Lorraine had never heard him so animated. "When there's a really low tide I'll take you out there."

Brenda studied the coral, and while she did so, Willis looked at her.

Lorraine bit the inside of her cheek and was glad of the pain. He looked at the bitch as if she were made of glass—gorgeous, blown glass. He looked as if Brenda was rare blown glass and he was an impressed connoisseur.

Brenda raised her face and Willis smiled at her. "Do you like it?" he asked.

"Very much."

The smile left Willis's marvelous face. He smoothed Brenda's hair, cupped her chin and bent to kiss her.

Lorraine edged farther forward.

When the kiss ended, Willis dropped to his knees in front of Brenda and offered her his hand. She took it and joined him on the mixture of sand and pebbles. Side by side, backs against the rock Brenda had vacated, they sat holding hands and watching the ocean.

He'd never kissed Lorraine with gentleness. She drew back her lips. She didn't want him to and he didn't want it either. Any more than he wanted to sit and hold hands, like a junior-high-school kid. For some reason, he was playing a game with the Amazon.

Lorraine slipped away. Her throat was tight because she'd been holding her breath. She didn't care if Willis was different with Brenda. She wasn't interested in sitting on the beach with him.

The Midgelys' cottage wasn't far from Pua-kali, the lodge Lorraine shared with Chuck. Both were inside the northern reaches of the compound walls and separated by carp ponds and towering clumps of giant bamboo.

Lorraine went straight to the back of the cottage and pressed her face to the kitchen window. There was no sign of Campbell and she quickly entered the room by a sliding-glass door.

What sounded like some sort of Far Eastern pipe music came from another part of the cottage.

Lorraine left the wine bottle and the glass in the kitchen and followed the noise until she stood outside a partially open door. She peered through the crack into the dim room beyond and saw Campbell. Dressed only in shorts, he sat cross-legged on the floor, staring at a candle that flickered inside a green glass holder.

She retreated several steps and said, "Campbell? Are you here? It's me, Lorraine." And louder, she called, "Are you home, Campbell?"

When she reached his door again and pushed it open, he was getting to his feet.

"There you are. Don't get up." Arriving beside him, she caught his shoulder. "I absolutely mean it. You are to sit right where you are. I've come to talk to you and I want you to be comfortable."

Campbell's tanned brow furrowed. "Is something wrong?"

"In a way. I was frightened for a while, but then I remembered I had you and now I'm not frightened anymore. You'll help me, won't you, Campbell?"

"If I can."

He wouldn't be anxious to do what she was going to ask. His stupid spiritual thing would make him say she shouldn't play games.

"I need to stay here for a while," she told him. "I need you to hide me."

His frown deepened.

Shit, he was going to be difficult. "It'll only be until after Chuck gets back, with Sinjun." Mentioning Angelica wouldn't be smart. When the time came, Sin wouldn't need to be begged to deal with Goldilocks.

"Why would you want to hide?" Campbell asked.

Lorraine inclined her head and studied his tanned, muscular chest. He was no Willis, but Campbell certainly had all the right equipment in all the right places. Or so it seemed from what she could see—so far.

"Lorraine?"

"All right, I'll explain. I need to talk to Chuck before I have to see Sin again. The only way I can be sure of doing that is to stay out of the way and have you bring Chuck to me. You'll have to get him on his own and make him come with you. He'll argue, but you'll be able to persuade him."

Campbell was already shaking his head.

"You will, I tell you. I'll make sure you know exactly what to say."

"Chuck doesn't like me."

The same old whining drivel. "Sure he does. He's reserved, is all. You'll have to convince him that he absolutely has to see me without saying anything to Sin."

"I don't think I can do it."

"Oh, you silly boy." Flipping open her long, emerald-green sarong skirt, Lorraine knelt in front of Campbell. "Forget I asked. It doesn't matter." It mattered more than anything had ever mattered. She was just going to have to make him forget everything but how much he wanted more of what she was going to give him.

"What's happened?" Campbell asked. "Why are you asking me to do this?"

"I'm not anymore," Lorraine said nonchalantly while she lifted the candle onto a low table. The jalousies were closed and the one small flame sent vague shadows flickering over white walls.

"Are you thirsty?" he asked. "Can I get you something to drink?"

"No. But you can make me feel better. Remember how you rubbed lotion on my back by the pool that time?"

He moistened his lips and looked away. "I remember."

Lorraine knew he wasn't remembering her back. She said, "Would you do that for me again? Now?"

He didn't reply.

Lorraine moved nearer and stroked the inside of his calf. Leaning, she spread her hands on his thighs and looked up into his face. "You don't have to if you don't want to," she said.

"I don't know if there's any lotion."

"If there isn't, we'll do without. You can help me relax and I'll help you relax. I'd like to do that, Campbell. I could do it for you, first, if you like."

"Chuck wouldn't like it."

"Why?" she asked innocently. "There's nothing wrong with two people making each other feel good, is there?"

"I guess not."

"Of course there isn't. What's that?" A bottle of pale-gold fluid stood beside a pack of matches near the tape deck responsible for the pipe music.

Campbell glanced around. "In the bottle?"

She nodded. "Mmm."

"Scented oil," he said. "You heat it over a flame and it smells good. It calms the mind."

To hell with calming the mind. Smiling, Lorraine reached for the bottle and unscrewed the cap. The scent that escaped was rich and musky, like cedar and sandalwood with a hint of cloves. She poured a little oil into her hand, set down the bottle and chafed her palms together.

"It already smells good," she told Campbell. "But it'll smell a whole lot better when we make it warmer."

She went to work rubbing his shoulders and chest. "It's wonderful. Doesn't it *feel* wonderful?"

He muttered, "Yes," and watched her hands.

When her forefingers centered on his flat nipples and she began to make tiny circles there, he jumped and looked surprised.

"Didn't you know that could feel good? Oh, Campbell, I'll bet there are a million really good things you haven't felt yet."

He reddened beneath his tan and began to get up. When he crouched, ready to spring to his feet, Lorraine caught his wrists. "Please don't leave me. I need you."

"Tell me *why*." He waited before letting his knees come down on the floor. "You know I want to help you. You know I'll do anything I can to make sure you're happy."

With very little effort, Lorraine made her eyes fill with tears.

"*Tell* me what's happening," Campbell insisted.

"I just need you, that's all. You make me feel safe. When you put your warm hands on me, all the tension flows out. That's what I need most now."

After a moment he said, "Okay. Please don't cry. Lie down on the couch. The floor's too hard for you."

Nothing was too hard for her. Smiling tremulously, she supported one of his hands and poured oil into the palm. Then she closed her eyes and said, "I don't want to lie down. Do it the way I did it to you."

For a long time she listened to his labored breathing. Finally, she heard him rub his hands together, then he lightly touched her shoulder above the neck of the sleeveless black bodysuit she wore with the sarong skirt on top. A lace held the front of the bodysuit loosely together from low neckline to a point below her navel.

Campbell spread a film of oil over Lorraine's neck and moved to her arms. Keeping her eyes shut, she began pulling the lace from its holes and managed not to smile when she heard his breath catch.

"You can't do it properly with this thing on," she said, tugging the lace, first from one hole, then another, keeping her back very straight and knowing what he was seeing. "Don't stop," she urged.

The bodysuit was open as far as the waist of her sarong.

Cautiously, Campbell dabbed at the tops of her breasts. "Why don't you turn around so I can do your back?"

Lorraine's answer was to unhook the skirt and let it fall. She pulled the lace all the way out.

"You . . ." Campbell's next swallow sounded painful. "You shouldn't do that, Lorraine."

But the thickening in his voice let her know her protégé was ready to advance to the next step, and the next. He was ready to become a performer in his own right.

Lorraine snapped her eyes open and fixed him with an intense stare. "I should do it. There are many kinds of love. You and I share one of those kinds."

He shook his head, but she moved nearer and held his face.

Campbell's eyelids didn't start to droop until she kissed him. She kissed him long and deep and wet.

Campbell was one hell of a talented apprentice. He was right in there, nibbling her lips the way she nibbled his, driving his tongue in and out of her mouth, just as she did to him—and from the panting she heard, he wasn't missing the lack of subtlety in their sexy parody.

She leaned away and rested her hands on his shoulders. His eyes were feverishly glazed.

"Do what I did to you," she said softly, and when he didn't respond, she returned a forefinger to his left nipple. "*Do* it."

Campbell looked at her breasts. Lorraine looked at Campbell. He passed his tongue over his lips, but made no move to push aside the suit.

"Oh, Campbell," she chided, and did the work for him. Her breasts sprang free and his mouth opened. "Do it, lover."

Slowly, looking as if he expected to be slapped, he raised his arms and settled each forefinger on a budded nipple. Twin jolts rocked her all the way to her feet. She curled her toes.

"God," Campbell breathed. "Oh, God."

"It's not fair," she said pettishly. "On you. There's so much more of me to make calm."

Veins at his temples stood out. His nostrils flared and his eyes narrowed. And Lorraine felt her own lips part. Campbell was definitely forgetting his spiritual hang-ups.

She didn't have to prompt him to smooth her breasts with complete, thorough absorption and he didn't flinch, even a little, when she slipped the suit from her shoulders and wriggled it down low on her hips.

Campbell replenished his oil and didn't as much as look at her face before going back to his task. This time he worked his way over her hips and around to her belly without faltering until his fingers encountered curly black pubic hair.

"Campbell!" Lorraine gave a little shriek of laughter and batted him away. "You may not do a single thing to me until I've done it to you. First. That was the deal."

"We didn't make a deal," he said, remarkably clearly.

"We did, too." Playfully, she tweaked at the crotch of his shorts and smiled with genuine anticipation. "You are a big boy, Campbell. Big enough to stick by deals. And our deal is, you first, then me."

He was watching her swaying breasts avidly. When he reached for them, Lorraine squealed again, but didn't stop him. Instead she opened the waist of his shorts and skinned them down around his knees.

"Jeez!" He turned bright-red but kept right on squeezing her breasts.

"Yeah," Lorraine said, pursing her lips. "*Jeez*. You really are a *big* boy. And you're ready, aren't you?"

He stared at her.

Lorraine slipped her arms around his neck and kissed him, gently this time, using her tongue like a feather rather than a mini-jackhammer. He held her and she layered her breasts against him. "We are so much alike," she told him during a breathing break. "We are kind and good where our hearts are. Where our spirits are. People can hurt us too easily. But now we have each other for special times like this and we'll always be able to make each other feel better."

"Lorraine, I want—"

"I know what you want. Stay right where you are."

Without further preamble, Lorraine bent down, gripped his tight butt with long fingernails that were going to leave marks, and opened her mouth wide.

He took about ten seconds to get over the shock.

Campbell became an instant devotee of her skills.

Afterwards, Lorraine didn't have to push him to make him lie down, and when she mounted him, he was already fully hard again.

"We are going to have lots of times like this, aren't we?" she asked him, loving the sobs that broke from him when she came down. "Aren't we, Campbell?"

"All the time." His eyes were flat and brilliant. "Don't worry about anything, Lorraine. We'll deal with the rest of them."

She started to move. "I knew you'd look after me, Campbell."

Twenty-three

"**W**ill you look at that thunderhead?" Chuck leaned forward and pointed over Sinjun's shoulder. "Whooeee!"

Sinjun looked south and saw the head rise high through a thick bank of clouds. "It's a big one, okay."

"I didn't think there were thunderstorms around the islands," Angelica said, breaking the latest and longest of a group of silences that had begun as soon as he'd told her they were returning to Hell.

"They happen," he told her. "But not very often."

He had chosen to pilot the Eurocopter out of Honolulu himself. Chuck had shown signs of arguing, but accepted the explanation that Sinjun needed a diversion. In truth, he needed to feel in control even if the feeling was only an illusion.

"Helicopters aren't great in bad weather, are they?" Angelica said. "Didn't I hear that somewhere?"

He glanced at her and smiled. "Don't worry. We'll beat the storm in."

"I think we're gonna have to batten down the hatches when we get there," Chuck remarked. "The thunder's gotta be a fluke overture. That front they were talking about is definitely on its way. They said seventy-five miles. I don't think so. I think I see the edges of it now."

Sinjun studied the southern skies again. "You could be right," he said, not wanting to heighten the alarm he felt in Angelica. He patted her hand where it lay clenched on her knee. "Always did enjoy a good island storm, myself. Wait till you see the way the world looks after it's washed clean."

"There she blows," Chuck announced as Hell came into view. "Prettiest sight on earth, right, Sin?"

"Just about." Sinjun looked at Angelica and kept on looking until she met his eyes. "I only know one sight that's prettier."

Predictably, her cheeks turned pink and she averted her face quickly.

He wanted to be alone with her again and he didn't want to wait. She wore a casual tan cotton shirt with the sleeves rolled up and tan linen slacks. A silk animal-print scarf tied her hair at the nape of her neck. She looked soft and clean and cool . . . and his mission for the day was to do away with all the cotton and linen and silk, to wrap himself around her soft, clean body and make sure they both forgot the meaning of the word *cool*.

"You planning to bring this bird in on Hell, Sin?" Chuck said from somewhere behind. "Or did you fancy a trip to Tokyo?"

Sinjun realized he was in danger of overshooting the pad and executed a flashy bank. "Just surveying the home front," he said nonchalantly.

Chuck laughed shortly and said, "Looks like a welcoming committee down there."

Sure enough, three figures, one with unmistakable red hair, converged at the edge of the landing pad.

"Here we go," Sinjun said, and grinned at Angelica's little shriek. "Scared?" he asked.

"Thrilled," she said loudly. "I just want to *be* there."

He wanted to be there, too, but he wasn't looking forward to dealing with Lorraine.

He didn't believe her story that she was about to become his salvation from the shadowy threat that had followed him for weeks.

Lorraine hadn't given up on getting into his bed. She couldn't handle it that he didn't want her. This would turn out to be one more trick. When Sinjun questioned Chuck, he'd also been in the dark and waiting to get back to the island to find out what she'd supposedly discovered. What in God's name would it take to either make Chuck realize he was being used, or to get the woman to leave—for good?

He set the chopper down.

"Not bad," Chuck yelled over the thudding sound of the blades. "For an amateur, that is."

Sinjun grinned. He grinned more broadly when Angelica released her belt and scrambled to kiss his cheek. "You are so good at that," she shouted—and laughed when he flinched.

Chuck was already pushing a door open. He ducked and dropped to the ground.

"You're relieved I didn't mash us all," Sinjun told Angelica. In their few moments of privacy, he slid a hand beneath the thick tail of hair at her nape and kissed her. When he drew back enough to see, her eyes were downcast. "We've got some things to get settled, Angel," he told her quietly.

She nodded slightly.

Last night, at his Queen Anne house, she'd been withdrawn and he had sensed she wanted to be alone. Lying awake, knowing only a few yards separated him from her, had been an unbearable test of willpower, but he'd schooled himself to let her come to him. She hadn't.

"I want you with me tonight, Angel," he said.

She bit her bottom lip.

"Okay?"

"Let's wait and see what's happening here," she said, turning her warm brown eyes on him again. "I'm frightened, Sinjun."

"I won't let anything happen to you." He prayed he could keep his promise.

"You always think I'm afraid for myself." Before he could respond, she pressed two fingers over his mouth. "I'm not. We've got so much to talk about. More than you know. I want a chance to do it."

"We'll get a chance. I won't let anything—"

"Hush. Please, Sinjun, don't say too much now." Pushing herself up to see past him, she said, "They're wondering why we aren't getting out. Let's go."

"Okay, sweetheart. The sooner I get this thing with Lorraine over with, the better. You and I have things *to do.*"

Angelica was already climbing from the helicopter. She looked back and said, "Nothing can happen to you, Sinjun. Do you understand?"

He started to answer, but Brenda was dragging her away and talking into her ear at the same time.

"Nothing can happen to you." Damn, but he could take on the whole world, chew up any fool who tried to get in his way and spit him out without noticing the bad taste in the meantime.

Sinjun took in a deep breath and stepped out into gusty heat that promised the coming storm. Of course he didn't believe in such things anymore, but he might be in love, completely, hopelessly, bloody fantastically in love.

The first words he heard as he approached the small assembled group were Chuck's "What do you mean, you don't know?"

"Exactly what we've told you," Enders said, and Sinjun was relieved to see the return of the familiar disdain.

"What ho, all," he said—deliberately cheerful—

and fended off Swifty's enthusiastic greeting. "Nice of you to roll out the red carpet, Enders. Don't usually see you in the honor guard, Mrs. M."

Mrs. Midgely's anxious face didn't engender peace of mind. "We're concerned, Mr. Breaker," she said.

"No need to be." He sought Brenda Butters's bright eyes and found them as serious as the rest. "Will you all *unwind*? Whatever's going on, we'll deal with it. *I'll* deal with it—with your help, of course."

He saw Willis emerge from the compound and start up the hill toward them.

Enders cleared his throat. "We have a problem, Mr. Breaker."

Coming from Enders, any sign of uncertainty was an ominous sign.

"Okay," Sinjun said. "What's happened here?"

"Nothing," Enders said promptly.

Suddenly, Chuck threw down the bag he'd been carrying. "Goddamn it, Sin. Haven't you noticed *anything*?"

"Yeah. This is not a happy homecoming."

"Mr. Breaker—"

"*Lorraine*," Chuck cut Enders off. "She isn't here. Doesn't that strike you as odd?"

"I guess—"

"She's gone, Sin," Chuck said through his teeth. "No one's seen her since this morning."

Something had gone wrong.

Standing against the wall, Lorraine risked a peek through the jalousies in Campbell's room. The sky had darkened and wind-driven rain streaked in horizontal sheets, beating trees and shrubs with slicing force.

Campbell had left over an hour ago. When they'd heard the chopper coming in for a landing, she'd hidden in his closet. She knew Chuck and Sinjun had searched Pua-kali lodge for her, and that they'd come here to the Midgelys', only to be told by Campbell that he hadn't seen Lorraine.

After waiting for the two men to get clear of the cottage, he had promised to find a way to make Chuck come here alone.

If Campbell panicked and spoke to Chuck in front of Sin, she'd lose everything.

A door slammed.

Lorraine spun around. She hadn't seen anyone approach. Rising to her toes, she crept across the room.

Her heart hammered and her throat ached.

Footsteps.

If it was Chuck, he'd have called out to her.

Casting about, she saw the open closet.

She never made it that far. The bedroom door smacked open so hard it hit the wall.

Chuck walked into the room. "What the fuck are you playing at?" he ground out. His khaki shirt and pants were plastered to his body. Water ran in rivulets from his drenched hair.

She took a step toward him and stopped. "Thank God you're here," she said, holding out her hands. "Oh, Chuck, I've been through hell waiting for you to come."

"Cut it, Lorraine. You know I don't buy the theatrics. You've really done it this time, lady. Sin's had enough. He's going to kick your ass so far off this island, you're going—"

"*Chuck!* Stop it. Listen to me. I know who's been trying to hurt Sin."

"Really? How did you manage to find out? With a crystal ball or did the culprit call up and volunteer? Why did you do this? Just to get me back here because you can't do without it for more than a few hours at a time?"

"Forget it." Fuming, she made to march around him.

Chuck grabbed her so fast she fell against him. "All right," he said. His eyes were cold. "I'm listening. Make it quick and make it simple. You've got about two minutes before I help you pack."

She was going to enjoy watching Chuck Gill's reaction when Sin told *him* to pack. "If we don't stop her, Angelica Dean will kill Sinjun."

Chuck's expression became fixed, then slowly changed to one of amazement. "You are really off your head," he said. "Yeah, this time you've completely lost it."

"Are you going to let me explain, or shall I just let you barge in and help that woman do what she intends to do?"

He released her and wiped water from his face. "Talk."

"I knew there was something about her. I couldn't believe that phony biography story and I was right. She intends to *remove* him. Don't interrupt me again, Chuck. I found a letter hidden under a drawer at the lagoon cottage. Right now she's probably making sure it's still there."

She had Chuck's attention now. He wasn't taking his eyes off her.

"First, I didn't come to the pad flapping the letter because I was afraid she might do something crazy."

"Like what?"

"I don't know. Like pull a gun." Spreading her arms, she managed to squeeze bemused fear out through every pore. "Chuck, I'm scared out of my mind. That woman's weird. Listen, and listen very carefully. Angelica Dean's working for Garth Lieber."

Amazement became disbelief. "That's insane."

"Tell me about it. According to that letter—from Garth—Angelica isn't supposed to make *any more* mistakes."

"But you're telling me it was here when she

left the island? You'll have to do better than that, baby. If that chopper was deliberately blown up and if someone tried to make sure Sinjun took a nosedive down an elevator shaft while we were in Seattle, then your letter's already a bit out of date, wouldn't you say?"

"Elevator shaft?" She had to be very, very careful. "Someone tried to push Sin down an elevator shaft?"

"As good as. So, you see, your story doesn't hold up."

Lorraine paced. "How am I going to make you believe me?"

"Show me the letter. That would be a great start."

"I *knew* you'd say that. Chuck, I didn't dare take it. I couldn't be sure I'd manage to talk to you and get you to warn Sin before Angelica went back to the cottage. If she got there and the letter was gone . . ." She let the sentence trail away.

Chuck braced an elbow on the opposite forearm. "You're telling me Angelica Dean is a killer? She's been hired by Garth Lieber to knock Sin off?"

"I think so." She had to make this sound believable. "He told her to deal with Breaker properly. Enders said there were several attempts on Sin's life before he came to Hell the last time. Is that true?"

"Yes."

"Oh, please go to Sin and tell him to get rid of that woman. And tell him to be careful."

"She's not exactly an accomplished hit woman, is she?" Chuck said. "What have we had? Three, four—*five* unsuccessful attempts?"

"It only takes one *successful* attempt, doesn't it? You didn't read that letter. I did. She's got to be afraid of not pulling it off. I never dreamed Garth could be capable of something like this." She mustn't overplay her hand.

Chuck rubbed his jaw thoughtfully. "Did I miss something, or didn't you say what it is Garth Lieber hopes to gain from having Sin killed?"

She hadn't thought of that. If she said it was something to do with business, he'd check and find out she'd lied. "Garth wants to punish me," she said simply. "He's angry because he lost me and he wants to make sure I suffer the way he has."

"I see." Chuck dropped his arms to his sides.

No, she'd said the wrong thing. "I mean, Garth wants to get at you because of *me*—because I'm with you. He knows how important Sin is to you, so he's having him killed to get even." She was stammering and babbling, but she couldn't seem to stop. "Garth knows . . . Well, he knows."

"That's that, then," Chuck said. "I guess I'll just go back to the house and tell Sin we've found the killer."

"Yes," Lorraine said eagerly. Thank God he hadn't noticed her slip. "Tell him, and tell him Angelica's very dangerous. Explain how I found the letter and make sure he knows he mustn't say anything to make her suspicious that we know about her."

He nodded. "Just keep everything nice and open, you mean? Make some excuse to get her back on the chopper and off the island?"

"Exactly." Excitement made her jumpy. "As soon as the storm passes over you can take her away. Brenda Butters, too. She's definitely involved in some way. Probably as Angelica's backup in case she gets into trouble."

"You've really worked this out."

"Oh, yes. Sin's going to be so grateful when he realizes I've solved his problem."

"Mmm. You're looking forward to Sin being grateful, aren't you?"

"Yes—" She hesitated. "You'll make sure he acts quickly, won't you?"

"Absolutely. Come here, Lorraine."

She pushed back her hair and smiled uncertainly. "We can't, Chuck. Not here. Not until you've warned Sin."

"Come here," he said, very softly.

Lorraine didn't like the way he sounded but she approached until she stood only inches from him. "I expect you've really missed me," he said.

"Yes." Why did he look different—*sound* different?

"I'm going to miss you, too."

"That's nice . . . What do you mean?"

"No need to work it out. It won't matter."

Lorraine took a step backwards, but Chuck's arm, snaking around her, stopped her from going any farther.

"What is it?" she asked him. "You're frightening me."

"It's all right now." He caught at the hair that hung down her back and pulled. "I'll make sure Angelica doesn't do Sin any harm."

"You're hurting me." Tears stung her eyes.

"Tell me you've been fucking Sin and I'll stop hurting you."

Her knees buckled but he jerked her upright.

"*Tell* me."

"No!"

"Say it," he ordered her through his teeth. "You want to get rid of Angelica because you're jealous, you bitch."

"I'm not, Chuck."

"You are. You want her out of here because you know he wants her now and not you. *Say* it."

She was losing control. "It isn't true." Chuck was dangerous. She could see it in his eyes and in the rigid set of his mouth. "I only want you."

He backed her to the door and through the house to the sliding door in the kitchen. "Let's go and ask Sin."

"No! No, we mustn't go to Sin."

"Why, because you know if I ask him he'll tell the truth and expose you for the liar you are?"

The second he forced her outside into the near-darkness, rain beat into her skin like fat needles. "Please, Chuck," she begged. Her scalp was on fire. He kept moving, pulling her hair to hold her neck arched back, half-carrying, half-dragging her toward the compound walls.

She struck out at him, sank her nails into his face. He plucked her wrist away like a useless twig and wound her arm behind her back. "Feel good?" he asked, and forced the arm up until he could clasp it in the same hand that tore at her hair.

Lorraine screamed.

Chuck drove his fist into her belly, and, when she choked and started to vomit, he crammed his free hand over her nose and mouth.

Lorraine didn't scream again.

Running, slipping on sodden undergrowth, Chuck made his way toward the lagoon cottage. Angelica would be with Sin. He believed Lorraine—partly. She wasn't inventive enough to make up her entire story. There was a letter and it said something incriminating. Whether or not it mentioned Lorraine was another question. She hadn't rehearsed her story quite well enough. If she had, she wouldn't have made the mistake of forgetting that Garth Lieber had never known there was any connection between her and either Sin or Chuck.

If she'd known of a real reason why Garth had supposedly sent Angelica after Sin, Lorraine would have told him, just as she would eventually have denied finding a letter at all if it hadn't existed. In the end, Lorraine would have told him anything . . .

He must put Lorraine out of his mind for now and get his hands on that letter before Angelica had a chance to move or get rid of it. He must find out exactly what it said.

Darkness hampered him. Only the sheen of water on slick leaves gave any perception of depth or the direction he must follow.

Winded by a fresh onslaught of rain, he paused, holding the rough trunk of a tree while he gasped for breath. Going too fast, not thinking each move through, could ruin everything. The first thing to do was to get Angelica away from Sin. Then Sin must be told about the letter—Lorraine's version— and, finally, Angelica had to go.

Like a mad magician's creation, lightning unzipped the sky all the way to the shuddering crowns of thrashing palms. Seconds passed before thunder bowled through the heavens. Chuck pushed away from the tree and staggered on toward the house. He approached from the south, along the edge of the jungle growth above the lagoon cottage.

He'd made the right decision. The letter could wait. The first order of business was to separate Angelica from Sin.

"Chuck?" A male voice came to him as a muted gasp, all but snatched away by the storm. "Chuck, it's me, Campbell. I'm over here."

The big flashlight Campbell carried ensured that Chuck saw him immediately. Only yards away, he stood beneath a dense arch of vines.

"What the hell are you doing, Campbell? Trying to drown yourself?"

"I didn't know what to do. I didn't know which way you'd go after you left Lorraine."

"Go home," Chuck told him shortly while lightning cracked again. "I'm getting out of this. You should, too."

Campbell leaped from his useless cover and grabbed Chuck's arm. "Is Lorraine all right? Did she . . . Do you understand what she had to tell you?"

A cool, calm place quieted the center of Chuck's roiling mind. "I understand perfectly."

"Good. *Good.* So you're going to do what she wants you to do?"

"Yes."

"She's had a terrible time, you know," Campbell said, speaking very rapidly. "Sinjun doesn't like her and he mistreats her."

This wasn't the first suggestion of its kind Campbell had made. "Sinjun doesn't like or dislike Lorraine," Chuck told him. That wasn't true, but neither was it up for discussion with this turkey.

"Lorraine told me you didn't believe it." Campbell's stance changed. He stood upright and raised his chin. "I'm going to make sure you change your mind. Did she tell you about Brenda Butters and what she's doing to Angelica as well as Lorraine?"

Chuck swiped ineffectually at his streaming face and frowned. "Brenda?"

"Yes. We think she's a private investigator. Lorraine—and I—we think Sin hired her to find out who's been trying to do something to him. Only Brenda's determined to turn everything around and get Sinjun for herself. We think Brenda was the one who did those . . . Whatever was done to Sinjun."

"Why don't you tell me exactly what she's been trying to do?" Chuck walked closer to Campbell. "Explain it all to me."

"Well . . . Well, Lorraine and Angelica are both in danger from Brenda. Lorraine explained it all to me and I'm sure she's got it right. Brenda should be gotten off this island as soon as possible."

"*Brenda* should be gotten off?"

"Yes."

"What has Brenda been up to while we've been away? Has she done anything to Lorraine?"

"I . . . No. No, not yet. She's been with Willis most of the time."

Chuck began to understand. "Lorraine told you all this."

"Yes. She's told me everything."

She hadn't told him she'd been fucking Willis, but then, she thought she was the only one who knew about that. He said, "You and Lorraine are good friends."

"Yes . . . Lorraine said . . . Someone had to look after her while you were away."

Campbell made no attempt to stop Chuck from taking the flashlight away. "I expect Lorraine asked you to look after her, didn't she?" He shone the light in the other's face.

Campbell's forearm came up to shade his eyes. He said, "She wouldn't have had to. I wanted to take care of Lorraine. She's sweet and gentle."

"And sexy," Chuck remarked offhandedly.

"And . . . I wanted to help Lorraine and Angelica. And you."

"Did she screw you yet?"

In the glare of the light's beam, Campbell blinked.

"I asked you a question." Leisurely, Chuck reached out, gathered the neck of Campbell's T-shirt into a bunch and twisted. "So answer me, you horny little boy. Has Lorraine screwed you yet?"

"I don't know . . . What are you asking me?"

Chuck tightened his hold on the shirt. *"Fuck,"* he said, drawing the word out. "Has she fucked you? Have you fucked her? How many times? And how? Did she find out how you like it best? Lorraine is a versatile woman—"

"Don't. Don't talk about her like that."

"You mean she didn't fuck you? Think carefully, Campbell. I'm a forgiving man, except when someone tells me lies. If you lie to me I get very, very angry."

The other man—the *boy* grappled, trying to free himself.

"Lorraine knows how to do everything, doesn't she?" Chuck remarked. "Do you like the way she sucks? Oh, yeah, nobody sucks like Lorraine. I bet you're hard right now just thinking about it." He felt for the boy's dick and proved his own point. "Oh, *yeah*."

Campbell flailed and cried, "Let me go."

Chuck gave a brisk shake and released him. "Admit it and we'll forget this conversation happened." When he didn't get a response, he shouted, "*Say* it. Now."

"All right. Yes. But it wasn't like—"

"It wasn't like that? Were you going to say it wasn't like that? Of course it wasn't. Lorraine specializes in the unique. No two fucks the same."

"We were comforting each other," Campbell said in a rush. "Everyone here is in danger from the forces of evil. Everyone—"

"Get out of my way." The kid was crazy but harmless.

"You aren't mad at me?"

"Don't push your luck."

"Oh, thank you. Lorraine is all right now, isn't she?"

He didn't have time for this. "She's perfect."

"Thank you."

"Go home to bed." Chuck thrust the flashlight back into its owner's hands and turned away.

"I will, Chuck. Thanks. Oh, Chuck, I just remembered something I meant to ask you."

"What?" He didn't stop walking, but the kid caught up.

"Did you lose your briefcase?"

Chuck stopped. "What?"

"Your briefcase. Did it . . . Forget it. It doesn't matter now anyway, does it?"

"It matters," Chuck said, closing in on Campbell once more. "What are you talking about?"

When Chuck's hand closed over Campbell's on

the flashlight, the boy frowned. "The briefcase that was going to be at Princeville. The one you said would be in a locker."

Chuck shook his head.

"You remember," Campbell said. "When you let me fly to Kauai with you and Fran. You gave her the locker key and told her not to forget to bring it . . . You told her to get the briefcase and take it on the chopper. You said she wasn't to tell Sin because there was a surprise for him in it. You said . . . *Jesus*."

"What a memory you have," Chuck said. "Did you mention this to anyone else?"

"No." Campbell shook his head vehemently from side to side. "No. Honestly I didn't. I just remembered it when you started walking away."

"I'm happy to hear it," Chuck said, reaching into his pocket. Some risks were simply too great. "What a pity you insisted on making that flight. Your poor mother's going to take this very hard."

Twenty-four

❧

*A*ngelica gave up trying not to watch Sinjun. He prowled, had been prowling, around his study for almost three hours. Three hours ago, Chuck, grimly white-faced, had insisted he be allowed to continue searching for Lorraine alone.

Willis had waited for Chuck to go before flatly stating that he'd walk the island's coastline. Brenda promptly decided to return to the apartment over the pool house and Enders made an excuse to go over some accounts with Mrs. Midgely in the kitchen.

Barefoot and minus a shirt, Sinjun wasn't difficult to watch. Angelica studied his wide, leanly muscular shoulders and the way his hair curled against his tanned neck. She tried to consider how she'd cope if things didn't work out between them and felt her chest grow tight. For now she couldn't face all the complications that stood a very good chance of separating them.

Sooner or later, the question had to be asked. "What do you think has happened to Lorraine, Sinjun?"

He checked his watch. "I think Chuck's got about ten more minutes before I contact the search-and-rescue people and the police in Hawaii."

"Do you suppose . . ." Of course he did. Voicing

aloud what they thought in private wouldn't solve a thing.

Still wearing the jeans he'd traveled in, Sinjun came to the side of her chair. "Lorraine isn't stable," he announced. "If she did manage to find whoever it is who wants me killed—and she decided to go and confront them—then I think she's probably dead." He dropped to his haunches and hung on to the arm of the chair. "Why keep on pretending? You and I both think Lorraine may be lying dead somewhere. Most likely on Kauai or Oahu, depending upon where she arranged her rendezvous."

"Nobody saw her leave," Angelica reminded him.

"She could have been taken off by boat."

Angelica sighed. "She isn't very diplomatic." How inane that sounded. "I mean, she's blunt and I think she could be impetuous."

"I don't like her," Sinjun said. "I've never liked her."

Angelica ran her fingers into his thick hair. "I don't like her, either." This wasn't the time to mention the suggestions Lorraine had made about her relationship with Sinjun.

"That doesn't mean we wish her dead," he said.

She shook her head vehemently. "No, it doesn't."

"I hope to hell she's still here. She could be hiding out—waiting to make a grand entrance. That would be exactly her style."

Angelica murmured noncommittally.

"I'm going out to look," Sinjun said.

When he started to get up, she wound her arms around his neck. "Stay where you are. Please. If Chuck can't find her, neither can you. He wanted you here in case some major decision has to be made about something. Don't forget Willis is out there, too. He knows this place better than either of you. You said as much."

"I'm no good at waiting and doing nothing."

"I know." She also knew they had more to talk about than Sinjun could begin to guess. With each second the idea terrified her more. Telling him the absolute truth about why she tracked him down in the first place would result in one of two outcomes: he'd accept and forgive or he'd tell her to get out of his life and stay out.

Resting his chin on her arm, he looked at her now. "Say you won't leave me tonight."

She fingered his hair away from his forehead and stroked a flaring black brow with her thumb. Touching him brought a barrage of intense, newly discovered sensations that made her want to touch more of him—and to have him touch her.

"Will you stay, Angel?"

If only all the decisions she had to make were as simple. "I'd like to."

His smile widened slowly. Such a wickedly suggestive smile. "We are so compatible," he told her. "You want what I want. You like what I like."

During the few hours she'd spent alone with him in his office suite, he had taught her to like a great many things she'd never even experienced before. "I need to go to the lagoon cottage. I need the clothes I left there."

"I'll ask Mrs. Midgely to have Campbell go and pack up all your things. He can—"

"No." She cut him off abruptly. "No, thank you."

"Does Campbell bother you? I could have Willis go when he checks in, but I doubt if he'd do a great job." He laughed. "How about Enders?"

"How about I pack up my own things?" she said gently. "I'd really rather do that." And there was a small task she couldn't entrust to anyone else.

He considered. "As long as I come with you."

Angelica clicked her fingers and Swifty rose ponderously from his favorite place beneath Sinjun's desk. "Come on," she told him. "You'll come with me, won't you, boy? I think you should stay here, Sinjun."

"Nothing doing," he said. "We'll have to wait for the storm to—"

"Sin!" Shouting, Chuck came into the study without knocking. "Holy shit, Sin. What a night."

Sinjun took Angelica's arms from his neck and stood up. "What happened to you?"

Chuck touched one of a series of long scratches on his face and winced. "I walked into a wiliwili tree. Those things have thorns like knives."

Sinjun said, "Yeah. They're mean," and cleared his throat.

Angelica moved to the front of her chair.

"You didn't find Lorraine?" Sinjun said finally.

Chuck unsnapped and unzipped the yellow oilskin jacket he wore over a dark shirt with jeans tucked inside rubber boots. "I found her," he said grimly.

"Thank God." Sinjun's hands fell to his sides. "Is she all right? Is she coming here?"

"She can't come. She's sick because she drank too much."

Embarrassed for the other woman—and for Chuck—Angelica looked away.

"Sick," Sinjun said, sounding confused. "So where is she? In bed?"

"Yeah."

"Was she there all the time, or what?"

The silence that followed was so long, Angelica couldn't help looking at Chuck again. He stood with the oilskin jacket pushed back and his hands sunk in his jeans pockets.

"Chuck?" Sinjun prompted.

"I searched this whole goddamn island," Chuck said morosely. "And Willis walked the coast. He's in the kitchen with Enders and Mrs. M. now."

"Lorraine may need professional help," Sinjun said. "The alcohol is a problem for her. I guess she wasn't up to explaining the information she said she had for me?"

"Look, Sin," Chuck said, sounding awkward. "D'you suppose we could talk alone?"

Angelica scrambled to her feet at once.

"What you can say to me, you can say to Angelica," Sinjun said, and she noted that the green glint in his eyes was more possessive than combative.

"I'd rather not," Chuck mumbled. He rubbed the toe of one boot against the heel of the other.

"I'll go back to the cottage," Angelica said quickly. "Is it still raining as heavily as it was, Chuck?"

"No. It's still blowing, but the rain's stopped."

"Wait for me, please," Sinjun said to her.

"Okay." Chuck took off the jacket and held it bunched in one fist. "I've got to say this before I explode. Lorraine was probably in bed when we got back this afternoon. She was certainly there when I finally found her. Unfortunately, she wasn't in *my* bed."

Angelica frowned and saw Sinjun do the same thing. "I don't follow you," he said.

Chuck crossed the room and poured himself a brimming glass of scotch. When he dropped in an ice cube, the drink slopped over and he cursed under his breath.

"You always fill it too much," Sinjun said.

Chuck flapped dripping fingers. "And you always behave like my damned father." He indicated Angelica. "Are you going to tell her to get out of here?"

"No."

"*Goddamn* . . . Okay. So be it. I'm sure you remember looking at Pua-kali. No Lorraine. Then we went to the Midgelys'. Remember that?"

"I remember," Sinjun said. "Campbell hadn't seen her, either."

"Wrong," Chuck said, sucking scotch across the

rim of his glass. "He *said* he hadn't seen her. She was there. She was in his bed."

"Christ," Sinjun muttered.

Chuck pushed his lips out in a philosophical pout. "Well put," he said. "*Christ*. There's more to this story, Sin, and I need to tell it to you." He glanced at Angelica and immediately lowered his gaze to the floor.

"Right," Sinjun said. "Angel, would you mind if Chuck and I—"

"No, of course not," she told him hastily. "I'll go on down to the cottage and . . . And I'll do those things I mentioned. Give me a call later, if you can. But don't worry if you can't get to it."

Swifty showed signs of following Angelica. She patted his head and pushed him gently until he flopped down again.

"I'll call you, Angel," Sinjun said. "Be careful how you go. It'll be slippery."

Angelica had been staring at the phone for more than an hour when it rang. She snatched it up and said, "Hi." Her voice sounded breathless. "How did it go with poor Chuck?"

"Listen to me," a woman's voice demanded. "And don't interrupt."

"Who is this?"

An exasperated sigh whistled along the line before the woman said, "Mary Barrett in Seattle. Sorry, I should have identified myself. Now, *please*, just listen. Sinjun asked me to call you."

Mary Barrett. Angelica had tried to put the woman's name and face—and the knowledge of what she'd been to Sinjun—out of her mind.

"Are you still there?" Mary asked.

There could be no question of forgetting how much the woman hurt Momma. "I'm here." Although there seemed nothing to be done now and at least she no longer blamed Sinjun for the wrong

Garth had set in motion years before Marlene took her life.

"Sinjun's afraid for you."

Angelica took the phone from her ear and looked at it. "What?" she said, mostly to herself.

The weak crackle of Mary's voice was inaudible. Angelica pressed the receiver to her ear again. "What are you talking about, Mary?"

"I'm going to tell you everything. Just *listen*. We know whoever's been trying to kill Sin is on Hell. Sin's afraid for you, too, and he wants to get you out of there."

"I'll go to him—"

"You will *not* go to him. And you won't call the house. If you do, you'll risk his life as well as yours. Do you understand?"

"I understand," Angelica said slowly.

"Good. You are to go directly to Sinjun's boat and hide in the aft cabin."

Boat. She'd never even seen the boat. "I don't know—"

"You don't have to know anything. Do as you're told. Do what Sin wants you to do. Go to the boat and hide in the aft cabin. Don't come out until you hear the engines start. Once you hear them, you'll know everything's okay because Sin will be at the controls. He'll get you both away to safety."

"But Mary, I don't—"

"Pray for the sound of those engines," Mary said, and hung up.

Sinjun put his elbows on the desk and buried his face in his hands. "I can't take this in," he muttered. "I don't *believe* it."

"Believe it," Chuck said. He set a glass in front of Sinjun and pushed it closer. "Drink that. It'll make you feel better."

Rather than the glass, Sinjun picked up the fax Mary Barrett had sent only minutes earlier. "How could Mary make such a monumental mistake?"

"We all make mistakes. People who only deal with little things make little mistakes. People who deal mostly with big things run the risk of making big mistakes. Mary deals with a whole hell of a lot of big things."

Sinjun glared up at Chuck. "Thanks for the lesson." He batted the paper. "This tells me Garth Lieber deliberately set out to rip me off. When I signed that agreement, he knew it was based on out-of-date data."

"Er—yeah. I think that about covers it."

"It begins to cover it," Sinjun corrected. "He already knew the release of Skins of Silk would be indefinitely delayed. *He knew because he had evidence that the damn stuff didn't do what it was supposed to do.*"

"Mary said they weren't sure it would—"

"Semantics," Sinjun said. "He pulled off a real coup when he got my name on the dotted line. Unfortunately—for me—he intended to make sure I didn't live to find out what he'd pulled and rescind the agreement."

"Right," Chuck said unhappily. "You've got it absolutely right."

"Thank God you had the sense to get right on to Mary. That son of a bitch Lieber withheld chemists' findings. Damn, but his audacity is amazing. If she hadn't been able to analyze all the stats, we still wouldn't know."

"I wanted to do it while Angelica was still in the house with you. I knew she wouldn't try anything here, with the others around. But you can bet your . . . You can be sure she's already working on the grand finale. She won't make another mistake, Sin. She can't."

"No. I can't believe I fell for it." Falling for her story wasn't what hurt the most. "I . . . She seems so special."

Chuck murmured, "I'm sorry."

Not nearly as sorry as Sinjun was. "All this was spelled out in the letter Garth wrote to Angel—?" Her name stuck in his throat. "It was all in his letter?"

"Not every detail," Chuck said. "Drink some of the scotch."

"I hate scotch. I want that letter."

"We may never get it. Lorraine was right to leave it where she found it, though. As long as Angelica doesn't realize we know what she's up to, we've got the advantage."

"Advantage?" Sinjun laughed shortly. "Yeah, I guess you're right." He'd just lost what he'd thought would be the best thing to happen in his life—ever— and that didn't feel like much of an advantage.

Chuck started pulling his jacket on again. "We can't hang around."

"What do you suggest we do?" He saw flashes, pictures of her face passing as if flipped through a slide viewer.

"We get you off this island while I deal with her."

Soft brown eyes that showed each changing emotion. Her smile. *"Nothing can happen to you, Sinjun. Do you understand that?"* Her heart and soul had been in her eyes when she'd told him that, or he'd thought they were.

"Go to the boat," Chuck said brusquely.

"You think I'm going to run away?" He stood up and walked around the desk. "No way. I'll deal with Angelica Dean myself."

"No, you won't." The tone in Chuck's voice stopped Sinjun. "The only dead body that woman wants is yours. Let's keep it that way. If you confront her and she realizes the rest of us know about her, we could lose some more innocent lives."

He didn't want to listen to reason, but he heard

it anyway. "We've got to make sure everyone else is safe."

"They'll be safe," Chuck assured him. "The best way to ensure that is by not alerting them. That way they'll behave as if nothing's wrong and I think that'll work. I want you to go to the boat. Cast off and get through the reef as soon as you can. Go. If she calls, I'll cover for you. Then I'll raise the alarm and say you're missing. That'll give us enough breathing space to make sure we get the police on board. We've got too much evidence for them to ignore us now. If we play our hands perfectly, we should be able to get her off the island and arrange for her to be arrested when she arrives in Honolulu."

Somehow, there seemed little or no satisfaction in the idea of winning against Angelica because whatever happened, he was going to lose—had already lost. "Why Honolulu?"

"Because I'll set her up. You don't need to waste time listening to me work out the details. For God's sake get going, Sin."

"Why don't I just take the Eurocopter?"

"She'd probably hear it take off. I may not need it, but I want the element of surprise on my side."

Sinjun reached for his shirt. "I hate this."

"Sometimes you have to give up control," Chuck said. "You haven't had much experience, but you're gonna have to learn tonight. The boat's our best hope. *Go.*"

Angelica switched off the bedroom light and went to look outside.

Midnight had come and gone. She should have left for the boat . . . Only she didn't have any idea where the boat was and this night was the darkest she ever remembered.

She needed to hear Sinjun's voice.

She needed to know he was safe.

A gust of wind hurled itself against the French doors, rattling the wooden frames. Big raindrops scattered the panes. The storm might gather strength again. If it did, any attempt to search for the boat would be made almost impossible and if she did find it and get aboard—and if Sinjun made it safely, too—surely navigating through the reef would be next to impossible.

All her things were packed and Momma's letter was hidden inside the lining of the jacket Angelica wore.

For Sinjun's sake, she would stuff down her fear and find his boat somehow, but not before making one call.

She walked through the cottage and used the kitchen phone. The sound of ringing at the other end of the line started almost before she finished punching in numbers.

The phone rang and rang.

Angelica closed her eyes and prayed for it to be picked up.

There was a click and the voice she'd hoped for said, "Yes?"

"Brenda," Angelica whispered urgently. "Something horrible is going on here. You already know someone's been trying to kill Sinjun, don't you?"

"That's what we were told."

"It's true, but I don't know what to do." She explained the elevator incident and went on to describe Mary Barrett's call from Seattle.

"Ruddy hell," Brenda said when Angelica finished speaking. "Sounds like a ruddy movie."

"I wish it was a movie."

"Aye, well, there's only one thing for it. Much as I hate to defer to the larger members of the species, we'll have to put this one on Willis."

"You trust him?"

"Abso-bloody-*lutely*. He's marvelous. Best thing that ever happened to me. He's *real*, Angel, and he'd die for Sinjun. I mean he'd really *die* for him."

"Where's Willis now? What are we waiting for?"

"He went to his place to make sure everything's secure. Evidently there's a fresh front coming through and it'll likely be worse than the one we just saw. Look, I want you to stay put. I wish I was with you, but I'll have to wait for Willis now. When he gets back, we'll come to you. Okay?"

"Okay." Angelica let the receiver fall back into the cradle. *Okay?* Nothing was okay.

The kitchen light went out.

Her heart rushed up into her throat and she whirled around. All the lights were out.

Fumbling, she got to the closest switch and flipped it up and down.

Nothing.

She had to remain calm. The storm must have cut off the electricity. She'd just give Brenda a quick call and make sure the power loss was general.

The instant Angelica picked up the phone and heard the sound of dead silence she knew her reasoning was faulty. She couldn't see the compound or any other outlying buildings from here.

There could be power to the rest of the island.

There could be severed lines only yards from where she stood.

There could be someone waiting outside, waiting for her to make a move.

The wind assaulted the cottage again. A drumroll beat across the roof as a new load of casuarina cones flew from nearby trees.

How long would it take Willis and Brenda to get to her?

The question, like the possible answer, was moot. All that mattered was whether or not she was about to be attacked.

The darkness was absolute.

Between the storm's batterings, only the distant whine of unnamed sounds broke the thick silence.

Feeling her way along the walls, Angelica made it into the bedroom and located the little Beretta in a side pocket of her tote. She fished around for a clip and snapped it clumsily into place.

The thing was loaded and ready to fire. The element of doubt lay in whether she *could* fire it.

Holding the gun aloft, as she'd seen done on film, she positioned herself in the hallway. There she had at least an equal chance of escaping whoever . . . If someone got in, she might have a chance of getting away.

An immense draft rushed through the hallway. Shuddering, Angelica turned toward the bedroom. The cold air had come from that direction.

As quickly as the current rose, it faded again.

The French doors in the bedroom had been opened and closed.

Angelica held her breath and listened. The wind slapped rain against the windows, and drew back to regain its strength.

The faintest creak reached her. Houses creaked, but the sound wasn't like that. This sound didn't belong.

Pressing her free fist against her chest, willing her heart not to beat so loudly it would be heard, she edged backwards.

Another creak.

Angelica froze.

She wasn't alone anymore. Someone moved, moved toward her as she moved away.

In the end, there was always a wall, real or perceived, beyond which there could be no more retreat. Angelica didn't know where her wall would be tonight, but, unless help came, there would be a wall. And then whoever was creeping through the darkness would catch up.

Could she shoot a human being?

Her shoulder slid from the wall into a space that was the open archway into the living room. Just inside the living room stood a peacock-backed rattan chair. Angelica located the scratchy cane, slipped to stand behind the chair and instantly regretted her decision. Now she was hemmed into a corner.

She felt the texture of the air shift and change, and, so near she could almost reach out and touch it, a deeper shadow slipped into the shades of black and dark-gray that filled the room.

Pull the trigger.

How could she? How could anyone shoot without knowing exactly who they were shooting at and why?

Shapes and air currents became confused. The silence was gone, without being gone. Angelica hovered, poised to make a dash for the front door, yet ready to run to the kitchen and through the side exit.

Something moved all about her.

It touched her face.

Angelica snapped her teeth together, squeezed her eyes shut and flailed her arms. She struck out and brought the gun down on solid flesh.

A male "Damn you" curled around her shattered nerves like a wild animal's snarl.

He grabbed for her gun, but she held on. Even when he used both big hands to clasp her wrist and drag her from behind the chair, she held on to the gun.

Struggling, she tried to drop her weight. He clamped an arm around her and jerked her upright, held her against a body that felt as big as the room, big enough to block all doors at the same time.

She kicked and brought no more than an "Oof!" from him.

Before she could aim another blow with her feet, he spun her around and closed a choke hold on her neck.

Angelica fought, and gasped, and saw wavering red before her straining eyes.

He was choking her—*killing* her.

She heard the sound of her own rasping breath, felt cold sweat slide between her breasts.

She would not die without leaving a mark on him. "Bastard," she screamed, and rammed a heel into his shins.

He groaned his pain and, for one blessed instant, his grip loosened.

"Let me go!" Rotating, kicking and punching, shrieking past a throat that felt afire, she attacked him. "I'm going to kill you," she shouted, working to push the gun into his side. "I will. I *will* kill you."

His fist, connecting with her belly, threw her to the floor. Angelica felt him coming after her. Retching, she covered her head, curled into a ball and aimed for where she thought his feet must be.

Cursing wildly, he overbalanced across her back and fell, smashing objects on the way.

"That's it," he ground out. He was too fast for her. His body hit hers, flattened hers beneath him. "That is *it*."

That *was* it. All over. Her breathing made great sobbing sounds that burst into her ears. Her arms were dragged from her head and stretched above on the floor. He held her legs down with one knee.

"Why did you have to play so dirty, Angel?" he said. "Why did you have to make me feel what I didn't want to feel for you?"

Sinjun. "Sinjun! Oh, Sinjun." She coughed. He was crushing her. "It's me. It's . . ." He knew who she was. He'd used her name.

He didn't have to wrest the gun from her fingers, she simply let him take it away. When he rolled over, he kept her hand above her head and her legs trapped by his.

"It's me," she whispered. "I thought you were someone else."

"Don't," he said. "I was going to leave, but I

couldn't. Not without knowing you couldn't hurt anyone else. If I stop you, I stop everything—at least for now."

She couldn't breathe. "I haven't hurt anyone."

His laugh made her flinch. "You mean I'm not anyone as far as you're concerned? Thanks to Chuck, I already figured that one out."

"I don't understand you."

"Of course not. You're just a journalist who wants to write my biography."

She forced her lungs to expand. "I'm just a journalist who fell in love with you."

Before she could regret the words, his hand came down over her mouth and she felt his face against her neck. He was a dead weight.

Angelica fought for breath. The fear she felt had nothing to do with death, not anymore. This was a nightmare and it was happening while she was wide awake.

"Damn you," he said into her shoulder. "Damn you for making me feel all over again."

She tried to form words, but his hand stopped her.

"How much is Garth Lieber paying you to kill me?"

Angelica blinked into the darkness.

"I'm going to take my hand away, and you're not going to scream again—or lie. You're just going to tell me how big a price Lieber put on my head. Then you'll tell me who you really are and why you didn't make a good job of killing me from the car that first time—in Seattle. You could have done it. You had time to line up again, but you drove away. The other times weren't meant to succeed either, were they? For some reason, you had to kill me here, on Hell. And now you're going to tell me why."

He took his hand away. "Tell me."

"I didn't do any of those things."

"*Tell* me."

"How could you think I . . . I couldn't do those things to you. Not ever. I love you, Sinjun."

"Stop. For God's sake, don't say it again. I'm not sure I can control myself if you do."

The tears came unbidden. They ran from her stinging eyes, ran hot down her temples and into her hair. "I don't know what you mean. Didn't you have Mary Barrett call and tell me to go to your boat? Didn't you tell her to make sure I didn't call the house first? And then all the power was cut. You must have done that. What are all of you trying to do to me?"

She felt him stop breathing.

"Brenda's going to come with Willis. I got through to her before the line went dead. I called her because I couldn't leave without warning her first. They're going to come. They'll be here any minute."

He was utterly still. "Mary called you?"

"Yes. She said—"

"I heard you the first time." Slowly, he eased away and pulled her to a sitting position. "You couldn't have made that up."

"No." She moaned and tugged on the wrists he still held.

With jerky, absentminded strokes, Sinjun began to chafe her bruised skin. "She told you to go to the boat?"

"And hide in the aft cabin," she told him. "And wait for the sound of the engines. She said that would mean you were aboard and we were on our way to safety. Only, I didn't know where the boat was."

"Oh, my God." He pulled her into his arms and held her so tightly it hurt. "Oh my *God!* I didn't touch the power. This is a total setup. Coming from every direction. There isn't any letter, is there?"

The pain didn't matter. "Letter?"

"Under a drawer in the bedroom? From Garth

Lieber? Telling you I'd better be good and dead the next time, or *you* would be?"

She tried to order her thoughts. "Who told you about a letter?"

"Lorraine told Chuck." He held her even tighter. "But there isn't one, is there?"

"Yes," she whispered. "There is. But it isn't from Garth and it doesn't say any of the things you just said. It's from my mother. She wrote to me about Mary. About Mary and you."

"Mary and me? Why would your mother write about Mary and me? I don't know your mother, do I?"

"No," she said simply. "But Mary met her. Do you want to see the letter?" Suddenly it seemed absolutely essential that he read her mother's words for himself. "There're some candles in the kitchen."

It took him a moment to respond, then he stood and helped her up. She leaned on him. Things hurt all over her body.

Supporting her, Sinjun guided a path to the kitchen and followed her directions to find candles in a drawer beside the sink. There were matches, too. He struck one and flickering light brushed his features.

Angelica looked at him and waited until he looked back. "I've cut your face," she said. "Again."

His laugh wasn't meant to be funny. "And I've turned you to pulp again. Are you all right?"

"I'm fine," she lied. "I keep telling you how tough I am."

This time Sinjun didn't laugh.

Her fingers didn't want to cooperate but she managed to work the battered letter from inside the lining of her jacket. Carefully, she pulled out all but the last two sheets and handed them to Sinjun. He didn't appear to notice that she'd held anything back.

Flattening the paper on the counter, he narrowed his eyes to read.

Angelica took a second candle and lit it from the first. Then she dripped a few drops of hot wax on a plate and fastened the stick in place. "It'll make it easier to read," she murmured, and he nodded slowly.

After what felt like forever, his eyes met hers. "Did your mother kill herself?"

"Yes."

"Was she the woman you told me about when you came to my offices?"

"Yes."

"And this friend of hers was the man who lied? He said he wasn't free to marry your mother, when he was?"

"Yes."

"I see." Wearily, he rubbed the back of his neck. "I'm sorry, Angel. That had to be tough, but I sure as hell can't imagine who the woman is who supposedly told her about me."

"I've already told you."

He stopped rubbing and said, "*Mary?*"

"Can't you work that out from what my mother wrote?"

"No, I can't. Who is this guy—this *friend?*"

She swallowed with difficulty. "Garth Lieber."

"You've got to be joking." His hand closed on her shoulder. "But you aren't, are you?" He shook the paper. "This *is* Garth Lieber, isn't it?"

"Yes. I told you it was."

"But when you saw him at that meeting, you pretended you didn't know him. And he didn't seem to know you either."

"And that makes me look guilty. Only I'm not guilty of anything but making a bad judgment about you. I came here to find a way to expose you for the louse you supposedly are. I didn't intend to write a biography, I wanted your blood—figuratively. I was going to write an exposé guaranteed to put you on the front page of every rag in the country—the

world. I tried you, Sinjun, and I found you guilty."
She paused for breath before finishing, "And I was
so wrong."

"Yes, you were," he said. "More wrong than you
know."

So, it was to be that way. He was telling her he
couldn't begin to forgive—*ever*.

"No wonder Lorraine put this back," he said,
almost to himself.

"Why did she put it back?"

"Where's the rest of it?"

She only hesitated an instant before giving him
the envelope. "Why not? You might as well know
it all."

He pulled out the last two sheets of Momma's
letter and Angelica's stomach rolled.

Sinjun read and she watched his face tense. Muscles in his cheeks flexed. When he finished, he
put the entire letter together, folded the pages and
handed them back.

Angelica stood on legs that tingled. "Mary went
to my mother and told her Garth didn't want her
anymore because she was too old. Momma had
been through so much, don't you see? She couldn't
take any more."

"I see," he said quietly. "I'm very sorry, Angel."

When his arms went around her, she couldn't
move.

"Was this really how you found out? Reading
this letter after your mother died?"

Gradually, Angelica relaxed, and once she started
to relax, she didn't want to stand up anymore. "You
understand how it was." She threaded her arms
around his waist and began to cry soundlessly. "I
thought I had to try to help Garth—for Momma's
sake and for mine. He's my *father*. And I *hate* him.
When Momma told him she was pregnant with
me, he arranged for her to marry Larry Golden.
The man I thought was my dad only took me on

because he worked for the man who really *was* my father. Garth *bought* a substitute father and husband to replace himself."

"Hush," Sinjun told her, rocking gently. "Don't fold up on me yet, sweetheart. I need you all in one piece until we're out of this."

"Out of *what?*" she asked, feeling hysterical.

"What made you think Mary was involved with Garth?"

"She . . . Things she said. Things Garth said to her in the corridor that day at your office. The way she behaved around him. And the letter."

"Your mother wasn't writing about Mary," he told her. "It was Lorraine who was having an affair with Garth. It must have been Lorraine who told lies to your mother—which fits. She told your mother what she wanted to believe herself."

It was all too much to grasp. "Lorraine as good as told me you were her lover as well as Chuck."

"Because that's what she wishes was true. Lorraine has difficulty acknowledging reality. But this does make it easy to understand why she invented an edited version of your mother's words, then put the letter back. She couldn't risk having either Chuck or me see it."

She wanted to kiss him, to have him kiss her, but fear still blurred the edges of sensation. "Why did Mary call and tell me to go to the boat?"

"For the same reason she persuaded Chuck to tell *me* to go there."

Angelica screwed up her face. "I'm sorry, I don't seem to be understanding very much, do I?"

"How would you? It's Mary who's working with Garth. Everything fits now. She falsified data to get me to sign something I never should have signed, and . . . Later, Angel. I'll explain it all later. Right now we've got to make sure we all stay alive. Come on."

Angelica didn't let him move away. "What are

we supposed to do? Mary's in Seattle. She can't hurt us here."

"She can't. But somebody can. I'm damned sure of that. Just as I'm damned sure we'd have died on that boat. Someone's waiting for us to go through the reef. That would have been as far as we got, sweetheart."

She was so cold. "They'd have found a way to kill us then?"

"You can bet on it. And if we don't act fast, they'll figure out we aren't cooperating and come after us here on the island.

"Come on. Back to the house. I want to get everyone together where I can try to make sure they're safe."

Angelica put her hand into Sinjun's and they went outside into the unkind night.

"Let's hope we run into Brenda and Willis on the way," Sinjun said. "Poor Chuck. When he finds out Lorraine fed him a complete line—and that Mary sucked him in, too—*he's* going to be in the mood to kill."

Twenty-five

❧

$\mathcal{T}$he house was in darkness.

Less force drove the wind, but rain still laced each gust.

Chuck had suggested Sinjun not take a flashlight when he left and, at the time, it had seemed a good idea not to risk catching the wrong attention. Now Sinjun wished they could have light if they wanted it.

Without being sure why, he drew Angelica against him and whispered, "Let's go in quietly, just in case."

"Just in case of—" She dropped her voice. "Just in case of what?"

"I don't know. We can't be sure someone didn't get here ahead of us. I wish I knew where everyone was."

"I didn't think I could get any more scared, but I was wrong." Angelica made a fist and pressed it into his chest. "I should have brought my gun."

He smiled to himself. "It's okay. I brought it and I've got mine, too. By the way, remind me to teach you how to take your safety off."

After a moment's pause, she giggled.

Sinjun held her hand and led the way around the house.

Angelica tugged at him and reached up to whisper, "There's no sign of anyone. Nothing. I'm scared for them all, Sinjun."

He was scared for the others, too, and for Angelica and himself, but he wasn't about to tell her. "The generator's housed near the desalinization plant. That's where the oil's stored, too. I'm guessing Willis would go directly there to work on the generator. That's probably why we didn't run into him. Brenda and the others could have gone with him."

Angelica said, "Why would they?" and voiced his own thought.

"They could have," he insisted. "Hold that thought and don't make another sound until we're sure there aren't any surprises in the house."

They entered through a door into the sun room. Hanging leaves brushed his face and he felt his way toward the step up into the kitchen.

Angelica's short nails dug deeply into his palm, and dug even deeper as she tightened her grip. The strength of his urge to protect her shocked him. So much had happened in the few weeks since they'd met. He wasn't completely sure what he hoped for, but he couldn't conceive of a future where he wouldn't see her again.

She touched his arm and he covered her hand.

Kitchen appliances gleamed dully.

A sense of unreality flooded in. This was like some twilight zone, a place abandoned by its inhabitants for no apparent reason—other than sudden darkness.

"Oh! Sin—" Angelica stumbled, yanking his arm, and he heard her muffle her own cry.

He caught her before she could fall, and realized what had tripped her.

"Swifty," he murmured, dropping to his knees beside the dog's still form.

Dreading what he would find, he started feeling the animal, expecting to encounter blood. Angelica joined him and he heard her talking softly, senselessly to the dog.

Suddenly, she grabbed Sinjun and whispered, "He's breathing. He *is*. Feel."

"He'd wake up."

"Not if he's been drugged."

"You think of everything. Have you ever thought of writing mysteries?"

She tugged on him, urging him to get up. "I've already started."

He didn't have to be told that she was talking about his life story. There was nothing to be done about Swifty now.

They continued creeping through the kitchen and pushed through the swinging door into the passageways at the back of the house.

Utter silence hemmed them in on all sides and Sinjun found himself feeling about with his toe before setting down each foot. Swifty was one of a kind around here. The next unconscious body they fell over wouldn't be a dog's.

He reached the hallway leading to his rooms.

Angelica stood close beside him. Then she jerked on his arm again.

He lowered his ear to her mouth and she said, "Is that light under your study door?"

Sinjun opened his mouth to say, "*Moon*," then remembered there was no moon. "Stay here," he whispered, but she promptly held his hand with both of hers and they went together to the door.

There was light, and it was obviously being carefully shaded. If the jalousies had been closed and the drapes drawn, from most angles the room would appear dark from the outside.

Sinjun closed his eyes and listened—and felt Angelica listen with him. The language of their entwined fingers ground out a reaction to muffled shuffling in the study.

Someone was going through papers.

Firmly, he set Angelica behind him, against the wall. He stroked her face, touched his lips to her brow and knew she understood that he must go on alone.

Subtlety now could kill them both.

Readying his gun, he kicked open the door and shouted, "Don't move!"

The Beretta was aimed at the desk—where nobody sat.

With his arms extended, Sinjun swung rapidly around.

A cloth-hooded battery lantern stood on the floor beside a man's feet. Sinjun's eyes flashed from the feet to the face, to the open wall safe.

"For God's sake," Chuck said, dropping his head forward. "You just about scared the *shit* out of me. Put that thing down."

Lowering the gun, Sinjun advanced. "What are you doing?"

Chuck shook his head slowly from side to side. "Jeez, cool it, will ya, Sin? Your bodyguard days are over. Don't ever scare me like that again."

"I asked you what you were doing in the safe."

"What the hell do you think?" Chuck snapped. "Ripping you off? Lifting Bruno's damned ace in the hole?"

"Just answer the question," Sinjun said shortly.

"You *gave* me the combination. Have you forgotten that?"

Sinjun's gut clenched. "I haven't forgotten. And you aren't answering me." He began to think about Chuck remembering to call Mary before coming to recount Lorraine's story about Angelica ... and Chuck telling him to go to the boat without alerting anyone. And Mary telling Angelica to go to the boat ... without alerting anyone.

"This is unbelievable," Chuck said. "We've known each other all our lives and you don't trust me."

The only person who had been in all the same places as Sinjun since this horror began was Chuck.

And Chuck had flown to Kauai and arranged for a test flight in the charter helicopter. Chuck had hung out the suggestion that Sinjun go and take that test flight, *knowing* he would grab the chance with both hands.

Chuck started to close the safe.

"Don't," Sinjun said.

On the day of the explosion, their schedule had gone awry and the later it got, the more agitated Chuck had become.

"Okay!" Chuck flipped the safe door wide open again. "I hope I'm going to be able to convince myself this is the result of too much stress. Otherwise, you've just lost an old friend, buddy.

"I was putting away the fax Mary sent. It seemed like a good idea to make sure there was nothing lying around to suggest we're on to Lieber and his people. Just in case one of them happens to show up and start looking before I can make this place safe."

Sinjun stopped holding his breath. "God." He shook his head. "God! I'm losing my mind." He put the safety back on the Beretta and shoved it into his pocket. "I'm so damned jumpy. You've got to know how you looked, Chuck. Listen, we're going to have to rethink everything. Lorraine lied about that letter. Angelica doesn't have any part in this, but Mary sure does."

As he spoke, Angelica came into the room.

Chuck stared at her and started closing the safe again. "Mary?" he said slowly. "I talked to Mary. She doesn't know a thing."

The bag containing Bruno's jeweled peony fell from the safe—where Sinjun had placed it a few hours earlier—and the flashing ruby flower with its fantastically wrought diamond-tipped gold stamens shot into view. A large envelope slipped after the bag and slid across the floor.

Ignoring the gems, Chuck stooped for the heavy

envelope but Sinjun was quicker. He turned the
packet over and realized he'd never seen it before.
In the upper left corner the typed words *Sinjun
Breaker, Last Will and Testament* were underlined.

"You can't believe her, Sin," Chuck said, but his
voice shook. "Lorraine was right. This woman is
dangerous."

Sinjun recalled the eighty pounds of hound dog
stretched out on the kitchen floor. "What happened
to Swifty?"

Chuck's eyes had lost focus. "Don't let her do
this to us," he said. "She lies like the pro she is.
She's sucked you in, buddy."

Ignoring him, Sinjun opened the envelope and
withdrew a bulky sheaf of papers.

"Stay where we can see you," Chuck said,
motioning toward Angelica. "Over there. Sit in
that chair."

Sinjun began scanning pages.

"You can still get away," Chuck said. "I'll keep
her here. You go."

Sinjun glanced up. The glow of the largest ruby in
the peony caught his eye and he looked at the empty
bag. The drawstring had to have been undone or it
would never have opened like that.

He continued riffling through sheets that coldly
stated the sum of his life's accumulation. "Interesting," he murmured, and flipped to the last page.
"I'm really going to have to work on my signature.
But I guess I'll wait till I'm older and have more
time."

"Sin—"

"Funny, I tend to forget Mary's a lawyer. She
would know all about drawing up wills, of course."

"What do you mean?" Chuck asked.

"I mean it's all over, *buddy*. Did you really think
you could get away with this?"

Chuck's hands flexed and made fists. "You *owe*
me."

"Do I?" Sinjun felt sick to the core. "Why is that? Because I took you on when you'd run everything Len left you into the ground? Because I said yes when the rest of the world said, 'You've got to be kidding'? Do I owe you everything I've worked for just because you didn't make out as well in life as I have?"

"You owe me because you *used* me." Chuck passed a shaking fist over his mouth. "You used your friendship with me to worm your way into my father's pockets. He treated you like a son. He thought you were worth more than me. He taught you to fly. If he hadn't, Bruno Kertz would never have met you and you *wouldn't* be where you are today."

"True," Sinjun said quietly. "Except for one thing. Len never thought I was better than you."

"Because of us. Because of what you got from *my* father, you became the big, rich man everyone wants to please. As soon as you saw something better than us, you left. If you'd stayed, we could have made everything work. You and me together. You had the know-how and you *owed me that.*"

Sinjun held up the will. "Because I didn't choose to stay on the ranch, you got together with my chief financial officer and *forged* a will? You forged a will and forged my *signature*."

"I didn't do that."

"Oh." Sinjun advanced. "Oh, I see. Of course. *You* didn't forge the signature. Mary did."

"I didn't say that."

"So you *did* do it? And I suppose the existing will is about to be deep-sixed."

"Mary did . . ." Chuck looked wildly around and pointed at Angelica. "It's that damn interfering bitch's fault."

"Really? You mean Angel arranged for you and Mary Barrett to destroy my existing will and forge a new one—a new one that leaves everything to *you?*"

"It belongs to me!" Chuck shouted, his voice climbing higher. "You treated me like a lackey. You got everything that was mine. Always. Everything that ever mattered to me, you took away."

"So you decided to kill me and take it back."

"Yes," Chuck screamed. "Yes, yes, *yes*."

"Where are the others?" Sinjun asked, and a new fear gnawed at him. "Enders and Mrs. M.? Where are they? And the rest of them?"

"They're not where they're gonna do you any good."

"Watch him!" Angelica cried. "On the desk."

Too late. By the time Sinjun retrieved his Beretta, Chuck had snatched up a matching weapon from the top of the desk.

He pointed it not at Sinjun, but at Angelica. "Bitch," he said, drawing his lips back in a snarl. "Bloody bitch. It would be all over if you hadn't showed up."

Sinjun took a step toward Angelica.

"Move again and I'll shoot her," Chuck said. "I'm probably going to kill her anyway, aren't I? But you can't afford not to hope I'll change my mind."

"Get out of here, Sinjun," Angel said.

Chuck laughed. "A real live heroine. How do you do it, Sin? Everyone wants to die for you, don't they?"

"Chuck," Sinjun said evenly. "Let's back up before it's too late. Let's stop this while everyone's alive and there's still some hope of finding a way to fix what's happened."

"It's too late," Chuck said. He blinked rapidly and muscles in his cheeks twitched. "We had it all worked out. Mary hated your guts because you told her *sayonara*. That's all it takes for a woman—a single blow to their damned sexual pride. With you and me, it's more complicated."

"It's more complicated because we go back forever," Sinjun told him. "We grew up together. You *saved* me. You and Gil."

"And you shit on us both."

"*No.*"

"Yes." He leaned against the desk and painted Angelica's outline in the air with the gun muzzle. "Lorraine left Garth because she wanted you, not because she wanted me. She thought she could *use* me to get close to you. Don't argue, because you knew it and I knew you knew it. And you must have laughed yourself sick over that one because you think she's a beautiful piece of garbage."

"I never laughed. Why didn't you let me in on what you knew? We could have sent her packing."

The gun muzzle moved fractionally in Sinjun's direction but returned toward Angelica. "I didn't want to. I was playing my own game and it would have worked without the journalist here. We had it all worked out. Stage a series of so-called murder attempts. Get you set up here on the island to supposedly lure the killer after you. Then arrange for you and Lorraine to turn up dead in a nice, tidy murder-suicide. The end."

Sinjun swallowed air and worked to grasp what he'd just been told. "If you kill Angelica and me, you'll never get away with it. Everything's ruined now."

"Mary's going to be happy with the payoff Garth promised her for turning a blind eye on the chemists' reports." Chuck's voice had become a monotone. "You have to die for that to work, too."

Hope flared in Sinjun. Chuck was losing it. "I couldn't have dreamed up anything this clever," he said, being careful to sound calm.

"Lorraine took me as second-best—and only for as long as she needed me," Chuck said. "Just like Dee-Dee."

Sinjun almost choked. He managed to swallow

and draw in a deep breath—and to say nothing.

"The baby she aborted was mine." Chuck smiled at Sinjun.

The gasp he heard was Angelica's. His own sounded deep in his brain.

"I loved her, but she loved the golden boy. So what else was new? She came to me when you wouldn't notice her, then, when she was pregnant, she managed to get you to sleep with her."

"Shut up," Sinjun said. "Don't say any more."

"Why not? *I've* had to live with it. She came back good and pregnant, told you the baby was yours and got you to marry her."

Sinjun closed his eyes. "She didn't have to get me to marry her. I wanted to. I wanted the baby."

"*My* baby? For once you were royally fucked, sucker. Dee-Dee used my baby to get you to marry her. Then she got rid of the baby because all she wanted was *you*." He swept wide his free arm. "And, yet again, I was supposed to bow quietly out. If she'd known she was dying, she'd have blown the whistle on me for punching her out."

He couldn't take in any more. Chuck was saying he'd beaten Dee-Dee. She'd had an abortion, but she'd been beaten, too, and that had probably caused the hemorrhage.

"Drop your gun." Chuck aimed his Beretta straight at Sinjun's face. "Drop it and get beside your new lady love."

Angelica started to get up. She said, "Don't do it, Sinjun."

"Sit down and shut up," Chuck ordered. "Or I'll change the way you remember his face."

She sat heavily.

"The *gun*, Sin," Chuck demanded, and wiggled the fingers of his outstretched hand.

Angelica made a headlong dive from the chair, and Chuck's first shot ripped open the top of Sinjun's left shoulder.

"Stay down," he yelled to Angelica.

Sound exploded all around.

Sinjun flipped off his safety and lined up. He hesitated, watching Chuck's gun make an arc in his upraised arm.

Angelica was crawling all over him.

Kicking at her, Chuck fired and hit a painting, shattering glass. A second bullet pounded into the upholstered back of the chair where Angel had sat.

"*Sinjun.*" She screamed his name and wrapped her arms around Chuck's legs.

Chuck turned a smile on Sinjun and took deliberate aim on the back of Angel's head. He beckoned. "Come and get me," he said, and his trigger clicked. "Come on, golden boy. You always win, don't you?"

In the quiet that followed, Sinjun heard his watch tick. He heard his heart beat . . . and he smelled fear.

From outside, a low wail sounded. The wail built to a moaning whoop. It swelled and swelled until it erupted into a mad banshee roar.

Chuck clutched a handful of Angelica's hair and looked over his shoulder.

The body that blasted the windows into a hail of glass shards, that splintered the jalousies into matchsticks and tore the drapes from their rods bore down on Chuck with the force of a human demolition ball.

Chuck got off another shot, but it was his last.

Sinjun barely managed to drag Angelica away before Willis sandwiched his quarry on the hard, wooden floor and began to punch.

Chuck screamed. He screamed when Willis wrenched away the Beretta and tossed it aside like a plastic water pistol. He screamed when Willis assaulted his head as if it were a disposable punching bag. And he screamed when Willis's blood fell from the wound in his neck to spatter the face of the man he was bent on killing.

"Stop him," Angelica whispered.

"Yes," Sinjun said when he gauged there had been enough damage to satisfy Willis and not enough damage to result in murder. "That's it." He dropped to the floor and pushed himself between Willis and Chuck.

Willis pulled back at once.

Chuck was unconscious.

"Propane," Willis said clearly. "Brenda told me what Angelica said about going to the boat and waiting for you. Then the power went out and Enders arrived with Mrs. M. He said Chuck sent them. Mrs. M. was to stay with Brenda. Enders and I were supposed to go to the generator to help you. Enders and I thought the same thing at the same time: We were all being kept away from the house. Enders went to the generator to check for you. I went to the boat." Willis paused in what was definitely the longest speech Sinjun had ever heard him make. "Propane in the engine room. He blocked the vents, opened the valve. You'd have gone aboard and switched on the ignition." He shrugged and pressed a hand over the wound in his neck.

"And Angelica and I would have been history. Blown out of the water."

Willis nodded and got slowly to his feet. "And so would Campbell and Lorraine. They were tucked up together in the forward cabin. They were gagged. He stripped them and beat them and tied them together. Or that was the general idea I got when I let them go."

"Why?" Angelica asked.

"I don't think you want to know." Sinjun said, aware of the welling stickiness on his shoulder—and the pain. "The cops can ask the rest of the questions."

It was over.

Twenty-six

❀

*I*t was over.

Angelica had just watched a lemon-yellow sun rise from a gunmetal sea. The sun swelled behind streamers of gray-blue cloud and tinted the water a warmer shade of steel.

The night's storm had slunk away, leaving the land as shiny clean as Sinjun had promised. Shiny clean and pungent with the scents of soaked earth and fallen fruits and wild white ginger.

"G'day, mate."

Angelica looked over her shoulder at Brenda. "Morning. I didn't hear you coming. How's Willis?"

Brenda grinned. "Abso—"

"Bloody—*lutely* wonderful," Angelica finished for her. Smiling, she faced the sea again.

Brenda dropped to sit beside her at the edge of the bank above the lagoon. She draped an arm over Angelica's shoulders and said, "Ruddy wild night."

"Wild," Angelica agreed.

"That Chuck had me fooled."

"Me, too." And his lifelong best friend, she thought.

"The coppers have got his number now, though."

"Mmm."

"I was glad they brought the doc to see to Willis and Sin."

368

"Mmm."

Brenda peered down into Angelica's face. "Would you rather I just jumped off this cliff?"

"Mmm? *No.* I'm sorry. I've got a lot on my mind."

"Haven't we all. Chuck blew up that chopper." Angelica leaned against her friend. "Unbelievable. And Campbell walked right into it with Chuck. I'd like to know how he made it all work."

"Willis says it was something to do with moving the briefcase. Set the mechanism in motion and Bob's-yer-uncle. The timer ran out and up it all went."

"Yes. Poor Fran. It was supposed to be poor Sinjun, too."

"Chuck'll get his, mate." Brenda rubbed Angelica's shoulders and kneaded her neck. "Lorraine's already getting hers, poor devil. She's going to hurt for a while."

"So will Campbell. I wish I could stop thinking about it."

Brenda hummed thoughtfully.

"I'm in a mess, Brenda." When had she become a mistress of understatement?

"You get any sleep at all?" Brenda asked.

"I don't remember."

"What'll you do about your . . . about Garth Lieber?"

While they'd waited their turns for police questioning, Angelica had finally told Brenda about Garth. Since then she'd put him out of her mind. What would she do about him? What *should* she do about him?

"Is that an off-limits question?" Brenda asked.

"No. Just a question I'm not sure how to answer. I probably won't do anything about him. He's the man my mother loved, the man who made her unhappy enough to kill herself. He also brought her a lot of joy along the way. I know that's true because I saw them together—without knowing exactly what I was seeing at the time."

"He's also your dad."

"Only in the biological sense. When I saw him in Seattle I realized I missed the times when he'd made me feel good. When I was a kid and he came with presents. He was like a favorite uncle—or maybe a doting grandfather. I think I'll leave the memory alone and try to forget the rest."

Brenda thought about that before saying, "You'll figure out what's best. How's Sinjun holding up?"

"The doctor stitched his shoulder. The bullet made a groove and ended up in the wall."

"I wasn't talking about his shoulder."

Angelica glanced at Brenda. "I know you weren't. I don't know about the other. After all those people left, he was very quiet. He wanted to be alone, so I came back here."

"How do you know he wanted to be alone?"

"I just—"

"You just made a wrong guess."

Angelica jumped and looked behind her—and up. Sinjun had joined them, his tennis shoes making no sound on the grass.

"Right-o," Brenda said, brilliantly jolly. She stood up. "That's it for me, then. I'll be off."

"Willis is going to have to keep the stress off that neck wound," Sinjun said. "He should probably have done as he was told and let them take him to the hospital on Kauai."

"Yeah, well, I tried to tell him. You know how ruddy obstinate he is."

Sinjun said, "I know he's waiting for you to go and hold his hand—or whatever."

Brenda assumed an expression of utter innocence. "Aye, well, I'll just run along and do . . . whatever." She winked at Angelica and ducked around Sinjun.

"I told Willis I thought his idea was great," he said.

"What idea was that?" she asked, walking backwards.

"Something about hanging out together when neither of you have anything better to do."

"Aye," Brenda said. "I'm giving it some thought. We may decide to look each other up from time to time. You never know, do you?" She turned away again and set off, her long legs quickly covering ground.

"Shouldn't you be wearing a sling?" Angelica said, staring at the sea once more.

"I don't need a sling. It's just a flesh wound. It doesn't hurt now."

"I'm glad." Her pulse felt erratic and muscles in her back ached. "I'm glad." She must be tired.

"I didn't hear you leave," Sinjun said.

"You were preoccupied with your thoughts." Muscles in her stomach also ached, and in her arms and legs.

"Aren't you?"

"What?"

"Aren't you preoccupied with your thoughts?"

Muscles she hadn't known she had were making themselves felt. "I'm . . . preoccupied." *With you.*

"Doesn't that mean I have to go away?"

"You own the joint. Around here you get to say who goes where."

"You don't sound happy about that." He knelt beside her. "It was a hell of a night, Angel."

"A hell of a night on Hell," she murmured. "You ought to change the name of this island."

"What shall I call it, Heaven?"

"Not for a while. Not till the negative energy wears off."

"What's on your mind?"

She could say *Nothing,* but they'd passed the point of useless games. "I'm sorry," she told him.

"I want you to know how sorry I am for not giving you a chance before I set out to punish you."

"You should be."

Angelica couldn't look at him. "I know," she said. "And I also know I can't take any of it back. I can't change it now. But I did want you to know how awful I feel. Fran would still be alive if I hadn't barged in."

"Possibly," he said. "I'd like to change that, too. I'd rather I was dead than her—which is what would have happened if you hadn't barged in."

It was true, and she was glad—and feeling glad soaked her with guilt. The sooner it was over, the better. "Well," she said brightly, slapping her thighs. "That's that, then. Off I go. Can we crank up the radio again to call for a charter out?"

He was quiet for so long, she turned to look at him. "Can we?" she repeated. They'd used the radio on reserve battery power to call for police and medical help.

"Get up, Angelica."

"I . . ." She saw the harsh light in his eyes and couldn't remember what she'd intended to say.

"I said, *up.*"

She swung her legs around and stood.

His face was on a level with her waist and that's where he fixed his attention.

"I'm up," she told him. "My things are already packed." And if she understood the meaning of heartache, she had a full-blown case.

"Why do you think you should run away without facing up to reality?" he said, still looking directly at the point where an inch or so of bare skin separated her short tank top from the waistband of her white gauze skirt.

"I'm chilly," she told him, avoiding the question because she didn't know the whole answer. "I'll go get a sweater and—"

"You're tired," he cut in. "You need some sleep."

"So do you," she said before she could stop herself. "You've lost blood. Go back to the house. I'll get Enders to make the radio call."

Sinjun stood up and began walking ahead of her toward the cottage. "That won't be possible."

"Of course it will." She caught up with him. "He was the one who called the police. He knows how to use the radio."

"I said it won't be possible." Sinjun reached the patio first and walked beneath the windswept petrea vines to open the door into the bedroom. "Hurry up, please."

Angelica hesitated at the edge of the patio. "I know how angry you must be."

"I'm going to lie down. You're going to make sure I'm comfortable."

"*Sinjun*." She ran toward him. "D'you feel faint?"

"Light-headed would be closer."

The difference wasn't clear to Angelica. She caught his elbow and urged him inside. "Lie down," she told him, shutting the door. "Stretch out and I'll make some . . . Damn. I forgot. The generator's still messed up. I can't make tea. I'll get some lemonade and put sugar in it. Sugar's supposed to help shock."

"Shock," he murmured.

"Please lie down," she insisted. "I'll be right back."

He sat on the edge of the bed and averted his face. "Why do you think I'm angry with you?"

Angelica's moistened dry lips. "I lied to you and I . . . I lied. And you think I deliberately set . . . I deliberately set out to use you." But that wasn't all of it. She ran her tongue over her lips again. "And you think I used sex to get close to you."

With that she fled the room and didn't stop until she stood before the open refrigerator door. Her breathing came in great heaves. Ever since the police had left and Sinjun became silent, she'd known he wouldn't want her once he'd had time to think everything through.

The jug of lemonade in the refrigerator was tepid. She took a can of still partially frozen concentrate from the freezer and went to the sink.

"Swifty's okay," Sinjun announced. He'd followed her into the kitchen.

She peeled the plastic strip from the top of the can, flipped off the lid and dumped the contents into the jug.

"I said Swifty's okay."

She massaged her temples. "I'm very glad."

"Chuck slipped him a dose of chloral hydrate. That's used in sleeping—"

"I know what it's in. I think you should go and rest. I'll bring you some lemonade."

"You don't get to give me orders, Angel." His voice was gravelly—harsh.

She began filling the can with water.

"I want you to tell me you used sex to get what you wanted out of me."

The water overflowed the top of the can. Angelica twisted off the faucet and held onto the handle. She felt Sinjun come to stand behind her.

"Say it."

She shook her head.

When he touched her, she dropped the can. Water sprayed her face.

He held her beneath the loose white top, clasped her rib-cage in his big hands.

Angelica wiped water from her eyes. Her heart pounded.

Sinjun pressed a hot kiss on the side of her neck and she couldn't help tilting her head away, couldn't help letting her eyes drift shut.

"Tell me, Angel."

"I can't," she whispered.

Sliding his hands up over the skimpy lace bra

she wore, he pulled the cups down and pushed her breasts together. His thumbs flipped over her nipples.

"*Say* it," he insisted, and jutted his hips against her. He was hard.

Her legs threatened to give out and she clung to the edge of the sink.

His thumbs did their work again, and again.

"You said I would do anything to get what I wanted," she gasped.

"Did I?" He found the bra's front fastening and unhooked it. "I guess I did. But I'm still waiting for you to admit it."

Angelica leaned farther over the sink and let it take more of her weight. The places he touched were points of fire.

"You can stop this anytime you want to," he told her.

He released her breasts and swiftly pulled up her skirt.

"Sinjun?" Cold followed heat in a race over her skin. "What are . . ."

She couldn't finish the sentence or the thought. He leaned his chest against her back and she heard him unzip his jeans.

Confusion made her try to turn around.

Sinjun held her still and jerked her panties down. Grasping her hips, he lifted her.

He was going to enter her from behind. Angelica opened her mouth . . . and closed her eyes.

Sinjun filled her up.

She received him.

He began to move her against his erection.

Angelica helped him.

He made a noise deep in his throat and said, "Tell me I'm an idiot. Tell me you've already told me all I need to know."

She couldn't speak at all.

"Remind me about sex being personal."

"Personal," she mumbled.

Her climax built.

"I'm scared out of my mind, Angel." He ground into her. "You were a virgin. You came to me because you wanted me. Say it."

"I came to you because I wanted you."

"Yeah." He pumped faster. "You wanted me because you loved me."

The climax broke and she clenched around him. "I love you," she told him.

"I like that," he said, and she felt him come. "I wanted you to say that."

As she began to slip, Sinjun caught her. Then he held them both against the sink. He sighed, long and deep, and said, "God, don't let this be a dream."

"Not a dream," she said. "Not a dream."

Sinjun rested his face on her back and said, "I'm not a well man. I think I'm going to pass out."

She stirred. "You can't."

"Why?"

"You're too heavy. I can't carry you."

They helped each other back to the bedroom. Angelica stripped back the comforter and pushed Sinjun down onto the bed. She lifted his legs onto the mattress and went no further. A very strong hand closed on her wrist.

"I'm not going to let you go," he said.

"At this moment, I don't think I could go anywhere."

"We've got a lot of talking to do."

She frowned down into his intensely green eyes. "We didn't get off to a great start, Sinjun. You're going to remember why I came to you in the first place."

"We got off to a perfectly good start and it got to be great in a hurry." He pulled her to sit beside him, caught the bottom of her tank top and shimmied it over her head. The bra disappeared without apparent help. "Is it okay if I lie here and stare at you?"

She felt the familiar rush of heat to her face. "Can I stop you?"

"No. Will you?"

"Will I what?"

"Whatever? Whenever? Everything? Always? All that stuff?"

"Sounds exhausting."

He pulled her on top of him and kissed her. He kissed her slow and hot and wet—and it was so easy to work out how to get him back where she liked him best.

Sinjun's hips came off the bed and she settled him deep inside her.

"Let's just stay like this for a moment," he said. "Just till I get my answer . . . No! No, damn it. Will you listen to me getting ahead of myself again."

Stretching down, grimacing as his shoulder must have hurt, he managed to reach his jeans without losing his link to Angelica.

"This is . . . Ah, God." His hips rose and he clenched his teeth. Then he smiled tightly and said, "I have to get a grip on myself. I have to be able to tell you no when I mean no."

Angelica made her own involuntary move. "But you don't mean no."

He found her hand, opened it and rested his fantastic ruby peony on her palm. "This is for you."

"Don't be ridiculous."

"Don't you ever call me ridiculous. Unbalanced, maybe, but never ridiculous. I don't need this anymore."

"Why . . . You can't just give away something so valuable."

"I damn well can, lady. And you're going to take it."

When she tried to push the ruby blossom back at him, he closed her fingers around it, with painful results.

"I told you when Bruno bought this in Singapore it cost him every dime he had. It was his security blanket, his ace in the hole."

"And he gave it to you because he wanted everything he had to be yours."

"Wrong. It was a symbolic act. He gave the peony to me when he made me his partner. He said I'd become his ace in the hole and I could keep the peony for the same reason he'd kept it: as a kind of lucky charm."

"Exactly."

"Exactly," he agreed. "Now I'm giving the charm to you, partner."